the Truth about Love

MAISIE MYERS

Copyright © 2022 by Maisie Myers

All rights reserved. No part of this book may be reproduced or used in any manner without written permission of the copyright owner except for the use of quotations in a book review.

ISBN: 9798802100950
Independently published

For Jess

Part I

Chapter One

AUDEN

The first time I see her, she's standing on the sidewalk beside the gas station. Her head is tilted towards the sky as clouds burst and raindrops splash heavy and warm into her open mouth. Her eyes are closed, her chest heaving. It's like she's trying to breathe in the downpour. She's beautiful.

Perhaps the most beautiful thing I've ever seen.

Even in the pale light from the station's canopy fascia, her skin takes on a golden glow. For anyone else it would make them look yellow, but not this girl. Nope. For her, the pale flickering light does what Midas's touch did to the world. Even her hair looks to be woven from long strands of gold.

I noticed her the second I pulled into the gas station.

Maybe it's because I could sense the sadness in her straight away. It practically bleeds from her. It's in the way she stands, I think, with her hands wrapped around her middle like she's trying to replicate the sensation of being held. Already, only seconds after laying eyes on her for the first time, I ache to do it for her.

Or maybe it's the expression on her face that betrays the darkness inside her head. A kind of pained serenity. Like she's in agony, but resigned to her suffering. I've seen the same expression on my Mama's face more times than I can count.

I know of the kind of monsters that haunt people. I've watched them eat away at my mother from the inside out for years, so I can tell that the girl has monsters too.

What I can't tell is why a girl who can't be any older than me is standing alone at a gas station in the early hours of the morning. Florida isn't always a safe place to be for a woman on her own. Especially at this time of night. I'm only here myself because I unwittingly landed the role of designated driver to and from a party that ended a little over twenty minutes ago.

A snore from beside me reminds me that my best friend Freddy is passed out cold in the passenger seat. The boy never has known how to hold his liquor and I'd be worried about him blowing chunks all over my dash, if he hadn't already done worse in my beat up old Chevy. But it's late and my bed is calling me home, so I refuel and pay at the kiosk where I convince the checkout clerk to sell me a packet of cigarettes for Mama.

All the while, I think about the girl with golden hair drinking in the summer rain just outside and by the time I've finished up inside the gas station, I've made up my mind to offer her a lift home. Maybe even learn her name.

But when I make my way back to my truck, whoever she was has gone.

Three days later, I see her again.

It's the first day of senior year and, as I stand beside Freddy loading books into my locker, the girl I've been thinking about for the past seventy-two hours stomps down the corridor.

I haven't been able to get the image of her standing in the storm out of my head all weekend. She's as beautiful as I remember, even wearing boots too chunky for her tiny frame and an expression that warns the world not to fuck with her. Her face has been forever burned into my memory and yet, I still don't know her name or even the colour of her eyes.

"Who is that?" I hiss to Freddy, who up until this point has been tapping away relentlessly on his phone. One glance at the screen confirms that he's arguing with his latest girlfriend. Again.

Finally, he looks up and scours the hallway until he finds the object of my fascination. "New girl."

"And?" I wait. The dude has more information than that. I know, because if there is one thing to know about Freddy Nelson it's that he knows everything there is to know about everyone.

He sighs, huffing like I'm an inconvenience. "She's a transfer from some private school in Cape Coral. Rumour has it her parents are loaded. Like *loaded* loaded. Surgeons or CEO's or some shit. Whatever, they're hot shit apparently. You'd have known this if you'd bothered turning up to assembly this morning."

My eyes roll.

I had some shit to deal with earlier that set me back an hour. I wasn't expecting to wake up on a Monday morning to my mother passed out cold in the kitchen with vomit in her hair and a half-drunk bottle of merlot trapped in the vice-like grip of her cold hand. She normally remains lucid long enough to make it up the stairs and collapse in her bedroom. I couldn't leave for school until I'd helped her wash the vomit out of her hair and tuck her into bed. On her side, obviously. Don't want her choking on her own vomit while my history teacher drones on about the Philadelphia convention.

So, Fred can forgive me for being a little late to school.

I ignore his pissy attitude and turn my attention back to the girl. Her hair is tied into a loose ponytail that swings back and forth with every step she takes. She stops at the locker directly opposite mine and curses when her combination doesn't work on the first try.

It's not an uncommon problem. The locks on these shitty things are so old it's a wonder they still work at all. Junior year, I started bringing a butter knife with me to school for the sole purpose of wedging open the door when the lock sticks. Of course, I couldn't get away with it when the school introduced metal detectors and bag searches, so I learned just to heave the thing open and hope it doesn't break.

I'm about to approach her when the bell for class rings and Fred shoves me by the shoulder down the corridor in the opposite direction.

Summer-Raine Taylor.

That's her name.

I learn it when our anthropology teacher calls it out during attendance and proceeds to humiliate her by forcing her to stand in place and introduce herself to the class using three "interesting" facts about herself. For a supposed expert in human behaviour, Mr Hanson is oblivious to her discomfort.

But I recognise the slight tremor in her voice when she begrudgingly does as he demands. I zero in on the way her hands clench into fists at her sides, the blush that creeps up her neck and the tightness of her jaw as she speaks. It all betrays her façade of confidence that she's working so hard to maintain even if I'm the only one in the room to notice.

She doesn't like to show weakness, that much is clear to me already.

"Yeah, hi," she says, gaze fixed on a random spot on the whiteboard at the front of the class. "I'm Summer, forget about the Raine part, it's stupid. Um, I played the harp when I was little but can't anymore, my favourite flavour of ice-cream is pistachio and I think the Beatles are overrated."

She sits down before she's even finished talking and rubs furiously at her hands on her lap beneath her desk. I only know, because she's sitting two desks adjacent to me and the one between us is currently vacant. It means I can watch her from my periphery while pretending to listen to whatever Mr Hanson is saying.

"Very good, aside from the practical blasphemy at the end of your introduction there." Mr Hanson clutches his heart with his hand and feigns a gasp. "Though I hate to be the bearer of bad news, Miss Taylor, we will be looking at the Beatles in quite close detail when we get to the ethnomusicology part of the curriculum later on in the semester. Considering music in its social and cultural contexts is an integral component of anthropological study."

Summer-Raine offers him a short smile, but doesn't respond. She's saved from further mortification when Marlowe Eriksen, a mousy girl with thick-framed glasses and braided hair, bundles through the door to the classroom and successfully distracts Mr Hanson long enough to put a stop his tirade about millennials and their disrespect of "music that isn't complete drivel".

"You're late, Miss Eriksen."

Marlowe, who until now has never arrived late to class in her life, blinks repeatedly and visibly shrinks in on herself. "S-sorry, sir. Won't happen again."

He assesses her down the length of his hooked nose and sniffs imperiously. "Tell me your favourite Beatles song and I might just let you off without a detention, only so long as I approve of your answer."

Marlowe's eyes widen in bewilderment before she stutters out, "Hey Jude, sir."

"Hmm." He sniffs. "It's not what I'd have chosen, but I suppose it'll do. You could have chosen Yesterday and then you'd have really been in trouble. Then again, you might have said the Beatles are overrated and then I'd have had no choice but to have you removed from my class altogether."

The class snickers. My eyes shoot to Summer-Raine, who scowls at the man like she's trying to kill him with the power of her gaze alone. Marlowe looks to and from them both in confusion.

"I'm only joking. We're all entitled to our own opinions, no matter how wrong they might be. Sit down, Miss Eriksen and close the door, will you? I know you weren't raised in a barn."

Thankfully, the rest of the hour passes with no further mention of overrated 1960s British pop bands. Mr Hanson busies himself by telling us what to expect of the curriculum this semester, Summer-Raine stares out the window and I watch her watching raindrops roll down the misty glass.

She's not in any other of my classes for the rest of the day.

When the bell finally rings for the end of school, my eyes are dry from searching for her in the hallways. I look for her in the parking lot and scan the rows of cars for a flash of golden hair, so distracted that I walk straight past my truck without realising.

"Dude, what's up with you?" Freddy asks, frowning at me as I double-back on myself, climb into the driver's seat and buckle up. "You've been super weird all day."

"What? No, I haven't."

"It's the new girl, isn't it? You've been all distant and shit since you saw her in the hallway earlier."

Jesus, the man can be so annoyingly perceptive sometimes.

"So what if it is?" I steer us out of the lot and drive us home along the beachfront. The rain stopped hours ago, the humid late summer air having dried up any trace of it, and the sand glistens like treasure in the mid-afternoon sun.

"I've never seen you lose your head over a girl before, let alone one you only just laid your eyes on. Even when you lost your virginity to Lana Sanders in junior year, you remembered where you'd parked your truck in the lot the next day. Have you even spoken to this girl yet?"

"You know her name. Use it. But no, I haven't." I frown. Truth be told, I have no idea what I'd even say to her if I had the chance. Something about her has me so hypnotised, I can hardly remember my own name around her.

"Well, now could be your chance," he says, motioning out the window. "That's her, isn't it?"

I look to where he's pointing. The unmistakable shine of her hair has my heart beating double time. Why do I react so strongly to her when I don't even know her at all? I don't believe in love at first sight, but if I did then I might just be convinced that's what this feeling is.

"Yeah, that's her."

"Pull up then, man. Look, she's heading to the beach."

"What? No, no, I'll just see her at school."

He sighs. "When have you ever been too chicken to talk to a girl? What happened to the dude who took the cheer captain out on a date last year? You're better than this. Pull over your damn truck, get her an ice cream to break the ice and talk to her before some other tool bag in our senior class beats you to it."

"God, I hate you sometimes," I grumble, but I do as he says anyway and pull into the small lot off the boulevard.

"Nah, you don't. You just hate that I'm right."

We climb out the truck and he lights a cigarette. "Tell me you're not expecting to come talk to her with me," I say, fussing with my very basic outfit of black jeans and a white t-shirt.

He rolls his eyes. "You'd be lucky to have me as your wingman, but no. I'll just wait here for you."

Nodding, I head towards an ice-cream parlour and order

two tubs of pistachio ice-cream before crossing over the sand to where Summer-Raine sits, staring out at the rolling waves of the Atlantic Ocean.

"Hey." She must not have heard me approach because her tiny body jolts at the sound of my voice. "Sorry." I grin shyly. "I recognised you from my anthropology class and thought I'd come over to say hi. You're new to the school, right?"

She nods, assessing me with suspicion.

"Can I sit?" She looks at the space I motioned to, thoughts running through her head so plainly she may as well be saying them aloud. "I'm not a creep or weirdo, I swear."

Finally, she must deem me safe enough because her face relaxes and she nods for me to join her. I hand her one of the tubs of ice-cream and her eyes widen in surprise.

Green. That's the colour of them. Like emeralds or spring leaves of four-leaf clovers. They're stunning. There was never any doubt that they would be.

"Pistachio?" Her voice is a breathy whisper laced with both surprise and distrust.

"Yeah." I shrug. "Remembered from class."

"Oh, thanks. That's, um, that's really nice."

"No worries." I make myself comfortable on the sand beside her. "So, you hate the Beatles, huh?"

She releases a surprised laugh, the suspicion that was so prominent in her gaze before finally starting to ebb away. She shakes her head. "No, not really. I quite like them actually. I just said it to get a rise out of him." She blushes. "I mean, you can't dispute their influence on pop culture or counterculture. Hell, their music practically redefined British identity."

Noticing the confusion on my face, she swallows and continues. "I was pissed at Mr Hanson for putting me on the spot like that. As an anthropology teacher, I figured he'd be a big fan of a band that had a fanatic phenomenon named after them. I know it was petty, I just..." She trails off.

I can't help it, I snort with laughter. "You're kind of a ballbuster, huh?"

Her face turns a furious shade of red and she tugs self-consciously at the sleeves of her sweater. It occurs to me that she must be boiling in this heat.

"Hey, I didn't mean anything by it," I rush to reassure her and she smiles in response. "It's Summer-Raine, right?" I ask, not because I need the confirmation but because we haven't been introduced and I need to change the topic of conversation. Besides, I haven't actually told her my own name yet.

"Just Summer," she nods. "I hate the Raine part. My parents can be pretentious and obviously fancied themselves poets when they named my sister and me. Winter-Skye, that's my sister. I'll leave it up to you to decide which name is worse."

I ignore her self-deprecation because I actually love her name, but I know now isn't the time to convince her of the beauty in it or how much I think it suits her.

"I can kind of relate, I guess. My Mama took a poetic route with my name too. I'm Auden." She blinks at me. "After W.H. Auden, the poet," I elaborate.

"'Stop all the clocks, cut off the telephone. Prevent the dog from barking with a juicy bone,'" she recites. "I know who he is, Auden Wells, I was just surprised you thought you needed to introduce yourself. I recognised you from class too."

Oh. She noticed me. Embarrassingly, that has me smiling in a way that definitely isn't cool for a guy my age.

"Anyone who's seen Four Weddings and a Funeral enough times can recite the opening lines to Stop All the Clocks." I wink and she blushes so slightly a less observant man wouldn't notice the way her cheeks are rosier now than before.

Summer-Raine smiles wryly. "And anyone who has read the poem enough times would know that the actual title is Funeral Blues."

She's got me there.

"'Some say love's a little boy, and some say it's a bird.'" She looks up at me through thick lashes, picking up a handful of sand and letting the grains drain slowly through her fingers. I can't look away. "'Some say it makes the world go round, and some say that's absurd.'"

My response is immediate, a reflex, as I pick up where she left off. "'And when I ask the man next door, who looked as if he knew, his wife got very cross indeed, and said it wouldn't do.'"

She takes another palmful of sand and drains it. "It's one of my favourites."

That surprises me.

The smile she gives me is soft and shy, but it doesn't hide the sadness that I know is simmering away inside her. She may not be giving me the same fuck-off-and-leave-me-alone glare that she was sporting in the school halls earlier, but her monsters are still there. They're still as real as they were when I saw her losing herself in the thunderstorm three days ago.

So, for one of her favourite poems to be 'O Tell me the

Truth About Love', a piece that is so light and playful compared to some of Auden's other work, is so at odds with the image I've painted of her that for a moment I think I may have been reading her completely wrong.

"Why?" I can't help but ask.

"I don't know really. It sounds like it should be a happy poem, but I'm not really sure it is. I don't see how it could be, anyway." She lowers her eyes to stare at her feet. "The guy basically spends his entire life searching for the meaning of love and never finds it. Sounds like a waste of time to me, to look so hard for something we don't even know exists."

"You don't believe in love?"

"No." She shakes her head.

"You don't believe that maybe you could feel it for yourself one day?"

"I don't know," she says. "I just don't think anyone will ever feel that way about me."

She doesn't think she's loveable? I frown, my heart breaking for her that she could even think that about herself. It makes me furious at whoever has led her to believe such bullshit.

"Why are you looking at me like that?"

"Like what?"

"Like you're mad at me."

I shake myself free of my thoughts and reschool my face into a wide smile. "I'm not mad at you, Summer-Raine."

"Just Summer," she says quickly.

I roll my eyes, but perk up as a thought comes to me. "I've had an idea. I'm going to take you under my wing and prove to you that love exists."

Her eyes narrow. "Are you hitting on me?"

I smirk. "Summer-Raine, if I was hitting on you, you'd know it." I shoot her a wink. "I just think that maybe if you see that love exists for others, you'll realise that it's possible for you too."

She doesn't respond, but her mystified gaze falls over me as I stand and dust the sand from my jeans. "Oh, and by the way," I pause. "Summer-Raine suits you just fine. Prettiest name I've ever heard for the prettiest girl I've ever seen."

Her eye roll is instantaneous. "What a line."

"Not a line," I call over my shoulder as I make my way back up the beach. "See you around, Summer-Raine."

Chapter Two

SUMMER-RAINE

Islamorada is a tiny whimsical village that stretches across six islands and is supposedly pretty famous for its sportfishing. I'm not entirely sure what that means exactly, except that the ocean surrounding the village apparently has quite a lot of fish. And clearly, from the copious number of signs hanging above every small-town business declaring Islamorada to be the "Sportfishing Capital of the World", it's a detail that the locals are pretty darn proud of.

That, and the dolphins.

My god, do the people around here love their dolphins.

There's museum exhibits and research centres and boat tours that leave every hour of the day. And I'd get it, I would, if there weren't dolphins playing with their prey or gangraping each other in every coastal town up and down the state. But from my brief experience living here, there isn't anything more special about the dolphins in Islamorada than the ones in Cape

Coral.

But whatever. It's fine. If people wanna brag about the fish in the sea or obsess over creatures that look cute but are actually pretty barbaric, then so be it. Live and let live, I say. Besides, I'm sure the people around here would have a multitude of opinions about me. People always do.

My parents more so than anyone.

It only seems fair that the prettiest name I've ever heard belongs to the prettiest girl I've ever seen.

Auden's words replay in my head for the millionth time since Monday afternoon and just like every time before, my heart races and my palms sweat. Compliments aren't something I know how to handle. I'd honestly have been more comfortable if he'd told me my name was ugly and matched my face.

But he had called me *pretty.*

And though I'm almost entirely certain he only said it to prank me, I find myself wanting to believe that he meant it. It makes me wonder what else he thinks about me. It makes me want to hear him call me Summer-Raine again, even though I hate it when people use my full name.

The truth is, it just doesn't sound so bad coming from him.

Auden Wells, with his eyes like sapphires and dimples that would make a grandmother proud. He's hijacked my every thought since he plonked himself down beside me on the beach three days ago. I swear, his smile is so sinful it could only belong to the devil. He's the quarterback who recites poetry, looks at me like he can see the shadows I hide from the world and makes promises to prove the existence of love.

But what would he want with me?

He didn't even strike me as the jock type and I had no idea he was even on the football team until I saw his photo on the wall by the gymnasium. As soon as I found out, I couldn't believe that I hadn't realised it before. It's a fact as clear as the Florida sky, he's the football star of the school. He sits with the cheerleaders and other jocks at lunch in the cafeteria, he wears his football jersey in the school halls.

And I sit alone on an empty table and wear long-sleeve shirts to school every day.

The more I see of him laughing with his friends, that sunshine smile so easy on his face, the more I doubt the truth of his words when he looked me in the eye and told me I was the prettiest girl he's ever seen. How can I be? When he hangs out with girls like the ones on the cheer squad with their blow-dried hair, manicured nails and perfect button noses. I bet he's slept with them all.

He looks the type to have left a trail of broken hearts and pregnancy scares behind him.

That's what I'm thinking about as I let myself into my empty house and lock the door behind me. My parents won't be home tonight, they're both away on business and my sister lives in the dorms of Florida State University, so it's just me.

The irony isn't lost on me that my parents moved us to Islamorada from Cape Coral for a supposed "change of scenery" and yet they've spent a maximum of maybe three nights here enjoying it for themselves. For the rest of that time, it's just been me in this huge monstrosity of a beach house all alone. At seventeen years old, I'm having to navigate my way through a town that I've never been to, start at a school with students

I've never met and try to make a home in a house I don't want to live in, all alone.

I shut myself in my bedroom and spend the evening getting as far ahead with my school work as possible and when I'm ready for bed, just like every night since I was fourteen, I use a razor blade to draw a line in crimson across the scarred skin on my forearm. And then I fall asleep.

Miss Rossi, if the name on the teacher's desk is correct, waltzes into AP English Lit wearing a yellow printed floral dress with a full skirt cinched in at the waist and an obviously inexpensive faux flower clipped behind her ear.

I watch, fascinated, as she individually places the books she was carrying onto her desk, arranging them at a perfect ninety-degree angle, all while humming what sounds like Dean Martin's 'That's Amore' to herself as she works. If her clear penchant for 1950s pop culture is anything to go by, I'd bet a large percentage of my parents' riches that she has a faded poster of James Dean on her bedroom wall and kisses it before bed every night.

Not that there's anything wrong with that. I'm not exactly in a position to judge other people's bedtime routines.

The door swings open and I don't even need to look in the direction to know who's just entered the classroom. It's like my body is intuitively aware of his presence. The skin on the back of my neck tingles and my breathing grows faster. It's like an instinct or a sixth-sense.

I was actually expecting to see Auden in this class, given our poetry recital on the beach, but I *wasn't* expecting him to make a beeline for the empty chair beside me and throw himself into it like he's claimed the seat for life.

Miss Rossi raises her eyebrows at his eagerness before swinging her feline eyes over to me. "You're new." She stares down her nose at me.

"Yes. Summer Taylor, Miss."

I hold my breath and brace myself for yet another awkward class introduction. Three teachers this week, not including Mr Hanson from anthology, have made me stand and recite three "interesting" facts about myself.

"Favourite book?"

Sweet Jesus, here we go.

I spend a moment debating whether or not to lie and say something that was published in the fifties like John Steinbeck's *East of Eden* just to please her enough to fuck off and leave me alone. But brown-nosing has never been my thing, so I opt for the truth instead. "*The Bell Jar,* Miss."

Auden audibly sucks in a breath beside me.

It's inconvenient that my favourite novel is often interpreted as a pretty damning critique of 1950s social politics when the woman asking is obviously obsessed with the decade, but what am I gonna do? She asked. I answered.

But its social commentary isn't the reason why *The Bell Jar* is my favourite, or at least not the *only* reason. The truth is, I just relate a lot to Esther, the novel's protagonist. Miss Rossi must see something on my face because she nods her head slowly in understanding before turning away to take attendance.

"So, Sylvia Plath, huh?" Auden nudges me, a few strands of his wild hair flopping onto his forehead. "Nothing like reading about the perils of outdated psychiatric treatments to put you in a good mood."

I cock an eyebrow "Would you rather I said something more cliché like *Twilight* or *Pride and Prejudice*?"

He chuckles. "Put your defences down, Summer-Raine. Your answer wasn't exactly surprising, but at least you didn't go for something like *Jude the Obscure*. That shit had me sitting alone in the dark for a week."

"And lemme guess, your favourite is *The Hitchhiker's Guide to the Galaxy* or something equally frivolous?"

Auden releases a breathy chuckle. "Hey, what dude doesn't love a bit of comedy mixed with science fiction? But no, Miss Judgemental, you'll have to guess again."

"Just tell me."

"*Great Expectations*. I fancy myself a bit of a Pip."

"Immature and romantically idealistic?"

"Christ, you really are a cynic, aren't you?" He winks to reassure me that there's no malice behind his words. "I was thinking more about his kindness and conscience, the way he's so critical of himself. Always looking to improve, to learn, to grow. I don't know. I know many of his motives are superficial but I respect his perseverance and determination to make a better life for himself, y'know?"

His words make me pause. I totally get why he'd be so fond of Pip. As nineteenth century book characters go, he's probably one of the least problematic. But listening to Auden idolise Pip for his ambition to leave his old life behind and build a better one makes me wonder what it is that he's trying to escape from himself.

Or maybe he's just ambitious and I'm reading into things too much. He's the star quarterback after all. He's probably just referring to his dreams of being drafted into the NFL or Superbowl or whatever it is that football players do.

But I don't have time to ask, because Miss Rossi fluffs her bouffant and claps her hands together, launching into a forty-minute monologue on why the 1950s was the pinnacle decade of American poetry. Afterwards, she declares *The Catcher in the Rye* to be the focus of the next few weeks and threatens us with corporal punishment if we don't keep up with the reading.

I spend the entire time attempting to ignore Auden's close proximity and the way his knee keeps gently brushing up against mine, but the woodsy scent of his aftershave makes it practically impossible.

"Are all the residents of Islamorada batshit crazy, or are Mr Hanson and Miss Rossi in a league of their own?" I whisper.

Auden smirks at my question. "Bit different from what you're used to back in Cape Coral?"

"Oh no," I grin, "plenty of batshit people there too."

"Including you?" He nudges me gently and my skin breaks out in goosebumps.

Stupid teenage hormones.

"I was the worst." I flash him a grin. "I bet they celebrated when I moved here."

"For sure. But their loss is my gain, right?"

I blink. "Are you flirting with me?" The words escape me before I have a chance to filter them and I burn in embarrassment. What is it about him that stops me thinking clearly?

"Maybe."

Oh.

"Why would you do that?"

He cocks his head to the side, assessing me with eyes so blue I'm half expecting to see the dolphins of Islamorada breaching the waves in his irises.

"I dunno, Summer-Raine. I think you're kind of cool in a standoffish, angry, renegade sort of way."

My heart stutters, but he was right when he called me a cynic earlier. "Has someone dared you to talk to me or something?"

"No, of course not." His eyes soften and it's as if he's looking straight into my soul. Like he can see everything that goes on in my head, like he knows of the poison in my veins and the monsters trapped within me. No one has ever looked at me the way he is now, like he can *see* me. "The whole world isn't rotten, but it's like all you can see is the ugliness," he whispers, almost as if he doesn't mean to be speaking aloud.

I've never felt so exposed.

"There are still beautiful things, Summer-Raine," he says gently, reaching out to tuck a loose strand of hair behind my ear in a gesture so intimate I'm not sure I'll ever be able to breathe again. "You just have to let yourself see them."

"And how do I do that?" I whisper.

"I'll show you."

The intensity of the moment grows too much to bear. I pull back, fighting to put distance between us and end whatever spell he's put me under.

"Proving the existence of love and showing me beautiful things," I say, hoping my voice doesn't betray just how affected I am by the conversation, "you've got your work cut out for you."

He stands up and shoves his hands into his pockets, revealing the empty classroom behind him. I didn't even realise that class was over, let alone that everyone had already left.

"I'm more than capable of getting the job done, Summer-Raine."

I stay rooted to my seat long after he's left, replaying his words over and over in my head until I'm dizzy. I don't doubt his ability to fulfil his promises to me. If anyone can prove to me that love is real, it's Auden Wells with his dimples and kind heart. My worry isn't that his efforts will be wasted on me.

It's that I can already feel them working.

My sister calls me on the walk home.

"Summer, hey." Her voice is breathless, like she's just got back from a run.

"You been working out?" I ask, crossing the palm-tree lined street towards the house, letting myself in through the front door and instantly reaching for the packet of Oreos I know are waiting for me in the cupboard.

"What, no?"

"Winter, you're panting." Something rustles in the background, heavy footsteps and a voice so distinctly masculine there's no way it belongs to my sister or her roommate. "Oh, you little hussy, I know exactly what you've been up to."

"Fucking sue me." She laughs. "Ain't nothing wrong with a bit of bump and grind at four o'clock in the afternoon."

For as much as I resent my parents, I'll forever be thankful to them for the existence of Winter-Skye. We fight like sisters do, of course, but she's the closest thing I've ever had to a best friend.

"Hey, I'm not judging. Who's the guy?"

"Brett, Brent, Ben, something or other."

I snort. "You're such a hussy."

"I'm just living the college lifestyle, baby."

"Tell me you're at least wrapping it up."

"Yes, *Mama*. I'm not an idiot."

"Mama would hardly approve of your extracurricular activities, Winter-Skye."

"Oh, spare me the double-barrel bullshit, Summer-Raine, I hate it as much as you do."

Trapping the phone between my ear and shoulder, I shove an Oreo into my mouth and carry my books upstairs to my bedroom, dropping them onto the bed.

"Speaking of Mama," Winter says. "How are the rents? They being good to you?"

"They haven't been here long enough for me to say either way. Some conference in Miami has had them gone since last week."

I imagine my sister rolling her eyes through the phone. She's as used to our parents' constant absence as I am. Back in Cape Coral, before Winter went off to college, we'd spend every night they were gone having slumber parties in each other's rooms, stuffing ourselves full of snacks and watching trashy Netflix original romcoms until we passed out.

The nights I spend alone now are starkly different.

"When will they be back?"

"Few days' time, I think." I keep my phone fixed in the crook of my neck and rifle through the homework I'll need to get done tonight.

"You got any new friends who can come and stay with you for a bit?"

I scoff. "You know I don't do friends, Winter."

Tutting, she asks, "What about a boy?"

A loose scrap of paper flutters onto the bedsheets from between the pages of my AP English Lit book. Unfamiliar, barely legible handwriting stares up at me. A quote. A message. A phone number.

"We must love one another or die." – W H Auden
That's lesson one.
Message the number for lesson two.

I can't help myself; a small smile curls my lips.

"Summer? Hello?"

"Sorry, sorry. I was just reading something. What were you saying?"

She sighs. "Boys, Summer. Have you met any boys?"

I hesitate a second too long.

"You have, haven't you?" Her voice is a high-pitched, disbelieving screech. "You've actually met a boy."

"Jesus, cool your jets. There's no boy," I say, and it's true.

Auden and I have had a grand total of two conversations. Sure, he's made some pretty promises and made my heart do that weird swoopy thing it does on theme park rides, but I can't claim that there's something going on between us when he hasn't given me any indication that there is. He probably calls every girl the prettiest girl he's ever seen. Probably hands his number out to anyone with a pair of breasts and vows to remind them of the beauty in the world. I'm nothing special.

And yet, the words leave a sour taste in my mouth. They make me feel like I'm unintentionally lying to my sister.

"But, say someone gave me their number..." I trail off.

"I knew it!" She squeals again and I can hear her slapping her hand excitedly against her thigh. "Is he cute?"

"Like a teenage dream, but that's not the point." I sigh. "I'm not gonna message him anyway. He's probably been dared to talk to me or is bored and wants to string me along as some sick kind of entertainment. I'm happier on my own. I'm just gonna keep my head down until senior year is over and I can finally join you at Florida State."

Winter releases a long breath down the line. "I know this is gonna sound a bit callous or insensitive cause I know you're battling things that you don't like to talk about, but babe, you've gotta get your shit together. Not everyone is out to get you, Sum. You can't keep shutting out the world because you're scared of letting people in, especially now I'm at college and not with you all the time. It kills me to think of you all alone. So, please, for me, try to make some friends. Text the boy. See what happens. Do it for me, yeah?"

It's not the first time she's lectured me on my reclusiveness, but it's the first time I haven't immediately shut down because I hadn't wanted to hear what she's been saying. It's the first time I've ever considered that maybe it wouldn't be so bad to not be on my own anymore.

So, after Winter has hung up the phone, I've done my homework, read most of The Catcher in the Rye and drawn my nightly line in red across my skin, I do something I never would have imagined I'd do. I follow my sister's advice.

And I text the boy.

Chapter Three

AUDEN

> **Unknown number:** I got your death threat. A little concerned I won't make it through the rest of the lessons alive…
>
> **Me:** Death threat?
>
> **Unknown number:** "We must love one another or die." Bit ominous, no? Sounds like you're threatening my life.

"What the fuck are you grinning so hard at?" Freddy asks as we pull into the parking lot of our favourite diner, Rosie's Place, on Saturday morning.

"Nothing." Slipping my phone back into my pocket, I fight to neutralise my facial expression but my lips remain rooted in a smile.

Admittedly, the note I scribbled for Summer-Raine during class yesterday wasn't my finest work, but I had to come up with something quickly if I was going to be able to slip it into the pages of her book undetected.

I never thought she'd actually text me.

I've had the same shit-eating grin on my face since I woke

up to her message this morning.

"Whatever." He rolls his eyes, looking over the breakfast menu despite always ordering the same thing. "But it's creepy, so cut that shit out."

I scrunch up a red napkin and toss it at his head. Thankfully, the sound of approaching footsteps saves me from getting hit with a fork in retaliation.

Auntie Rosie, who isn't in fact an aunt at all but insists that her patrons call her it anyway, smiles down on us with fondness and red lipstick on her teeth.

"What can I get y'all?" she sings in her southern drawl that can't possibly be real considering she's a village native. "Don't tell me. One cappuccino and one glass of freshly squeezed OJ. Two breakfast burritos. Hold the salsa for my Freddy-bear and extra cheese for the angel with baby blues?"

She may be pushing eighty, but Auntie Rosie is a woman confident in her sex appeal, despite Fred and I being a couple of years outside her target age demographic. Regardless, she's brought a blush to my cheeks more times than I can count and Fred always humours her flirtation every time we come here to eat.

"You know us so well, Auntie Rosie," he says, handing over the menus and winking when her fingers brush against his and linger there for a few beats too long.

My eyes roll.

Rosie struts off to the kitchen to place our orders with far more swing in her step than I knew a woman her age could be capable of.

"What?" Fred asks, catching me eyeing him with mirth.

"You're as bad as she is."

"Nothing wrong with a flirt once in a while with an attractive woman."

"Seriously? You'd really go there?" I shake my head in disbelief. "She's older than your grandmother."

"You know I'm not one to discriminate, dude."

"And Mia wouldn't mind if you started fooling around with a woman four times her age?"

"Oh man." He sighs. "Don't talk to me about Mia right now."

If I've learnt anything about Mia during her and Fred's brief relationship, it's that she's impossibly difficult to please. Possibly even more so than her predecessor, Bethany, who made him delete all his social media accounts and wouldn't let him watch movies with any hot female characters.

Fred's little black book reads like a Yellow Pages for emotionally abusive and overly-controlling teenage girls. And yet, he jumps from one relationship to the next with very little time in between. For someone who claims to hate commitment, my best friend is a serial monogamist.

"Trouble in paradise?"

He snorts. "You can call my relationship a lot of things, man, but paradise ain't one of them."

I say nothing, knowing that if I wait long enough, he'll start talking about whatever shit is bothering him.

And I'm right.

"She wants us to move into my parents' pool house." He drags a hand through his short dirty blonde hair. "We've been together two months. I'm not even eighteen yet and she wants us to live together. I can barely handle Saturday nights with her, let alone every damn day."

I'd ask him why he bothers to stay in a relationship that makes him so miserable, but I already know the answer.

Like most of the rich kids round here, Fred's parents are largely absent. They're not necessarily bad parents, hell, they're far better than mine and I'm dirt poor, but they're stern and often cold and if I'm totally honest, I'm not sure he's ever received a hug from his mother.

So, he stays with Mia because even though she gives him headaches, she also gives him affection. And when their romance eventually goes to shit, because it will as it always does, he'll move onto the next toxic relationship in his never-ending pursuit of intimacy. He'll check out other girls and make a show of flirting with Auntie Rosie to keep up his ruse that girlfriends suck and commitment is useless so no one knows that all he wants in life is love.

Even if he's looking for it in all the wrong places.

I don't say any of this, of course. Doing so would only make me a hypocrite. Because it's not as if I'm prepared to sit here and have a deep conversation about my own mommy issues.

And boy, do I have a lot of them.

Auntie Rosie comes over with our order and sets the plates down in front of us, followed by our drinks. Cappuccino for me, OJ for Fred.

"I brought y'all some of my famous cinnamon rolls too. On the house, of course. Baked 'em fresh this morning. Y'all are good to me and it ain't never hurt anyone to show some appreciation once in a while."

"I can think of a way to show *you* some appreciation, Auntie Rosie," Fred tells her with the cocky smirk he's mastered that brings girls to their knees.

Anticipating the flirt-fest that's about to begin between the two of them, I take out my phone and answer Summer-Raine's message.

> **Me:** First of all, you don't need to worry about survival with me, Summer-Raine. I'll keep you safe. Secondly, it was the only W H Auden quote I could come up with at the time. Would you judge me if I told you I can't quote anyone else?
>
> **Summer-Raine:** Wow. Are you really admitting to only knowing the work of your namesake? Have you been tested for narcissistic personality disorder?
>
> **Me:** Of course, and my results were off the charts. I've always been an overachiever.
>
> **Summer-Raine:** You are something else, Auden Wells.

Rosie finally saunters off, leaving Fred and I to our food. My shit-eating grin is firmly back in place, making Fred tut and shake his head every time he looks up. Eventually, he stops looking at me altogether, inhaling his burrito and three of the four cinnamon rolls before downing his orange juice like he's just lost a round of beer pong.

"You ready to go?" he asks before I've finished chewing my last mouthful. "I have to dash. Mia's pissed at me again and I need to go do some damage control before she loses her shit and breaks my PlayStation or something."

"Don't worry about it, man." I wave him off. "Gotta do what you gotta do."

"Yeah." He nods, resigned to whatever nightmare awaits him when he gets home. "Yeah, guess so."

Poor bastard.

If I could, I'd find a girl actually deserving of him to claim his heart, or force his Mama to give him a hug every once in a while.

But I'm not a magic man.

Fred's Mama won't ever change, and he'll just keep latching onto undeserving women in an attempt to fill the void she's left in him until one day he finally realises that he's worthy of a better kind of love. I could try and convince him until I'm blue in the face but it wouldn't make half a bit of difference. He's gotta figure that shit out for himself.

We settle up the tab and leave a hefty tip for Auntie Rosie before walking silently to my truck. He says nothing the entire ride back to his place, too lost in thoughts of Mia and the headache that's waiting for him, and that's fine by me.

Because Fred's not the only one who's dreading going home.

There's no way to know what will be waiting for me when I walk through the front door. Mama's moods are about as unpredictable as Donald Trump's rise to presidency. They're either good or really fucking bad. And bad days can have me doing anything from rocking her while she weeps to locking myself in the bathroom when her psychosis convinces her I'm an intruder who's trying to kill her.

No son should ever have to worry about forcefully disarming his own mother.

Since that particular episode, I've taken to hiding all the knives in the house as soon as I see signs of a bad day. But, thankfully, today seems to be a good day.

When I walk through the door twenty minutes later, having dropped Fred home, Mama is standing in the kitchen manically whisking sweet-smelling mixture in a bowl. A thick layer of flour coats every surface like snow during an Alaskan winter. There's some kind of beige paste smeared on Mama's face and clumped in her hair, though she hasn't noticed or if she has, she doesn't care. Her hair is pinned up in a bun on top of her head, a red gingham apron wrapped around her waist. She looks like a 1950s housewife that Miss Rossi would be proud of.

"Baby!" Mama sings when she notices me watching her from the doorway of the kitchen. "I'm baking cookies."

"I can see that." It's impossible not to return the smile on her face when she's looking at me like a child visiting Disneyland for the first time. "Need any help putting them in the oven?"

"No no no, you're not old enough to use the oven." She waves me away with a tea towel, bustling me out of the kitchen. "You're too little. Go and get into your pyjamas while Mamamy bakes the cookies and you can have one with your milk before bedtime."

My heart sinks.

I guess today isn't a good day after all.

"How old am I, mama?" I ask gently, conscious of how lightly I need to tread.

It's not uncommon that she mentally reverts back to a time when she was happier, back when her monsters didn't scream as loudly and Dad was still around. This is the kind of episode that's okay while it's happening, it's when reality comes crashing back that shit really hits the fan.

"You're four, silly billy." She cups my cheek softly, stroking her thumb back and forth across my skin. "Now go and get changed, that's a good boy."

"Okay, mama."

I turn to go upstairs, planning to lay low in my bedroom until she inevitably gets distracted with some other task and forgets all about the gloop in the oven, but a knock at the front door has Mama snapping her fingers round my wrist.

I can hear her terror in her fast breaths and I don't need to turn around and look at her to know her eyes are as wide as a deer that's been shot from behind.

"Baby, listen real close to Mamamy, okay?" she whispers shakily into my ear. "Get down and crawl nice and slow to the living room. Find somewhere to hide and stay there until Mamamy comes to get you. Can you do that for Mamamy?"

All I can think about is the poor delivery guy trying to deliver a package that Mama undoubtedly ordered during one of her manic episodes earlier this week. I can imagine him scratching his head and looking at the house in confusion when no one comes to the door. Mama would have specifically arranged delivery for today because she never goes out on Saturdays.

But trying to reassure Mama that there isn't a threat would only make the situation worse. She'd grow hysterical. Probably accuse me of conspiring with whomever has come to kill her by luring her into a false sense of security. Maybe even attack me before I could potentially attack her. That's happened before.

But I learnt young that the only thing to do when she gets like this is to go along with whatever bizarre behaviour she's asking of me and wait it out. So, I do as I've done countless times before. I crawl as quietly as my six-foot-two frame can manage and sit on the floor beneath the window, making a mental note to pick Mama's missed package up from the depot on my way home from school on Monday.

The first time this happened, I was probably around seven and just as terrified as she was. I'd spent hours and hours trembling in fear from inside the TV cabinet that she'd folded my tiny body into to "keep me safe". But the more often stuff like this happened, the more I wondered why nothing ever happened to us beyond a few knocks on the door, and the more I realised that the danger on our doorstep wasn't really danger at all. And the fear I once had of being murdered by strangers in my own home slowly morphed into fear of my mother. Not because I was worried that she'd hurt me, though she had on some occasions when her hallucinations were particularly bad, but because I was too young to understand how to navigate my mother's mental illness and I was terrified of making it worse.

My school teachers were oblivious to what I was dealing with at home and I would never have gone to CPS off my own back for fear of us being separated. She may not have been the mother I needed her to be, but she was still my Mama and I'd never turn my back on her.

A little after my sixteenth birthday, she finally received a diagnosis. Schizophrenia. She was prescribed anti-psychosis medication to help with her hallucinations that would have made life more bearable for the both of us if she'd have ever actually taken it.

But for the past year and a half, those pills have sat untouched in the bathroom cabinet. And I have continued to care for her, despite not having the depth of knowledge or understanding of the condition needed for me to actually help her. I've tried requesting emergency mental health assistance multiple times, but nothing has come of it. She's not deemed a big enough risk to herself to be involuntarily admitted to hospital.

So, life moves on.

And I make it through by spending as much time out of the house as possible. At football practice. Parties. The library. Fred's place. Auntie Rosie's Diner. I throw myself into sports and my studies because college is the only solution there is for us. I'll study psychology and specialise in schizophrenia and psychotic disorders.

And then, once I'm a licensed therapist, I can help Mama and make her better.

Later, once I've cleared up the mess in the kitchen and put Mama to bed, I text Summer-Raine.

```
Me: Are you ready for lesson number two?

Summer-Raine: Depends what it is.

Me: A surprise. Keep next Saturday night
free for me.
```

Summer-Raine: Sorry, can't make it.

Me: I can smell your lies from here. You know what W H Auden would say? "The way to read a fairy tale is to throw yourself in." Come on, Summer-Raine, don't make me beg. Throw yourself into the fairy tale with me.

Summer-Raine: You need to start reading other poets.

Summer-Raine: Fine.

It takes considerable effort not to burst into a celebratory dance. I don't give her a chance to change her mind. I text her back instantly.

Me: I'll pick you up at seven. It's a date.

Summer-Raine: Not a date.

Me: Oh baby, it absolutely is a date.

And despite all I've dealt with today, I fall asleep with a smile on my lips, dreaming of a smart-mouthed girl with golden hair and eyes the colour of spring.

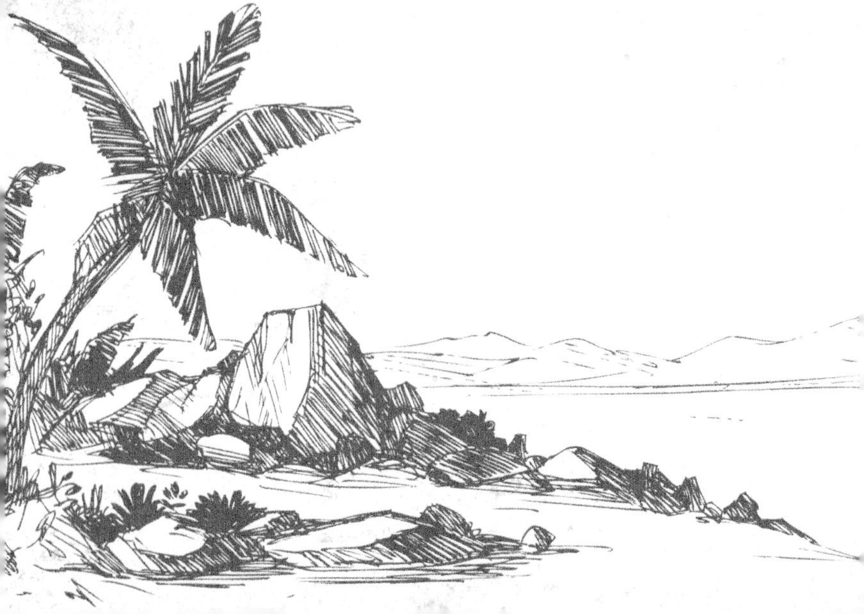

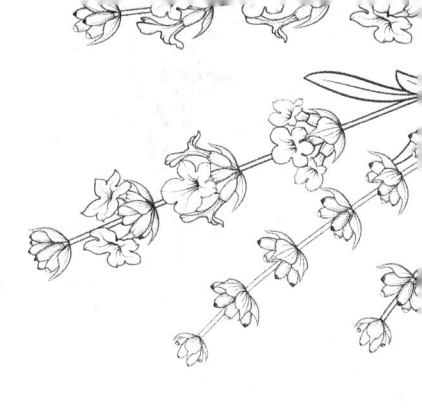

Chapter Four

SUMMER-RAINE

Monday morning, my sister's advice to make some friends is fresh in my mind like a headache that won't fuck off.

Having friends, plural, isn't something I have ever imagined being plausible for me. After years of being relentlessly bullied at my previous school, it became pretty clear that I'm not someone people tend to like. And after a while, I stopped liking people too.

But if I scrunch my eyes shut tight and focus really hard, I can maybe see myself tolerating the frequent presence of one person. Maximum. Auden not included.

I don't know what he is to me exactly, but he is definitely not my friend.

My experience is limited, I know, but I'm pretty sure friends don't lay in bed at night imagining what it would be like to touch the skin of the other, to feel their heat and their lips and their breaths on your neck as they fall asleep beside you.

Maybe Auden sees me as a friend. But I don't see him as

one.

But the more I think about it, the more I think that maybe it wouldn't be so bad to have someone to spend time with, talk to and confide in now that my sister is away at college.

I just have no idea where to start or how it even works to build a connection with someone on a friendship level. Even as a small child I didn't have friends. I'd play by myself in the corner and eat my sandwiches in the classroom with the teacher while the other kids played outside.

When I went to high school, cold shoulders in the school yard turned into cruel words in the cafeteria. Fictitious rumours were spread about me, my name was slandered in gel pen on the walls of the restrooms and my locker was vandalized more times than I can count.

It didn't take long for me to realise that I must not be a likeable person and I guess I've just always accepted that loneliness is an inevitability for me.

But something about this little town has created a shift inside me and left me with a nagging little voice in the back of my mind that says maybe my misery isn't written in the stars. Maybe I'm not fated to spend my life alone in darkness. Maybe I can have some colour in my life if only I let it in.

And that voice in my head, the one that sounds suspiciously similar to the seventeen-year-old boy with eyes the same colour as the waters surrounding this place, is the reason I find myself approaching a table in the cafeteria at lunch and hesitantly taking the seat across from Marlowe Eriksen.

I decided this morning during Anthology, as she rolled her eyes at some bullshit Mr Hanson was spouting about Gen

Z's ruining American culture with their lip fillers, TikTok and condemnation of side partings, that she would probably be my best shot at finding someone with common ground.

From what I've noticed of her over the past week, Marlowe, like me, is a loner. Less hostile, sure. Doesn't have the resting bitch face down like I do either, but she's a loner nonetheless.

She keeps her head down and her nose tucked into her chest, her index finger continuously holding her round-framed glasses to her face. She walks through the hallways like no one can see her and she's totally oblivious that some floppy-haired, smirky douchebag from the swim team called Tyler can't take his eyes off her whenever she walks past.

At the sound of chair legs dragging against the old wooden floor she looks up at me.

"Hi." My voice is quiet. Sheepish, even.

"Hey." Marlowe tilts her head to one side, watching me with narrowed eyes and a crinkled brow.

"Can I sit here?"

Perhaps the question is a little belated considering I'm already sitting, but she's looking at me with such wariness that it wouldn't feel right not to ask permission.

"Why?" she asks, shifting further back in her seat.

I freeze. What can I say to that?

Can I sit here, because my sister said I need a friend and you're pretty much the only option I've got and actually, now I've been thinking about it, maybe she's not being totally off base when she says that I need to sort my shit out? Maybe I really could do with a friend. Maybe if we just sit together in silence at lunch, even if we don't bother making small talk or acknowledging each other at all, life would be a little less grey not having to eat alone every day.

No.

I obviously can't say that. So, even though my mouth opens, I say nothing at all. I just nod my head.

This was a bad idea. She doesn't want me here. Who would be interested in building a friendship with a girl who acts like she hates the world and cuts herself before bed each night?

People don't make friends with people like me.

I nod my head again, more for myself this time, as I push my chair back and turn to leave.

"Wait."

I turn slowly at the sound of Marlowe's hesitant voice.

"It's Summer, right?"

Her expression morphs from suspicious to quizzical, the silent accusations that were written there before having seemingly disappeared.

"Yeah."

She stares at me as she thinks something over in her mind before coming to a decision. "You can sit with me."

"Really?"

"Yeah." She motions towards the chair I just vacated and nods her head reassuringly. "So long as you've not been sent here to fuck with me."

Her statement gives me pause.

"Who would send me to fuck with you?"

Her gaze moves slowly to somewhere behind me and I follow it over my shoulder, spotting the table where Auden sits with some guys from the football team and a couple of cheerleaders still in their uniforms.

She's as distrustful of people as I am, it seems. It makes me think that maybe she's had similar experiences growing up as I have.

"Why would they send *me* if they wanted to mess with you?" I ask, turning back around to face Marlowe.

She shrugs. "You're close with Auden, aren't you?"

I frown. "What makes you think that?"

There's no way she could know that we've texted back and forth this weekend and that he's plagued my every thought since I first set eyes on him and that I dream of his lips every night even though I'll probably never actually taste them, but… close? Not enough for somebody else to notice, surely.

"He spent all of Anthropology class this morning trying to get your attention," she says. Ah, I forgot that she sits in the desk directly between Auden and me.

"You noticed that, huh?"

"Yep." She pops the 'p'. She's surprisingly sharp-tongued for someone who appears so meek. "That, and I heard him talking to Freddy Haines about you in Psych earlier."

My cheeks heat and anxiety churns in my gut. "What did he say?"

She takes a bite of her sandwich, chewing thoughtfully before saying, "Nothing really. Just that he asked you out. So, is it true?"

"Is what true?"

"That he asked you out."

"Kinda," I say, eyes trained on my bowl of chilled pasta in front of me. "I don't think I'm gonna go though."

"Why?" Her mouth falls open. "It's Auden Wells, the

quarterback of the football team, the guy every single girl in senior year wants to date. Why wouldn't you go?"

I look up at her then. "For the same reason you didn't want me sitting here just ten minutes ago. What if he only asked to fuck with me? You said yourself he's the damn quarterback. There's no feasible reason why he would want to go out with me."

"Nah." She shakes her head. "Auden doesn't date. Ever. I mean, I'm pretty sure he's slept with a couple of girls on the cheer squad, if the rumours are true, but he's never taken anyone on a date. Besides, I don't think he's the sort to play with someone like that."

I swallow down the bile that inexplicably burns my throat at the mention of his sexual history. "Sorry, but how can you say that when a minute ago you accused him of sending me over here?"

"Guess I'm just a cynical bitch like you."

A surprised snort escapes me.

I'm not even offended by her words. If anything, I'm impressed with her audacity and want to see more of it. "Fair enough."

"Go on the date, Summer." She sighs. "Don't be an idiot."

The bell rings for the end of lunch and the sound of metal chair legs on wooden floors echoes like a siren as everyone packs up their shit to get to class.

"Reckon I can sit here again tomorrow?"

Marlowe shrugs her shoulders in an attempt to appear apathetic, but I catch the slight tilt of her lips before she covers it. "Yeah, guess so."

My sister would be so proud.

The end of the week arrives before I'm ready for it.

My parents got back from their conference on Tuesday and every night since they've insisted on having a farce of a family dinner. It wouldn't be so bad if Mama didn't insist on cooking despite having about the same kitchen prowess as a monkey or if we didn't sit in awkward silence the entire time. But I'm used to that, the silence. My parents stopped knowing how to talk to me when I became a teenager and they never cared enough to learn.

But at least the dinners have afforded me some time spent away from staring at my phone while I wait for a text from Auden. Apparently, I'm willing to waste my life away wishing he'd reach out to me again, but I'm too chickenshit to message him first.

When I mentioned it to Marlowe during lunch, she told me that I was embarrassing her with my pathetic pining. I didn't realise that was what I was doing, but I didn't argue. Apparently, I need to get a grip.

By the time I walk into AP English Lit on Friday morning, I'm convinced that our lack of communication means Auden has moved on from whatever interest he had in me and that whatever we were is no more. And for the most part, I've made my peace with it, so colour me surprised when he saunters in and takes the seat beside me again.

"Summer-Raine." The sound of my name on his lips is a

sacred prayer I want to hear him say over and over again.

I can't even lift my eyes to look at him. Somehow over the last two weeks, this damn boy has robbed me of the essence that made me the stone-cold bitch I was. And I want it back. Truth is, I don't know who I am without it.

I'm not the girl who sits with friends at lunch. Who goes to sleep at night and wakes up every morning thinking about a boy. Who pretends that she doesn't get jealous every time he smiles at a girl who isn't her.

I prefer the Summer-Raine with a black heart.

It's safer being her.

"Hey," Auden says, gently touching my arm and forcing me to finally look up into his hideously beautiful eyes. "You okay?"

"Yeah." I try to sound nonchalant, but my voice comes out cracked and raspy like I've just smoked a carton of cigarettes or hiked across the Serengeti without water.

"You sure?" He cocks his head to the side, watching me with amusement.

"Uh-huh."

"Still on for tomorrow?"

"Oh, um." My gaze shoots to my lap, my palms sweating feverishly as panic seizes my body. I was so sure he'd forgotten all about it. "Sure, yeah."

I sneak a glance back at him.

He nods, perfect mouth curled into a knowing smirk. "Good."

The smell of him assaults me. It's woodsy, warm and familiar. Like old books and forest floors, November nights and Christmas trees. I can hardly bear it. It makes it impossible to concentrate on anything else. No one should be allowed to smell like that.

Thankfully, Miss Rossi sashays herself through the door and gives me something else to focus on. Today, she wears a flowy white dress with her hair coiffed into a pageboy style just like Marilyn Monroe in *The Seven Year Itch*. She's even drawn herself a beauty spot on her cheek. Some jerkface in the front row snickers and asks her if it's Halloween already.

"Perhaps if you were more secure in your own individuality, you wouldn't feel the need to tear down others for theirs." She scathes, utterly unflustered by his ridiculing. "Jordan Miller, isn't it?"

"Yes, Miss." He nods, lacking half the confidence he had only minutes ago.

"Since you're so enthusiastic to contribute to discussion today, how about you kick off by talking to the class about the theme of artificiality in *The Catcher in the Rye?*"

Jordan gapes, panic flashing across his face. Hesitantly, he pulls out his chair and moves to the front of the room to address the class.

"I – I – um – artificiality, right."

If he wasn't worthy of it, I might have found his humiliation painful and difficult to watch. But Jordan Miller is a mouthy douchebag who deserves every second of his comeuppance.

And sure, I may not totally understand Miss Rossi's devotion to 1950s America, but I respect her right to express herself. Champion it, even. Especially when conceited jerks like Jordan Miller try to rob her of the liberty.

At his stuttering, Miss Rossi cocks a brow and says, "If you're struggling with that one, perhaps try discussing a theme you're more familiar with. Like Holden's sexual confusion, perhaps?"

Snickers sound throughout the class. Auden beside me covers his smirk with a clenched fist, eyes wide like he can't believe the scene unfolding before him.

Jordan's face grows red as a fire hydrant.

"Anything to say?" Miss Rossi probes.

"No, Miss."

"Did you do the reading as I instructed?"

"No, Miss."

"Thought not." She fluffs her hair and sighs. "Sit back down, Mr Miller, I'll see you in detention on Monday."

The rest of class passes by with less spectacle. I spend the majority of that time holding my breath for fear of breathing in too much of Auden's air and doing something mortifying out of sheer delirium, like holding his hand beneath the desk or pressing my face into his neck.

I'm already manically stacking my books together when the bell finally rings.

I can see Auden in the corner of my eye gathering his own things, hoping to hell that one of his friends will steal his attention so I can slip out without having to talk to him.

But no such luck.

He turns to me with that all-American smile, eyes twinkling in amusement as if he can see straight into my soul and read all the thoughts I've ever had of him.

I hate that he can do that.

That he can see me in a way no one else ever has.

It's unsettling.

So why do I feel myself melting into him whenever he looks at me, willing him to see the things I'm too frightened to show him myself and tell me that he accepts me for them anyway? Why do I find comfort in the way that he holds my gaze? Why do I feel safe whenever he's around?

"I'll see you tomorrow, Summer-Raine," he whispers, reaching to brush a strand of hair behind my ear, fingertips grazing my cheek. My heart stutters. I can barely see when he touches me like that. "Text me your address."

I nod wordlessly and watch as he picks up his books and walks out of the classroom.

Heart thudding like a freight train, hands still trembling at my sides, I grab my books and force my legs to carry me out of school, doing my very best to pretend that Auden Wells didn't just nearly kill me with the softest touch of his fingers to my skin.

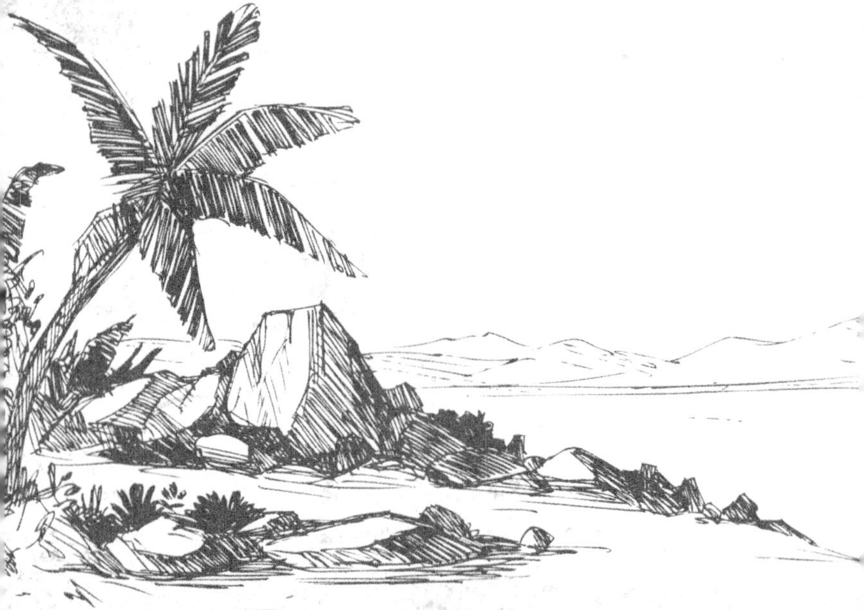

Chapter Five
AUDEN

I pull up outside Summer-Raine's house at five minutes to seven, with my best cologne on my neck and a bunch of wildflowers sitting on the passenger seat beside me.

Set away from the path, behind a small greenwood of plumeria trees and buttonbush, her house is three stories of blue weather-beaten cladding and white balustrades. Beyond it, ocean waves wash up on a private beach.

As homes on this side of town go, it's one of the more modest but a mini-mansion nonetheless.

It is everything my house isn't.

Per Summer-Raine's adamant instruction to not meet her on the doorstep and despite it going against the laws of gentlemanliness that Mama has instilled in me since I was a child, I stay in the truck while I wait for her.

I turn the music on, then turn it off again. Blow into my hand and smell it. Check my hair in the rear-view mirror. Turn the music back on and flick through until I land on 'Seeing Blind' by Niall Horan and Marren Morris. Then I turn it off again.

It's ten minutes later before I finally see her.

She appears in the gentle glow of her porchlight wearing a thin cream jersey tucked into a black denim skirt, fresh-faced and hair pulled into a ponytail. I watch slack-jawed as she walks across her front yard towards my truck. She tugs at the sleeves of her top and keeps her eyes trained on the ground beneath her feet.

Her obvious nervousness makes me smile. Not in a sadistic way, but I find it kind of flattering that she drops the fuck-you mask around me that she wears for the rest of the world. Like she saves her truth just for me.

Maybe she's not even aware of it, but I can read that girl's emotions like an old beaten-up paperback.

When she's a few steps away from the truck, I lean across the passenger seat and open the door for her, moving the flowers off the seat so she can sit down.

"Thanks." She gives me a small smile, slipping into the seat and eyeing the flowers in my hand. I present them to her with a flourish.

Her eyes widen. "For me?"

"Well, they wouldn't be for anyone else." But she doesn't reach to take them. "They're for you, Summer-Raine. I got them for you. Picked them myself and everything."

"Really?"

"Yup." I nod enthusiastically. "Right from my neighbour's garden."

She laughs. It's a beautiful, melodic sound that I want to hear over and over again.

Finally, she reaches out and takes the flowers. "Thank you. You didn't need to do that."

"I know."

Her eyes meet mine and she searches them, looking for signs of bad intent. But she won't find anything. There's nothing behind my actions other than an inexplicable burning need to be near her and make her smile.

I want to see happiness on her face and know I was the one to put it there.

She clinks her heels together in those Doc Martins she wears to school every day. It must be unbearable wearing long-sleeve shirts and chunky boots in the heavy Floridian heat, but I don't comment.

Instead, I tell her how beautiful she is and instantly turn the music on to stop her from trying to disagree. That earns me the side-eye. Girl knows my game but lets me get away with it.

It isn't long before I'm parking the truck in the lot of the restaurant I've chosen for tonight. She was silent for the entire journey.

"Something's up, Summer-Raine." I say gently. "What is it?"

I'm expecting her to blow me off with a shrug or lie, but she surprises me with the truth. "I've never been on a date before. I don't know what to do or how to act. Fuck, I even had to google what to wear tonight and I'm not even sure if I've got it right."

I tuck a non-existent hair behind her ear, losing the fight with myself not to touch her, and stroke my thumb across her cheek. Her eyelids flutter shut.

"You don't need to be nervous. Not with me, okay? Never

with me." I pull my hand back before I get carried away and start petting her like a cat. "Anyway, I thought you said this wasn't a date." I punctuate my sentence with a wink.

"Oh, shut up." She swats at me, but finally smiles.

There she is.

"Come on." I hop out the truck and dash to her side to grab the door, taking her hand as she climbs out. "You really do look beautiful. You could wear an orange jumpsuit and still be the most beautiful thing I've ever seen."

"What a line." She rolls her eyes, reminding me of our very first conversation on the beach a couple of weeks ago.

And because I've always been a fan of symmetry and it's the goddamn truth, I reply with the same words I spoke to her then. "Not a line."

Hand still holding her tiny one, I lead her into the restaurant and straight over to the table in the window I've had reserved for us since last weekend. Overlooking the dock where local fishermen moor their boats, this table is my favourite in the house. I pull out Summer-Raine's chair, giving her the one with the better view and settle into my own.

"Wow, aren't you quite the gentleman." She rests her elbows on the table and smiles at me.

The gentle flickering of the candlelight from the single sconce in the centre of the table catches on her face and turns her skin to gold. I can't take my eyes off her. Her radiance is unlike anything I've ever seen before and the fact that she's so completely unaware of it only makes it more profound.

How can someone look the way she does and have no idea?

"One of the few good things my Mama taught me."

If I thought Summer-Raine would skip over a statement like that, then I'd be wrong. "You don't get along with your Mama?"

"No, I do," I backtrack, guilt nicking at me. "That was unfair of me. Our relationship is… dysfunctional. She's not very well, but she tries and does the best she can. I shouldn't have said that."

"Don't hide your truth from me, Auden, if you're expecting me not to hide mine from you." Her words are firm, but her voice is soft. "Your Mama is sick?"

"Not physically," I say, unsure whether or not I want to tell her more. But she's right. I can't expect her to reveal herself for me if I'm not prepared to do the same. And I want to. I want her to know everything there is to know about me, it's just that I don't know how she'll react to learning about my Mama's illness and this is quite a heavy subject for a conversation straight out the gate. But I tell her anyway. "She's schizophrenic."

"Oh."

I search her face for a reaction. I find no pity, but concern swims in the depths of her green eyes.

"Which is fine. Obviously. She can't help it, it's not her fault. But having to carry your mother off the roof of the house at twelve years old because she thinks the world is flooding kind of changes the parent-child dynamic."

"Yeah, I get that." Summer-Raine nods in understanding, eyes widening slightly at that last part. "But it's okay to resent her for it sometimes. Sometimes a kid just needs their Mama."

"Sounds like you're speaking from experience."

She shrugs. "My parents aren't around much."

"How come?"

"They work a lot." She pauses and I wait for her to continue. "They're doing things more important than raising their kids, I guess."

"That's shitty."

"It's fine." She smiles, but it doesn't reach her eyes. "It's the same for every rich kid, right?"

"I wouldn't know."

Which is the truth. I wouldn't *personally* know if it was the same for every kid born to a wealthy family, but I do know that Freddy's home situation is pretty similar to Summer's.

But where Fred tries to compensate for his parents' shortcomings by latching onto the wrong girls and claiming it's love, Summer-Raine works hard to keep everyone around her at an arm's length.

Apart from me, it seems.

Somehow, in the space of only two weeks, I seem to have clawed my way inside her comfort zone, even if only for a few moments at a time. And those glimpses she gives me of the girl no one else gets to see makes me desperate to find a permanent home for myself inside that icy exterior.

The waiter, a dude called Elijah who is a year or so older than us, approaches the table and fist bumps me in greeting.

"Auden, my man." He grins at me genially before turning his eyes to Summer-Raine.

I watch the moment he registers the sheer scale of her beauty. He takes a step back as if literally blown away, thick eyebrows almost hitting the ceiling.

I get it, buddy, I get it.

"Damn, dude. Who's this and what the fuck is she doing with you?" And then… "I'd hide every chair in the world just so a girl like you could sit on my face."

Summer-Raine's cheeks burn red and I have a sudden, uncharacteristic urge to punch Elijah. Hard.

"Back off her, man," I say, but that's as far as I get in my valiant attempt to defend my date's honour. Should've known Summer-Raine wouldn't need someone fighting her battles for her.

"Then I'd probably just sit on the floor."

Elijah's eyes widen, both amused and thunderstruck. "Ouch. I feel like you've stolen my manhood. You have successfully robbed me of my scrotum with your scathing words and laser-beam stare."

"Are you aiming for a sexual harassment lawsuit?" Summer-Raine asks, sitting straight in her chair as she stares Elijah down.

"W-what?"

"In less than a minute, you've made a lewd joke and referenced your genitalia twice."

Elijah swings panicked eyes over to me. But if he thinks I'm going to help him out here then he will be bitterly disappointed. Even if I didn't agree with everything she was saying, I'd stand by Summer-Raine with a battle axe ready to take on the world beside her.

"She's got a point, man." I shrug.

Elijah pales. "I'm sorry. Jesus, that line usually works on girls."

"Wanna just take our order, dude, and get out of here?" I

prompt.

"Yeah, yeah, sure. What can I get y'all?"

"You cool if I order for you?" I ask Summer-Raine, and when she nods with a surprised but grateful expression, I order us both Philly cheese steak sandwiches, a pitcher of fresh lemonade and a portion of tropical coconut shrimp to share.

Elijah scurries off immediately, tail tucked between his legs, and I breathe a sigh of relief that he's finally left us alone.

"I'm sorry about him. He's actually a pretty decent guy, but sometimes he doesn't know when to stop, y'know?"

"Oh, he's nothing." She waves me off. "But it was fun to deflate his ego and beat his arrogance around a bit. He can't be serious about that pickup line working though, right?"

I grimace. "Um, yeah. I've actually seen it happen a few times."

Her jaw drops. "Jesus."

"Yeah."

Her gaze flicks over the room, breathing in the faded whitewood panelling, low hanging lights and nautical décor. She lingers for a second on a couple sitting adjacent to us, their hands held together on the table in front of them, faces aglow with the magic of being in love.

"This is my second lesson in the existence of love and beautiful things, right?" she says quietly, dragging her eyes back to me.

"It is."

"So, what was Elijah? An example of the type of man to avoid on my quest for love?"

I chuckle quietly, but the smile I force falls flat. Doesn't she realise that the only man she should be looking for is me?

It's the first time I've considered that maybe she doesn't feel the same way about me that I do for her. That maybe she doesn't experience the same crackle of electricity in the air whenever we're close, or realise that our souls are connected in a way that some people spend their entire lives longing for.

I can't be the only one of us to feel that.

I'd just assumed she was on the same wavelength as me since it's so goddamn obvious. That pull between us. That thread binding us together.

And now I have to know if it's all in my head or if she can feel this too.

"Happy coincidence." I shrug. "But I was kinda hoping that you wouldn't have to look further than me to find out that love exists."

Surprise flashes across her face, stretching her eyes to saucers.

"I don't mean already," I say hurriedly. "But one day if you were to find what you were looking for with someone… then maybe that someone could be me?"

The words are barely out my mouth before I realise in blinding horror that I may have just royally fucked up by laying my cards on the table so openly.

She actively rejects personal connection and human relationships. Hell, she doesn't have any friends apart from Marlowe Eriksen and even then, I don't really see them talking to each other.

And I've just gone and stuck my big foot in my mouth by telling her after only two weeks of knowing her that I hope she falls in love with me someday.

Fuck, I'm such an idiot.

"So, that's what all this is about, huh?" She smiles coyly. "Giving me lessons in love is just a play at getting laid?"

I blanch. "What? No. Th-That's not even on my mind."

She raises a brow in challenge.

"But I'll admit that maybe I had ulterior motives bringing you on this date tonight. I do actually have something to show you, but I was hoping that if you had a good time tonight that I could take you out next week. But right now, we're just a girl and a guy having dinner together for the first time. That's all. No pressure, no expectations."

I heave in a deep breath, relief coursing through me when I see that she's not looking as if she's about to make a run for it. In fact, she doesn't look scared at all.

"Okay," she breathes. "What am I looking for?"

I motion my head to a table by a window that overlooks the ocean. In the centre, a tiny vase with a single beach sunflower sits beside a flickering candle. On one side of the table, in the seat with the least beautiful view, Captain Arthur Harris sips at a glass of red wine and gives his undivided attention to the empty chair opposite him.

Despite there being only one person dining, the table is made up for two. There are even two glasses of wine, one still full, the other half-drunk.

Summer-Raine looks at me in confusion.

"That's Captain Harris," I tell her. "But we mostly just call him Cap. He's a war vet. Comes in every Saturday night, sits at the same table and eats the same meal. The lovebird's seafood sharer. It's supposed to be shared between two people, but only ever eats half."

"Then why does he order it?" She asks without judgement, looking at the elderly gentleman with softness in her eyes.

She already suspects the answer, but I tell her anyway. "He used to come in with his wife every week and that's what they always had. She died two years ago."

"And he keeps coming? Every week?"

"Yeah."

"And he pours a glass of wine for her?"

I nod.

"Does he talk to her?"

"Sometimes."

She's silent for a moment, eyes locked on the empty chair where Mrs Harris used to sit to eat dinner with her husband of fifty-plus years.

"But… why?" Summer-Raine's voice is little more than a breath whispered into the air between us. "Doesn't it just make him sadder and remind him that she's not here anymore?"

"I don't think so." I shake my head. "I think it makes him feel close to her. Like if he keeps doing the same things they always did together, then she'll always know where he is."

The sight of tears welling in Summer-Raine's eyes hits me like a thunderbolt. She blinks them away quickly, casting her eyes downwards to hide them, but I see them anyway.

I see her.

I don't believe for a second that she doesn't think love exists. She wouldn't look at Cap like her heart was breaking for him if she didn't. I think she's too scared to admit to herself that love is real because it's easy to protect yourself from something that you don't believe in.

"That's love," I say gently, hesitantly reaching across the table to rub my thumb across her wrist. "A love like theirs can outlive even death."

Green eyes meet mine, sparkling in the soft light. "So, is that the truth about love? That it lives even longer than the hearts who are touched by it?"

"Maybe. Would you be mad if I told you that I don't know what true love is either? Not personally, anyway."

"You mean to say that I'm being taught about love from a man who has never experienced it himself?"

I smile shyly.

"I might not know what it feels like, Summer-Raine, but I know what it looks like." My gaze falls upon Cap again. "And I know that I want it."

With you, I want to say.

But I don't.

I'll keep that to myself for now.

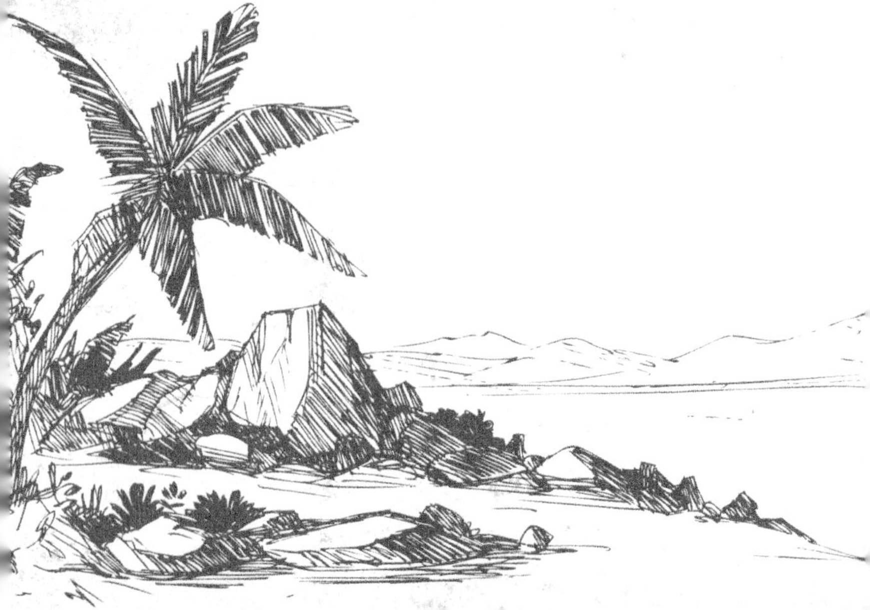

Chapter Six

SUMMER-RAINE

"So how come you know about the Captain?" I ask, carrying my boots in hand as we walk barefoot along the beach.

Auden insisted on buying dinner. I tried to argue, offering up the credit card in my wallet that's charged to my parents' bank account, but he told me I'd only be insulting him. Still, I feel guilty for giving in. I get the distinct impression that he doesn't have a lot of money and I don't want him spending what little he does have on me.

But the boy is a gentleman through and through. Not that I've ever actually met one in the flesh before, but I've seen enough costume dramas and chick flicks to know what one is supposed to look like.

"I worked there over summer." He kicks the sand at his feet as he stares down at the ground, one hand carrying his dress shoes, the other shoved into the front pocket of his chinos.

He looks edible.

"You don't anymore?" I ask.

"Nah, couldn't keep it going once school started. Between classes and football practice, it'd be impossible to pick up the shifts." He shrugs a shoulder and honours me with a heart-stopping smile that has dimples appearing on his cheeks. "But I saved up enough during summer break to keep my truck running and take pretty girls out for dinner."

"Pretty girls, huh?" I ask playfully, but my stomach churns with the idea that I'm just one of many.

I know Marlowe told me that he doesn't date anyone, but what if she was wrong? It'd be easy enough to have missed the gossip when her only source of information is what she overhears in the girl's bathroom at school.

"Just the one."

A sigh of relief escapes me and Auden, ever the perceptive man that he is, shoots me a knowing smirk. He saw my jealousy and it pleased him.

"You don't date a lot?"

"Or at all."

I don't know what possesses me to say it, but I find myself asking, "But you sleep with girls?"

His eyes widen in surprise at my question and he cocks his head to one side while he thinks his answer over.

"I'm not a stereotypical football player, Summer-Raine," he says finally. "But I'm not a virgin either."

My heart dips. It shouldn't upset me that a boy I barely know has had sex before.

It *shouldn't* upset me, but it does.

Auden stops in place and turns to me, reaching his hand out to run a long finger down the side of my face. "Does that bother you?"

"No," I lie. "Why would it?"

I should have known better than to think he wouldn't see right through me.

"It's okay that it does," he says, fingers running over the pulse at the side of my neck. My breath hitches, my heart thunders like a storm between us. "The thought of anyone touching you makes me blind with jealousy."

"No one has touched me," I whisper.

His nostrils flare at my words, his pupils black and blown. I can see it, that blaze of possession in his gaze is the same as the one he had when he told me earlier that he hopes it's with him that I realise the existence of love.

I try desperately not to show him how his close proximity is affecting me. He's so close that it'd be easy for him to see how far gone I already am. It would be so easy for my heart to fall hopelessly into the palm of his hand.

Two weeks is a ridiculous amount of time to feel this way about someone. And I reason with myself that it's probably just infatuation born out of being shown some attention from the hottest guy in school.

It's not real.

It can't be real.

"What, *ever?*" he asks.

I shake my head.

"Anywhere?"

"No."

"Even here?" My breath turns ragged as the brush of his finger moves across my face to the seam of my lips.

But I can't answer him because he's dragging my bottom lip down with the tip of his thumb, staring at my mouth in a way no one ever has before. Like he's hungry despite having just eaten.

"I'm not sure I'll survive you, Summer-Raine." His voice is so soft and quiet that I almost don't hear it.

But I'm glad I do. Because the truth is, I feel the same way. Maybe more so.

But my untrained, untrusting heart isn't built to withstand romantic trauma. And Auden Wells, with his poetry and dimples and lessons in love, is everything I've been hiding from in order to keep it safe.

Because living with the monsters in my head already causes me enough pain without the addition of heartbreak. I'm already too damaged, too corrupted by the evil of clinical depression to expose myself to the danger of falling in love.

I realised earlier as Auden told me about his mother's illness that I'd have to tell him about my own. It was an epiphany that scared me to the core, because for the first time I'd be opening myself up to the very real possibility of rejection.

It wasn't quite the same when I approached Marlowe last week. This isn't me reaching out to someone because my sister called me a loner and told me to try and make friends.

This will make me vulnerable in a way I have never allowed myself to be before with anyone.

"Auden," I choke out, his thumb falling away from lip.

"Mm?"

"I need to tell you something." My hands claw at the sleeves of my jersey as I search wildly for the right words to say. "After what you told me about your Mama, I feel like it'd be wrong to keep this from you. I'm sick too."

"Shhh," he pulls me to his chest and runs a flat hand up and down my back in soothing strokes. "I know, I've seen your monsters Summer-Raine. They don't scare me away."

I pull back to look at him, but his arms stay locked around me. Even in the dim glimmer of the moonlight, his eyes are as blue as the midday sky.

"When?"

"The Friday before school started," he admits. "You were standing in the rain by the gas station. I saw them then as I see them now."

I remember little from that night, but I do remember the rain. I'd had a bad day, that much I know for sure. I imagine that I'd done what I usually do when the darkness takes over, and left the house in a trance with no sense of direction. Rain has always had a way of grounding me, of bringing me back from the brink when I've needed it to. And that night was no exception.

I remember standing somewhere, the gas station apparently, with my head tilted to the sky as I waited for the water to bring me back to life. Raindrops had fallen heavy on my skin, washing away the poison that flowed through my veins.

It was the early hours of the morning before I found my way back home.

"And you're okay with that? With my depression?" I ask, the scepticism clear in my voice.

"Why wouldn't I be?"

"Because you're already dealing with your Mama's illness."

"That's completely separate." He sighs, shaking his head. "We all have baggage, some people's just come with a label."

"But I don't want to add to yours."

He rubs a hand across his jaw as he gazes down at me.

With him standing so close, it's the first time I've really been able to appreciate his height. Standing about a foot taller than me, he could comfortably rest his chin on the top of my head if he wanted to.

Perhaps if it were someone else, I'd find it intimidating. But around Auden, I've never felt anything other than safe and our vast height difference only adds to that.

"Mental illness doesn't make you a burden. Only a weak person would think that of you."

His words whittle away at the ice around my heart, making my eyes heat. I blink before tears have the chance to form, but pull my gaze away from his anyway. I'm too vulnerable right now, too exposed. It's like Auden can see every insecurity I have. And although he's saying all the right things, I can't help but doubt the truth of his words.

I don't doubt for a second that he *thinks* he means them, but would he be saying the same thing if he saw me at my lowest? If he saw what my monsters are truly capable of?

Would he still not consider me a burden then?

"You don't believe me." He cups my cheek, bringing my eyes back to his. "That's okay. I'll just have to prove that you can trust me."

"You're trying to prove a lot of things to me at the moment. Maybe you're taking too much on."

"Nah." He smirks and I melt under the heat of it. "See,

I realised tonight that you don't need me to prove to you the existence of love, or anything else. You already know it to be true, you just don't want to admit it to yourself."

How can he see through me so clearly?

It's as if he knows what I'm thinking before I even think it.

"I think you pretend that it doesn't exist because it's actually the very thing you crave and that scares you."

God, I wish he'd stop looking at me like that.

Instinctively, I feel my defences rise. My heart beats frantically and my palms sweat at my sides, so much so that I have to wipe them dry on my denim skirt.

"I'm sorry if I've made you uncomfortable, maybe I should've just kept what I was thinking to myself." I huff in agreement. "But, Summer-Raine, I *see* you and you might hate that, but it doesn't stop it being true."

I avert my gaze but he immediately tilts my face back up to his with the touch of two fingers to my chin.

"Don't hide from me."

But it's hard. It's so goddamn hard to stand here as he studies me, as he speaks my secrets aloud into the summer air, without shrinking in on myself or biting his head off in self-preservation.

I wish he would look somewhere else. Anywhere but at me.

"Please."

Behind him, inky ocean waves roll up the sand towards us. The tide is coming in and it won't be long before I feel the lick of it at my ankles.

I finally meet his eyes. "You're kind of intense, you know that?"

"Sorry." He shrugs, smiling at me bashfully. "I just lose my filter when I'm around you. I can try and reel it in."

"No," I say quickly. "I don't want you to hide from me either."

"Yeah?"

I nod mutely.

His intensity scares me, but only because I'm not used to it.

I've never had anyone look further than my perpetual resting bitch face, let alone right into the very depths of my soul. But it's not as if Auden is saying anything that isn't true. So, although it's hard to hear, I can't really be mad at him for that.

And maybe, if I'm truly honest with myself, I actually like it.

"Yeah."

The smile he gives me is brighter than the lights on the boulevard behind us and it's impossible not to return it.

Long fingers reach out to brush hair behind my ear, the way they always do when Auden and I are within touching distance, and I lean into them.

"I'm going to kiss you now, Summer-Raine." His hand moves to cup my cheek. "Is that okay?"

I'm momentarily stunned. My mouth opens to speak but no words make it out.

Do I want Auden to kiss me?

My initial reaction is stone-cold fear, causing my entire body to seize in panic. But the soft back and forth of Auden's thumb on my skin brings me back to the moment the way rainfall usually does.

And I realise, yeah I do.

I *really* want Auden to kiss me.

He must see the answer on my face because he blinks slowly as if to prepare himself before slowly lowering his mouth to mine.

And then it's happening.

His lips, softer than silk, move against me. Gentle. Sweet. Coaxing. The hand on my face is warm and safe, and he brings the other to my waist, wrapping around me and pulling me into him.

Sparks shoot through me, heat burning at every point where his skin meets mine. When he nibbles at my bottom lip, I gasp, sucking in air like I'm drowning. He takes full advantage, slipping his tongue into my open mouth and sliding it against mine.

This, right here, his tongue, his hands, his body against me, it's *everything*.

The mix of his sweetness with the tang of the lemonade we drank at dinner is a dizzying cocktail that intoxicates me more than any liquor ever could.

"Goddamn, Summer-Raine," he rasps, breaking our kiss.

But I wind my fingers into the hair at the base of his neck and pull him back into me. I feel his chuckle against my lips, though it morphs into a low groan the moment I tentatively brush my tongue up against his.

I can't get enough of this feeling.

It's like every atom in my body is trembling with the ecstasy of it all.

Auden must feel the same because when he finally

wrenches himself away from me, his pupils are dilated and his chest heaves.

"Gotta stop, baby," he breathes.

I eye him quizzically.

"Can't take all your firsts in one night." He winks and I giggle, still drunk on the taste of him. "Come on, it's time I get you home."

The drive back to my house is quiet. We listen to late night radio, driving with the windows down and his hand on my thigh.

When I climb into bed, the wildflowers he bought for me arranged in a glass of water on the table beside me, I dream of the town's star quarterback and the taste of citrus on his lips.

And it's the first time in four years that I don't make myself bleed in order to fall asleep.

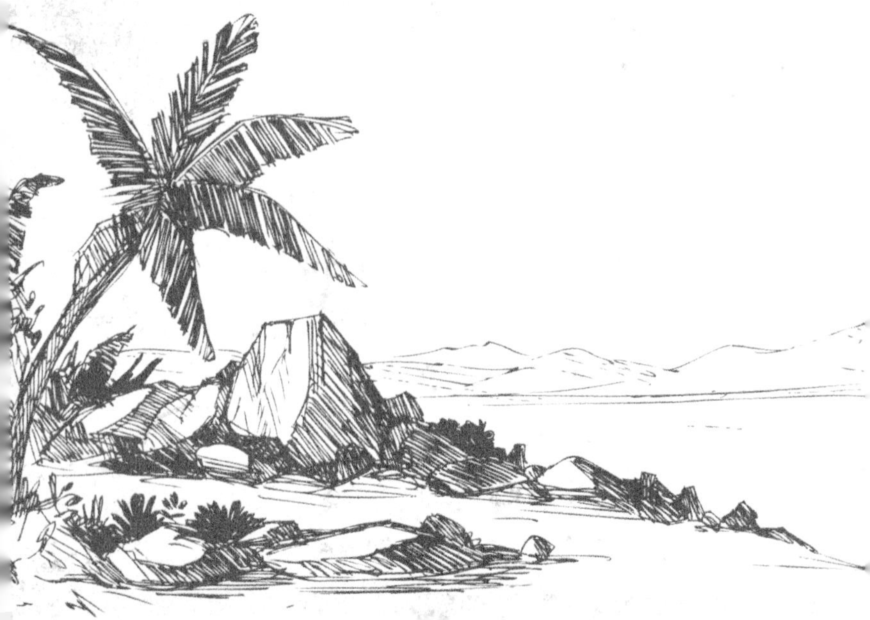

Chapter Seven

AUDEN

"So, I heard something interesting in homeroom this morning," Freddy says, looking at me coyly over his half-eaten BLT.

"Yeah?" I ask, not really listening.

My gaze stays locked on the other side of the room where Summer-Raine sits with Marlowe.

"Lana Sanders saw you on the beach on Saturday night." He pauses to wiggle his eyebrows. "All over some blonde, apparently. Didn't say who it was, but it ain't hard to work out considering you've been staring at a certain golden-haired goddess for the better part of half an hour."

I roll my eyes, but don't deny it.

"You kissed her, huh?"

Sighing, I prepare myself for a conversation I'd rather not have. But Fred is my best friend and we've always shared everything. It's not as if I've ever had an issue with kissing and telling before, but Friday night with Summer-Raine was different.

It was ours.

And I kinda just wanted to keep it that way for as long as possible.

Guess I should be grateful that we made it all the way to Wednesday without it being brought up.

"Yeah, man."

"And? Was it good? Did you use tongues? Slip a finger in? Holy shit, did you fuck?" With every question, Fred grows more animated, face lighting up like a damn Christmas tree.

"Fucking hell, Fred. You're worse than the cheerleaders for gossiping." I drag a hand down my face. "But no dude, chill. It's not like that with her. I'm not looking to fuck her."

"What? You can't tell me you're not attracted to her."

I've never been more attracted to anyone in my life. Her tiny waist, plush lips, legs that go on for days despite her being kind of short, everything about her slays me. But it's more than just her body that entrances me. It's her heart and her soul and her secrets too.

"That's not what I said. It's just that I'm not looking to get my dick wet, or whatever." I pick thoughtfully at the sandwich on my plate. "If that's what I wanted, I know where to go, you know? But she's not like that. She's different."

"Wow. You're really gone on her, huh?"

Shrugging, I reach for the food in front of me and take a bite. "Too early days to say."

"You're an idiot." He shakes his head, seeing straight through me. "But whatever. She coming to the game on Friday?"

The first game of the season is in just two days' time and

adrenaline pumps through my veins at the thought. Football in senior year is serious shit. College scouts will be making the rounds throughout the season and I've got my heart set on securing a full ride to the University of Florida. Being quarterback for the Florida Gators is a dream I've had since even before my dad left.

"Haven't asked." I shrug, my eyes seeking her out again.

Today, she wears a plain white tee tucked into ripped jeans with a thin cardigan covering her arms. Her hair is pulled off her neck in a messy bun and she doesn't wear a speck of makeup, yet she is by far the most beautiful girl in the room.

"Why not?" Fred's eyebrows pull together in confusion. "You don't want your girl there?"

"She's not my girl."

But I wish she was.

"Course she is. I know it, you know it, she knows it. You just haven't publicly claimed her yet and Friday's game is the perfect place to do it. Then you can walk into the after party at my place fresh off the glory of the win with your girl on your arm."

"Jesus, Fred. *Claimed her?*" I gape at him. "But seriously, it's only been a couple weeks. I don't wanna scare her off with too much too soon."

She already thinks I'm intense. But damn, if the image of her in the stands wearing my number doesn't have my heart beating double time and my mouth salivating like one of Pavlov's dogs.

"Whatever. Just hurry up and wife her so we can go on double dates."

Yeah, that's a no.

I can't think of anything worse than dragging Summer-Raine to dinner where we'd have to listen to Fred and Mia argue all evening.

The bell rings for the end of lunch and I wrap up my unfinished sandwich, stuffing it inside my satchel. On the walk to my last class, with Fred's words echoing in my ears, I text Summer-Raine.

> **Me:** Pretty girl, are you coming to the game on Friday?
>
> **Summer-Raine:** "Pretty girl?"
>
> **Me:** I couldn't find an Auden quote to call you beautiful, so I had to wing it.
>
> **Summer-Raine:** *Gif of Dwayne "The Rock" Johnson rolling his eyes*

I snort, drawing the attention of a group of girls in their freshman year who giggle as they pass by.

> **Me:** So, the game?
>
> **Summer-Raine:** Probably not.
>
> **Me:** Can I persuade you to come cheer me on?
>
> **Summer-Raine:** Wouldn't waste your breath, but I'll be cheering you on from the comfort of my bedroom. Go kill it, Quarterback.

Disappointment settles in my gut that she won't be

cheering me on for real, but I get it. She's still new in town, her only friend is Marlowe who I never actually see her talk to and whatever is going on between us is still in its very early stages. I also get the feeling she had a rough time at her old high school.

So I understand why she wouldn't want to come.

But it doesn't stop me wishing that she would.

I'm met with the stench of cheap booze and gyrating bodies the moment I turn up at the afterparty. It's Friday and as Fred predicted two days ago, the team and I are riding the high of the first win of the season.

We're at a house on the very same street I was waiting on last Saturday night to pick up Summer-Raine for our date. But though she lives only a few doors down and can probably feel the thrumming of the music vibrating her floors, she won't be here. She wasn't invited.

Am I an asshole for not mentioning it to her? Probably.

I would have done so if she'd come to watch me play, but I figured if she wasn't up for a football game, she sure as shit wouldn't be ready for a seniors-only house party. Especially as the ones around here can get a little crazy.

I cut around a couple fucking against the wall in the entryway and a group of guys snorting lines of white powder off the console table, and head straight for the kitchen, pouring myself a beer from the keg on the centre island. Fred steps up behind me, pouring his own beer and clapping me on the shoulder.

Bringing the red solo cup to my lips, I shift my eyes across the room.

"Man," Fred whistles. "Have you seen Elena Bodega tonight? She looks fine as hell."

I find the girl he's talking about standing with a small group of her friends that I recognise from the volleyball team and cast my eyes over her.

A scrap of electric blue material wraps around her body, leaving almost nothing to the imagination. Her hair, long and mahogany, tumbles down her back in manmade waves and her lips are painted the boldest shade of red.

"Yeah, she does," I agree.

She's gorgeous, but she does absolutely nothing for me.

"Mia know you're here?" I ask, cocking an eyebrow in his direction.

"You kidding? She'd freak if she knew where I was." He scoffs. "Told her I was visiting my grandparents in Key West this weekend."

"So, you've got a completely Mia-free weekend?"

He grins. "Damn right. Need the time off, to be honest."

I smile to humour him. Ten bucks says he gets lonely tomorrow night and tells her he's home early. Wouldn't be the first time.

"Why don't you just sack her off and go for someone like Elena?"

"We've talked about this, man." He sighs. "Mia drives me crazy, but I still love the psycho."

I gulp down some of my beer, wondering why I bothered to ask when I already knew what his answer would be. "Yeah.

Yeah, I know, man. Sorry."

He shrugs off my apology.

Our attention is stolen by the team's mascot, still kitted out in full costume, singing the national anthem at the top of his lungs as if the team just played in the NFL. Before long, everyone around us is joining in. Fred in particular goes hell for leather and I take the opportunity to slip outside while he's distracted.

The fresh night air fills my lungs and I instantly relax. I didn't even notice how tense I was back there. Considering I scored the winning touchdown of the game tonight, I should be in a better mood. But for some reason, the idea of partying into the early hours of the morning isn't as appealing as it usually is.

In fact, I'd rather just go home and text Summer-Raine. Maybe tease her until she hits me with some sassy remark that would have me falling asleep with a smile on my face.

For the first time, getting drunk off my ass and fucking a cheerleader to celebrate the team's win doesn't feel like a decent use of my time.

Sighing, I go to head back inside to let Fred know I'm heading out when long fingernails grip my shoulder. Turning, I find Lana Sanders looking up at me through false eyelashes and heavy makeup.

"Hey, Lana."

"Hey, you." She drags her acrylics across my chest to play with the neckline on my t-shirt, bleached blonde bob catching the early Fall breeze. "You're quiet tonight."

I force a smile. "Not feeling it today, I guess."

"Anything I can do to cheer you up?" The tip of her finger

trails down my body, tracing the hard ridges on my stomach before settling just above the waistline of my jeans.

I catch her wrist and gently move it off me.

"I'm actually about to leave," I say thoughtlessly and instantly regret it.

Her face lights up, completely misinterpreting my words. "Meet you outside in ten?"

She spins in her stilettos without waiting for an answer and disappears inside the house, to say her goodbyes, I assume.

"Lana, wait," I call after her, but she's already long gone.

Fan-fucking-tastic.

Sighing, I decide to text Fred to let him know that I'm leaving instead of telling him in person. At least this way I can hopefully slip out without Lana catching up to me.

I slide my phone from my back pocket and my heart stutters at the notification blinking at me on the screen.

Summer-Raine: Congratulations, Quarterback. You killed it like I knew you would.

I text her back immediately. Does that mean she watched me on tv?

Me: You saw?

Summer-Raine: Every minute.

I fire off a quick message to Fred before slipping into the shadows at the side of the house.

Summer-Raine: Enjoy the party, Auden. You deserve it.

Me: I'm actually heading out.

Summer-Raine: Somewhere better to be?

Me: Just home. Not feeling it tonight.

The speech bubble appears and then vanishes.
Appears.
Vanishes.
Appears.
Vanishes.

Me: Something you wanna say, pretty girl?

Summer-Raine: My parents are out. Wanna sit with me for a bit?

I don't even need to think about it.

After messaging Lana on social media with an apology to let her down gently, though I never had any intention on going anywhere with her, I sprint to the blue-slatted house on the opposite side of the street.

The front door opens before I even raise a fist to knock.

"I didn't tell you I was coming." I smirk, leaning an arm against the doorframe.

Summer-Raine looks adorable in an oversized sweater, pyjama shorts and odd socks that come up to her knees. She's kept her hair loose for once and it tumbles over her shoulders and down her back. I reach out and rub a golden lock between my fingers.

"You didn't need to."

"That confident, huh?" I cock a brow.

She grins. "Maybe you're just predictable."

"Maybe." I tuck the hair I'm holding behind her ear and wink. "So, are you going to invite me in or are we staying out here all night?"

She rolls her eyes with a chuckle, heading inside the house without a word and expecting me to follow. I do. Predictably.

I'm led up a lightwood staircase to the first floor and down a hallway to a room at the very end.

It's obvious the second I step through the door that I'm standing inside Summer-Raine's bedroom. If the incredible smell of bergamot and peaches isn't indication enough, the postcards with literary quotes lining the otherwise blank walls are a clear giveaway.

Among the wisdoms of Tolstoy and Brontë, one card in particular catches my eye.

"'All sins tend to be addictive, and the terminal point of addiction is damnation.'" Summer-Raine's voice tinkles through the fresh evening air. "Should've known the W H Auden card would be the one to get your attention."

I turn to her with a grin. "My narcissism is showing again."

She opens the door to her balcony and steps out into the night, leaning over the balustrade to stare out at the sea beyond. "Do you have any addictions, Auden?"

"Just the one," I reply, moving to stand beside her.

You.

"Would you ever give it up?" she asks, her gaze fixed firmly on the inky waves.

"I don't plan to."

"Even if it means you'll be damned in the end?"

I stay silent for a second. The sound of our soft breathing and the occasional scream from the party across the street is all that exists between us while I wonder what her addiction is.

"Maybe he's wrong," I say finally. "Maybe not every addiction ends in damnation."

She thinks on that a moment.

"Yeah maybe," she whispers. "Or maybe we're all just damned anyway."

"Bit of a fatalist attitude to have, isn't it?"

"Maybe I'm just realistic."

Today must be a bad day. It's like the colours of her have waned, the vibrancy of them weakened by her mood. I don't know what's triggered her tonight, but I do know that I can't bear to see the defeated look on her beautiful face any longer.

Folding myself backwards into one of the two wicker chairs, I wrap my fingers around her wrist and tug her into my lap. She tenses immediately, finding herself in a position she's never been before and not knowing which direction I'm going to take this.

But there's nothing sexual about my intentions. I simply want to hold her.

"Relax, baby," I whisper into her hair.

And that's all it takes for her body to melt into me. She brings her knees up towards her, shifting so that I'm cradling her like a child and she tucks her head into the space beneath my chin.

For a while, we just sit there like that.

She traces tiny circles on my chest with her index finger, branding me with the lightest of touches. I stroke my hand absentmindedly through her hair and breathe in the sweet, citrusy smell of her.

It takes some time, but gradually the tension in Summer-Raine starts to ebb away. The pace of her breathing slows to match mine, the movement of her fingers on my chest grows lazy and languid.

"I've never been held like this before," she whispers into the silence.

The caveman in me celebrates, but the truth is, I've never held anyone like this before either.

"What do you think?"

She sighs, nuzzling into my neck. "I think I could stay here forever."

"Me too."

She melds into me perfectly, fitting the shape of me as if we're puzzle pieces. It's like her body was made for mine to hold.

"How did you know what I needed?" she asks hesitantly after several moments of quietness.

Something in my soul told me what she needed before she knew herself.

"I don't know." I run my hand down her back and hold her tighter, brushing my lips across the top of her head. "Intuition, I guess."

We fall back into comfortable silence, looking out over the dark waves that wash up on the small beach beneath us.

The stars are out in their thousands tonight, sparkling against the blackness of the late-night sky. What I would do to spend every evening like this with her.

"It's my birthday the beginning of November," I say, speaking gently into the softness of her long hair. "We're having a bonfire on the beach. Nothing big, not like the party tonight, just a small group of people chilling out and shit. Will you come? As my, um, date?"

The stroking of her fingers on my chest stills. I hear her suck in a nervous breath and I swallow down the fear that I've pushed her too far too soon.

"You don't need to answer now," I say hurriedly. "It's weeks away, but maybe you could think about it?"

"Okay," she breathes. "I can do that. I can think about it."

It's damn hard to stop the smile from spreading across my face. My birthday isn't for another five weeks, that's plenty of time for Summer-Raine to make up her mind that she doesn't want to come, but hope blooms in my chest regardless.

It'd be the best present to have her celebrating my eighteenth birthday with me.

I check the time on my phone and groan. "I've gotta go, baby."

She yawns, stretches and climbs off my lap. By her slow blinking, it's clear that she's only minutes away from falling asleep.

"You okay if I stay here while I wait for an Uber?" I ask, willing to wait on the street if she'd rather just go to bed.

"You don't have your truck?"

I shake my head. "Was planning on having a drink."

She closes the balcony doors behind us as we step back inside her bedroom. Padding across the floor, she flops herself into bed and throws back the covers, taking off her sweater to reveal a thin long-sleeve pyjama top underneath.

"Just stay here," she says with a yawn.

"What?"

"It's late, you'll be waiting ages for a cab, so just stay here." She pats the empty space beside her as if this isn't a highly uncharacteristic suggestion of hers.

"You sure?"

"Yeah, just hurry up. I wanna go to sleep."

Chuckling, I loosen the fastening on my jeans and shuffle them off, leaving me in just my boxers and t-shirt. "You okay if I sleep like this?"

"Yeah." She says, but her eyes are closed, sleep already pulling her under.

With an amused shake of my head, I switch off the light and slide in beside her, wrapping an arm around her waist and curling my body around hers. She lets out a contented sigh and nuzzles further into me, her hand finding mine beneath the covers.

"Goodnight, pretty girl," I whisper.

"Goodnight, quarterback."

Just like that, with our fingers entwined and my face buried in the crook of her neck, I fall asleep. And though only two hours later I wake to my Mama summoning me home with a psychosis-induced emergency, it's still the best night sleep I've had in a long time.

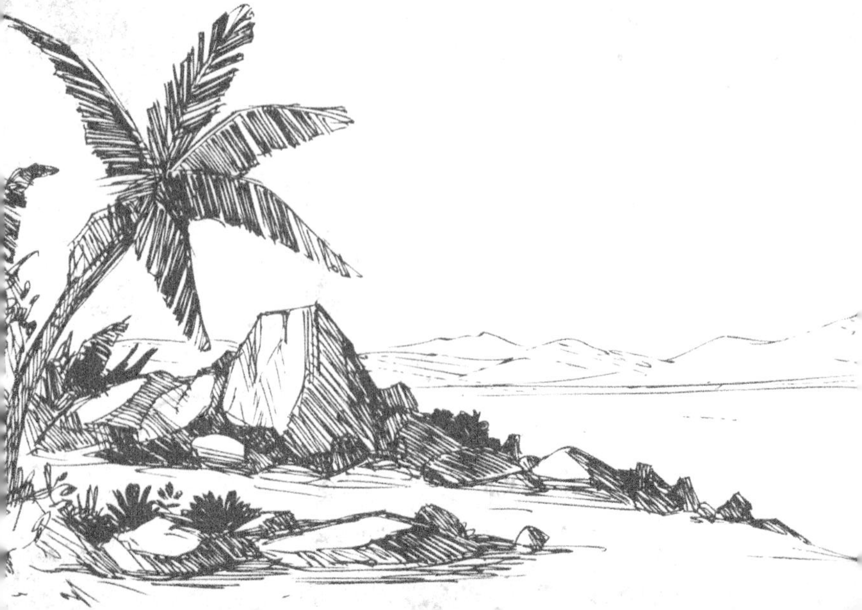

Chapter Eight
SUMMER-RAINE

Naked branches replace falling autumn leaves as September ends and October begins only to slip seamlessly into November.

Since that first night Auden stayed after his football game, he's gone to multiple parties only to find himself sitting on my balcony again. Always, he sits in the same chair with me cradled in his lap and always, he sleeps in my bed afterwards.

But he hasn't kissed me.

Not since our first date all those weeks ago.

And yet, when we're together, he can hardly keep himself from touching me. His hands are constantly on me, in my hair, around my waist, rubbing gently up and down my back. In AP English Lit, he links our pinkie fingers together underneath the desk or brushes his foot along my calf. Even when we sleep, he's touching me. Holding me to him like he's scared of what would happen if he let go.

But still, no kiss.

In the short few months that we've known each other,

Auden has shown me more affection than my mother ever has and though I'd have expected to be overwhelmed by it, I find myself constantly leaning into his touch or seeking out his body heat. I find myself constantly wondering why he hasn't kissed me again. And wishing that he would.

Somehow, about two weeks ago, he convinced me to go to his bonfire that's happening tonight. It took some begging on his part and I finally agreed, but only on the condition that I could drag Marlowe along with me. She was pissed at first, but when I told her that Tyler from the swim team, the one who's always checking her out, would be there she begrudgingly accepted the invitation.

And that's how Marlowe and I end up standing in my closet, staring at the rows upon rows of clothes my Mama insisted on collecting for me over the summer as we desperately try and work out what one is supposed to wear to a bonfire.

Like me, this'll be her first time hanging with people from school. And like me, she's nervous as hell.

"What about this?" she asks, pulling out a red dress with a plunging neckline.

"For you?"

"Oh please." She rolls her eyes. "There's no way in hell I'd ever wear something like that."

"Yeah, well same," I say, taking the dress from her and hanging it back on the rail.

"It's in your closet." She gives me the side-eye, confused why I'd refuse to wear something that she assumes I picked out myself.

But I don't really want to get into how my Mama buys

me clothes because she thinks that materialistic purchases will make up for her continued absence in my life. Even if they were the style that I'd choose for myself, which they never are, designer clothing could never compensate for her being a shitty mother.

"Think I'll just go casual," I say. "I'd rather be comfortable and underdressed than feel self-conscious in a skimpy dress."

"Yeah, me too."

Marlowe finds a pair of dark skinny jeans and an old Rolling Stones t-shirt that I haven't seen in years, and she knots it at her side to reveal her naval piercing.

She's swapped her glasses out for contacts and with her winged eyeliner and raven-coloured hair, she looks edgy. Cool. Nothing like the meek and quiet girl she makes herself out to be at school.

She'll turn heads tonight, that's for sure.

And if she actually allows anyone to have a conversation with her, I think they'd be shocked by the fierce lioness she keeps hidden beneath her shy exterior and patent penny loafers.

I settle on a cream turtleneck sweater dress that I pair with my Doc Martins and a black blazer, hanging it off my shoulders the way I've seen influencers on Instagram do. I even take the time to curl my hair and clip some of it away from my face in tumbling waves.

"You look hot as sin, girl." Marlowe winks. "If Auden doesn't, I'll take you in the bed of his truck tonight and show you a good time."

Our friendship has been founded on our mutual hatred of small talk and neither one of us ever wants to fill the silences with sob stories or profound conversation. But occasionally there are moments of easy camaraderie between us and I'm surprised by the joy it brings me each and every time.

I snort, shoving her shoulder playfully. "Will you shut up?" I apply some light makeup and a subtle swipe of lipstick across my mouth. "You ready?" I ask and she nods, nerves replacing her previous playfulness.

Twenty minutes later, we're following the smell of burning wood and ash as we trudge our way across the sand. The night sky is a deep indigo, lit up by the millions of stars that get harder to see the closer you get towards the city. Swirls of smoke billow upwards, reminding me of the log fire my grandparents had in their living room back when they were alive.

Around the bonfire, I can just about make out the shapes of a dozen or so people sitting in foldaway chairs. Music blares through wireless speakers and already drunk girls dance barefoot on the sand with their hands in the air. Elsewhere, people stand in small groups chatting, smoking and having a good time.

"This is way more than the small gathering Auden told me it would be," I mumble loud enough for Marlowe to hear.

"Bitch, this isn't a gathering. It's a whole damn party."

Her face is a picture of horror.

"Yeah, I can see that."

Anxiety twists in my gut, but I refuse to let it turn me around and make me go home. This is way, way, *way* outside my comfort zone, but I made a promise to Auden that I'd be here to celebrate his birthday with him. And though it's looking like he purposely misled me in order to get me here, I feel too much for him to break the promise I made.

This isn't Taylor Swift's twenty-first birthday, and I'm not Jake Gyllenhaal.

"Come on," I tug on Marlowe's hand, "let's do this."

She stumbles along behind me, but I don't loosen my grip. I have a feeling that the second I release her, she'll be shooting right back across the sand to catch an Uber and get the fuck home.

But if I have to do this then you bet that she does too.

I find Auden reclined in one of the camping chairs around the fire, a bottle of beer suspended between his finger and thumb, his expression animated as he laughs with his friends from the football team.

When he spots me, his face lights up even more.

"Pretty girl!"

I'm suspicious by nature, but when Auden looks at me the way he is now, it's only genuine happiness I see. There's no malicious intent, no smuggery over tricking me into coming to the party tonight, no arrogance or signs of ill will. He's just simply happy to see me.

It's also clear that he's already drunk.

I move in the direction of an empty chair, but he's quick to tug me into his lap and position me the way he does on my balcony when we're home alone.

"This is a bit more than I was expecting," I whisper, checking for Marlowe and relaxing when I see that Tyler has taken her to get a drink.

"Oh no," Auden sighs and buries his face in my neck. "I didn't know, I swear. Fred invited them all. You're mad, aren't you? Oh, baby, please don't be mad at me."

Am I mad at him?

Surprisingly, no.

I believe him when he says he didn't know, but a heads up still would've been nice. That said, if he'd told me in advance then I probably wouldn't have shown up at all.

"No." I smile, stroking a hand through his hair to soothe him. He's pretty cute when he's drunk. "No, I'm not mad."

The sigh of relief he releases is almost comical.

"Oh, thank fuck for that. I think I'd die if you were mad at me."

"Well, it's a good thing I'm not then," I say, shifting to place a kiss on his stubbled cheek. "Happy Birthday, quarterback."

His face brightens with a full tooth grin that could rival the smile of a small child waiting in line for an ice cream cone.

It's adorable.

And it makes my heart swell with an unfamiliar feeling. A feeling that has me leaning to brush my lips against his, capturing them in our second ever kiss, and forgetting all about the fifty or so other people surrounding us for the brief few seconds we're connected.

For those precious moments, it's just us.

Just a boy and a girl and a kiss on the beach.

And though it doesn't occur to me until later, it's at this very moment with our lips linked together and his hand on my cheek that I fall in love.

Because he was right all along. Of course, he was. I never believed that love didn't exist, I just didn't think that I'd ever be blessed enough to experience it for myself. I refused to acknowledge its existence because I've never deemed myself worthy of it.

And I still don't.

But right now, I don't care about anything other than my quarterback and the way his gentle touch fills my heart with warm golden light.

"Best birthday ever," he breathes, blinking slowly in his rose-tinted drunken haze.

I laugh and ruffle his hair.

Scanning the beach for Marlowe, I find her walking towards me across the sand, beer bottle in one hand and Tyler in the other. I raise an eyebrow and her eyes widen as if to say *I don't know what the fuck is happening right now.* Her terror at the situation is palpable, but I know that if she wasn't okay with what's going on then she'd make it more than clear. I mean, the girl called me a cynical bitch in our first ever conversation, so I have faith that she's okay.

They both collapse into empty chairs around the fire and continue with whatever conversation they were having. So, I turn my attention back to Auden, who's head is resting on my shoulder with his nose stuffed into my hair.

"Are you sniffing me?"

"Mmm," he moans. "So good. Like peach cobbler."

"You like peach cobbler?"

He nuzzles into my neck and I'm pretty sure he's minutes away from falling asleep. "I like you, pretty girl."

"You do, huh?"

"More than I've ever liked anyone ever."

I giggle, dropping a kiss to his forehead. "I like you too,

quarterback."

He falls silent, his chest rising and falling with slow heavy breaths and just when I think he's fallen asleep, he whispers, "Sometimes I think I more than like you."

My heart stops.

Is he really saying what I think he's saying?

Am I even ready to hear it?

Not like this. Not when he's drunk and will forget in the morning. Not when almost the entire senior class is around us and he's barely coherent enough to keep his eyes open.

As endearing as he is right now, as giddy as he is making me feel, I don't want this to be the moment he tells me those three words that no person other than my sister has ever said to me before.

"Shush," I say gently. "Don't say anything else. Not now. Not here. Okay?"

But I needn't have worried, because soft snoring tickles the side of my neck. The birthday boy has fallen asleep.

"Dude, is he asleep?" Marlowe hisses from the chair beside me, turning her back on Tyler.

"Looks that way."

"What are you gonna do with him?" she asks, trying and failing not to laugh at the enormous and undignified snort that escapes Auden as his head lulls forward.

"Who the fuck knows?"

Would I be a total bitch if I took him home early from his own birthday party? Especially as I've only just shown up and it's not even nine o'clock yet. I'd look like a psycho rolling up and instantly stealing the man of the hour to take him home.

And yet, what else can I do?

It's not like I can just leave him here to sleep it off while the party carries on around him.

"I think I need to take him home."

"Oh, thank fuck for that." Marlowe throws her hands up in the air. "I've already ordered myself an Uber, I'm *that* ready to get out of here."

"And here I was thinking you were having fun with Tyler."

"I got a drink with him, that was it."

She tries to appear casual, but her burning cheeks and panicked glance to check he can't overhear us say otherwise. I call her out on her bullshit with a cock of my eyebrow.

She sighs, knowing I'll just keep staring at her until she gives me the truth. "…And he asked me for my number."

There it is.

"And what did you do?"

"I gave it to him."

"So, why do you want to leave? Stay and chat to him or something. Listen, I'm gonna give you the same advice you gave me, okay? Don't be an idiot, Marlowe. Go on the date."

She looks at me, confused. "He didn't ask me on a date."

I shrug the shoulder Auden isn't sleeping on. "He's got your number, so it's only a matter of time."

"I don't talk to people, Summer, certainly not boys. Hell, until tonight, yours was the only contact from school that I had in my phone." She releases a long sigh and scrunches her eyes shut. "It's just a bit overwhelming and I wanna go home. Is that okay?"

I give her a gentle smile. If anyone understands how

difficult it is to step outside the safety of social isolation it's me. And I'm not the kind of person to pressure someone into something they're clearly not ready for.

Truth be told, I'm ready to get the hell out of here too.

"Of course, it's okay. I'm just grateful you let me drag you here in the first place."

Her shoulders relax as the tension slowly leaves her body. "We're friends, right? Coming with you to your boyfriend's birthday party is the sort of shit friends do, or so I've heard."

Friends.

The word, still so unfamiliar to me, makes me feel a little brighter when Marlowe uses it to describe us. It's the ultimate compliment. I might not have a lot of experience with them, but yeah, Marlowe Eriksen is definitely my friend.

My first and only friend.

Maybe even my best friend.

I don't say this, of course. We're not the kind of friends who tell each other mushy shit or cuddle when one of us is crying. We're straightforward, no nonsense, uncomplicated kind of friends.

We're simple.

And it's perfect.

"He's not my boyfriend."

"Girl, look at him." We both glance to Auden, who now has his lips and nose pressed into my neck, his arms clinging to me like he's a child and I'm his comfort blanket.

Yeah, I'm sure we look pretty cosy right now, and I know he all but told me he thinks he loves me just minutes ago, but I'm not kidding myself into thinking he's my boyfriend.

Marlowe's phone dings with an alert that her Uber has arrived and she disappears into the night with the promise to let me know when she's home.

For a while after she's left, I just sit and watch the party going on around me. Auden snores gently into the crook of my neck and I absentmindedly run my fingers through his hair as I people watch.

Freddy Haines stumbles across the sand towards the bonfire, a petite girl with dark hair marching along behind him. Her face is a putrid red, her screwed-up mouth firing off venomous words that I'm not close enough to make out, but the hostility in her tone is loud and clear.

When I catch his wrist to get his attention, I swear the girl actually snarls at me.

I ignore her.

"Hey, Freddy?"

His red eyes blink slowly as they focus on my face. "Summer, hey." It takes him several more moments to notice his best friend slumped on my shoulder. "Oh, damn, is he asleep?" He coughs a laugh into a closed fist.

"I'd say so, yeah." But my sarcasm is lost on him as he picks up one of Auden's arms and lets it drop. "Think you can help me get him to his truck?"

I saw Auden's red Chevy parked up on the boulevard on the walk here earlier.

"He's way too hammered to drive, Summer," he says, all too stern and serious.

"You don't fucking say." I roll my eyes. "Obviously, I'll drive."

He grimaces. "I don't think he'll like that. He's never let me drive his truck before."

"Well, he's not really in a state to give me his permission right now, so he can suck it up. You gonna help me or what?"

The girl with the black hair is still shooting daggers at me.

"Yeah, yeah. I'll help."

Together, we hoist Auden out of the chair and drag his comatose body up the beach. I lift the keys out of his front pocket, checking that he's still got his phone and wallet on him, before climbing into the driver's seat while Fred gets him settled in the passenger side.

I drive us back to my house, thinking he can just crash in my bed like he does sometimes since I have no idea where he lives. I don't know how the fuck I'm going to get him up to my bedroom though.

Thankfully, I don't have to worry for long.

Auden cracks his eyes open just as I turn the truck into the driveway.

"Pretty girl?" he slurs, his head flopping against the window.

"Hey, sleepyhead." I can't help but smile at him. "We're at my house, think you can manage to make it up the stairs on your own?"

"Wh-what? Yeah. Yeah." And then his chin hits his chest as he falls immediately back to sleep.

I jostle him awake.

"Come on, birthday boy. I can't get you up there on my own."

He nods slowly and slips from the cab, following me to the

door with uncoordinated, stumbling steps.

As soon as we make it to my room, I take him to my bathroom and force him onto the toilet. He can piss sitting down tonight. I'm not cleaning up piss, not even for the boy looking up at me with the brightest, most bashful, drunken smile.

"I wish you were my girlfriend," he sighs wistfully.

"What?"

"If you were my girlfriend, you could come see me play and wear my football jersey and stand with the other girlfriends and scream my name and then when I win, I could kiss you in front of everyone. Man, that would be so awesome. Wouldn't that be so awesome?"

His wide dopey eyes blink up at me and I'm not even sure he knows he's speaking out loud.

"So awesome, quarterback," I whisper, surprising myself.

You couldn't get further outside of my comfort zone than a public display of affection, but the whimsical picture Auden paints makes me more excited than it does anxious.

After he's done and washed up, I help him out of his jeans and into bed, climbing in beside him wearing an old t-shirt and fresh panties.

Like always, his arm instantly curls around me and pulls my body into his. "Hey, Summer-Raine?"

"Mm?"

"Will you be my girlfriend?" His voice is just a slur murmured into my hair, reminding me that the question is nothing more than a product of the alcohol in his bloodstream.

"Tell you what," I whisper. "If you can remember asking

me in the morning and you still feel the same, I'll give you my answer then."

And despite the monsters raging wars in my mind and the fact that I'm still very much the same cynical renegade I've always been, I know exactly what my answer will be.

Just so long as he remembers.

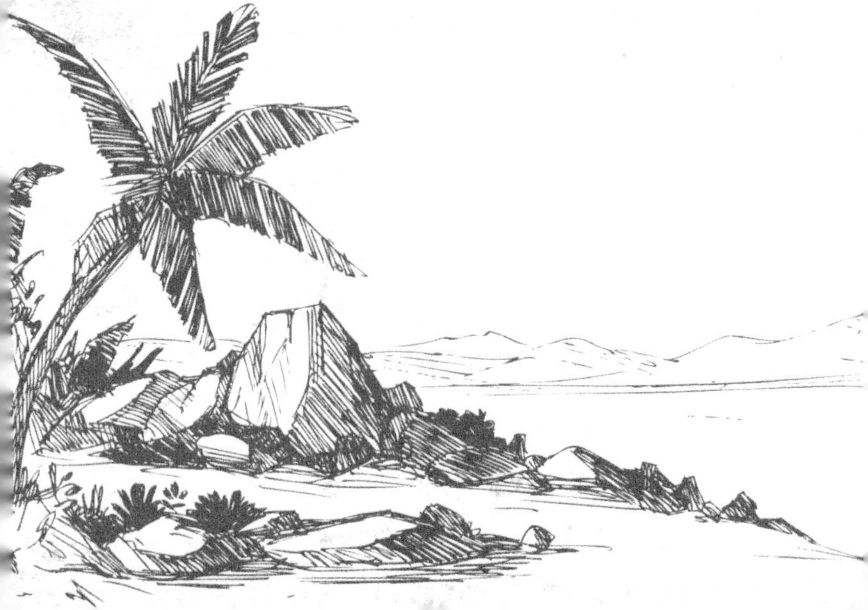

Chapter Nine

AUDEN

The worst hangover of my life hits me before I've even woken up.

I don't know what the hell I had to drink last night, but I know that whatever it was I never want to drink it again.

What even happened last night?

I remember arriving at the beach, having driven myself because I was an idiot who trusted Fred when he said it'd just be a small get together of our close friends, so I wasn't expecting to drink more than one beer. I remember the dread that filled me when I saw everyone scattered across the sand. It took me so long to convince Summer-Raine to agree to the bonfire back when it was only ten or so people, I knew that there was no way in hell she'd ever come if she knew that half the senior class had shown up.

And just that thought alone almost ruined my night.

Because, even surrounded by so many of my friends who had come to get drunk in honour of my birthday, the only person I actually wanted to spend the night with was her.

Did she turn up? Did she see everyone on the beach and go straight back home? Is she mad at me now?

If only I could remember anything after the seven shots Freddy poured down my throat.

I crack open my eyelids, wincing instantly when the dappled morning light hits my retinas. Jesus. My head booms like a bitch. I try again, slower this time, so my eyes have a chance to adjust to the offensive brightness.

I'm not in my bedroom.

But the instinctual panic that rises at that realisation quickly ebbs away the moment I register where I am. Walls dotted with literary postcards, doors that open to a balcony I've sat on countless times and windows overlooking the sea. I should've realised sooner where I am from the smell of citrus and peaches in the air alone.

And then it hits me. If I'm in Summer-Raine's bedroom, then she must have come to the party last night.

I know how uncomfortable she would have been to have seen all those people, to have realised that she'd arrived at a party and not just a chilled-out night talking with friends around a campfire. And I wasn't even sober enough to help her deal with the situation.

But still, she showed up.

It's hard not to read too much into that. I know that I shouldn't get my hopes up. I know that she's a flight risk with nomadic tendencies and a very real, but unnecessary fear of love. But does it mean that maybe she feels the way about me that I do about her?

Because isn't that basically what love is?

Not wanting to do something but doing it anyway because you care more about the other person's happiness than your own.

Is it possible that Summer-Raine might actually *love* me?

The thought makes my heart thunder in my chest, so loud I'm surprised it doesn't wake her. But I'm glad it doesn't. Because for the very first time I've woken up beside her without having to run home to Mama in the middle of the night. So, I take the opportunity to study her.

She sleeps facing me, one hand tucked under her cheek, the other resting on my bare chest. Thick lashes rest atop her soft cheeks, fluttering like wings every time she takes a breath. Her hair is so golden, it practically glows in the dark and it fans around her head like a halo.

She's the perfect sleeping angel.

She must feel my gaze on her, because she stirs and begins to wake up. I watch enchanted as her sleepy eyes blink away the remnants of her dreams and eventually focus on my face.

If she thinks I'm creepy for watching her sleep, nothing in her expression gives her away. She simply smiles at me. And it's so bright, so goddamn beautiful, that I want to kneel at her feet and beg to see it every morning.

"Good morning, pretty girl."

"Morning, quarterback." She yawns, sitting up against the headboard, and stretches her arms in the air above her head. "How are you feeling?"

The thrill of waking up beside her had made me forget all about the hangover from hell and it instantly crashes back the moment I'm reminded of it. "Like shit, but better than I would've done if I'd woken up without you."

I know what she's going to say before she says it.

"What a line."

"Not a line."

She grins, the easiness of her smile mirroring my own.

"So," I start, "how did I get back here last night?"

"You don't remember?"

I shake my head.

"None of it?"

"No."

Her face falls but she catches herself quickly, fixing a smile back on her face that isn't even half as bright as it was a second ago.

God, I wish I could remember last night.

"Just after I arrived you kind of fell asleep." My eyes widen. I must have been really out of it. "So, Freddy helped me carry you to your truck and I drove it back here."

"Jesus."

"Yeah." She chuckles. "You were pretty drunk."

An image of Summer-Raine nestled on my lap and me whispering something about cobbler flashes through my head. I try so hard to catch it, but it escapes me as quickly as it came.

"Did we talk about cobbler or something?"

Her eyes widen in surprise. "Um, yeah." She laughs nervously. "You told me I smell like peach cobbler."

"Sweet Jesus." I groan, covering my eyes with my hands in shame. "Tell me that's the worst of it. Tell me I didn't say anything more embarrassing than that?" I'm practically begging at this point.

Tell me I didn't do something stupid like tell you I love you. Because I do, of course I do, but that's not how I wanted you to find out.

She assesses me quietly, chewing the inside of her cheek as she thinks about something. There's an uncomfortable feeling in the pit of my stomach telling me that I'm forgetting something important, but Summer-Raine shakes her head and relief fills me instantly.

"Relax, quarterback. You were worried I was mad at you and you were quite emphatic about your relief that I wasn't. After that and the peach cobbler comment, you fell asleep."

I ignore the niggling feeling saying that there's something she's not telling me and push it to the back of my mind, because I'm a coward and it's easier that way.

"I wasn't wrong though. You do smell like peach cobbler."

"And you smell like Christmas trees," she says, turning her blushing face away as she climbs out of bed.

I try to be a gentleman and not concentrate on the way her t-shirt barely covers her ass or the extraordinary length of her legs. The way her pretty toes are painted white and how they complement the natural tan of her skin. But I can't stop my eyes from raking over every inch of her. Can't stop my body from responding to what I see.

Absolute perfection.

She pads over to her closet, disappearing inside but forgetting to close the door behind her.

I should look away. I know I should. But my eyes stay fixed on the vixen taking off her pyjama shirt, leaving her in nothing but a scrap of black underwear.

But it's not the bareness of her breasts that catches my eye or even the torturous curve of her spine. It's the lines that cover both her arms from wrists to elbows. Red, angry scars. There's hardly a millimetre of skin that hasn't been touched by them.

I know instantly that she's put them there herself.

She's always completely covered up, never wearing anything short-sleeved or loose enough that could fall down and reveal her scars. So, I've had my suspicions before. But it's one thing to think it and another to see it.

I don't know what to do, but I have to make this better somehow. Have to cover every inch of her scarred skin with my lips, kiss away all of her suffering and replace it with unyielding love. Her pain, so clearly carved into her body, hurts me more than if I'd taken a knife to my own skin.

Though I shouldn't, I push open her closet door and step up behind her.

"Auden, what the fuck?"

She scrambles to cover herself. Not her body, as you'd expect, but her arms.

There she stands, naked all for a scrap of lace covering the space between her legs, breasts bared to me, her figure completely exposed, and yet her instinctual reaction is to hide her scars from me.

"What did I tell you?" I growl, reaching for her hand and stretching her arm out in front of me, scars facing the sky. "Don't ever hide from me, Summer-Raine."

She tries to pull away, but I don't let her.

Her eyes, wide and fearful, track my movements with the same expression a field mouse would give a cat right before it pounces.

"Shhh, baby, it's okay," I whisper.

She flinches at the first touch of my lips to her scars, but I don't let it stop me. I trace kisses over her perfectly imperfect skin, breathing all my love into her to somehow counteract her trauma. And when my lips have loved every inch of her arm, I move on to the other and start all over again.

Finally raising my eyes to hers, I find that her terror has dissipated and turned into awestruck astonishment. Her mouth is frozen in a gasp. Her face is pale and her limbs are shaking, her breathing fleeting and erratic.

Our hands are still clasped together between us and I run my thumb back and forth over her knuckles until she begins to calm down. And when she has, I simply turn around and walk back into her bedroom. Because there's nothing to say. My lips said all I needed to and not with words. I accept her for who she is and love her for all she is. I just hope Summer-Raine understood.

Is it too soon to love her?

Probably.

But it was obvious from the moment I saw her at the gas station that my heart would become hers someday.

It might not have been love at first sight, but it was pretty damn close. It was more like the recognition of souls. Like my soul saw hers and knew instantly that it had found its home.

It's ten minutes later that Summer-Raine finally emerges from the closet. She's covered her legs in gym leggings and her top half in a formfitting t-shirt that surprisingly doesn't hide her arms.

"You've seen them now," she says, shrugging.

"Yeah."

I don't want to make a big deal out of it, and yeah, I see her point that there's no point concealing something that I now know to be there, but I can't help secretly smiling. She could have easily put on a cardigan or long-sleeve tee and pretended the last twenty minutes never happened. And I'd have followed her lead. Wouldn't have brought it up, would never have talked about it again if that's what she wanted. It would have been the easy thing to do.

So, the fact that she's so openly baring herself to me, leaving her scars unhidden for me to look at whenever my eyes stray that way, it's like she's telling me that she trusts me. And I know that that isn't something she finds easy to do.

In fact, I'm not sure there's anyone other than her sister who she's ever put her trust in before. And I'd bet money I don't have that Winter has no idea about her sister's affinity for razor blades.

"You got any plans today?" I ask, perching on the end of her bed as she busies herself around the room.

"Not really."

"Wanna hang out with me for a bit? I have to nip home and check on Mama, but we could go together and then go get some breakfast or something?"

I've never introduced a girl to Mama before. Hell, Fred's never even met her. He's been round the house, of course, but only when she hasn't been in. But Summer-Raine trusted me with her pain today, so it's only right that I trust her with mine.

An amused smile tugs at her lips. "It's midday."

"Lunch then."

"Yeah, okay."

She disappears inside her closet again and emerges with a thin cotton cardigan.

"For lunch," she says, and I just answer her with a smile. She doesn't need to

explain herself to me. Especially after all she's already shown me this morning. "They're not fresh," she follows up so quietly I almost miss it.

"What?"

"The cuts." She shifts awkwardly from foot to foot. "They're old. I haven't – haven't, um, added to them in a while. Not since the night you took me to dinner."

I swallow.

How do I react to that?

There is no response adequate enough that I can give to that revelation.

Because, *holy shit*, what a revelation it is.

"You don't have to say anything," she whispers, stepping between my open legs and running her fingers down the side of my face. "I just wanted you to know."

I wrap my arms around her thighs and hug her tight to me, telling her with my body what I'm unable to say in words.

That she's brave. That she's extraordinary. That she's *everything*.

My truck grumbles to a stop outside my tiny ramshackle

conch house. The blinds are open downstairs, the windows open to let in the air, confirming that Mama's home. And if she's feeling brave enough to have the windows open, then I can probably assume today's a good day.

Summer-Raine sits beside me rubbing her clammy palms together. She chews at the inside of her cheek, brows furrowed as she stares at my house in dread.

"You seem tense," I say, stating the obvious.

Wide eyes swing to mine. "What if she doesn't like me?"

"That won't happen." I snort. "But even if it does, she'll have forgotten all about it tomorrow."

"Her condition gives her amnesia?" she asks.

"No." I shake my head. "But the alcohol does."

"Gotcha."

I jump out the truck and rush round to the passenger side to open Summer-Raine's door, only to find her already swinging herself onto the sidewalk.

"If Mama's spying on us right now, then I hope you realise you've just got me in deep shit."

She looks at me in confusion.

"Told you she raised me to be a gentleman. But it's kinda hard to be one when you refuse to let me every time I try."

She swats me on the arm and then immediately shoots a worried glance towards the house. I take her hand and pull her up the front path. The closer we get to the door, the more her steps falter and the quicker her breathing becomes.

I unlock the door and lead us inside.

Rotten floorboards creak underfoot as we make our way to the kitchen. I watch Summer-Raine as she takes in the house, breathing in the chipped and faded wallpaper, the old wooden flooring and flickering lamplight. There's no pity in her expression, there never is, but her eyes shine bright with concern.

"Do you not get any financial aid?" she whispers.

"Mama gets alimony, but it mostly feeds her drinking habit."

I steer her into the kitchen, finding Mama on her knees on the tiled floor as she clears out one of the cupboards.

"Hey, Mama."

The sound of my voice surprises her and she smacks her head on the countertop as she shunts herself out of the cupboard to stand up. "Oh, darling, hello." Wiping her hands down on her apron, she finally raises her head to look at me.

And then her eyes catch on Summer-Raine and my breath hitches.

Because I wasn't exactly truthful when I assured Summer-Raine that Mama would like her. There's no way I could predict what her reaction would be to meeting a girl of mine for the first time. She's a tornado, my mother. She can be anywhere from weak and harmless to wild and treacherous. And this is the first time I've ever put someone else at risk of getting caught up in her storm.

Mama drags her gaze up and down Summer-Raine's body, taking in her branded Stella McCartney gym leggings and Tommy Hilfiger tee. Her clothes don't scream rich kid as much as they could do, but it's clear as day that she comes from money. And Mama fucking hates people who come from money.

"Who the fuck is this?"

"This is Summer, Mama." I say, knowing Summer-Raine would hate me to introduce her using her full name. It's only me who's allowed to call her that. "My girlfriend."

I hear a sharp intake of breath behind me, but I don't take my attention off of my Mama.

"I see."

She stares at Summer-Raine down the slope of her nose.

But my girl doesn't allow herself to be intimidated. "It's really good to meet you, Ms Wells," she says, stepping around me to stand in full view of my mother and peeling the cardigan off her shoulders, exposing her secrets to the woman she's only just met.

Part of me aches to pick up Summer-Raine and carry her somewhere far from here, but my feet are anchored to the floor. I don't know what she's doing, but I have faith that she does. All I'm able to do is just watch whatever's happening play out in front of me.

To her credit, Mama's eye contact doesn't falter. But I know for a fact that she can see Summer-Raine's exposed arms in the corner of her vision and I watch the moment her opinion of my girl changes. Like tectonic plates moving, the shift is monumental and strongly felt.

And suddenly I understand why Summer-Raine did what she did.

By showing Mama her arms, she put her demons on display. She showed a part of herself that she knew Mama would recognise as also existing inside herself. A part of her that Mama would understand.

It's a warped, fucked up kind of olive branch, but an effective one nonetheless.

"He's a good boy, Summer," Mama says, extending her hand for Summer-Raine to shake. "Heart of fucking gold, that one. Don't ever take it for granted, or worse, do something to break it."

"Never." Summer-Raine's promise is a whisper that echoes all around us.

Hiding my smile, I take my girl's hand and lead her upstairs to my bedroom, calling out to Mama on the way that I'm just stopping to change before we head out for lunch.

In the safety of my room, Summer-Raine releases a long, relieved sigh and sinks herself down onto my bed. I give her a moment of peace to collect herself after the intensity of that introduction and quickly change out of last night's clothes into an exact, but clean, replica of the outfit.

"Girlfriend, huh?" Her voice is playful and confident, but I can still hear the slight tremble of nervous anticipation.

I grin.

I was wondering how long it would be until she brought that up.

"Did you really think I'd forget asking you something like that?"

Memories of Summer-Raine arriving at the party last night, me almost confessing my love for her, telling her how awesome it'd be if she was my girlfriend and then finally asking her if she would be came screaming back in full technicolour during the drive over here.

She just looks at me, stunned.

"So, what's your answer, baby?" I give her a wink, striding over to where she sits at the foot of my bed looking up at me with beautiful, panicked eyes.

"My answer?"

"You said if I still remembered asking you this morning, then you'd give me your answer then."

She can barely hold my gaze, her cheeks flushed a stark pink, a tiny smile pulling at the corner of her lips. "Technically, it isn't morning anymore."

"You're totally right." I fake a defeated sigh. "What a missed opportunity."

Summer-Raine blinks like she can't work out if I'm joking.

So, I put the poor girl out of her misery. "Summer-Raine, even though it's past twelve and no longer morning, I'd really love it if you could give me your answer."

Her blush burns impossibly brighter as she shifts her gaze to the Rolling Stones poster on the wall behind me. I gently reach out and tilt her chin up so that she's forced to meet my eye again.

"Yeah, okay," she whispers.

"Okay, what?"

I'm an asshole for dragging this out, but damn if her shaking hands and shy smile don't make my soul sing like all of heaven's angels carolling at once.

"Okay, I'll be your girlfriend."

I finally end her suffering, cupping her cheek and covering her mouth with my own. We make out like teenagers on my tiny twin bed and then, once I've finally found the self-control to pry my lips away from hers, I take my girlfriend out for lunch.

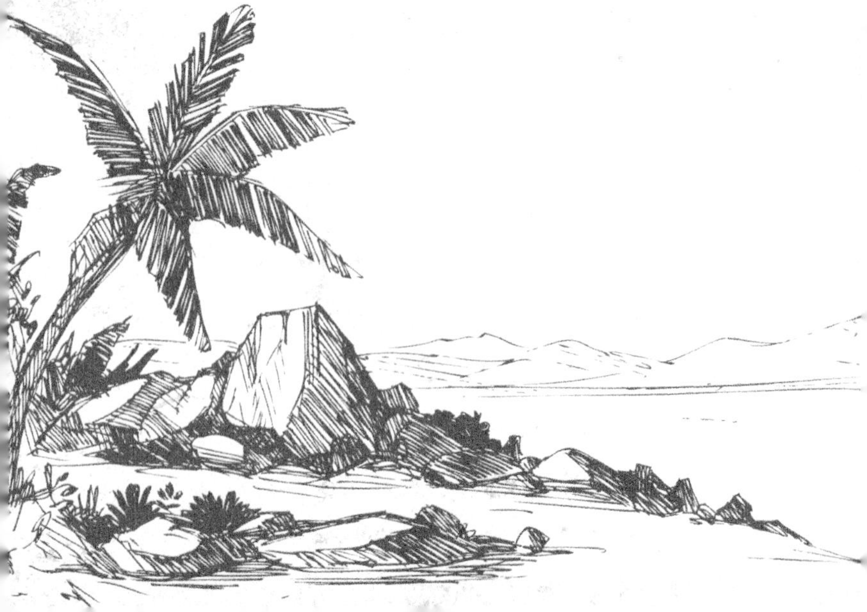

Chapter Ten

SUMMER-RAINE

"What are you doing for New Years?" Auden asks, looking at me from where he sits on a wicker chair on my balcony. The breeze rolling off the sea catches the loose strands of his hair and blows them across his face.

It's brisk despite Florida winters never being particularly cold and the late December air makes me want to grab a blanket from the bedroom to wrap around my shoulders. We're in that weird purgatory between Christmas and the New Year when everything just feels kind of uncomfortable and no one can ever remember what day it is.

For once, I'm not curled up in Auden's lap like a baby with my head tucked into his neck. Instead, I sit cross-legged on the floor, fluffy socks warming my feet, as I sift through the pile of literary postcards that he gave to me for Christmas.

We didn't spend the day together like the both of us had wanted, but we had our own mini-Christmas just the two of us a couple of days later. We hung twinkling lights from every wall in my bedroom, ate leftover turkey subs and pretended the holly vine suspended from the top of my balcony was mistletoe just so that we could kiss underneath it.

Before we went to sleep, I gave Auden a framed print for his room with a quote from his favourite book, Great Expectations, that said, "You are part of my existence, part of myself." I don't have the guts to tell him that I love him yet, but I thought that line might give him an inkling as to the way I feel about him.

I'd wrapped it up in brown paper and string, adorning it with a sprig of lavender that I'd saved and dried from the bouquet of wildflowers he'd given me on our first date.

And he'd loved it all.

He'd stared at the print, studying the words, for several long moments before giving me a smile so breathtaking, it's been seared into my memories forever. He'd brought the lavender to his nose to smell before slipping it into his wallet, promising that he'll keep it safe for the rest of his days and never lose it or give it away.

Then, he'd passed me a bundle of postcards with the most beautiful designs I'd ever seen, all tied together neatly with ribbon. He didn't have any wrapping paper, he'd said, but he still wanted it to look like a gift, not just a stack of small papers.

I'd rolled my eyes at that.

He could have given me a rock from the driveway of my house and still I'd have treasured it. Because it had come from him.

"It's actually my birthday," I say, answering his question.

"On New Year's Eve? How come I never knew this?"

I shrug. "Didn't come up, I guess."

"I was going to ask if you'd spend it with me," he says, that signature smirk of his fixed firm on his lips, but there's disappointment in his eyes. "But if it's your birthday, then I assume you have plans already?"

"No, actually."

I'm usually dragged along to some kind of ostentatious event hosted by my parents or one of their friends to celebrate the New Year, but this year will be different.

I guess my parents decided that since I'll be turning eighteen it won't be necessary to burden themselves with my presence, so they're going to a party in Miami and didn't extend the invitation to me. Not that I'd have wanted to go anyway, but it's nice to be asked. The fact that it'll be my birthday wasn't mentioned, but then, I guess, it never is. Winter tried to insist on spending the evening with me instead, but I knew how much more fun she would have if she were to stay at FSU and I didn't want to be the reason for her missing out.

I give Auden the CliffsNotes version of all this and he listens with both an empathetic expression and a hopeful one.

"Does this mean I can spend the day with you?" he asks, struggling to keep the excitement from his voice.

"If you want to." I try to be casual about it when really I can think of nothing better than spending my entire birthday with my boyfriend by my side.

That's still a concept I haven't quite adjusted to yet. Having a boyfriend.

Sometimes I psyche myself out, panicking that I'm not doing the relationship thing right or that I'm a shitty girlfriend, or even that this whole thing is one big hoax designed to humiliate me and break my heart.

But then I remember that it's Auden we're talking about.

I force words like boyfriend and girlfriend out of my head and concentrate on the one thing I know to be true, the goodness of Auden's heart. He may be the popular, all-American football player with floppy hair and a smile that makes women of every age fall panting at his feet, but his soul is as pure as glacier water.

It's just him and me.

The labels don't matter.

And when I remember that, I calm down instantly.

"Don't be an idiot," he says, seeing straight through my cavalier bullshit. "Prepare for the best birthday of your life, baby."

I climb off the floor and fold myself into his lap. "Oh yeah?"

"Yeah." Instantly, his lips are on mine, soft and searching. His tongue slips inside my mouth, only briefly, but it makes my body erupt in goosebumps. "From the moment you wake up to the moment you fall asleep, I will blow your fluffy socks off with all the birthday festivities."

I smile, already feeling like the luckiest girl in the whole world.

"You got it, quarterback."

He wasn't lying.

On the morning of my eighteenth birthday, I wake to the

smell of sweet pastries and freshly made coffee. When I crack my eyes open, Auden is wafting the tray of goodness in front of my nose, so giddy with excitement you'd be forgiven for thinking it's his birthday instead of mine.

"Rise and shine, pretty girl." His grin is brighter than the morning light. "It's your birthday."

I bury my face in my pillow and groan. "Please God, don't start singing."

"I will if you don't get up right now and eat some breakfast." He rips the pillow from beneath my head and hits me with it. "We have a crazy day ahead of us, baby, and you need to fuel up."

I grab a croissant, tearing off a chunk and shoving it into my mouth. The buttery pastry flakes away on my tongue and I chew with my eyes shut, thinking that if the rest of the day is half as good as breakfast, then it will be the best birthday I've ever had.

Though, in truth, we wouldn't have to leave my room to make that happen. Just the fact that he's here with me is enough to have me glowing from the inside out.

I demolish a further two croissants, down my coffee in one and then drink Auden's before it has a chance to cool. My tongue burns from the heat, but I'm so excited for what he has planned for us that I hardly feel it.

"What should I wear?" I ask, swinging my legs out of bed and heading straight for the closet.

"Nothing fancy," he calls after me. "Something comfortable."

I pick out a pair of light wash jeans and a floaty white

blouse, throwing a thick-knit cardigan around my shoulders like a cape. I don't bother with makeup, just throw my hair into a ponytail on the top of my head, the natural curls falling to my mid-back.

"Wow." Auden blinks. "I don't think I've ever seen you in anything other than boots."

I look down at my feet, having swapped out my faithful Doc Martins for sneakers that, until now, had never seen the outside of my closet.

I knock my ankles together. "I dread to think what your reaction would have been if I'd chosen to wear my clogs."

He barks out a laugh, stopping short when he sees my straight face. "Wait, you're serious?" His eyes widen to a comical degree. "You actually have clogs?"

"I have a lot of shit in that closet, quarterback." I wink. "But yeah, Winter brought them back for me when she went to Amsterdam last year. Maybe I'll try them on for you one day, but I'm not sure that you could handle it."

"You underestimate me, baby," he smirks, "but the clogs will have to wait because there's birthday fun to be had."

Ten minutes later, we're in his truck and heading out of the Florida Keys.

Birthday privileges mean I get to control the music, so I hook my phone up to the speakers and blast the Beatles, because they remind me of the first day Auden and I met. My ankles are crossed on the dash in front of me as I ride shotgun, the windows down and his hand on my thigh.

This is what teenage dreams are made of, I realise.

Girls in the ninth-grade pin photos of moments like these

to their Pinterest boards of relationship goals, before doodling their crush's name in their diary and kissing their Noah Centineo poster before they go to sleep.

This is what Taylor Swift sings about in her early country music.

This is everything I never thought I'd have.

Two hours later, I find myself clinging to Auden as he leads me across the ice at a skating centre. I'm sure when he planned this, he had a far more romantic vision in mind. He probably thought we'd look like something out of a holiday card, but unfortunately for him, the reality is far different. I'm a hot mess. Like a giraffe fresh from the womb learning to stand for the first time. Except, I'm an eighteen-year-old girl in ice skates trying to move across a surface that should only ever be touched by arctic animals.

Auden, to his credit, seems to be having the time of his life. The boy can't stop smiling, whether it's at my expense doesn't matter, his joy is infectious. And it makes this activity, that could very easily be one of the worst things I've ever done, so incredible that I don't ever want it to end.

But it does eventually as all things do.

And once we've returned our skates and I've regained the ability to walk on solid ground, he takes me for Pistachio ice-cream that we eat on the seafront. Together, we sit on the warm sand, me situated between his legs with my back to his chest. He tells me about his dreams for college, to go to Florida State on a football scholarship and study Psychology so he can learn how to help his Mama. And I tell him that I'm hoping to go to FSU too.

There on the beach, with our pinky fingers crossed and our ice cream melting in the small plastic pots at our sides, we make an oath to go to Tallahassee and make a life for ourselves there. Together.

With the promise of forever floating heavy in the air, the afternoon drifts slowly away. I must fall asleep, because I wake up cradled against Auden's chest as he carries me to his truck, the way a groom would carry his bride.

An hour into the drive home, we stop for dinner in Florida City, where we share a plate of dirty fries and sip from enormous glasses of strawberry milkshake.

It's early evening and the sun is beginning to set, the sky bleeding as night closes in. I watch the colours blending above us, my feet tangled with Auden's underneath the table, as I bathe in the comfort of our silence.

Perhaps that's why everything has always been so easy between us, because of our ability to be quiet together.

We don't need words to fill the space. We're happy just being in each other's presence, breathing in the same air. We understand each other, I guess. Always have done. From the moment he sat beside me on the beach all those months ago, it's been that way. Like our souls knew each other long before we did.

Auden wraps his fingers around my wrist on the table in front of us, drawing my attention from the sunset to his face.

"Have you had a good day?" he asks, almost anxiously. It's important to him that this day is special for me and he's made that clear every single step of the way.

"The best." I grin.

And I have.

I've never had a birthday like it.

Even when I was a child, I don't ever remember my parents going to the effort to make the day especially noteworthy. Once, when I was about four or so, they hired a bounce house for a party where they'd invited more of their own friends than mine. One particularly unpleasant guest of my Father's had used it to snuff out the ashes of his cigar, burning a hole in the plastic and deflating the entire structure, all before most of my kindergarten friends had even arrived.

That same friend had groped me on my fourteenth birthday, ten years later.

But I'd have a thousand more of those birthdays if it meant being able to live this one again.

"Good." Auden's smile takes up his entire face. "I got you something. A gift."

My mouth falls open. "But I didn't get you anything for your birthday."

The look he gives me is a scathing one and I snap my mouth shut instantly. "You coming to the bonfire was more than enough."

"As is everything you've done for me today."

"Baby, will you just shut up and let me give you your gift?" He reaches into the satchel beside him and pulls out a small present wrapped in bright red paper with an obnoxiously large bow, thrusting it towards me. "For you."

"Should I open it now?" I ask, my cheeks flushed and heart fluttering.

He nods wordlessly, sucking his bottom lip into his mouth

to chew on nervously while he watches me finger the gift wrap.

Trembling, I untie the bow and pick at the tape binding the paper together. The busy sounds of the diners around us fade to nothing as the gift is unveiled. All I can hear is the thudding in my ears and the slight shake in Auden's breath.

It's another literary postcard. Framed this time. And while I loved every single one in the bundle he gave to me for Christmas, the words on the card in front of me provoke a reaction that the others didn't. My cognitive function, the beating of my heart, my entire fucking nervous system is plunged into total chaos.

I'll love you, dear, I'll love you
Till China and Africa meet,
And the river jumps over the mountain
And the salmon sing in the street

"It's W H Auden," he whispers.

"Of course, it is."

No other words come to me.

I can't think through the deafening sound of blood whooshing in my ears. Can't breathe because my damn heart is beating so hard. Can't feel anything but tingles in every extremity in my body, as if I'm experiencing pins and needles everywhere. And yet, the feeling isn't uncomfortable.

It's thrilling. Electrifying. Euphoric.

"Summer-Raine," Auden's warm hands take mine, "is that okay? I know it's kinda terrifying, *fuck*, it scares me so much I can't sleep at night. But I needed you to know, you know? And you don't have to say it back, not right now, not until you're ready. I know how you feel without needing to hear those words from you, but I wanted you to hear them from me. So, is it okay, baby? Is it okay that I love you?"

Words are lost to me. For the first time since I learned to speak, I find myself without language.

It's as if I'm a child again. Like his beautiful confession has reverted me back to a time before I knew who I was. Because I suddenly don't know anything other than the way his words feel settling in my soul.

They are fatal and life affirming all at once.

With his confession of love, he has both murdered the old Summer-Raine and given life to a new one.

Because, from this moment on, I will forever be the girl who is loved by Auden Wells.

And I'll never be the same again.

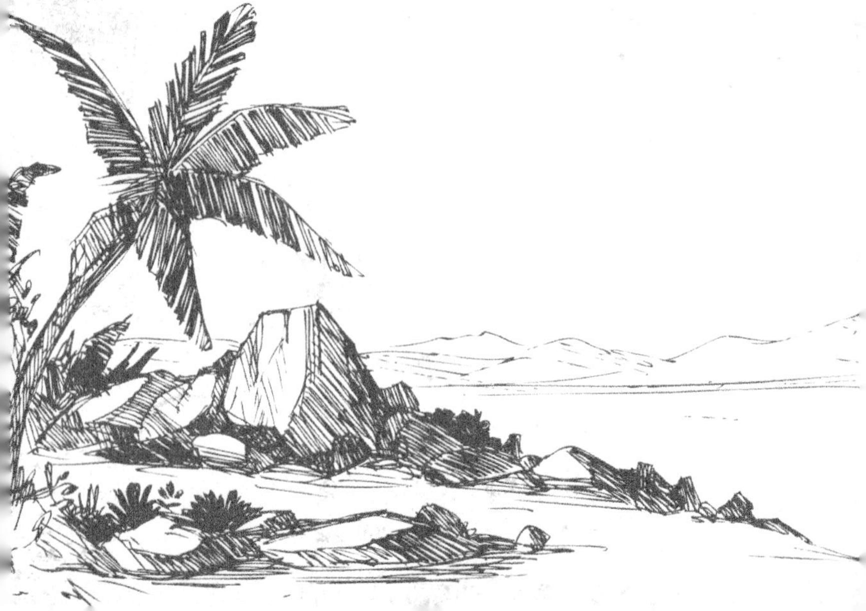

Chapter Eleven

AUDEN

We're sitting on her balcony, cuddled up together in the old wicker chair like we always are, as we wait for the New Year's firework display to start. They're being set off just a little way across the bay, so they should be as clear for us to see than if we were watching from the beachfront directly underneath them.

Summer-Raine has been quiet since I gave her my gift at the diner. Not awkwardly or solemnly so, just calmly pensive. Like she's giving herself time to absorb my words and adjust to her new reality.

I know that no one other than her sister has told her that they love her. She confessed that truth in a breathy whisper as I drove us home, worrying that she'd disappointed me because she hadn't known how to react.

She worries too much about what I think.

I wish she'd accept that I love her for her, for all her quirks and whimsies and idiosyncrasies. For both her darkness and her light.

All I want is to take care of her. To keep her so safe that her monsters wither away, to love her so fiercely that I can heal every hollow in her heart.

"It's starting," Summer-Raine whispers, pulling me from my thoughts.

Base thrums as a voice comes over a booming sound system, beginning the countdown to the New Year.

Together, we count down from ten, our lips getting closer with every passing second until finally the first firework explodes and her mouth is on mine.

We miss the entire display. The sparks flying between us are so much brighter, so much more explosive than the bursting lights in the sky above. My hand winds into her hair, clutching her head to me in fear of her disappearing into thin air. Because, surely, she's too good to be true. Too beautiful to ever belong to me.

And yet, she does.

She's mine, just as I am hers. And I don't ever see a time in our lives when that will be different.

We may be young, but your heart knows when it's found its home. Eighteen isn't too early to know that for certain, despite what grown adults like to tell us. They assume we know nothing, but that couldn't be further from the truth. I'm not old enough to drink, but I'm old enough to love Summer-Raine. And I know that I'll never stop.

I'm breathless when she pulls away, skimming her fingers down the side of my face.

"This really has been the best birthday I've ever had," she says with a gentle smile.

"I did good?"

"So good." She leans forward and presses the tip of her nose to mine in an Eskimo kiss, her eyes shut tightly as she prepares herself to say something. "Tell me again."

"Tell you what again?" My eyes scrunch in confusion.

"What you told me at dinner, Auden. Tell me again."

Oh.

"The once wasn't enough for you, baby?" My fingers find hers and slip between them, joining our hands together.

"Don't play with me right now, quarterback," she huffs. "Just say it."

I pull back, wanting a clear view of her eyes so that I can watch the way her pupils dilate as I utter the three words that she's seemingly desperate to hear.

"I love you."

Her eyes close and she sucks in a deep breath. I can feel her entire body trembling on my lap, her fingers quivering inside mine. When her eyelids finally open, it's as if my words have caused her irises to change colour. They're still that same deep, precious kind of green, but now they've been set aglow with millions of flecks of gold.

She moves her hand back up to my face, cupping my cheek and stroking my skin with the pad of her thumb.

"I love you too," she says finally.

And my whole world shifts on its axis.

I knew already, of course I did, but nothing compares to hearing those words fall from her lips.

The rhapsody of the moment has my body shuddering uncontrollably. I can't help myself; I pull her back towards me to capture her lips again, kissing her until I'm dizzy and gasping for breath.

"Auden," she whispers against my lips. "I know you've already done so much for me today, but could I ask for one more thing?"

"Anything."

"Be with me."

Her meaning doesn't sink in. Not immediately. Not anywhere near as quickly as it should. I look at her, confused. We've been together for months now, so what could she possibly mean?

And then I notice the way she chews frantically at her lip. The impossible size of her pupils. The way she keeps shifting on my lap.

"You mean…" I trail off, terrified to say what I'm thinking, because it would be awful if I was wrong.

But she nods, reading every one of my thoughts, understanding everything that I'm thinking and knowing what I need to hear.

"Yeah, that's what I mean," she says. "Be with me. Be my first, Auden. I want it to be you, if that's what you want too?"

"What I want too?" I repeat, mystified. "I want everything you'll give me. But baby, I don't want to just be your first, I want to be your *only*."

The smile she gives me in return is small and shy. "I want that too."

"Are you sure?" I ask.

I need her to be absolutely one hundred percent certain that this is what she wants, because once it's done, she can't take it back. I'd know. I'd give anything for this to be my first time too.

Not because losing my virginity was traumatic or disappointing, but because no one will ever measure up to Summer-Raine. I want her to be my first, my last, my only. Just like I'll hopefully be for her.

"I'm sure."

That's all I need. I stand, keeping my girl cradled tightly against me, and carry her into the bedroom, where I lay her down on the bed as gently as if I was handling the English crown jewels.

Her hair fans out on the pillow, a halo of gold around her head as she looks up at me with an expression I haven't seen from her before. Her eyes are set ablaze with longing and I know without seeing them that mine look the very same.

I'm buzzing with anticipation. The realisation of what's about to happen between us, of knowing her in this new way, of touching her where she's never been touched before is almost too much to bear.

This is completely unchartered territory for us.

The most we've ever done together is making out and even then, I've always pulled myself back as soon as I thought things were going too far, not wanting to make Summer-Raine feel pressured to take it further.

We've been together for months and I'm yet to learn what the curves of her body feel like under my hands, or the softness of her skin beneath her clothes, or the sound of her breath as she comes.

But I'm about to discover it all.

Even if I don't feel worthy of any of it.

My fingers skim her stomach as I gently raise the hem of her blouse. I watch as tiny goosebumps scatter across her skin, growing even more prominent when she sits up to help me pull the material over her head.

But I don't allow myself to look at her.

Not yet.

I know that once I set eyes on her body, I'll lose all rational thought. My self control will snap and I'll be overcome with the ache to bury myself inside her. And then the night would be over before it had really had a chance to begin.

I've never had an issue with restraint in any of my previous sexual experiences, but then, I guess that's because none of those girls were Summer-Raine. They didn't set my soul aglow with yearning the way only she can.

So, I don't take my eyes off of hers.

Not when I reach for the button of her jeans and they pop open with the faintest sound. Not when she arches off the bed so that I can roll them off her. Not even when her legs fall open to let me slide my body between them. Through it all, my eyes stay firmly fixed on hers.

"Auden," she whispers, my name like an oath on her pillowy lips.

Her trembling hands tug on my shirt and I tear it over my head, throwing it in a heap on the floor beside the bed. She tentatively reaches for my chest and skims her fingers across it, scolding me with every featherlight touch.

It's treacherous, this thing between us. This connection that we have.

The ache that fills me, the pain of craving her nearness, the desperate, wretched need to be as close to her as possible could start world wars, I swear it. You can roll your eyes and call it teenage melodrama, but I know as surely as I know my own name that there are no two people on this Earth more tightly tethered together than me and Summer-Raine.

I shuck my own jeans off then. And I can tell from the widening of her eyes, that the proof of my excitement, though covered by my boxers, is standing proud for her to see.

Leaning up on her arms, she tilts her chin to kiss me.

It surprises me, though it shouldn't, that despite the foreignness and vulnerability of the moment, she still stands so tall, so self-assured. She'd be forgiven for feeling tense and apprehensive in a situation so new to her, but that's just not Summer-Raine. Every new challenge or experience put in front of her she faces down with fortitude. It's one of the many reasons I'm so crazy in love with her.

Reaching behind her back, she frees the clasp of her bra with one hand. The lacy straps fall over her shoulders achingly slowly until she's completely exposed to me. And finally, because I just can't help myself any longer, I allow my gaze to fall upon her body.

My God.

For a girl with such a small frame, her body has curves in the places only women do. Her hips are set wide, made more pronounced by the slightness of her waist. Her stomach, taught and lean, gives way to full, heavy breasts that swell with every inhale and her nipples, a kind of watermelon pink colour, are drawn tight with the evidence of her desire.

I need to know what they feel like in my mouth. There's no point in fighting it, not when Summer-Raine seems as desperate for the touch of my tongue to her skin as I am. So, I lean forward, peppering soft kisses from her throat down across her chest, before tracing the roundness of each flushed breast with my lips. But the urge to properly taste her is too much. I can't hold myself back from pulling one of those tiny rosebuds into my mouth and laving my tongue over it again and again before moving on to the other.

Bergamot and peaches. She tastes just the same as she smells and the discovery draws a deep groan from my lips.

She thrusts into my touch, her back arching off the bed as she chases the sensation she's only ever felt at my hands. At my lips.

I'll be damned if she ever experiences this with anyone else. The thought of another man seeing her like this is sickening. This here, her pleasure, her arousal, the flames blazing in her eyes, is all for me and only me. Just as it will always be, should things go my way.

I run my palms across her body, down her waist to her hips. She shivers with every caress, her body so beautifully responsive it's as if she was made for me to touch her. My mouth follows the path of my hands, my lips brushing ever so softly against her skin as I shift myself down the bed to settle at the crest between her thighs.

"What are you doing?" Her voice shakes, her legs closing reflexively, but I keep them splayed open with my hands.

"Have to get you ready, baby," I whisper, rubbing my face over her panty-covered pussy. "Trust me, okay? You'll like it,

I promise."

She nods hesitantly, biting down on her lower lip as she finally relaxes her legs.

"Good girl."

I hook my fingers into the strip of lace and tear it from her body. Not giving her time to second guess herself, I run my tongue along the length of her slit. She bucks, hands shooting out to grab fistfuls of my hair.

Her breath quickens. Shallow, little gasps that shake the more I lick at her and when I suck her clit into my mouth, they transform into low, breathy moans. My tongue traces patterns over her swollen bud and I pay close attention to the shapes that elicit the biggest reactions, repeating them over and over again until her entire body is quivering.

So responsive.

It's as if her body is an orchestra and I'm its conductor, controlling the rhythm of her pleasure and leading her closer and closer to a climax that I know will be symphonic with every flick of my tongue.

"Auden, I… I'm…" Her legs shake, her back bows off the bed. "I don't know what's happening to me."

"I've got you, baby."

I lick at her faster, my hands gripping her thighs to keep them apart. When I slip a finger into her wet heat, followed shortly by a second, her body convulses, her lips falling open on a silent scream.

Wow.

I've never seen anything so beautiful as Summer-Raine falling apart.

It's an adrenaline rush like no other, a power trip I could easily get addicted to.

I lick her through it all, refusing to stop until I've drawn out every single tremble and moan her body has to offer.

"Oh my god," she whispers, once the last of her orgasm has washed over her. "That's never happened to me before."

"You've never made yourself come?" I ask.

"Yeah, I have," she breathes. "But never like that."

I grin, sitting up on my knees to pull my wallet out the pocket of my jeans that I'd discarded earlier. Finding the foil wrapper, I slide off my underwear and situate myself back between Summer-Raine's legs.

"Are you ready?" I ask, leaning over her to place a kiss on her bruised lips. "You can still change your mind."

Her skin is flushed, glowing from the effects of her climax. She's radiant. So exquisitely beautiful that it hurts for me to look at her, and yet I can't look anywhere else.

"I'm ready, Auden."

"If you want to stop at any point, just tell me and I will, okay? I won't be mad. We can just cuddle and go to sleep."

She strokes her fingers down the side of my face. "I want this. I want you."

Her words have my eyes closing and I suck in a deep breath through my nose to prepare myself. Because even if I'm not losing my virginity tonight, this will be a first for me too.

I've never had sex with someone I'm in love with.

Slowly, I roll the condom down the length of me and line myself up at her entrance.

I hold her gaze as I push into her. Her eyes widen. Her

breath stutters. I'm so terrified of hurting her that I barely move an inch at a time. She's so tight, she's basically strangling me.

When she releases a pained cry, my body stills. "Oh, fuck, baby." I cradle her head in my hands, stroking her hair and ghosting my fingers across her forehead as she fights to breathe through the pain. "I'm sorry, I love you. I'm sorry, I love you. I'm sorry, I love you." I whisper these words over and over again, comforting both her and me.

It's a bizarre paradox. The indescribable pleasure I feel at being inside of her partnered with the horror of causing her pain. I'm stuck between the urge to pull out to stop hurting her, and the feeling of never wanting this experience to end.

"You can move now," she whispers, a lone tear leaking from the corner of her eye.

I brush it away with my thumb before covering her mouth with mine as I slowly slide the rest of the way inside her. I give her a second to adjust before pulling my hips back only to thrust back in again.

All too soon, tingles begin erupting at the base of my spine, but I refuse to come this early and leave her behind. She needs to enjoy this too. Needs to experience the same ecstasy that I'm feeling at us finally being part of each other.

I slip my hand between us to draw lazy circles over her clit with my finger as I continue to move inside her. Her strangled rasps turn to gentle sighs. I can feel the fluttering of her pussy around me as the pleasure builds. It makes everything tighter, makes every sensation more intense.

It's as if my whole body is burning. I'm alight with glowing flame, my skin tingling and hypersensitive as my orgasm draws closer. I rub at her faster. My hips snap against her harder and more urgent. I've lost control, my body totally overcome by instinct. All I know is the euphoria of being surrounded by Summer-Raine and the sound of our synchronised gasps.

Her body tenses.

Her eyes snap shut.

Her pussy squeezes me impossibly tight, pulsing and quivering, as she comes around me, forcing an orgasm from my own body. With my face buried in her neck, I spill myself inside her, chanting her name over and over against her skin.

Afterwards, I clean her up and pull her naked body flush to mine. Our skin is slick with sweat, our bodies still hot and flushed. Her fingers stroke tiny circles on my bare chest as our eyelids grow heavy and sleep promises to pull us under.

"Happy Birthday, pretty girl," I whisper into the starlit night. And together, we fall asleep, my palm cupping her cheek and her hand covering my heart.

Much of senior year passes the same way. She comes to my football games, wearing my number on her back as she cheers me on from the stands. We go together to the afterparties where she hangs out with my friends and drinks cheap beer, before we bow out early to go home and make love until morning.

I take her to drive-in movies, though we never make it beyond the opening credits before we're fucking in the back of my truck. It's a wonder we haven't been thrown out of one yet.

We go for breakfast with Fred and Mia and I introduce her

to Auntie Rosie, whom she falls in love with instantly.

She even spends every other weekend at my house and deals with Mama's episodes like a seasoned professional, reading her moods and behaving accordingly. When Mama's psychosis convinces her that the house is under attack again, Summer-Raine hides with me in the living room for hours without complaining. And not once does she ever pass judgement.

I ask her to be my date to senior prom. We talk about corsages and what colour my tie should be to match her dress.

She laughs at how much different she is now than when we first met. She credits me for the change in her confidence, for encouraging her to break outside of her comfort zone and try new things. She seems to forget that I'd still love her even if she was the same reclusive girl with heavy boots and fresh scars on her arms that I'd met way back in September.

We're so in love, it feels like I'm constantly walking on rainbows and for a while, everything is perfect.

Until, one day, it isn't anymore.

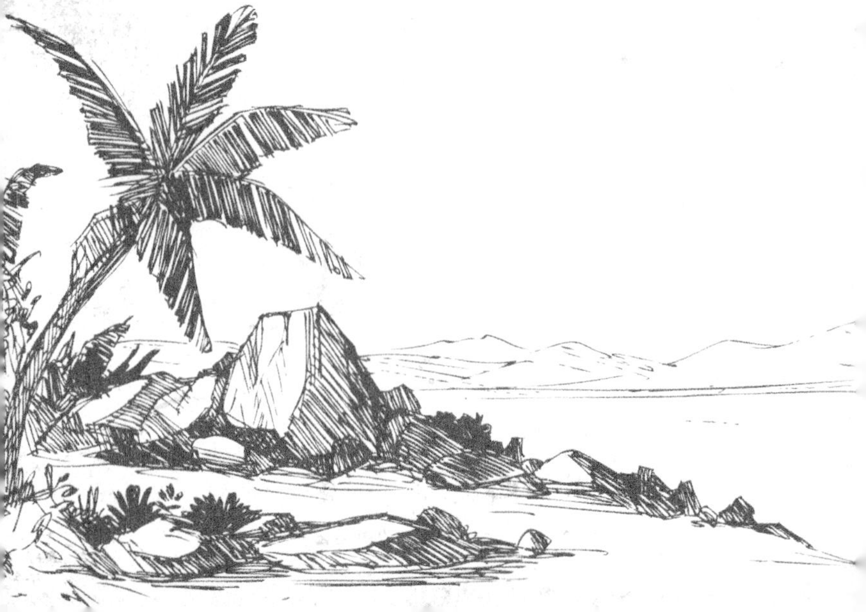

Chapter Twelve

SUMMER-RAINE

I don't know when it starts exactly.

It creeps up on me so quietly that I don't even realise it's happening until it's too late. The darkness seeping in at the corners of my vision, the feeling of emptiness that begins to swell within me like a growing wave.

It isn't until one night when I'm in bed alone, staring at the ceiling and unable to sleep, that it even occurs to me. The sound of Auden's breathing has always acted as the perfect lullaby, so it's not unusual for me to struggle when he's not here, but not to this extent. Never this badly.

Because it's not just the silence that's bothering me tonight.

It's the unbearable numbness that has smothered my soul, suffocating my ability to sleep, to feel, to *love*, even.

Of course, I know that I'm still in love with Auden. I know it because my heart tells me so, but that sensation of lightness and warmth in my chest that was always so dominant before has been engulfed by a blanket of nothingness.

That's the crux of it, I guess.

That I feel nothing.

Even when, for the first time in nine months, I take a blade to my skin and slice a deep line across the width of my arm, I feel nothing. I can imagine Auden's face when he sees what I've done, the pain that will be there, the disappointment, and still…

Nothing.

I should have known better than to think falling in love would magically cure me of my sickness. Up until this point, loving Auden has had a more profound impact on my mental health than any medication I have ever taken.

And I thought he'd sent the monsters away.

But he hadn't. Of course, he hadn't. They weren't gone, they were only sleeping. Waiting in the darkest shadows of my mind to jump out at me when I least expected it and ruin everything. Depression doesn't disappear just because you meet a boy. And I'd been stupid to think any different.

But, my god, had I been so happy.

The morning after my eighteenth birthday, when we'd made love for the very first time, I didn't think life could get any better. I was tired and sore, but every twinge of pain between my legs only served to remind me of the magic I'd experienced the night before. The incredible insanity of becoming one with the boy I love so deeply.

And every day afterwards had been just as special, just as utterly maddening.

The things that used to frighten me, like parties and making friends and actually smiling in public, didn't bother me anymore. Once Marlowe and Tyler finally made things official between them, I even started sitting with Auden and his group of friends at lunch.

I was a completely different person than the girl I was at the start of the year.

I was sociable, untroubled, *happy*.

But then, just as abruptly as Auden came into my life and changed it completely, I regressed back to who I was before. It's like for the better part of a year, I've been possessed by an imposter who's lived everyday for me, going to parties and football games and making love in the back of my boyfriend's truck.

And now whatever it was is gone.

And I'm left even worse than before. Because at least that miserable girl from September still had the capacity to feel misery. I still had emotions; they were just always the bad kind. But whatever version of myself I am now is just a vacuous void. An empty, desolate, shell of a person.

My phone dings with a text message, but I don't read it. I know who it is. Auden's been trying to get hold of me all night, ringing me every hour or so and leaving messages. I haven't answered a single call.

He's worried about me. It's not normal for me to be so quiet. I always find time to text him back no matter how busy I am. And I know it's not fair for me to ignore him, but talking seems too much effort right now. I don't have the strength to make conversation. Not even with him.

I guess he deserves a text back though.

Sighing, I pick up my phone and read the most recent message.

Auden: Baby, I know something's wrong. Do you need me to come over? I want to be there for you.

Me: No, I'm fine. Just not feeling well. See you at school tomorrow.

Auden: I love you, pretty girl. Feel better soon.

Me: Back at you, quarterback.

That's all I can handle tonight. I toss the phone onto my bedside table and stare at the ceiling until morning.

School is abuzz with excited chatter as I walk through the halls to my locker. It's early June, graduation is just around the corner and every senior I pass is talking hurriedly about their plans for ditch day and summer vacation.

Back when things were better, Auden and I had talked about driving up to Sunshine City and sleeping every night in the bed of his old Chevy underneath the stars. We were going to see the Sunken Gardens, pretend to care about art at the Dalí Museum and eat pistachio ice cream for breakfast every day. We'd been so excited about it.

But I'm not sure I want to go anymore.

I doubt he'd still want to go with this version of me anyway.

At lunch, I sit at Auden's table with him and his friends, surrounded by laughter and preppy smiles, our hands clasped together on my lap, his thumb brushing circles over mine.

But the sounds of their conversations blur together as if I'm listening to them through glass or while standing in another room.

I may as well not be here.

They'd all prefer it if I went away, I can see it in their shifting eyes and snarly lips.

We all just want me to disappear.

And that's how the rest of the week passes. Auden tries to include me in conversations I can't even hear while I struggle through every lunch period with my teeth clenched, wishing I would turn to ash and scatter away in the wind.

It's another week of the same before Auden addresses the issue. We're sitting cross-legged on my bed sharing a family pack of chips while we stare at the television mounted on my wall, neither of us actually watching whatever cartoon comedy is playing.

I know a conversation is coming that I don't want to have when he sucks in a deep breath through his nose, preparing himself.

"You wanna talk about whatever's going on with you?" he asks finally.

My automatic response is denial. "Nothing's going on with me."

He shakes his head, tutting like a disappointed parent. "Don't lie to me, Summer-Raine. Not only is it insulting, but it breaks my trust in you. Something's changed, I'd be an idiot not to notice. Just tell me what I can do to fix it."

I stare blankly at the wall behind him. I hate this. Hate that he's right, that something has changed. Hate that he wants to talk about it.

I really don't want to talk about it.

I want to ignore it, lock whatever bullshit my monsters have created in a box and throw it into the sea.

But he won't let me do that, I know he won't. Auden is nothing if not persistent. That's how we ended up together, after all. He saw me, pursued me and got me. It's the same with everything he wants in life. He goes after it until it's his.

But I can't let that happen, not this time. He doesn't really want to hear about how I've been cutting myself again, or how I spend hours at a time doing nothing but fantasising about what it would feel like to die. It would only hurt him.

"Do you think I haven't noticed that you've been wearing cardigans again? It's June, Summer-Raine. It's ninety fucking degrees outside, don't tell me it's because you're cold."

I say nothing.

He doesn't want me to lie to him, so I won't. But I won't confirm it for him either. I don't want him to give me that look he gets when his Mama is having a bad episode.

He told me once that I could never be a burden. I didn't believe him then. I still don't.

My eyes stay locked on the wall.

"Baby, please," he begs. "Give me something."

I look at him then. I breathe in the sight of his fallen face, his wide, sad eyes and downturned lips. The way his entire body seems to sag in defeat, his shoulders bearing the weight of the world and collapsing under the shear force of it.

I wish I could feel my heart cracking at the sight of his pain.

"Make love to me," I whisper finally, crawling across the bed to climb into his lap. "Just touch me and love me and maybe it'll go away."

It won't go away.

I know that. He knows that. But still, he does as I ask, just like I knew he would.

I'm a coward for initiating sex to avoid a conversation I don't want to have, but I don't have the capacity to care. Don't have the ability to feel guilty for manipulating the person who loves me most in the world.

He brushes a loose strand of hair behind my ear, the way he always has done, and I close my eyes as if it brings me comfort, when really, I'm only pretending.

God, I'm not worthy of this extraordinary, beautiful man.

If I was a better person, I'd let him go. Set him free to find a girl who can love him the way he truly deserves. A girl without baggage or monsters or darkness that destroys everything good in her life. She'd make him happy in a way I'll never be able to, not if I live the rest of my days with this poison in my blood.

He kisses me. One hand cups my face, the other falls to my arms to roll up the sleeves of my cardigan. When his fingers trace the raised slashes, he hisses.

"Fuck, baby." His forehead presses against mine, his eyelids screwed shut. "Why are you doing this to yourself?"

I bring my hands up to his face, coaxing him to look at me. "No talking," I whisper. "Just kiss me."

His laboured, shuddery breath warms my lips as he covers them with his own. I close my eyes, wishing that his kiss could revive me from the bleakness of my existence like Prince

Charming bringing his one true love back to life.

But I'm not Sleeping Beauty or even Snow White.

This isn't a Disney movie and no matter how magical the previous months have been, this isn't a fairy tale either.

We lose our clothes and tumble together down onto the bedding. When he rolls a condom down his shaft and aligns himself at my entrance, I press a flat palm to his chest, stopping him.

"Can we do it from behind today?" I ask.

We've always gravitated towards positions that allow us to look into each other's eyes, to hold that connection and experience the ecstasy of our lovemaking together. Not that we don't enjoy it in other ways, but that's just always been our preferred way of being with each other, rather than the animalistic, rawness of fucking on all fours.

But I don't want to look at him today.

I don't want him to see the lie in my eyes when I pretend to be lost in the feel of him like I have been every time before.

He nods silently and I slide out from underneath him to get settled on my knees.

"You might need warming up first if you want it like this," he says, stroking a hand softly down my back.

"I'll be fine."

"It might hurt."

Good. I hope it does.

I respond by wiggling my ass, wishing he'd hurry up and fuck me so that I can cut a fresh line in my skin and go to sleep.

Finally, he pushes into me. His hands stroke over my skin, his hips thrusting against me as he leans down to press tender kisses to the base of my neck. Even in the midst of all my bullshit, he still wants to make love to me. This isn't fucking for him, despite how easier it would be if it was. With every press of his lips to my body and slide of his cock inside me, he's telling me how much he loves me.

And it makes me want to die.

Because this isn't what I deserve right now. I can't give him the same affection and intimacy that he's so intent on giving me. All I have to offer is coldness and detachment.

Fuck, if only I could feel something.

He's been pumping into me for minutes now and though I know my body is responding in the way it's biologically programmed to, whatever pleasure I should be feeling is lost in the fog of my depression.

"Harder," I whisper, thinking maybe it will help.

His hips piston more forcefully against me, his fingers gripping my waist.

Nothing changes.

"Harder," I say again.

His thrusts grow stronger still, his hold on my body tighter, and yet, I still feel nothing. Absolutely nothing. It's as if I've been put under anaesthetic, my whole body desensitized, though my mind is still very much awake.

"Harder, Auden," I yell this time.

"Fuck, Summer-Raine, I can't."

His hips are snapping against me with such incredible power, every drive of his cock into me sends my body shunting up the bed. We've never had sex like this before. I'm not even sure he's enjoying it. My brain isn't registering whether he's making his usual noises or not. But he's doing it because I asked him too. Because he'd do *anything* I ask him to.

"Then bite me, hit me, anything. *Hurt me*, Auden."

He freezes.

Turns out, I was wrong. Maybe he wouldn't do anything I asked of him.

Because I feel the change in him the moment the words are free of my mouth. The coldness that settles over him, the sickened shock he feels at my request.

He pulls out of me, looking at me like I'm a stranger. "I can't do this."

And then he's gone.

I hear the slamming of the back door. The way the sound echoes through the old house, rattling the rafters and shaking the floors. If he's gone out the back then he hasn't gone home.

I give it five minutes before I throw on my discarded clothes and follow him out to the backyard. I find him sitting on the sand on our little strip of private beach, his arms resting on his bent knees and head bowed to his chest.

I know he knows I'm here. He's always been able to sense my presence. Can work out where I am in a room without even looking round. Up until recently, I could do the same with him.

Sand crumbles beneath my bare feet as I move up beside him and sit down. I watch him from the edge of my vision as he raises his head to stare out at the black sea in front of us, his eyes glistening with fresh tears.

I made him cry.

His silent disgust at what I asked of him echoes around me, not even the crashing waves can wash away the noise of it. Looking away, I wait for him to say something. Anything.

Does he still want to be with me after that? Would I even feel the breaking of my heart if he didn't?

When he finally speaks, his voice is little more than a shaky whisper. But regardless of how quiet it is, the resentment sewn through each word is deafening. "Don't ever ask me to do that again."

"I just wanted to try something different," I lie.

"God damn it, don't do that. Don't lie to me." I've never seen Auden angry before. I didn't even think he was capable of feeling a hostile emotion, but apparently, he is when pushed far enough. And that's what I've done. I've pushed him to this. "That's bullshit, you know it is. What just happened had nothing to do with trying new things."

"Yes, it did." I'm trapped in my denial and lying is all I'm capable of now. "I was just mixing things up."

"*Stop lying.*" He picks a rock out the sand and hurls it at the sea. "I'm up for experimenting and shit with you, Summer-Raine, you fucking know that. So long as we're both comfortable and it's about trying out what feels good. But that had fuck all to do with pleasure and everything to do with pain."

"I don't know what to say, Auden." I stand, turning to him, combative and cold. "Everything is numb, like I've been paralyzed on the inside. I'm so blank I may as well be dead and I just wanted to fucking *feel* something."

"Then talk to me!" He stands to his full height, his hands clawing furiously at his hair as he stares me down, eyes aflame with rage and hurt. "If you need me to help you feel something, tell me and I'll love you harder. And if that's not enough we can ride a rollercoaster, go skydiving or even fucking shark diving, but don't ever ask me to hurt you again."

"I'm sorry," I say weakly. "I didn't think it would be a big deal."

He looks at me like I've broken him. "Not a big deal? You think I'd ever be okay with causing you pain? You tried to manipulate me into hurting you and by doing that, you've hurt me. You've fucking *destroyed* me."

A tear falls, followed by another and then another, until they rain violently down his face. I should reach out to him. Should do what he would do if I was crying and pull him to me, stroke his back until he calms down and his breathing slows.

But I don't.

I just watch on silently as he fights to choke back sobs on his own.

Finally, he calms down enough to face me again. "I love you, but you fucked up tonight." He takes a heaving breath, catching the last of his tears with the palm of his hand. "I need some space to think about shit, Summer, so I'm just gonna go home. I'm still here though, I still love you, I just can't be around you right now. Text me if you need me, but otherwise I'll probably see you in a few days, yeah?"

I nod mutely as he drops a chaste kiss to my cheek and leaves, walking round the side of the house to get to his truck on the driveway. I watch him go, the smallest flickering of *something* burning in my chest.

And then it hits me.

For the first time ever, he didn't call me Summer-Raine.

He called me Summer.

It makes me want to charge after him and demand he never uses the shortened version of my name again. Because that's not what we do, him and me. He's the only person in this world who calls me Summer-Raine. It's our thing.

So, I need him to come back. I need him to make it right again.

But I let him go.

Because knowing the pain I've caused him, hearing him calling me Summer and then watching him walk away has rekindled the smallest spark in my barren heart.

No matter how mildly, right now I can feel something.

So, I'll replay tonight on repeat in my mind and I'll remember the look of devastation on Auden's face, clinging onto the minuscule slice of pain it brings me and hoping it's still there in the morning.

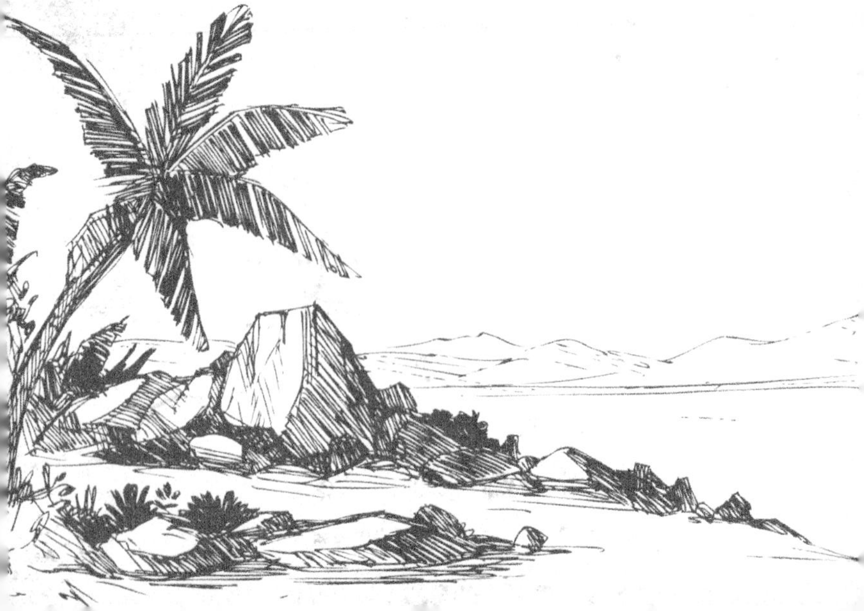

Chapter Thirteen

AUDEN

My parents split up when I was five. Dad was never around much anyway and, looking back now, I actually think he was cheating on my Mama a long time before they finally divorced, so his absence at mealtimes didn't come as too much of a shock.

But it was still a big change for a child of that age to deal with. Especially as all of a sudden, I found myself having to care for a woman whose mental stability was declining by the day. And though Mama has never admitted it, I've always suspected that her condition was the reason for him leaving.

Shit got hard and Dad bowed out.

He couldn't handle it. Couldn't find it in himself to support his wife when she needed him. So, like a coward, he divorced her. Found a woman somewhere who didn't have a mental health disorder, stood at the alter for a second time and promised to love her in sickness, health and irony. Then he left his five-year-old son to pick up the shattered pieces of the broken woman he'd left behind.

It's a young age to realise that you hate the man who raised you. Even then, I couldn't see past his betrayal. Though I was barely old enough to tie my own shoelaces, I knew that I didn't want to grow up to be like him.

So, I haven't seen him since the day he left. I only know he remarried because he had the carelessness to send a wedding invitation to his ex-wife's house, not six months after their divorce was finalised.

That's when things got really bad.

For the first time ever, Mama struck me during one of her episodes. She started drinking heavily, stopped taking her medication and would scream this awful piercing cry into her pillow at night.

It used to terrify me.

For a long time, I'd cry alone in my plastic racing car bed, wishing my stuffed toys would come to life and take care of me the way my parents should have been. Every night, it was the same. She'd scream for hours like she was being murdered and I'd sob in petrified silence underneath my covers.

Until one day, it just stopped.

Not the screaming, but my fear of it.

I acclimatised. Learnt how to block out the noise until I could sleep through it. No five-year-old child should have to deal with that. And truthfully, I'm not sure if the screaming ever really stopped or if I just stopped being able to hear it.

But the experience shaped me, I guess.

Because of it, I'll never be a man who breaks his promises. I'll never leave when things get tough or abandon someone when they need me.

I will *never* be my father.

And that's why, despite how broken I am over what she did, I've texted Summer-Raine every day since I left her on the sand four days ago. Once in the morning to wish her a good day and once before I go to bed to tell her that I love her.

But I miss her so much.

It physically hurts to be away from her for so long, but I don't want to see her until I've moved past what happened. Don't want to risk hurting her with something I could potentially say in anger or without really thinking it through.

Mama's sitting in the living room sipping from a cup of coffee as she sifts through an old magazine when I go downstairs to get myself a drink of water. The smile she gives me as I pass is brighter than I've seen from her in a long time. So much so, that I stop in my tracks and just look at her.

She's always been beautiful, my mother, but years of alcohol abuse and mental torture have worn at her features, making it easy to forget the woman she is underneath all the darkness.

The torture that usually screams in her eyes, eyes that were once as blue as mine but long ago turned a lifeless grey, the barrenness of her figure from weight loss, the slow, drawn out way that she speaks. I've gotten so used to seeing her that way that her skeletal face and translucent skin are as familiar to me as the sound of my name.

But right now, I don't see any of that.

For the first time in years, I just see her.

My Mama.

I fill two glasses of water before taking them through to the living room and passing one to her. She accepts it with a grateful smile and the two of us settle into silence, her reading whatever trashy magazine she found in the wastepaper basket and me staring quietly at the wall, plagued by thoughts of Summer-Raine and the darkness that haunts her.

"So, you gonna sit there looking all suicidal or tell me what's on your mind?"

I turn to Mama with wide, surprised eyes.

"What? You think because I'm fucked in the head that I can't tell when something's up with my boy?"

I don't mention how she has spent the majority of the last thirteen years oblivious to the tribulations I've been forced to survive alone. All those times I lay crying in bed while she screamed into the night. The heartbreak of watching her mental health deteriorate. The anguish of pubescent teenage melodramas.

But Mama seems completely lucid today.

Almost like her schizophrenia doesn't exist at all.

"Just shit with Summer-Raine, Mama."

She signals with her hand for me to elaborate and, surprisingly, I do. I tell her about the other night with Summer-Raine. How sick it makes me feel to think I'd have been complicit in her warped attempt at self-harm had I not realised what was happening when I did. How angry I am with her for trying to make me do something she knows I'd never have been comfortable with.

Mama listens to it all.

And when I'm done, she takes my hand and holds it gently in her lap.

"Baby," she says, rubbing her thumb up and down my

pinkie finger the way she used to do when I was very little. The way she sometimes does when her illness has taken her back in time. "She's a lot like me, you know? Has those demons in her head that make her do crazy shit sometimes. That's how demons work. They fuck you up, make you do shit you don't really want to do, until you don't even know who you are anymore."

"But she hurt me, Mama." I drag my hands down my face, sighing. "The idea of causing her pain like that, of causing her pain *at all*, makes me wanna throw up. And she knew that, but she did it anyway."

Mama sighs, reaching up to softly pull my hands away from my face. "I hate that you feel like this. But that girl loves you, I can promise you that. She might be going through shit right now, but I've seen how she looks at you." She takes a breath, thinking. "I'm not saying you don't have a right to be pissed, cause baby you do, but I know she'd never hurt you on purpose. I know how hard she's trying to protect you from the shit inside her head."

I blink.

"I know, because every day I'm the same. You think I don't see the way I hurt you sometimes? I can't fucking help it and it kills me. But it's the monsters that make us this way."

My eyes burn unexpectedly.

Hearing that she's aware of what's happening sometimes, that even during the darkest moments, my Mama is still there, buried somewhere deep beneath her diagnoses and psychotic episodes and the blankness in her eyes, is so startling, so staggering, that suddenly all I want to do is cry.

I curl myself up into a ball and lay my head across Mama's lap as I process all she's just said. She strokes my hair and whispers gentle words. And for a little while, I'm just a boy being comforted by his mother.

"Look at me," she says eventually. "Go to her and give her hell for making you feel like this. And then forgive her. Cause she loves you, Auden, almost as much as I do. It's clear as the damn day to see." She sighs and cups my cheek in her cold hand. "And please, always know that I love you too. I know it's hard to remember, but I do, baby, I love you. So much."

It's the first time in years that my mother has been lucid enough to tell me that she loves me. I didn't realise how much I needed to hear those words from her until now.

And for the second time tonight, I want to cry. Though this time with tears of relief, because I've been reminded that my mother still loves me.

But I don't.

Because, as if a switch has been flicked, I watch as the clouds close in across her eyes. The sparkle of life that was glittering there before has been replaced by a barren stare. The colour of her fades, the essence of her lost once again to the darkness, until all that's left of her is the colour grey and a chasm of nothingness.

I may as well be alone in the room.

Leaving her there, I go up to my bedroom and lay down on the bed. I need to call Summer-Raine. It's been long enough now. The distance between us is eating away at me and *fuck*, I just miss her so much.

There's a message from an unknown number blinking at

me when I pull out my phone.

> **Unknown:** Hey, Auden, it's Marlowe. I got your number from Tyler, who got it from Fred. Hope you don't mind me messaging, but I just had this really weird conversation with Summer. She was saying something about cliff-diving and wanting to do some dangerous shit, I don't even know, but it worried me. I'd go find her myself, but Tyler's taken me to Miami and it'll take a few hours to get back. Thought you might wanna know. Maybe go check on her? Let me know if you do.

Shit.

I check the time stamp and see that she sent the message twenty minutes ago.

That's plenty of time for Summer-Raine to have done something stupid in her pursuit of trying to feel something.

What the fuck have I done leaving her alone for four days?

I've been such a selfish asshole, licking my wounds for so long when she's been needing me.

I should have seen how bad she was the other day, should have stopped things as soon as she'd initiated sex.

I'd known what she was doing, after all. Using sex to distract from the conversation. And though I'd known, I'd gone along with it, not wanting to upset her by forcing her to talk about things she wasn't ready to.

That was my first mistake.

My second was agreeing to fuck her from behind when I could already feel her detachment. It's not that I have an issue with that position. *Hell,* I'm a teenage boy. Head down, ass up is a wet dream come true. But sex with Summer-Raine has never been about just getting each other off. It doesn't matter how many times we've done it, where we've done it, how dirty we've done it, our connection has always been just as powerful as it was the very first time we were together. But that night, she was so absent I may as well have been fucking a sex doll.

I should have just stopped, pulled her into me and held her for as long as she needed me too.

Instead, I let it go too far.

If I'd have just put an end to it, the night wouldn't have ended how it did. We wouldn't have spent the last few days apart, my heart wouldn't be aching with regret and Summer-Raine wouldn't currently be doing something dangerously stupid.

She hasn't been living in the village long enough to know the safest spots for cliff jumping. You have to know the water depth, ocean current and rock formations before even thinking about going. And you should absolutely *never* go on your own.

But Summer-Raine is reckless right now. She wouldn't have thought about any of that and even if she had, the risk would only have spurred her on.

I have to find her.

I'd never forgive myself if she got hurt.

They're the thoughts screaming through my mind as I drive my truck to the cliffs nearest Summer-Raine's house.

I abandon my car and go hunting for her on foot.

Being midsummer, the sun beating down is devastatingly hot. As I walk, the harsh light bounces off every reflective surface, blinding me and making it even harder to stay calm. The heat of the day and the stress of the situation combine until sweat has my clothes sticking to my skin. I tear my shirt over my head and use it to dab at my forehead.

Where the fuck is she?

I try calling her, but it doesn't even ring before going straight to voicemail.

She's turned off her phone.

If that's not a red flag, I don't know what is.

I'm wheezing by the time I make it to a point on the cliffs high enough to allow a clear view of the crags fringing the shoreline. Squinting my eyes, I search as far as my eyes can see.

I can't see her.

My heart thunders harder, anxiety rising like a tsunami in my gut as the time ticks on. Thoughts of what could be happening to her, of her lying somewhere hurt and alone or gasping for breath as she gets caught in a rough current, riot in my head.

And then I see her.

A few hundred metres away, Summer-Raine toes her shoes off as she stares down at the drop below her. I watch her, her body blurred in a shimmering haze as the light around her diffracts and glimmers as a result of the hot air.

She was there all along. It was simply the light playing tricks on me, obscuring her position and hiding her away.

I've never been diving here. I don't know if it's safe, don't know if there are rocks hidden in the water or if it's even deep enough to cushion her fall from this height.

I can see her readying herself, preparing to throw herself

from the cliff's edge into the ocean waves below.

I don't wait another second.

I run.

But the closer I get to her, the closer she gets to the cliffside. She hasn't seen me yet. She doesn't know I'm here. Doesn't know that I've forgiven her, that I just want to hold her, that nothing matters more to me than loving her hard enough to conquer whatever it is she's going through right now.

I'm so close, but it's too late.

"Summer-Raine!"

I watch in horror as she turns her head at the sound of my voice. Her eyes widen, surprise and relief painting her face.

But she's already stepped over the edge.

The shock at seeing me here has forced her to slip from her streamlined position. Her arms flail, her back curves, her legs bend as she falls backwards. There's no worse position for someone to enter water from a height like this.

And there's nothing I can do but watch as the girl I love more than anything tumbles off the cliffside.

I don't know what's worse, the silence as she falls or the sound of her body slapping the sea when she hits it.

She screams.

And then there's nothing.

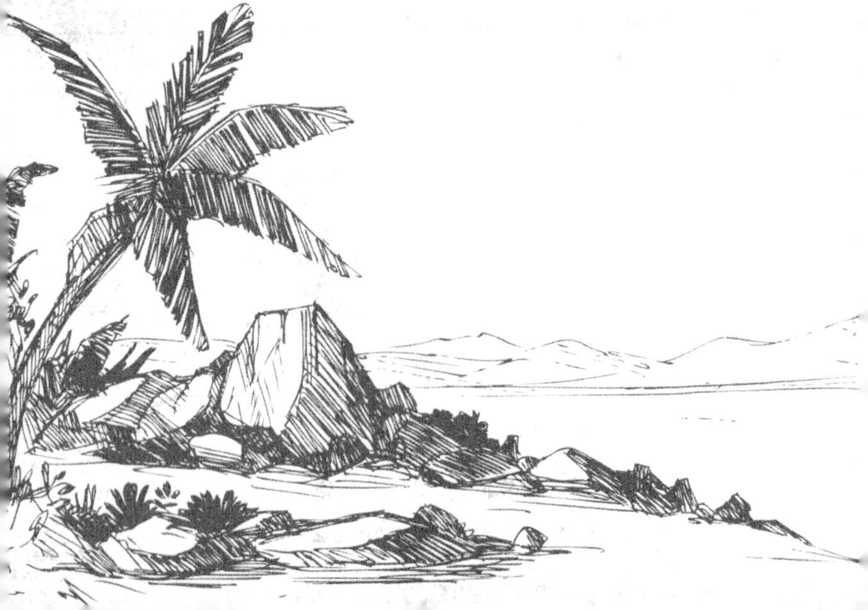

Chapter Fourteen

SUMMER-RAINE

I should have died.

That's what the doctor said.

That I'm lucky to have survived an impact like that with only the injuries I sustained. Six skeletal fractures—including three out of four limbs—two dislocated vertebrae, a collapsed lung and internal bleeding in my abdomen.

Dr Acherley says it's a miracle I'm not paralysed or severely brain damaged. She told me that the jack-knifed way I hit the water would have felt the same as falling from a building onto concrete.

I'm lucky I didn't choose a higher cliff, she said. Then I certainly would have died.

Apparently, several broken bones and a handful of internal injuries was the price I had to pay to finally puncture the blackhole of numbness I've been haunted by for the last few weeks.

Because the second my back slapped the ocean waves, sensation came screaming back to me. Suddenly I could feel everything. Pain. Fear. Regret at how I'd behaved with Auden several nights before. The guilt at hurting him so badly, at doing something so selfishly dangerous to myself, was so powerful it was more painful than the feeling of my bones crushing.

Still is.

He's here, of course. In the waiting room, so I'm told. Has been camping out there since I was rushed into the hospital some time yesterday. He told the hospital staff that he's my brother to make sure they let him in.

But I haven't seen him yet.

I'm not entirely sure I want to.

How can I face him after all I've put him through? I saw the look on his face as I tumbled backwards of that cliff, the raw panic in his eyes like nothing I'd ever seen before. The terrifying fear in his voice as he'd called my name to stop me.

What can I say to him after that?

Besides, it would only hurt him more to see me like this.

I haven't had the chance to look in the mirror since I woke an hour ago, but I imagine I look like absolute shit. Most of my body is wrapped in white cast and wires tangle together as they protrude from multiple parts of me. Between my legs, a catheter drains my pee into a transparent bag at my bedside.

There're so many fluids pumping into me, what they're for I haven't asked, but Dr Acherley told me they're likely to make me sleepy and she's right. My eyelids are heavy and I'm asleep before they close completely.

I blink my eyes open sometime later to find Auden sitting in the beaten blue armchair beside the bed. His head is in his hands, his elbows resting on his bent knees. He doesn't know

I'm awake and I don't say anything to get his attention. I just listen to his shuddering breaths and the quiet sobs that slip from him.

It's the second time this week I've seen him cry.

Though my fingers ache to reach for him, to stroke his hair and soothe him, I don't. Not mainly because both of my hands are encased in casts, but because I know that I'm the source of his pain. I can hardly comfort him when it's my fault he feels this way.

If I wasn't such a mess, if I was just a normal, easy teenage girl, then he wouldn't be here right now crying softly into his hands.

All he has ever done is pour his love into me. He cherishes me with every touch, adores me with every caress of his fingers and brush of his lips over mine. He loves me with an unconditionality that I'm not worthy of. And there is no one in this world less deserving of my poison than him.

He deserves a kind of love that I can't give him. He deserves to be with a girl who can return all of his tenderness and devotion with the same ardour he shows her. Who treasures his Midas touch and turns his gold to diamonds.

Because all I'm capable of is turning it to coal.

But he would never turn his back on me. His heart is so damn pure and good that walking away from our relationship wouldn't ever be an option for him, even though I'll never be able to make him truly happy.

A silent tear slips down my cheek as I realise what has to happen now.

Auden would never leave me.

So, I have to leave him.

The truth is, I'll probably never live a happy life. Auden can, but he won't if he chooses to love me for the rest of it. Setting him free is the only way to make sure he lives the incredible life he deserves.

But I'm a coward. I'm not strong enough to look him in the eye and break his heart. Just one word from him would make me change my mind and backtrack, and I can't let that happen.

So, I take a moment to breathe him in. If this is the last time I'll ever see him, I'll use it memorising every millimetre of him, searing the shape of him into my mind so that there's no way I'll ever be able to forget it. Classes are over now, graduation and senior prom are the only school events left and I'm not in any shape to go to either. Summer will pass and Auden will go off to college in the fall. I don't know what will happen to me, but I know that I can't go to FSU with him like we'd planned.

This really is it.

This is the last time I'll ever breathe in the same air as the boy who stole my heart.

I suck air in through my nose, filling my heart with the safe, woodsy scent of him until my lungs are bursting. Tears leak from my eyes unrestrained and it's getting harder and harder to stay silent.

I can't risk drawing his attention and having him see me, so with one last lingering look over him, I close my eyes and pretend to sleep.

For hours, we remain that way. At some point he reaches for my hand, curling his fingers around it, and it takes everything in me not to throw my eyes open and beg him to climb into bed beside me.

The warm touch of skin only reminds me that I'll never feel him hold me again. Never again will I feel the softness of his lips or the way he worships my body with his hands.

My heart shatters.

The longer he stays sitting beside me, the more my heart splinters into tiny unmendable fragments.

I wish he would just leave.

Ironic, isn't it, that this is only happening because I was trying to force myself to feel something and now that I finally do, I want nothing more than to lose the ability again. Because nothing has ever hurt more than saying goodbye to Auden, even if he doesn't know it's happening.

Eventually, I fall asleep and when I wake up again some time later, he's gone.

But I'm not alone in the room. My sister, Winter-Skye, smiles worriedly up at me from her place in the same chair Auden was occupying only hours ago. Her long, mahogany hair is piled into a bun on top of her head and looks as if it hasn't seen shampoo for a little while.

She was blonde once, like me, but she's been dying it for as long as I can remember because she claims that, contrary to popular belief, it's brunettes who have more fun.

I can't argue with that. Look at me. Look at where I am. I'm as blonde as the angels in heaven and I'm hardly someone you'd enjoy spending time with.

Maybe I was for a minute or two not so long ago, but that girl wasn't really me. She was an imposter. A happy, carefree pretender who doesn't exist anymore and never will again, not without Auden.

"You okay?" Winter asks, cringing at the sight of my bandages, IV's and urine drainage bag.

"Just peachy." I press a button at the side of the bed to help me into a sitting position, looking around at my small room. "Where's Mom and Dad?"

She grimaces. "You know them, super busy."

Of course, they are. Their daughter is immobile in a hospital bed with a multitude of serious injuries after effectively falling off a cliff, but I'm sure that whatever business lunch they're at or team meeting they're in is more important than checking to make sure I'm okay.

"Sorry I didn't get here sooner. I didn't see the messages on my phone until this morning, left as soon as I did." She pauses. "Was that your boyfriend I passed on the way in?"

Another piece of my heart breaks at the mention of Auden, making it harder to breathe than my collapsed lung does.

"No," I whisper. "Not anymore."

"What?" Her eyes widen. "*Why?*"

I turn my eyes to stare at the wall on the opposite side of the room. It hurts too much to look at her in that chair when the image of Auden sitting there crying is still as vivid as if he was really here.

"Because it's the right thing to do," I say simply.

"You don't love him anymore?"

That couldn't be further from the truth. I've never loved him more than I do now that we're over. "I do, but I can't keep hurting him like this. You should have seen the way he looked at me when he found me on that cliffside, Winter. It was like

I'd broken him. I can't do that to him again."

"But he loves you," she says. "After everything you've told me about him, I can't believe he'd just let you go."

"He doesn't know yet."

"What?" She can't hide the shock in her voice.

"He didn't let me go, because he doesn't know we're over yet."

"When are you going to tell him?"

"I'm not."

I finally allow myself to look at her.

Her eyes are wide with disbelief, astonishment and disappointment. "I really don't think you should do this, Sum."

"Have to." She doesn't get it. "If I don't, he'll be stuck dealing with my bullshit forever, because he'd never leave me of his own accord. I'm not right, Winter. I'm not the kind of girl who can make him happy like he should be. I'm broken and selfish and fucked in the head and he deserves so much more than that."

I can't bear the look of pity I see on her face.

"Sum—"

"Don't." I cut her off. "Please don't. You don't have to agree with me, but please don't try and talk me out of this because you won't."

She nods sadly.

"Okay," she whispers and we fall into silence.

Now that I'm looking at her, it occurs to me that she looks different than the last time I saw her. The sleeves of her varsity sweater are pulled over her hands as she jostles them on her lap, but that's not what's got my attention. Her cheeks are flushed, her skin glowing and her stomach, though mostly hidden underneath her loose sweater, swells in a way it didn't before.

Holy shit.

"Winter?" Her eyes snap to mine, panic filling them as she realises what's caught my attention. "Win, are you…?"

She sucks in a sharp breath and averts my gaze. For a while, it seems like she's going to ignore my question, but finally she nods. Just once, almost imperceptibly, but it happens and I see it.

"Oh my God." My mouth falls open in shock.

"Don't freak out, Sum."

"I'm not." But I kind of am. "How far along are you?"

"Sixteen weeks," she says it so quietly I almost miss it.

I gasp. That's nearly four months pregnant. "How long have you known?"

Her face falls. "A while."

I feel a twinge of hurt that she didn't tell me sooner.

As if reading my thoughts, she says, "I didn't keep it from you on purpose, Sum. I've just been so scared, you know? I'm still in college, I'm not even old enough to drink yet and I'm gonna have a baby. I just needed some time to process it and make a decision before I told anyone."

I can hear the desperation and fear in her voice. I can understand that. Fuck knows how I'd react if I found out I was pregnant, so I'm hardly able to judge her for how she's chosen to deal with it.

"You're keeping it then?" I ask.

Her hands fold over her stomach and she strokes it absentmindedly. "Yeah." She smiles. "Yeah, I am."

"What about the father? Is he in the picture?"

"Yeah." She nods. "He's a good guy, Summer. You'd like him." She worries her bottom lip between her teeth. "Are you mad at me? Disappointed?"

"Not at all." I reach a cast-covered hand out to her. "Congratulations, Win, I'm so happy for you. You're going to be the most amazing Mama."

"You think so?" she asks, a shy smile on her lips.

"I know so."

And I do. It might be a shock at first and take her some time to adjust to life with a new-born baby, but I have no doubt that she'd be the most incredible mother.

She squeezes my fingers. "And you'll be the best Auntie."

That I'm less sure about, but I'll try. There's no way I'd let that little life grow up feeling anything less than loved by me, so I'll do my damndest to do right by them.

We're interrupted by the door opening and a nurse coming in to take my vitals. She smiles at Winter before turning sympathetic eyes onto me.

They all look at me like that, like I'm someone who needs pitying, with their sad eyes and tilted heads. I suspect it's because jumping off a cliff looks suspiciously like a suicide attempt, as well as the scars on my arms that they'd definitely have seen before they were covered up in casts. But there's nothing worse than people looking at you like an abandoned puppy in a pound.

"Your brother's outside," the nurse says, wrapping the strap of the blood pressure monitor around the top of my arm. "Want me to send him in?"

Winter swings her confused gaze to me. "Brother?"

"Auden," I answer.

"Oh."

"No." I look back to the nurse.

"Really?" She gives me a quizzical look, finishing up my vitals and wheeling her trolley back across the room. "He was here most of the morning. Think he only went home to shower. He hasn't been gone long."

She means well, I know that. I know that she's only concerned about my welfare and making sure I'm getting support from my family, especially as the absence of my parents is clear as the damn day, but irritation swells within me.

"I don't want him in here anymore," I say quietly, the words burning like acid in my mouth. I can feel the sharpness of Winter's glare stabbing into my skin, her undisguised disapproval like a blinding light in the room. "Can you please have him removed from my approved visitor's list?"

My sister gasps behind me.

The nurse's mouth drops open in surprise. "That's what you want?" she stutters, disbelief and a hint of judgement colouring her tone.

No, that's not what I want.

Of course, that's not what I want.

But I don't have a choice.

I can't keep hurting him like this and I know that I will over and over again so long as he stays with me. And I refuse to burden him with my darkness anymore. He already has so much to deal with at home with his Mama.

So, I just nod, because I'd be lying if I said yes.

The nurse leaves without another word and I sag back into the hospital bed, desperately trying not to imagine the confusion and pain on Auden's face when he's told that I don't want to see him. My eyes burn at the image.

He won't understand.

But I guess, he doesn't need to.

Setting him free is the best thing I could ever do for him.

"He deserves better, Summer," Winter whispers into the silence.

I lay back and turn my face to the side, hiding myself away as I finally let the tears fall. "I know, that's why I have to do this."

She says nothing and I'm grateful. I'm not strong enough to defend my decision or even open my mouth to speak another word.

All I can do is lay in the jagged pieces of my broken heart, grieving the love I never thought I'd have and mourning the loss of the boy who gave it to me.

I never planned for us to end. If only I could have stayed that happy, carefree girl I was at the start of the year. If only the monsters would have stayed away so I could keep him for the rest of my life.

But I guess life just doesn't work like that.

I know that Auden will eventually move on. He might struggle for a while, but one morning he'll wake up and realise the sun is still shining, the sky is still blue and happiness is still possible. He'll find someone new and fall in love again.

In fact, I hope he does.

Even though I never will.

I hope his life is filled with sunshine and blue skies and bright smiles. I hope the girl he meets can give him everything I never could. That she'll make him laugh instead of cry, that she'll hold him when he's sad and lift him up when he needs her to. I could never do that for him. And maybe one day, she'll even give him a family. The children will get their blue eyes and dimples from their father and be just as staggeringly beautiful as him.

And Auden will be happy without me.

But that's okay.

Because if I've learnt anything from this it's that sometimes to truly love someone you have to let them go.

Part II

Five years later

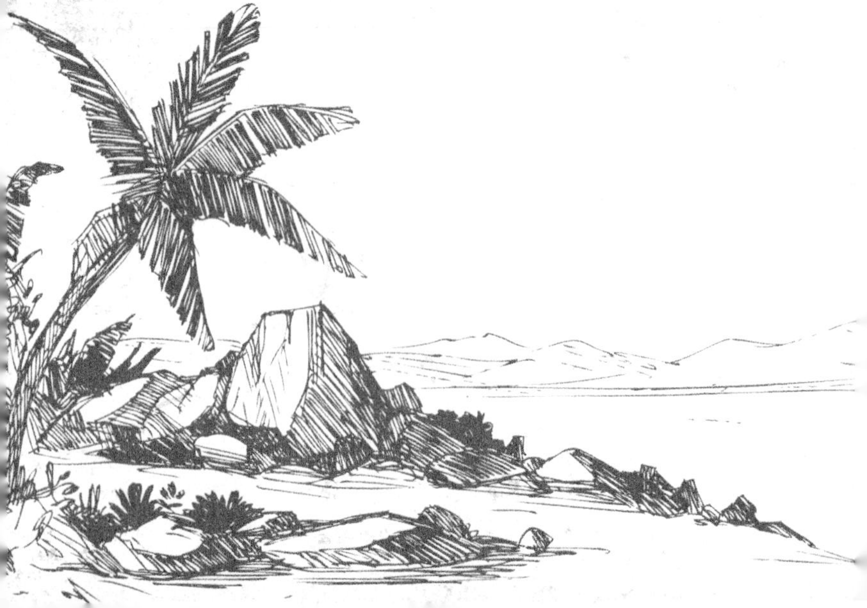

Chapter Fifteen

AUDEN

The cursor blinks at me from the blank page I've been staring at for the last two hours. It taunts me, mocks me with its relentless, unhurried flickering, making me want to drive my fist through the computer screen and render it unblinkable forever.

Your creative writing professor was right, it says.

I scrunch my eyes shut, shake my head to silence the imaginary voice and stretch my fingers out over the keyboard. If I can just get down a hundred words, today won't be yet another wasted day.

The cursor blinks.

My brain echoes with the absence of ideas.

Fine.

I'll settle for one sentence, one word even, I just need *something* other than "Chapter One" to take up some of the empty space on the document.

How can you call yourself a writer when you're not even able to write?

Coincidentally, my cursor's imaginary voice is the exact same condescending drone that belonged to my creative writing professor in college.

"You'll never make it as a writer," he'd told me more than once. "You probably have enough talent to get a couple of poems published in an anthology, maybe even a short story in The New Yorker, but you'll only wind up in a classroom just like this one, teaching a group of pathetically hopeful students how to structure manuscripts that have no hope in ever being accepted by a publishing house."

I'd been so desperate to prove him wrong, but gradually over the last eighteen months my confidence has waned. The blinking cursor on the blank page delights at this, of course. But I still show up every evening, hoping that today is the day inspiration strikes and the words pour freely from my fingertips.

"Come to bed, babe."

Small feminine hands reach over me from behind and slide down my chest. I sigh and rest my head on the back of the chair to look up at my girlfriend, who bends down to drop a soft kiss over my mouth.

I stroke my hands down her arms and rest my thumbs on the pulse point at her wrists, tugging her closer to feel her lips on mine again. Her dark hair falls around us like a canopy as our tongues meet, the kiss growing feverish as it does every time.

Cara and I met six months ago at a bar in downtown Tallahassee. Memories of the past were heavy in my mind that day and I was looking to drown out the noise of them with several fingers' worth of amber liquid. I'd drunk until I couldn't see. Then I'd eaten from a steaming plate of grease that Cara had set in front of me to sober me up and afterwards I'd taken her home and used her body to forget what the liquor had failed to.

It didn't work.

But then, five years of trying has taught me that nothing does.

I guess the difference between Cara and the other countless women I've used in the same way since the end of senior year is that she refused to accept it was a one-time thing. So, that one night became two, then three and before I knew it, it had been three months of seeing each other multiple times a week and I was suddenly referring to her in conversation as my girlfriend.

And the craziest thing? It didn't feel wrong.

The jasmine scent she always left on my bedsheets, the hair ties scattered around my apartment, even the hairs clogging the drain in the shower, none of it bothered me. In fact, after such a long time of being on my own, I even came to find the constant reminders of her comforting. I actually came to like them.

Now, she spends more nights in my bed than she does her own.

When I pull away, Cara's cheeks are flushed and her pupils are blown. I let her spin the desk chair around, snapping my laptop closed as she rotates me. She takes my hand and leads me across the tiny studio apartment to my king bed, tumbling us onto the sheets in a mess of tangled limbs, wet kisses and wandering hands.

The moonlight streaming in through the parted curtains

sets her body aglow in silver light. She's stunning with her porcelain skin, dark eyes and rosy mouth. She's like a real-life Snow White, possibly one of the most beautiful women I've ever known, but it's not her I see as I sink inside her body.

It's not raven hair fanned out on the pillow below her, but gold.

It's not brown eyes looking up at me, but the deepest green.

And when she comes, it's not Cara I hear sighing my name, it's the girl who broke my heart.

I leave Cara in bed in the morning with a soft kiss to her forehead and head out to work, diving into Starbucks on the way to pick up two triple-shot venti lattes with soy milk, no foam and four pumps of hazelnut syrup.

The first time I'd been forced to order my boss's obnoxious coffee, I'd almost died of shame. The second time, I'd spilt it on the way into the office and almost faced disciplinary action. By the third, I'd learnt my lesson and ordered two of the same over-caffeinated cups of vegan crap with my head held high.

Two years on and I've grown accustomed to the taste. I haven't needed to make use of the backup coffee since that second day, but I'd still rather drink the shit stuff than order what I actually want and have another accident.

Martha Goodman, CEO and founder of Goodman Publishing Group, didn't get to where she is today without being a hardass and believe it or not, despite my daily trip to Starbucks, I'm not her personal assistant. But being the youngest junior editor in the company seems to have landed me the coveted position of being her coffee bitch.

Not that I'd ever argue.

I respect everything about Martha, but I'm not ashamed to say that she terrifies me to the very core. So, I'll carry on humiliating myself in Starbucks every morning, buy two of the same piss-tasting drinks and spend more time making photocopies than doing my actual job, simply because I don't want her to yell at me in front of everyone. Again.

I make it to the office building twenty minutes before my official start time, waving at the blonde behind the front desk who blushes as she does every morning and take the elevator up to the fifteenth floor.

For a publishing company with such a large, infamous client list, Goodman Publishing Group only hires less than fifty members of staff. I was lucky enough to land an internship right out of college, which eventually resulted in the offer of a full-time position. And though I know how incredibly fortunate I am to be able to work here, it's not what I really want to be doing.

What I really want is to write.

I want some chump like me at a publishing house to spend hours editing my manuscript. I want to see my books displayed in a store window, or spot someone reading one on the subway or sitting at a bus stop. I just want to make a living doing the thing I adore.

If only I could get some words down on a page.

The elevator doors open to a full view of the office floor. Opposite me, an entire wall of windows looks out over downtown Tallahassee. Everywhere, books pile on surfaces. On shelves, sideboards, even stacked into towers on the floor. Three obtrusively large meeting tables take up most of the centre floor space, where the staff are forced to sit together to do their work.

Having read an article about the benefits of community work environments last year, Martha had all the office cubicles removed and replaced with the three whopping planks of mahogany in the hopes that it would encourage collaborative work and offer more learning opportunities. I'm not sure I've seen the benefits myself yet, but she seems pleased with the new layout.

The day passes slowly. I spend most of it with my head buried in manuscripts, copy editing and proofreading until my eyes sting. By the time I look up from my work, half-light bathes the office space in a purple-orange glow. The sky looks like it's been set on fire and for a while I sit and watch it burn.

It doesn't matter how much time has passed, sunsets always remind me of Summer-Raine. Those evenings we spent wrapped together on her balcony as we watched the night come in with the tide. I remember them so vividly that I can almost feel the tickle of her hair on my cheek and smell the salt of the ocean in the air.

Despite what ended up happening between us and how much she hurt me, I still feel something akin to homesickness when I think of her. Nostalgia is a funny thing. Time passes but a yearning for the halcyon days never ceases. It's what makes me reach for my wallet and pull out the sprig of lavender that I've held onto for the last five years.

Shortly after Summer-Raine gave it to me, I had it preserved in resin and then set in glass. It probably wouldn't have lasted the test of time without it. And though life has moved on, I'm not sure how I'd feel if I ever had to part with it. It marks the time in my life that I was happiest and it's nice to remember that feeling sometimes.

As deep as my feelings for Cara are, she doesn't set my soul on fire the way Summer-Raine used to.

The office has slowly emptied, leaving me sitting alone at one of the vast meeting tables. I turn the lavender keepsake over repeatedly in my fingers as I stare out the window at the twilight.

It's been a month since I last called Winter Taylor. A month since I last asked for an update on how her sister is doing. I told myself I wouldn't call again. I figured five years is long enough to go regularly checking up on someone who broke my heart so momentously, yet my fingers twitch to pick up my phone once more.

And because I'm a weak man with no self-control, I do.

Winter picks up on the third ring.

"Auden, hey." Her voice is breathless, as if she'd been running before picking up the phone.

"This a bad time?"

I can hear the babble of little voices in the background, giggling and squealing as they run rings around their mother.

"No, no," she pants. "It's fine."

I cringe at the sound of Winter cursing under her breath, then yelling after one of her kids. It doesn't sound like it's a good time, but I'm not about to argue with her.

"You doing alright?" I ask.

"Sure." She sighs. "But that's not what you called to ask, is it?"

Perhaps I should feel guilty, or at least a little sheepish, about calling Winter simply to ask about her sister, but we've done this song and dance enough times. Denying it would only be lying and she'd know it too.

So, I ask the question I really want the answer to. "How's she doing?"

I hear her suck in a breath through her nose, her momentary hesitation causing my gut to twitch in apprehension. "She's not well, Auden."

My heart plummets. How after all this time does it still ache so much to know that Summer-Raine is hurting? I react the same every time Winter tells me she's having a bad day or going through a particularly dark period. It causes me actual physical pain.

"What's going on?" I ask, a slight tremor in my voice.

"She's just kind of checked out, I guess. Like she'll look at me, but I never know if she can actually see me cause her eyes are glazed over. It's kind of scary. It's like she's a zombie. I've had to go out in the middle of the night a couple times to find her after someone's rung me to say they've seen her wandering around somewhere."

Hearing this kills me.

If she hadn't suddenly started refusing to see me after her accident in senior year, it would be me chasing Summer-Raine around town at all hours of the day. I'd have found her, taken her home and held her to me until the sun came up. I can say that with certainty. If she hadn't ended us the way she did, I know for a fact that we'd still be together.

There was no way in hell I'd have ever wanted a life without her.

But as angry and hurt as it still makes me, I can almost understand why she did it. If I hadn't called out after her on the cliff that day, she wouldn't have fallen the way she did. If I hadn't called out after her, maybe she wouldn't have gotten hurt the way she did.

God, the memory of her floppy, jack-knifed body hurtling towards the water still haunts me even now.

It's something I'll never forgive myself for.

So, yeah, maybe I can recognise why she'd blame me for what happened, but I'd truly thought that she'd loved me enough to at least break my heart herself. Not just left some random nurse to tell me that I'd been removed from her approved visitors list.

At least Winter took pity on me and offered to stay in touch.

"Jesus, Winter." I scrape a hand down my face. "That's so fucking dangerous. She could get hurt or into trouble. *Fuck*, why do you let her get out?"

"*Let her?*" Winter yells through the phone. "I'm a mother to two kids, Auden. I do what I can for my sister, but those kids are my priority. She's living in my house, for god's sake, I'm doing my best. How dare you suggest otherwise."

"Christ, Win, I'm sorry." I sigh, shame instantly washing over me. It's not her fault that Summer-Raine is a loose canon and, if she's anything like she was five years ago, there's not a lot someone can do to help her once she's in that place anyway. "I didn't mean to insinuate anything. I know how much you do for her. But surely there's gotta be something else we can do if she's got this bad again."

"You know what she's like. She refuses to accept the help she actually needs and they won't commit her involuntarily because she's not a big enough danger to herself." Winter sounds as resigned as I feel.

"That's fucking ridiculous," I growl, frustration at the mental healthcare system mounting. It failed my Mama and now it's failing Summer-Raine.

"You know what it's like," she says. "They won't admit her unless she makes an actual attempt on her life. That's just the way it is."

"Bullshit is what it is."

She sighs. "Yeah, I know."

For a little while, neither of us says a word. The silence through the phone is thick with unspoken thoughts of Summer-Raine, both of us worrying about the same special girl and wishing things were different.

"Hey, Auden?" Winter says finally. "Can I ask you something?"

"Hmm?"

"Do you still love her?"

My eyes scrunch shut. It's a question I've been asking myself for five long years and refused to answer. *Do I still love her?* I'd be an idiot if I did. But then, I've always been an idiot when it comes to Summer-Raine.

"It's not like that anymore." My voice breaks, but if Winter notices she doesn't mention it. "It's not been like that for a long time."

She seems to accept my response, though both of us know I didn't really answer the question.

When she hangs up, I let my forehead fall to the table in front of me and suck in heavy breaths through my nose. I don't know why I torture myself like this. Hearing that Summer-Raine is suffering only causes me pain and it's pointless. Because the truth of the matter is that there's nothing I can do about it anyway. So, I just have to harbour the knowledge that she's out there somewhere, standing alone in the dark with her monsters, maybe even at the gas station where I saw her for the first time, hurting and scared and alone. And I just have to deal with it.

So, I do what I do every time I speak to Winter.

I brush myself off and try to resist the overwhelming urge to go wherever Summer-Raine is and fix everything for her.

I go home. And later, after dinner at an Italian restaurant with Cara, I use her body once again to try and forget about the girl with golden hair and demons in her head.

And just like always, it doesn't work.

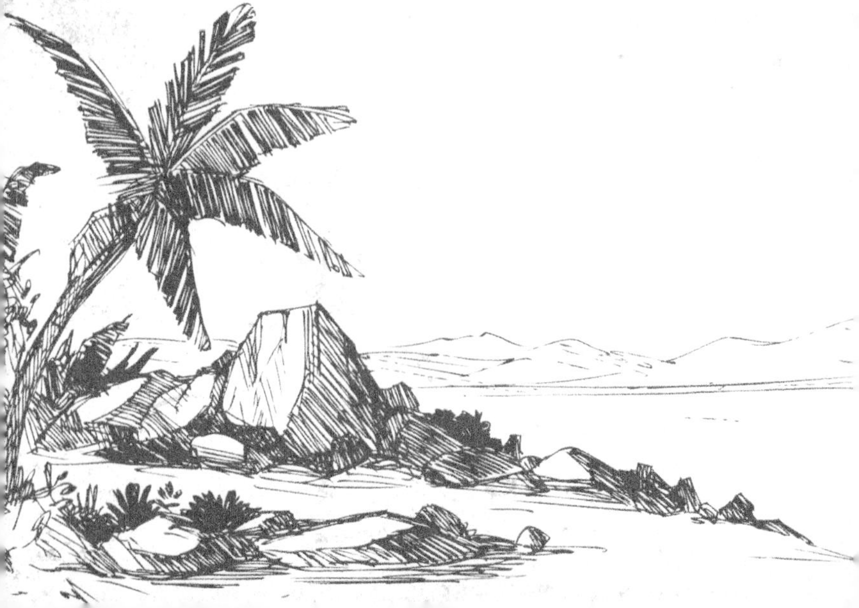

Chapter Sixteen

SUMMER-RAINE

*I*t didn't work.

That's the first thing I think when I wake up.

Around me, I can hear the incessant beeping of medical machines, a sound I've grown used to over the last several years. Harsh light beams down on my closed eyelids and the lingering smells of citrus scented cleaning agents, stainless steel and questionable microwaved dinners fill my nose and make my stomach churn.

I can feel long fingers wrapped around my own, and they tremble as I slowly blink my eyes open to look into the devastated face of my older sister.

Tears fall freely down her cheeks and she releases a loud sob before resting her forehead on top of our entwined hands resting on the bed beside me.

It's not the first time I've woken up in a hospital bed to find her holding my hand, not even the second, but it's the first time I've woken to find her so emotional. I guess that's because all my previous trips to hospital have been accidental.

This is the first time I've hurt myself like this *on purpose*.

Except... I was never supposed to wake up in a hospital bed to my sister weeping next to me.

I wasn't supposed to wake up at all.

"Hey, Winter," I croak, forcing a reassuring smile on my face in the hopes that she'll stop crying.

She doesn't.

Her eyes lift to mine, worn out and defeated, before more tears rain down and stain the scratchy linen bedsheets.

"Why did you do it?" She asks between sobs.

"Thought it would be fun," I deadpan.

"That's not fucking funny, Summer. Do you think this is a joke?"

"Well, what do you want me to say?" I sigh, refusing to look her in the eye. "You know why I did it. To die, Winter. I wanted to die."

She sucks in a sharp breath like my admission has come as a shock.

Why else would someone throw themselves off a pedestrian bridge into oncoming traffic?

"But, *why?*" she whispers. "I don't understand. Help me understand."

I sigh and burrow my head into the pillow. Talking about this is too much. I don't want to revisit the thoughts I had before I took that step, don't want to relive those moments or remember what drove me to do what I did.

Not now, not today.

And not with Winter, who already shoulders so much of the weight of my mental illness.

Though I've never asked her to, she's been there each time I've fallen to pick me back up again. It was her who insisted I stay at her house for a while so that she can keep an eye on me, despite having two young sons to care for. It's been a year now and I'm still sleeping in her spare room, so I'm not blind to the fact I'm a burden.

I refuse to add more to that.

Thankfully, the door opening distracts Winter from the conversation and she rapidly wipes her eyes before turning to the doctor with a forced smile.

"Oh, great," the doctor says. "You're awake."

Dr Harrison, according to the lanyard hanging from her neck, is a woman in her late forties with greying hair and a stern yet benevolent face. She steps up to my bedside, clipboard in hand and pencil balanced behind her ear, and fiddles with the tubes of one of my IV's.

"So," she starts, studying her notes. "A fractured ankle, one deep skin laceration on your left thigh, some soft tissue damage and a healthy dose of road rash. I imagine you're probably feeling pretty sore right now but count your lucky stars to have gotten off so lightly."

Huh.

Lucky.

Why is it that I've been feeling the exact opposite since the second I opened my eyes?

"I don't understand," I say, my voice hoarse. "How is that even possible?"

"According to a couple of people the paramedics spoke to, you landed on the roof of a car which significantly reduced the height of the fall. Traffic was luckily slowing anyway, so by the time you rolled onto the road, the car behind had enough time to stop before hitting you."

I should have just taken an overdose.

Speaking hurts, but I don't have words to say anyway, so I turn my head to stare out over Winter's shoulder through the small window behind her. The sun is beaming, birds chirp from branches in evergreen trees and cotton candy clouds whisper softly against a bright blue sky.

It makes me nauseous.

If only it would rain.

"You wanna tell me what happened last night?" Dr Harrison asks. "And why you were standing on the wrong side of the barriers on a pedestrian bridge at one in the morning?"

I don't answer. Don't turn to look at her either. I just continue staring out at the depressingly glorious summer day, wishing that I never had to look at it again.

It's like they think I've been planning my suicide for a while. But truth be told, there wasn't a whole lot of thought that went into it. There wasn't a trigger or something that pushed me over the edge. It's just that when I found myself on that bridge, looking down at the oncoming traffic below, I realised that the thought of throwing myself over was more comforting than the thought of going back to Winter's house and living another day.

"What was the outcome you were aiming for, Summer?" She asks, softer this time.

I roll my head in her direction and narrow my eyes. "With respect, doctor, you know exactly what I was aiming for."

"Very well." She nods solemnly, then changes the direction of the conversation. "How are you coping pain wise?"

It's as if her question awakes all the receptors in my body, because pain pours through me in a torrent of pure agony like a damn breaking.

"Not great," I answer honestly.

She grimaces. "Hmm, you're on some pain meds already, but I'll have a look at what I can do to up the dosage."

I nod my thanks.

"What happens to her now?" my sister asks, her eyes dry but cheeks tear stained.

She answers my sister's question, but talks directly to me. "The neurologist will be coming to see you in a bit to talk over some of your injuries and discuss a treatment plan, as well as nurses to take your vitals and redress that nasty friction burn on your thigh, so it'll be somewhat of a circus in here for a little while."

Her pen scratches across her paper as she notes down some numbers blinking on the monitor behind me.

"But what happens now in terms of why she's here?" Winter asks hesitantly. "You know, in terms of what she did?"

Dr Harrison pauses and taps her lips several times with the tips of her long fingers, looking over at me with thoughtful eyes. "I'll be completely transparent here, okay? We're in a difficult situation. If your notes are correct, this isn't the first time you've attempted something like this. There was a similar incident five years ago in Islamorada, correct?"

Winter nods, but I interject. "That was different," I whisper. "I didn't jump, I fell."

Dr Harrison cuts me a dubious look but continues. "State law allows us to involuntarily commit patients for seventy-two hours if we deem them a risk to themselves or others." She stops and my heart sinks. "However, you'll likely be here for a few more days anyway so that we can continue to treat your physical injuries, and I'll use that time to monitor your mental state and assess whether or not I believe it safe for you to return home. The likelihood, however, is that I'll only feel comfortable with you going home if you have someone to be with you round the clock."

"Like a carer?" I gape.

"Not really. Just a friend or family member to keep an eye on you and support your recovery. You'll need a strong support system over the next several months or so to make sure something like this doesn't happen again."

Winter sits up in her chair. "She's been staying with me recently, but I have two kids, a job and a husband. It's made it hard to be there for Summer when I should have been. But I'll see if I can cut back on some shifts or ask to work from home or something, so I can be there with her as much as possible."

My heart pangs. Winter has so much responsibility already, so many people relying on her, that her beautiful face is already beginning to look weather-beaten despite being only twenty-five.

I can't be a burden to her anymore. It's not fair.

Just like it wasn't fair to Auden all those years ago.

"Don't say shit like that," I say, taking my sister's hand. "There's nothing more you could have done."

Dr Harrison smiles gently, looking between Winter and

me. "Use the next few days to think it over. You don't need to make any decisions right now."

"Thank you," Winter replies diplomatically, whereas I give the doctor a curt nod and turn to look out the window again.

The door clicks shut and I breathe a sigh of relief.

My reprieve, however, is short-lived. Winter looks at me with wide eyes and a hesitant expression, making dread build in my stomach in anticipation of whatever she's about to say to me.

"Can I say something without you jumping down my throat?" she asks.

I don't answer, but motion with my hand for her to go ahead.

"I think it might be time to look at maybe going into inpatient care."

"No."

"Please, just hear me out," she begs. "I know it's not an idea you like the sound of, but I can't be what you need, Sum. I'm trying, I am, but I'm not trained in this shit, I don't know what I'm doing and you need someone who does."

"I said no," I say through gritted teeth. The last thing I want to do is snap at her right now, but rage at the suggestion flares within me.

"Summer, please, just think about it."

"No," I bite. "I get it, I can't stay with you anymore, but I'm not gonna let you ship me off to some fucking nuthouse, okay? We're done talking about it now."

I shift myself in the bed to angle my body away from her and do my best to ignore the quiet sounds of her crying and the guilt gnawing at my heart.

Sometime after the door stopped revolving, I must have fallen asleep, because I wake to the sound of hushed voices. I know without looking that they belong to my sister and her husband, Ben. They're whispering, but I can hear the hostility between them and the bite in their tone as loudly as if they were speaking at a normal volume.

They're arguing.

Perhaps it isn't the right thing to do, but at the sound of my name I keep my eyes closed and pretend to still be sleeping.

"Summer's my sister, Ben." Winter's voice is shaky, like she's whispering while crying. "I can't just turn my back on her."

"I'm not asking you to turn your back on her, Winter, but things have gone too far now. I don't want her round the boys anymore. This shit is affecting them, you know that as well as I do."

"So, you want me to just turn her out onto the streets?"

"Of course not, but the kids should be our priority and I'm putting my foot down. She can't stay with us anymore."

Winter chokes on a sob. "Where the fuck do you expect her to go?"

"I don't know." He scoffs, his exasperation evident. "Your parents? Rehab? Back to her own fucking apartment?"

"Christ, Ben. Our parents didn't even look after her as a kid, they're not going to be interested in helping her now. And rehab? You know I've spoken to her about it and she's adamant that she won't go. Not now. Not ever."

"Her apartment then. It's been sitting there unoccupied for months now, she may as well get her fucking money's worth."

"And who will look after her? The doctor says she can't go home unless there's someone around to keep an eye on her."

"Fucking hell, Winter. Just hire some nurses or something. You've got all that trust fund money rotting in your bank account, it's not like you're using it for anything else."

I hear Winter gasp. "Oh? Apart from the house that you live in and the car that you drive?"

"You fucking love throwing that in my face, don't you?" He pauses. "She's not staying with us anymore and that's final."

"God, you're such an asshole."

"Why? Because I want what's best for my children?" Ben releases a dark laugh. "Fuck, maybe it would have been better for everyone if she'd actually died."

The sound of the resulting slap is deafening and echoes hauntingly around the room.

"If you don't want a divorce, then I suggest you never say anything like that about my sister again."

Angry footsteps storm across the room, followed by the sound of the door slamming. And then silence.

But I know my sister is still there. I can feel the anger, sadness and frustration rolling off of her and my fingers twitch to reach out for her, but if I were to do so then she'd know I've been awake and listening this entire time. And it would break her heart if she knew that I'd overheard it all. Especially Ben's parting words.

As cruel as they were though, I don't blame him for saying them. It's not as if he's wrong.

I know that it would be easier for everyone if I wasn't here anymore, that's why I did what I did. The world would be a better place without me in it. So, I can't be mad at Ben for thinking the same thing, for voicing the truth, no matter how hard the words are to hear coming from someone else's mouth.

My sister sniffs and I pretend the noise wakes me.

Blinking slowly, I turn to look at her sitting in the chair by my bedside, rapidly trying to dry her eyes so that I don't suspect her of crying. It's obvious though, even if I hadn't been eavesdropping on their argument. But I don't mention it. She clearly doesn't want me to if she's going to such an effort to hide her tears, so I smile at her sleepily and pretend I don't notice the way her mascara runs in lines down her swollen cheeks.

"You okay?" she asks.

"Just dandy."

She sucks in a breath, rubbing her hands together in her lap as if she's preparing for something and then opens her mouth to speak.

I know what she's going to say.

I know she's trying to find a way to tell me I can't stay with them anymore and I know how much it's going to kill her to do it, so I don't let her.

"Hey," I say before she has a chance to speak. "I've been thinking, I don't think it's a good idea if I keep living in your house anymore."

"What?" She blinks at me, eyes narrowing suspiciously.

"I just think that I won't get better if I'm always depending on you, you know? I can't live with you forever, it's not fair on you and your family and it's probably not what's best for me either. I need to stand on my own two feet, learn to get by on my own again and you guys need to be a family without the crazy auntie pulling her bullshit all the time."

"Summer…" she starts, but trails off.

I think she knows that I overheard the argument, but neither of us bring it up.

"Really, it's okay." I smile reassuringly. "I know that Cooper's been having nightmares since I've been staying with you and Carter barely ever makes eye contact with me anymore. I don't want to ruin the relationship I have with my nephews and I will if I keep living with you guys."

A tear escapes from the corner of her eye. "But the doctor said you need someone with you to keep an eye out and support your recovery. Who, if it's not me?"

"I'll figure it out, Winter." I reach for her finally, curling my fingers around her hand. "But I won't let the burden fall on you anymore. You've done too much. I need to take responsibility for my own recovery and you need to focus on living your own life now."

"You know I'm always here for you, right?" she asks.

"I know."

"And that I love you?"

"I know that too."

She squeezes my hand, eyes closing as she heaves in a deep breath. The relief pouring off her is palpable, I can feel it as powerfully as the rain on my skin during a storm.

But my gut twinges with guilt.

I know the only way for her to agree to letting me move out of her place is if she believes that I'm really invested in making changes for myself. But truthfully, recovery isn't something I think is possible for me. I haven't felt even a slither of happiness since senior year, before my fucked-up head went and ruined it all for me. I know I'm never going to "get better", know I'm never going to get to feel the way I did for those nine perfect months five years ago, so why even bother trying?

All I care about is Winter and her boys no longer having to bear the weight of my behaviour. I swore when she was pregnant for the first time with Carter that I'd do anything for his little soul, shield him from the cruelty of the world, protect him from things that could hurt him. And when she fell pregnant with Cooper two years later, that oath extended to him too.

So, I don't care what happens to me now, don't care who the fuck ends up taking the ridiculous role of my babysitter, so long as my sister and nephews are far away from me and the monsters inside my head.

Without me, life will be better for them all. They'll be free and happy and safe.

Because protecting them from the things in the world that can hurt them sometimes means protecting them from *me*.

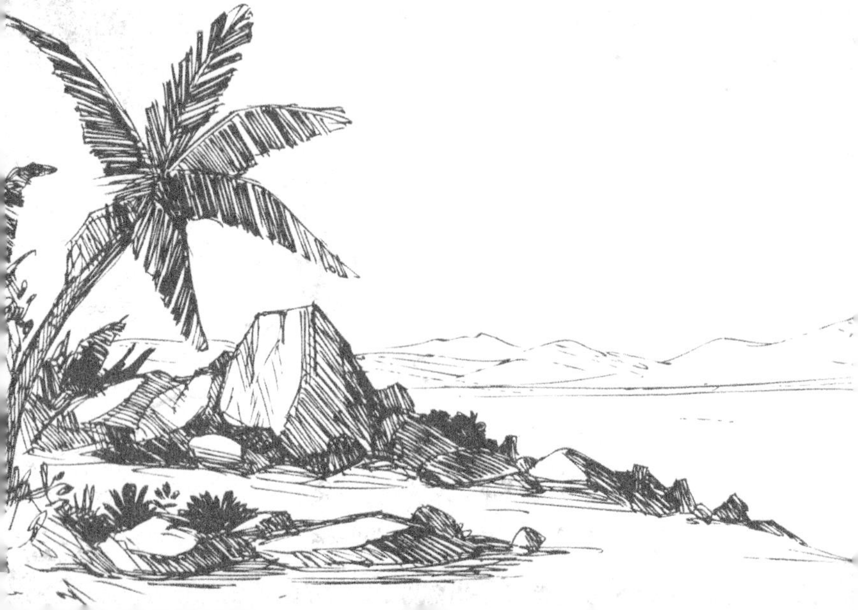

Chapter Seventeen

AUDEN

I slam the lid of my laptop closed.

Another night, another three hours of my life wasted.

Chapter One are still the only words I've been able to write since I opened that document for the first time a year and a half ago.

Maybe it's time to face the truth that my goal is just too big for me. That maybe I don't have it in me to write a full-length novel, let alone convince a publishing house to take it on and turn me into a world-renowned author.

I rest my head on the desk and suck in a deep sigh.

Tonight is one of those rare nights that I'm alone in my apartment. Cara's gone out for dinner and drinks with a few of her girlfriends and though I told her I'd miss her, I'm actually glad for the temporary reprieve.

As much as I enjoy her company, sometimes I just need to be alone with my thoughts. Or lack thereof, as the empty document would signify.

It's late—just after eleven according to the time display on my microwave oven—but sleep still feels far off. For the last couple of weeks, I haven't been able to shake the conversation I had with Winter and the lingering concern for Summer-Raine that it left me with.

I know it's pathetic that five years later I'm still thinking about the girl who ripped out my teenage heart, but even with all the time that's passed and the way that things were left between us, there's still that connection there. Like a thread of gold tying our two souls together even though we're worlds apart. I can't say if she feels it too, or if it's just my pitifully feeble heart clinging onto something that hasn't existed for half a decade, but I feel it as profoundly as I did back when we were in love.

Since that phone conversation with Winter, my dreams have been haunted by images of Summer-Raine wandering lost and alone down dark roads and woodland paths, the gnarly branches of trees clawing down at her as the sky turns black and shadows slither out of corners to play in the gloom of the night.

I've woken up every morning with a racing heart and a sweaty sheen on my skin.

But I have to keep reminding myself, as I have done for so long now, that Summer-Raine isn't for me to worry about anymore.

My thoughts shouldn't be overwhelmed by images of her, but of the woman who warms my bed at night and tells me that she loves me every single day despite never hearing it returned.

I shouldn't obsess over what Summer-Raine is doing, but

instead daydream of Cara and the wide-eyed, rosy way she looks at me when she thinks I'm not paying attention.

What does it say about my relationship that I spend more time thinking about a woman who isn't my girlfriend?

And yet, I can't stop.

It may not be fair to Cara, but I can't imagine a time when I won't think about Summer-Raine and hope that she's doing okay. But that's fine, right? It's not as if I'm still in love with her or fantasising about her in ways I shouldn't be, with the exception of every single time I've slept with a woman over the last several years.

But my daytime thoughts, the ones that really matter, aren't of an illicit nature, nor of something inappropriate or disrespectful to my relationship. They are simply ones of concern for someone that I used to know. The way you worry about an old college friend you haven't spoken to for years, or a distant relative who lives overseas somewhere.

I'm sure Cara does the very same with people from her past.

With that in mind, I go to pick up my phone for a late night check in with Winter, when she bizarrely beats me to it. Her name flashes on my screen and my stomach dips.

She never calls me.

Especially not at this time.

"Winter, hey." Confusion and unease are clear in my voice. "Everything okay? What's going on?"

She waits a beat too long to answer. "Hey, no, yeah, um, everything is fine. It doesn't matter. Forget I called, okay?"

"What? No," I yell, stopping her before she has a chance to

hang up the phone. "Something's up. What is it?"

She sighs and I can hear her defeat and resignation through the receiver.

"Summer's in hospital." My stomach plummets. I open my mouth to ask why, but Winter carries on. "A couple of days ago, she... um, well she made an attempt on her life."

The world falls out from beneath my feet as pain seers through my heart.

Summer-Raine tried to kill herself.

I feel sick. Acid rises in my chest and burns in the pit of my throat. I can't breathe. Can't move. Can't think of anything but Summer-Raine and the incredible pain she must have been in to do something like that to herself.

"She's okay," Winter says hurriedly. "Got lucky actually. Should've been much worse than it was."

"What happened?" I croak, swallowing down a mouthful of acid.

I hear her suck in a breath. "She jumped off a bridge into traffic."

"*Fuck.*"

"Yeah."

"And she survived that?"

"She fell onto a truck which kinda cushioned the fall, I guess."

"And she's really okay?" I ask, needing to hear her say it again. Because how can she possibly be okay after something like that? "She's not too hurt?"

"Oh, she's hurt plenty, but nothing life threatening."

I stand up and pace the length of the apartment, my hand

not holding the phone scratching relentlessly at the fabric of my trackpants that cover my thighs. They're loose, but I feel like they're suffocating me.

"Look," Winter says after a long period of silence. "I called because I need your help."

"Anything."

"You're gonna wish you hadn't said that." She laughs gently, but there's no joy behind it.

"Winter, what is it?"

I can't imagine anything I wouldn't do to help her and her sister right now. Not after what she's just told me. Not after what Summer-Raine's done.

"The doctor won't discharge her until she's confident Summer has enough support at home." She pauses. Sighs. "But my husband refuses to let her stay with us anymore."

"Okay," I say slowly, not understanding where this is going.

"She needs someone with her twenty-four hours, Auden, and I'm not going to be able to do it."

"Right, so what does this have to do with me?"

She sucks in a long breath. "Well, I was hoping that you could do it."

I blanch. "What?"

"Look, I know it's a huge ask. Ridiculous, really. But I don't know what else to do. She won't agree to inpatient care even though it's the best thing for her, I'm not in a position to be able to look after her anymore and I'm terrified that she's going to try to do something to herself again if I don't find a solution. You know her, Auden. She loved you once, she trusted you. There's no one else I can ask to do this."

I listen to her talk, can hear the desperation in her voice, and though I told her only moments ago that I'd do anything to help, I know that I can't do this.

"Winter." I sigh, but she cuts me off.

"Please, Auden. I wouldn't ask if I had any other choice."

"But what about your parents?" I ask, though I already know the answer. Their parents didn't give a shit about them five years ago, I can't imagine they've started caring now. "Or Marlowe. Have you asked Marlowe?"

"Who's Marlowe?"

"Her best friend."

"Summer doesn't have any friends. She stopped talking to everyone after high school. You're literally my last hope."

"But what about my job and my apartment?" Admittedly, the lease on my shitty studio is up next month, but Winter doesn't know that.

"You can still go to work. There'll be nurses with her when you're not and I think it's a good idea if Summer volunteers at an animal shelter during the week or something. She's been living off her trust fund since she lost her job last year, so it'll do her some good to get out and do something."

"And my apartment?"

"I'll pay whatever's left on your lease."

"You've really got it all figured out, haven't you?"

She scoffs. "Told you, you're my last resort."

The despair in her voice punctures my heart like a dart. And I get it, her hopelessness. She really must have exhausted all of her options if she's asking me to move in with my ex-girlfriend, whom I haven't seen for five years, in order to make sure she doesn't hurt herself again.

But would I really be able to move past the pain and heartbreak Summer-Raine put me through all that time ago and look after her without those memories tainting the way I act towards her? Would I be able to forgive her enough to do this?

I don't know.

"And she knows you're asking me this?" I ask.

Winter's silence tells me all I need to know.

"She doesn't know, does she?"

"Not exactly."

"How do you think she'd react if I turned up on her doorstep ready to move into her apartment for the next however long? Winter, she'd lose her shit. You know she would. She broke up with me, for fuck's sake. She hates me. I'm literally the last person in the world she'd ever want to do this for her."

Winter releases a resigned sigh. "You don't know how wrong you are, Auden."

I snort indignantly, but say nothing.

"Look," she says. "We both know that you're going to do it and it's late and I'm tired, so let's stop pretending like you're not."

"I'm not pretending. I can't—"

"You can and you will. You've called me every month for five years, sometimes more than that, to ask how she's doing. You might be lying to yourself and everyone else, but you're just as in love with her now as you were when you were both eighteen, so let's just cut the bullshit, okay? She needs help and you're going to give it to her. You know you are."

Shit.

She's right.

I know she's right.

Maybe not about me still being in love with Summer-Raine, because I'm not, of course I'm not, but about me helping her. Because the truth is, there isn't a universe in existence in which I wouldn't help Summer-Raine if she needed it. And Winter knows it. It's why she asked, because she knew I'd end up saying yes.

My heart somersaults at the thought of seeing Summer-Raine again. I wonder if her hair is still as golden as it was when we were young, if her eyes are still the same extraordinary shade of green as they were in Islamorada.

It's killed me, all these years, knowing that we live in the same city. That she could be just around the block from me at any time and I wouldn't know. I've spent hours upon hours staring out the vast windows at the office, wondering where in the city she is and what she's doing. I've even strained my eyes to try and see if I could spot her.

But not once in the time I've lived in Tallahassee have I seen her.

And now I will.

"When?" is all I ask.

"Saturday."

"That's three days away."

"I know."

Three days. It's so soon and yet, at the same time, feels so far away.

Three days until I see the girl who broke my heart again.

Three days to try and work through the lingering resentment I feel towards her for leaving me the way she did. Three days to work out what the fuck I'm going to tell Cara.

She'd flip her shit if she knew I was about to move in with my ex-girlfriend, the girl who I'll always consider the love of my life. But she deserves my honesty. Even if that means she decides to cut things off between us, telling her the truth is the right thing to do.

But worrying about that can wait.

Summer-Raine needs me and that's the most important thing right now.

I told Cara that Summer-Raine is my cousin.

I'm not sure why.

It's not as if the thought of her breaking things off between us worried me so much that I couldn't face telling her the truth. Honestly, I just couldn't summon the energy to have a conversation that I knew would end in a fight.

Maybe that makes me an asshole, I don't know. But in the moment, sitting across the table from her at her favourite sushi restaurant, lying seemed like the most logical thing to do.

I'm not proud of it. I've always taken pride in doing the right thing, in being a gentleman and keeping my promises, so I don't know why I prioritised convenience over honesty in that moment. Or why I've kept the lie going since.

Even more surprisingly, I don't feel guilty. My thoughts have been too occupied with seeing Summer-Raine again after such a long time to have lingered on my deception. And that *definitely* makes me an asshole.

But even now, pulling my truck up in a parking spot outside an apartment building in uptown Tallahassee, I can't find it in me to worry about Cara and how she deserves better. Because my breath is coming in short gasps, my heart thuds like a thunderstorm and my palms are so sweaty, they slip from the steering wheel.

I'm only moments away from finally laying eyes on Summer-Raine. And truthfully, I don't know if I'm ready.

Not for the first time, I wonder if I'm doing the right thing. It took me so long after we broke up to get myself back into a good place, to adjust to life without her and accept that she didn't love me anymore. In my naïve, eighteen-year-old mind, I honestly thought that we'd last forever.

So maybe agreeing to do this was a stupid thing to do. If I was still in love with her, which I'm not, it would be the perfect way to get my heart broken again. At the very least, I'll end up with more bruises on my soul.

And yet, that doesn't stop me from pulling my luggage out the back of my truck and nodding at the doorman, whom Winter has already approved my arrival with. It doesn't stop me boarding the elevator, pressing the button for Summer-Raine's floor and walking the corridors until I find the door with her number on.

And when I raise my fist to knock, listening for the sound of footsteps as she shuffles through the apartment to answer the door, it doesn't stop a smile spreading across my face as after five years of missing her, worrying about her and picturing her face as I make love to other women, I finally lay eyes on her again.

And fuck, if the sight of her doesn't steal the breath straight from my lungs.

I want to stand and stare at her forever. Take in the sight of her wide, surprised eyes and cheeks that are flushed from rushing to answer the door.

But I don't.

Because that's not what I'm here for.

And it's in my best interest to remember that.

So, I ignore how she's just as beautiful as she was in highschool, if not more so, and swallow down the urge to pull her into my arms and breathe in the smell of her. Instead, I let my smile melt into a smirk as I feign total confidence and control.

And with a voice as steady as I can muster, I finally utter the words I've been practicing for the last three days.

"Hello, Summer-Raine."

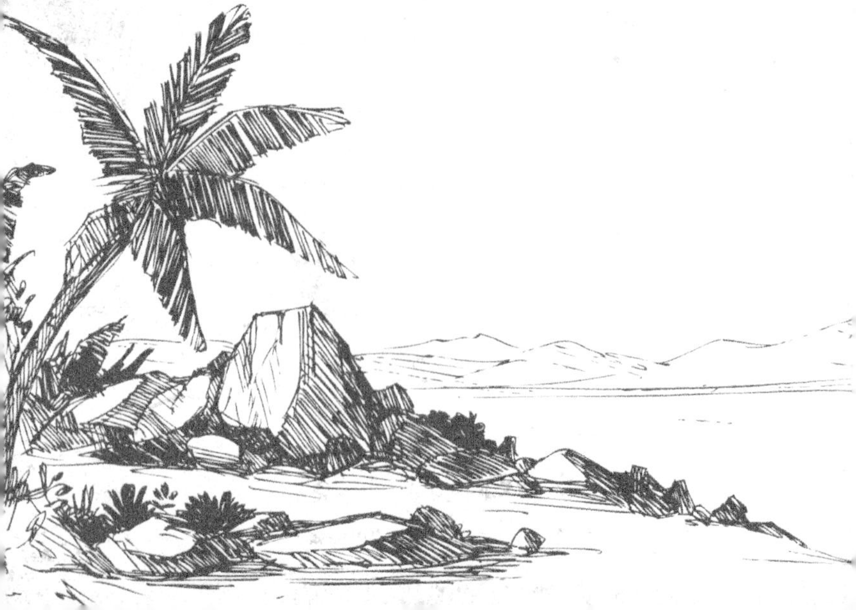

Chapter Eighteen
SUMMER-RAINE

"Hello, Summer-Raine."

I stumble backwards, a strangled gasp escaping me as I knock into the coffee table in the middle of my living area.

No.

I can't breathe.

It's like someone's got their hands around my neck, slowly choking the life out of me.

Because the man on the other side of the door looks exactly like the boy I've loved for so long, only aged by five years. He still has the same woody shade of hair that flops too long over eyes blue as sapphires. Same dimples on his cheeks. Same muscular arms that used to hold me while I slept, only bigger now and more toned.

It's not him. It can't be him.

I've had hallucinations before, but never like this. Never this viscerally. Like I'm trapped inside a lucid dream, the delusion refusing to disappear no matter how many times I tell myself he's not really here.

This isn't real.

I can't tell if I'm shouting or whispering, or even talking aloud at all. I just know that if the image of Auden Wells and his gut-wrenchingly beautiful face doesn't disappear soon, I'll probably start to scream.

I scrub at my eyes with the back of my hands and look to the open door again.

The fake Auden is still there. Still leaning against the door frame, but with concern in its eyes now rather than the cocky glint that shone there when it first appeared.

"Are you alright?" it asks, and even its voice has the same caramel-smooth lilt to it that I remember so well. "Summer-Raine?"

Why won't it stop talking?

I slam my hands over my ears and squeeze my eyes shut, repeating the same three sentences over and over and over until my voice turns hoarse.

Go away.

Leave me alone.

You're not real.

When I feel the warm touch of hands on my skin, I scream. I scream until there's no air left in my lungs and my body is drained of energy, weak and limp as my legs give out beneath me.

My eyes are still closed. I don't dare open them. In all my life, I don't think I've ever experienced pain or fear quite like this. Even during my episodes of disassociation, when I've wandered off in the middle of the night as if I'm sleepwalking, have I ever felt such a loss of control over my mind.

I guess nothing can turn me inside out quite like the image of Auden Wells and the reminder of what I gave up so many years ago.

I don't regret what I did, I never have. Letting him go was the best thing I could have ever done for him, but that hasn't stopped my heart from beating his name every second of every day for the last five years.

Over time, the absence of him from my life got easier to manage, so long as I didn't see him unexpectedly on social media or bump into him around town.

Once, when I was grocery shopping, I saw him in the vegetable aisle loading yams into his basket. It was coming up to Thanksgiving, maybe a year or so ago, and the sight of him standing there analysing root vegetables had me running back out the way I came. He hadn't seen me, but even so, it took several minutes of heavy breathing in the alley beside the store to calm the panic attack that was swelling inside me like a tidal wave.

But that was nothing compared to this.

"Summer-Raine, I need you to breathe."

I can't.

"You can. Copy me, okay? In for four seconds out for eight, can you do that for me?"

But the voice of the hallucination is beginning to ebb away. Even behind my eyelids, coloured spots dance dizzyingly in my vision. My head feels light and heavy all at once, like I'm made of both helium and steel. I must bite my tongue, because it's iron I taste as I lose consciousness, the soothing notes of fake-

Auden's voice lulling me into oblivion.

It's Winter's face I see when I wake up.

I'm lying on the couch, my legs and feet propped up on a pile of throw cushions, with a wet flannel drooped across my forehead.

"You're always here when I wake up. Do you just enjoy watching me sleep?" I say in a lame attempt at a joke.

She smiles, but it doesn't reach her eyes.

"What happened?" she asks, taking the flannel from my head and dabbing it down my cheek. It's cool and damp and feels phenomenal against my burning skin.

"Had a crazy hallucination and freaked out." I shrug. "Must have fainted."

She hums in response, looking everywhere but at me. Her fingers twitch in her lap, before tucking her hair behind her ear and repeating the action, something she does when she's nervous.

"You're being weird." I narrow my eyes, slowly lifting myself up into a sitting position. "Why are you being weird?"

"Um," she looks down at her hands, "it wasn't a hallucination, Sum."

"What?"

"You weren't hallucinating. It was real. He was here."

I laugh, because *what*? There's no way Auden was really here. He couldn't have been. It's not possible.

"No, he wasn't."

I scratch at my neck as shivers creep along my skin, running the length of my body.

She finally looks at me and I can see in her eyes that she believes what she's saying. She doesn't say anything, just nods as if to say *yeah, he was.*

"Don't be stupid." My tone is biting. "Why would he be here? We haven't spoken in half a decade. He doesn't even know I live in the city, let alone my address."

"Please don't freak out, okay?" she says and instantly, my heart begins to thunder again. "I called him. Three days ago, when I went home from the hospital your first night. I called and asked if he could stay with you. I didn't know what to do, Sum, or who else I could ask."

"No." She wouldn't do this. She wouldn't go behind my back and betray me like this. "No, you didn't."

She's joking, she must be. She's never been very good at pranks and this is just another one of her misfired attempts, because there is no way in hell that she'd call the last person in the world that I would want to see me like this.

But her eyes fill with tears as she nods to validate her story.

"Why would you do this to me?"

"Because you need the support and I know you'd refuse to let me hire anyone."

"That doesn't mean you could go behind my back and ask my ex-boyfriend. What the fuck, Winter? Are you trying to hurt me?"

"What? *No.*" A tear slips free down her cheek. "I did it because I love you. And I'd rather you hate me for this then throw yourself off a bridge again. I can live with you being angry with me, I can't live with you being dead."

Rage still burns hot inside me and I cling to it. If I focus on being angry at my sister's betrayal, I won't think about the fact that Auden was really here. On my doorstep. Talking to me. *Touching me.*

I remember the warmth of his hands on my arms as I collapsed on the floor. It was the first time since senior year that he's touched me, that *any* man has touched me, and I was too far gone in the throes of my panic attack to take notice of the way it felt. I hadn't even thought that it was real.

How long have I ached to feel the touch of his hands on my body again? It's all I've dreamt of since I had him removed from my visitors list after the accident on the cliffs. I never thought I'd get the chance to touch him again.

"Where is he now?" I ask.

Winter eyes me cautiously, chewing on her lip as she thinks her answer over.

And then I realise.

If her lack of response doesn't confirm my suspicions, then the way my body tingles in awareness does. I should have realised sooner. From the way I was burning up, the goosebumps on my skin, the way I kept shivering despite feeling so hot.

I may not have picked up on it, but my body certainly had. Just like it had always done back in high school whenever he was near.

"He's still here, isn't he?"

Her eyes widen and then she nods. "In the guest room."

Holy shit.

Another panic attack threatens as I realise that this is really happening. Auden is really here, in my apartment, in a room just down the hall.

"Do you want me to stay?" Winter asks on a whisper, still unable to hold my gaze for longer than a few seconds at a time.

"No." I sit on my hands in a bid to stop them shaking. "You've done enough."

She nods, then stands, wiping her hands down the front of her jeans. "I really am sorry for upsetting you, Sum, but I'm not sorry for calling him."

"Just go."

We can talk this out another time, but right now, there's more pressing matters. Like the man in my guest room who still holds my heart in the palm of his hand, whether he knows it or not.

Winter lets herself out and I listen to the fading sound of her footsteps until all that surrounds me is a deafening, stifling silence. My heart hammers painfully against my ribcage as I steel myself for coming face to face with Auden again.

I'm not ready for this.

I'd need years to adequately prepare myself to see him again, not mere minutes. Part of me still thinks this is all just a figment of my imagination. At the very least a dream that I'll wake up from in the next few moments. But when a minute passes, then another, and nothing changes, I finally accept that this truly is my reality.

"You can come out now," I whisper into the stillness.

I close my eyes as the sound of cautious footsteps fill the room.

I smell him instantly. The scent of pine and well-read

books floods my senses and makes me dizzy. Even after all this time it's as familiar to me as my own perfume. In fact, in all the Christmases that have passed since I cut things off between us, I haven't been able to put up a tree because they remind me too much of him.

"Open your eyes, Summer-Raine," he says gently, his voice as comforting as a blanket to a small child.

And I do.

My eyes find him and my breath catches.

If it's possible, he's even more beautiful now than he was back then.

I say nothing as I trace the lines of his face, memorising every new freckle and crease that the last few years have gifted him with. He still has the same boyish features, but there's rough stubble on his jaw and a crookedness to his nose that hadn't been there before.

And all the while, he studies me with the same intensity that I study him.

I stand stock still as he breathes me in, watching his eyes trail over me from head to toe. His gaze is hot as he takes in my body like he remembers what it looks like beneath my clothes, but his gaze is nostalgic rather than lustful or predatory. For a long time, he only looks at me from my chin down, as if steeling himself to meet my eyes.

And when he finally does, it's as if the last five years never happened at all.

I may have broken his heart so coldly, but he looks at me only with warmth. His eyes shine only with happy memories of us, so brightly I can almost watch them play out in front of me. His lips tip upwards at the corners, his smile as dazzling and easy as I remember.

Our worlds may have changed, we may not know each other anymore, but that magic that was always between us is still there. We don't belong to each other anymore, but our souls still reach for each other as if we do.

He's still Auden.

And when he looks at me the way he is now, I'm not the same Summer-Raine who tried to kill herself just days ago or the one who broke his heart back when we were eighteen. I'm the Summer-Raine I was when we spent our nights wrapped together on my balcony in Islamorada, reciting the poetry of W H Auden and imagining the future we were supposed to have together. It's like I'm eighteen again.

But then he looks away and reality comes crashing down.

I'm still just the damaged girl with baggage a mile high and he's just the guy my sister called to stop me trying to kill myself again. He's not here because he loves me, he's here because Winter asked him to be. Because I'm crazy. Because I'm fucked up. And that's all I'll ever be.

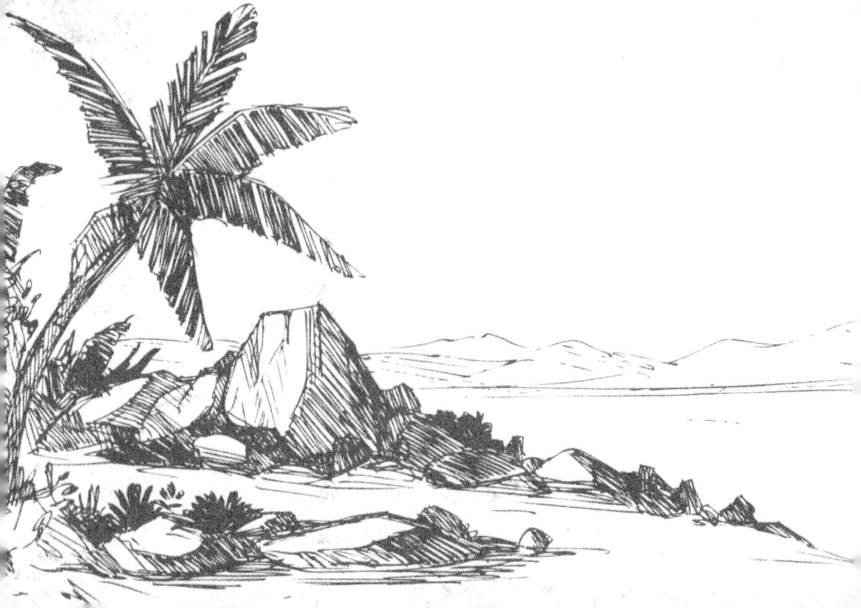

Chapter Nineteen

AUDEN

She looks at me through the corner of her eye as she sits on the sofa sipping coffee.

It's been hours and neither of us have spoken. The tension in the air is so thick I could choke on it, both of us thinking about the heartache of the last several years but neither taking the step to talk about it.

For so long I've imagined what I'd say if I were to ever see her again.

Why did you break my heart?

Why didn't you just talk to me?

Didn't you love me enough to try and get through it?

I'd have been patient if time was what you needed.

But now I finally have the opportunity, it's like I've lost the ability to speak.

Occasionally, I cast a glance at her. My eyes can't seem to stop themselves from seeking her out, but it's too painful to look at her for any longer than a few seconds at a time.

Her beauty is too bright. It always has been, but it has

intensified with age. It blinds me even from the edges of my periphery. It's as if I'm scared to look at her for too long for fear of being turned to stone.

"Why are you here, Auden?" she asks finally.

Her voice is the same sultry husk that I remember, only a little deeper and with more grit. Almost like she's taken up a smoking habit. I hope not, but it wouldn't surprise me.

"Winter asked me to be," I say, as if that's explanation enough.

She huffs and looks down to pick at the corner of her thumbnail until it starts to bleed.

"Did she offer you money or something?"

My eyes shoot to hers, wide in shock.

She thinks I'm here for money? It may have been a long time since we last saw each other, but I'd have hoped that she knew me better than to think I'd be here for any other reason than to be here for her. But the fact that she even has to ask the question reminds me of how much has changed. We don't know each other anymore. We're nothing really more than strangers.

"No, Summer-Raine. I wasn't offered money."

"Then why?"

I contemplate just telling her the truth. That even though she ripped my heart straight out of my chest and hurt me more than anyone ever has, she needed me and so I came. That I will always come running if she needs help, like the pathetic heartsick boy I am.

But I don't say any of that.

For the second time in only a couple of days, I lie.

"I had nothing better to do."

Though she does nothing more than nod, I know she isn't pleased with my response. Unlucky for her though, that's all she's getting. I might not be able to resist running to her side when she's in trouble, but I'm still harbouring a fuck-tonne of resentment towards her for leaving me the way she did. I'm not about to go back to treating her like she's the centre of my universe. She isn't, not anymore. And she only has herself to blame for that.

My legs begin to ache from standing. Summer-Raine never offered me a seat, so I didn't take one, but it's been hours now and it doesn't look like an invitation is coming to make myself at home.

She scowls at me as I flop into one of two brown leather armchairs surrounding the oak coffee table. When I pinch the fabric and rub it between my fingers, it feels just like butter. Expensive leather. Proper designer shit, not just something you can pick up at Pottery Barn.

It surprises me.

The Summer-Raine I knew was never into materialistic stuff. Sure, she wore designer clothes, but she told me once that's only because her mother bought them to sweeten the fact that she was a mostly absent figure in her life.

In fact, this whole apartment drips with luxury. From the armchairs to the flat screen television mounted on the wall, to the twelve-person dining table by the floor-to-ceiling windows that looks to have been handcrafted from reclaimed teak root. A bespoke piece, I imagine. Probably cost thousands.

"My mother decorated," Summer-Raine says.

"Ah." I nod. "Makes sense."

"Yeah."

Silence stretches between us once more, neither of us knowing what to say.

Maybe this was a bad idea. Maybe agreeing to move in with Summer-Raine and be on suicide watch wasn't actually the right thing to do. She'd have kicked up a storm, but hiring round the clock care was probably what should have happened.

Because there's this awkwardness between us that never existed before. We don't know how to be in each other's company anymore. And if this is how the next several months are going to go, I can't imagine Summer-Raine will make any progress.

My phone buzzes in my pocket and I answer without checking the name.

"Hey, baby." Cara's voice tinkles in my ear. "Did you make it to your cousin's place okay?"

I glance at Summer-Raine who watches me quizzically.

"Yeah, I made it here fine."

"You told me you would text me when you got there, but you didn't." I imagine her pouting at the other end of the phone.

Lying and breaking promises, what the hell has happened to me?

"Sorry, babe. I completely forgot."

She harrumphs like a toddler who hasn't gotten their way.

"When can I see you?" she asks on a whine.

I close my eyes and rest my head on the back of the armchair. My patience is already running thin. "I don't know. I think I'm gonna be busy for a while."

I can almost hear her sulking through the phone. "Bleh. You suck."

"I'll make it up to you, yeah? But I gotta go. I'm sorry."

"Whatever. I'll see you later. Love you, baby."

"Yeah. Bye babe."

I cringe as I shut off the phone, keeping my eyes closed for a few more beats before opening them to meet Summer-Raine's questioning stare.

"Babe?" she asks with her eyebrows raised.

"My girlfriend."

I don't miss the way she flinches. It must have been pretty obvious given the phone conversation, but I guess it's one thing to suspect it and another to have it confirmed.

I don't know how I'd react if I knew Summer-Raine had a boyfriend. Maybe it makes me a hypocrite, but the thought of another man touching her the way I used to makes my stomach churn in jealousy. But in all the time I've kept in touch with Winter, no boyfriend has ever been mentioned. I'm not naïve enough to think that that means there never has been one, but it's a relief that there hasn't been anything serious enough to mention.

"Are you seeing anyone?" I ask and grit my teeth while I wait for the answer.

She chews on her lip, contemplating the idea of lying maybe, but then she dips her head and whispers, "No."

I exhale in relief, not having realised I was even holding my breath.

"So, your girlfriend," she says with a slight grimace, as if the word tastes sour in her mouth. She's never been very good at hiding her emotions from me. "Have you been together long?"

I tilt my head to the side, surprised by the topic of conversation. If the shoe was on the other foot, I wouldn't want to know anything about the man who had taken my place in her life.

But then, I guess, maybe our relationship hadn't meant the same to her as it had to me. It was her who ended things after all. Maybe she doesn't see what we had as anything more than a relationship she had in high school, one that was built off of hormones and the naivety of a teenage heart. Just because she was the love of my life, doesn't mean that I was hers.

"Six months," I answer.

"What's her name?"

"Cara."

She nods thoughtfully. "Nice name."

"I guess."

But I prefer yours.

"Is she pretty?"

I pause for a moment and picture Cara with her alabaster skin and hair dark as raven feathers, her willowy legs and supermodel body.

"She's beautiful."

But not like you. No one ever comes close to you.

"Are you happy?"

Am I happy? That's a question with too many possible answers. I have a good job and a girlfriend and friends that I can drink beer and shoot the shit with. For all intents and purposes, I'm happy. So why am I finding it so hard to answer the question?

"I can't complain," I say finally.

Summer-Raine smiles, but it's not a real one. Her nostrils flare slightly with the effort of it, her eyes glimmering with the promise of tears though none actually appear or fall.

"Good." She nods and then raises her eyes to look at me with total sincerity. "I'm happy for you, Auden. I really am."

And despite the slightly crestfallen expression on her face that she's trying so hard to hide, I believe her.

We fall back into silence. A relief, as I don't want to talk about Cara anymore. Not with Summer-Raine. I may have moved on, but they are two parts of my life I want to keep completely and utterly separate. Talking about my current girlfriend to my ex feels wrong in so many ways.

I glance at the large gilded clock hanging from a wall above a lightwood sideboard. It's early evening. I should have guessed from the low position of the sun, but I was too caught up in Summer-Raine to notice the dimming light in the apartment and the slight tinge of pink to the sky.

"Hungry?" I ask and she nods. "Fancy ordering a pizza?"

She nods again.

"You still have it with pepperoni, mushrooms and extra cheese?"

Another nod.

"Have you forgotten how to speak in the last fifteen minutes?"

She scowls, then looks down at her hands.

"Well, alright then." I stand and walk into the open-plan kitchen, where I rifle through her drawers until I find a pizza menu. "I'll just order then, shall I?"

Still no answer.

I don't know why she's suddenly turned into a mute, but I'm not about to grill her. So, I dial the number for the pizza place and put in an order for two extra large pizzas, a portion of chicken wings and a side of garlic bread and all the while Summer-Raine watches me with rapt attention.

"Are we expecting company?" she asks with raised eyebrows and a slightly amused expression on her face.

"Nope. That's all for us."

She snorts. "I'll never eat all that."

My eyes trace the lines of her face that are sharper now than they were five years ago. I should have noticed it before, but she must weigh at least ten pounds less than she did back then and that was weight she couldn't really afford to lose. Her arms are thinner, her cheeks hollowed and her body—which she's tried to hide beneath the oversized flannel shirt that looks vaguely familiar—is so slim I could wrap my arms around her twice over.

"Try." I frown. "You need the calories."

I excuse myself while we wait for the pizza to arrive and start unpacking my small suitcase in the guestroom. I didn't take much notice of the room when Winter showed me in here earlier, telling me to stay hidden until she'd calmed down Summer-Raine, so I take a moment to fully breathe in my surroundings.

Like the rest of the apartment, the room screams money. The walls are decorated with textured gold paper that reflects the light coming in through the large window and scatters it like stardust across the room. The wall behind the bed is dominated by an ivory upholstered headboard that is arguably too big for the space and double doors lead off the room to a hotel suite style bathroom.

I knew her family had money, but I didn't realise how much until now.

It makes me wonder if Summer-Raine pays for this herself, albeit out of her trust fund, or if her parents are financing it directly from their bank accounts. I guess it doesn't matter either way.

An hour later, I'm back in the living room watching Summer-Raine take tiny bites out of her pizza and pick off the toppings despite them being her favourite. She watches me between chews, sucking her bottom lip into her mouth and scowling.

"I can hear you thinking from here," I say with a wink.

She blushes, averting her eyes and staring down at her lap. *Don't hide from me,* I want to yell at her. But she isn't mine to demand that of her anymore. She hasn't been for a long time.

"What's on your mind?" I ask, swallowing my last mouthful and tossing my crust into the box.

Her brow furrows, her gaze still locked on her lap. "You never called me babe." Her voice is timid and quiet.

I mask my surprise with a cocky grin. "Disappointed?"

"No, I hate it."

"Then why do you care?"

"I don't care." But the thunderous expression on her face says otherwise. "It was just an observation."

"Mmhmm."

"Shut up."

"I didn't say anything." I hold my hands up in mock surrender, my lips twitching in amusement at her obvious jealousy.

It feels so natural to poke fun at her just like I used to when we were together, that it doesn't occur to me to question why she would be jealous at all. Sure, I didn't miss her reaction to finding out about Cara, but I figured that it would be uncomfortable for anyone to discover the existence of their ex's new partner by overhearing a phone conversation. It didn't occur to me that there could be anything more to it than that.

"How's your Mama?" she asks in an obvious bid to change the topic of conversation.

My stomach drops. I don't want to talk about Mama. It will only dredge up the memories I've tried so hard to bury in the furthest corners of my mind. It will only serve to remind me of how epically I failed her.

"She died," I say, turning to look out the imposing windows at the bleeding sky above the city, "during my first year of college."

Summer-Raine gasps. "Shit, Auden, I'm so sorry. What happened?"

I scrunch my eyes shut as images of my Mama laying grey and cold on the kitchen floor come screaming back to me. The shards of broken glass around her. The empty cannister of pills on the counter.

"Accidental overdose."

That's what the coroner ruled it anyway. But I know differently.

"But you don't think it was," Summer-Raine whispers.

I open my eyes to find her watching me closely.

"Accidents don't come with a note."

It was the first day of Spring break of my freshman year. I'd come home from college and found my mother dead in a puddle of vomit, piss and faeces, her blue hand still clutching the neck of a five-dollar bottle of merlot. It hadn't been until days later that I'd found the note she left me, slipped between the folds of my pillow case. I hadn't turned it over to the police. They didn't need to see it.

I'm sorry, I love you, it's better this way, she'd written. *I can't do this to you anymore.*

That's basically the gist of the whole letter. I'm the reason she killed herself, all because I'd made her feel like a burden.

I must have said that out loud because one second, Summer-Raine's sitting on the couch with her legs crossed beneath her and the next, she's crouching down in front of me with one tiny hand cupping my face. "Oh, Auden. No, that's not true," she says, tears brimming in her eyes.

"You are not the reason she did that, understand? It doesn't matter what she wrote in that note to you, she made that decision for herself. She did it because it's what she wanted to do. Do not blame yourself for this, *please.*" Her voice breaks on a sob.

My eyes shutter and I lean into her touch. *Home.* That's what she feels like.

I nod because I can't find it in me to speak right now. But I don't believe her. Mama wouldn't have felt like a burden if I hadn't had made her feel like one.

I blink my eyes open and look at Summer-Raine. We're so

close, our mouths only inches apart and my lips tingle with the memory of what it felt like to kiss her. When she moves her hair over her shoulder, I'm hit with the scent of her. *She still smells like peaches.* It's a fact that hits me like a cupid's arrow to the heart.

I reach for her, twirling a golden lock of hair around my finger the way I used to do when we were eighteen and in love. So much between us has changed. Our minds don't know each other anymore, yet our bodies still gravitate towards the other as if we've never been apart.

We're a study in paradoxes, Summer-Raine and I. We're strangers and soulmates and ghosts from our pasts. I've moved on from her, yet I've loved her every single day since she left.

"It would have been an insult to call you babe," I whisper, moving my fingers from her hair to trace a delicate path down the side of her face.

"What?" Her voice is as gentle as mine.

"Babe is a word men use when they forget the name of the girl they're fucking. It's easy. It's impersonal. It lacks intimacy. Babe isn't the name you use to refer to the love of your life."

She inhales sharply and her eyes close as if she's in pain. I brush my thumb along her cheekbone, but her hand snaps up to stall my movements.

"Please don't," she rasps, eyes still closed.

I bring my hand down as she stands and walks away from me, her footsteps disappearing down the hall until I hear her slam her bedroom door.

I get it. The intensity of the moment grew too much. The air was so thick with memories of us and words left unspoken that I feel like I need to open a window to let some of it out, so if she needs space to work through whatever just happened between us then I'm not going to hold it against her.

I spend some time clearing up, putting our leftovers in the fridge and taking out the pizza boxes. If I'm going to be living here, I'll treat the place with the same respect I do my own apartment and maybe in doing so, it will lessen the blow for Summer-Raine.

As I load our dirty plates into the dishwasher, it occurs to me that as furious as she was that I'd be staying with her, not once has she asked me to leave.

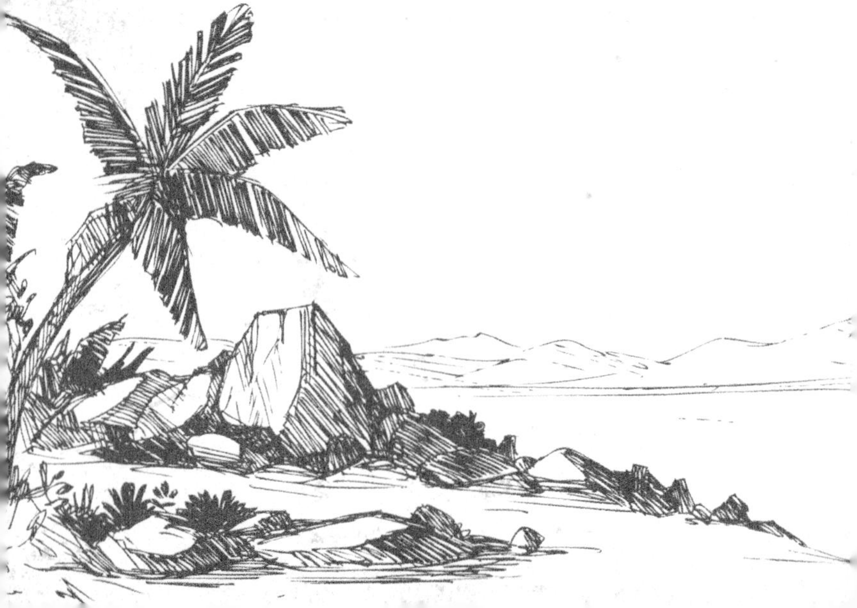

Chapter Twenty

SUMMER-RAINE

It's been two weeks since the first night Auden stayed and my skin is still tingling from the touch of his fingers on my face.

I'd been so mad at him for crashing back into my life at a time that I have never felt so vulnerable, but any anger I'd felt in that moment had dissipated when he told me about what happened with his Mama. My heart had screamed in pain for him.

I've always known that he'd had it rough at home, given the severity of his mother's condition, but he loved her as fiercely as any son loves their Mama. Perhaps even more so. Because out of the two of them, he was the parent.

I didn't know what I was doing when I knelt in front of him and cupped his face in my hand. Instinct had taken over. In that moment, I'd forgotten that he isn't mine to comfort anymore—not that I ever did a good enough job of it when we were together. All I knew was that I couldn't sit there on the couch across from him as he told me how he blamed himself for his mother's suicide, without doing something to get through to him that it wasn't his fault.

But then he'd called me the love of his life and *God*, how much it had hurt to hear that.

There was once a time that hearing those words would have set me alight like fireworks on the fourth of July, yet now they only bring me pain. I don't deserve to be the love of his life, not after how I treated him and the shit I put him through. But that doesn't stop me wishing that I could be worthy of the title, that I could be the love of his life now and forever, not just once upon a time five years ago.

I've spent the last fourteen days doing my damndest to avoid him. But it's pretty hard to hide from the guy who's been tasked with watching over me twenty-four-seven. He wakes in the mornings when I do and refuses to go to bed until he's confident I'm asleep. When I try and camp out in my bedroom, he makes me keep the door ajar. When I use the bathroom, I'm thankfully allowed to close the door but he makes me keep it unlocked, and he won't go to work on weekdays until a nurse or my sister arrives to take over. He even follows my GPS on the days I volunteer at the animal shelter Winter set me up with.

It's stifling.

Not simply because I feel like a bird in a cage, but because it's so damn hard to be around him without crumbling. Oh, how desperate I am to fold myself into his lap the way I used to do on my balcony in Islamorada and bury my face in his neck. It's been torture to be constantly surrounded by the scent of him without being able to smell it directly from his skin. To have to hold myself back from touching him. So many times,

I've almost slipped up and called him quarterback, only to face the crushing disappointment when I remember it's not okay for me to call him that anymore.

And, *God,* the pain that cuts through me every time I'm forced to listen to another one of his phone conversations with his girlfriend. My apartment is nice but it's not overly big, so it doesn't matter where he is, I can still make out the words exchanged between them. I can still hear him call her babe.

Babe is a word men use when they forget the name of the girl they're fucking. Babe isn't the name you use to refer to the love of your life.

If I weren't so sickeningly jealous, I'd feel bad for his girlfriend for being with a man who so clearly doesn't love her. And it makes me wonder why Auden is even with her at all. But then I remind myself that I had my chance with him and I fucked it up so epically that it would be hypocritical of me to pass judgement over their relationship.

Maybe they're not in love, but I bet she makes him happier than I ever did.

"Want some coffee?" Auden asks from where he sits in the leather armchair that he seems to have claimed as his own.

I nod and watch him walk into the kitchen, my gaze not faltering as he sets about making us a latte each from my integrated coffee machine. My stomach flips as I breathe in the sight of him. Faded sweatpants that have seen better days hang low on his hips and a white t-shirt with NASA branding clings to his biceps that have grown significantly since I saw him last.

My mouth runs dry. *Why must he be so beautiful?*

I look at his face in profile, at the sharp lines of his

cheekbones to the slight crookedness of his nose to the gentle wave of his chestnut brown hair. Then he turns and I'm too slow to look away.

"Wipe your mouth, Summer-Raine." He grins, bringing the coffee back over to the living area and setting a cup down in front of me. "You're drooling."

"I have no idea what you're talking about." I scowl, but wipe my hand across my mouth anyway.

He chuckles. "Sure, you don't."

His lips tilt into a cocky smirk, taking a seat in his chair, and I wonder if it affects Cara as much as it does me whenever he looks at her like that. Part of me hopes he's never looked at her like that at all, but the rest of me knows that's just wishful thinking. Of course he's looked at her like that. She's his girlfriend. I'm sure he even looks at her like she's his entire universe the way he used to do with me.

"You always think so loud," he says, leaning forward to study me with his elbows resting on his parted knees. Every so often, he raises his coffee cup to his lips and I watch his throat bob each time he swallows. I still remember what it felt like to kiss him there.

"Do I?" I shrug and force myself to stop looking at him.

"You always have done."

I don't know what to say to that, so I turn and look out the window at the setting sun. The sky is beautiful tonight. It's like a watercolour painting of bleeding reds, purples and oranges, with birds flying like little black silhouettes that have been stencilled straight onto it.

"Sunsets always remind me of you."

I freeze as I'm assaulted by images of the two of us wrapped up in each other as we watched the sun sink over the sea on my balcony.

"Do you remember, Summer-Raine?" he whispers. "Do you remember watching the sunsets with me?"

I can't breathe.

I can feel him watching me, but I don't turn to look at him. I don't want him to see how his words have undone me or the pain on my face from hearing him talk about the only time in my life that I have ever been happy.

The memories hurt so much.

"I remember."

He falls silent, but I can still feel the burn of his gaze on the side of my face. For the last two weeks, we've managed to avoid the subject of us. We haven't tried to reminisce about old times or brought up the fact that once upon a time we were young and desperately in love. Not until now.

And all of a sudden, I feel a shift in the atmosphere.

"Why did you do it, Summer-Raine?"

There it is.

The question I've always hoped I'd never have to answer. The question I ask myself every night when I climb into a cold bed and try to imagine the feeling of his arms around me to help me go to sleep.

I squeeze my eyes shut.

He doesn't have to say anything more for me to understand what he's asking, but he does anyway. "Did our relationship not mean as much to you as it did to me? Did you not love me anymore? Did you ever even love me at all?" I can hear the hurt and desperation in his voice, his need for me to answer his questions, but I can't. "You didn't even say goodbye."

I can't have this conversation with him. Not now, not ever. But it breaks my heart that he thinks I never loved him.

"I loved you more than anything."

"Then why did you leave?"

I shake my head, pain slicing through me. I don't want to remember the day I ended things, the way my heart splintered as I heard the nurse outside my room tell him he wasn't allowed to visit me anymore. I don't want to remember the sound of his voice as he called out to me through the door in confusion or the sound of his feet scuffing the floor as security carried him out.

I grip my heart.

This is too much.

"I can't talk about this with you."

My eyes are still locked on the scene outside the window, but the sunset has long given way to darkness.

"Bullshit," he snaps, angry now.

But still, I say nothing.

"You broke my heart, Summer-Raine," he growls, coming to stand in front of me and forcing me to meet his eyes. "You ripped it straight out of my chest and you never even told me why. I mourned our relationship for *years*. So you *will* talk to me about this, or are you the same coward now as you were back then?"

Until now, I've only seen him angry once, on the night I tried to manipulate him into hurting me. But that was nothing compared to the rage I see on his face now. The grief, the anguish, the sheer, unadulterated fury. His eyes blaze with it all. It makes him look like a different man altogether.

"You didn't even have the courage to break up with me yourself," he says, shaking his head as he drags a calloused palm down his face.

"I couldn't," I say, the words coming out strangled and breathless.

He scoffs. "More bullshit."

Tears burn in my eyes and I don't even try to blink them away. "I couldn't," I suck in a deep breath, "because I knew that if I saw you, I wouldn't have been able to do it."

Auden blanches, his nostrils flaring as his hands curl into fists at his sides. His stance may be aggressive, but I know he'd never hurt me. "What the fuck are you talking about?"

But I just shake my head. I've already said too much.

I stand up and push past him, desperate to put distance between us. But a large hand closes around my wrist. The touch of his skin on mine sends electricity humming through me and renders me paralysed.

"You're not going anywhere, Summer-Raine," he warns. "Not until we've had this conversation. I know how much you love running away from me, but I don't give a damn how hard it is for you right now, because I guarantee whatever discomfort you feel at having to answer my questions is nothing compared to the pain you put me through when you left without a word."

And now he's not the only one who's angry.

Like a switch that's been flicked, my eyes snap to his and the despair I was feeling just seconds ago morphs into white hot rage.

Fuck this.

"You think it didn't fucking hurt me too? You think that doing what I did didn't break my heart too? Jesus, Auden, I've ached for you every second of every day. It *kills* me that I hurt you, that I gave up our future, that I let you go." He towers over me, his eyes ablaze with tortured fury, but I don't look away. If he's so damn desperate to have this conversation, then so fucking be it. "You really think that you're the only one who wears the bruises from that day?"

He laughs. "Well, what the hell am I supposed to think? *You* left *me*, remember? I get that you blame me for getting hurt that day. If I hadn't have called out your name, you'd never have fallen like you did, but *fuck*, did I not at least deserve a conversation? I thought we loved each other enough to get through anything, but I obviously couldn't have been more wrong given how easy it was for you to leave me."

His words destroy me.

He's spent all this time thinking I blamed him for what happened on those cliffs?

"You've got it all wrong." I shake my head. "I didn't leave you, Auden. I set you free."

He freezes.

"Say that again."

"I didn't leave you," I whisper. "I set you free."

He moves so suddenly that I don't know what's happening until my back hits the wall and I'm caged between his arms.

"You set me free?" he growls, low and stormy.

But I can't speak. Not when he's standing this close to me, looming down on me with wildfires burning in his eyes.

Maybe I should be intimidated, but I've never felt anything but safe with him and now is no exception.

"And why would you do that?"

I pull my eyes away, focusing my gaze on a pulled thread on his t-shirt so that I don't have to see the expression on his face when I speak. "Because I knew that you'd never leave me, so I had to do it for you."

A hand beside my head clenches into a fist and bangs against the wall, but I don't even flinch. There's nothing he could do to scare me.

"Why, Summer-Raine?" he chokes, the sound something close to a sob. I keep my gaze trained on his t-shirt, knowing if I were to look into his eyes right now and see tears that I would break. "Why did anyone have to leave? Why couldn't we have taken my truck to Sunshine City like we talked about and gone off to college together? No, actually, I don't even care about Sunshine City and Florida State. We could have gone fucking anywhere, wherever you wanted to go. I'd have followed you to the ends of the Earth. I only ever cared about us being together."

"Because of the monsters in my head, Auden. I've got so much goddamn baggage."

"What's that got to do with anything? I'd have looked after you forever if that's what you needed."

"Don't you see?" I look up at him then and when I see the shine in his eyes, my hand lifts of its own accord and cups his stubbled cheek. "That's exactly why. What kind of life would that have been for you? You deserve so much more than I could ever give you, Auden. You deserve a woman who can make you truly happy." I pause. "A woman like Cara."

I don't know why I say that last bit. Maybe because I need the confirmation that I did the right thing, that breaking both our hearts wasn't in vain. But maybe part of me just enjoys torturing myself.

For a long moment, we stand and stare at each other, my thumb gently stroking back and forth on his cheek. His eyes close and he lowers his forehead to press against mine.

"*God*, I'm so angry with you," he says, but there's no trace of it left in his voice.

"I know," I whisper.

And nothing more needs to be said.

He got the answers he wanted and I hope they bring him the closure he needs. Maybe now he can move on properly and give his heart completely to Cara. He can stop calling her babe and start calling her baby, just as long as he doesn't call her pretty girl.

That one will always belong to me.

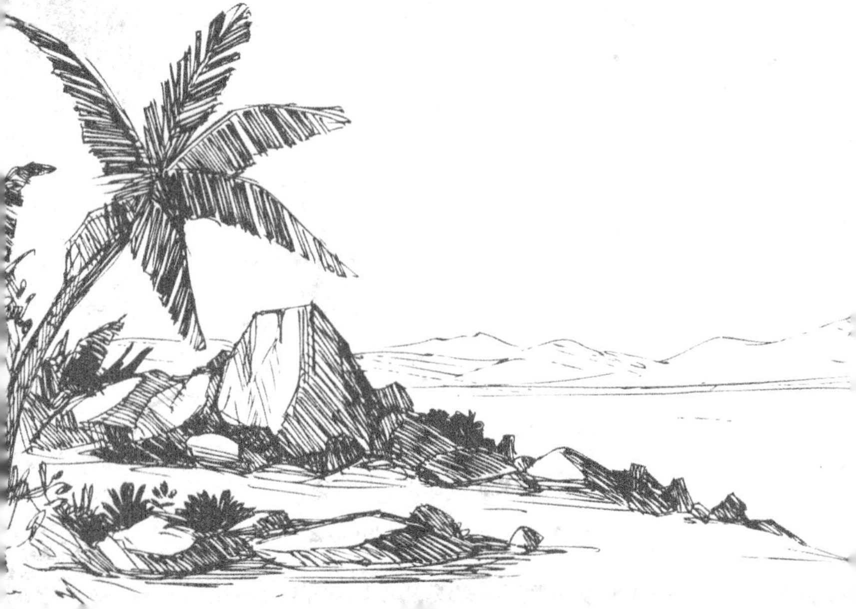

Chapter Twenty-One
AUDEN

I spot Winter's car parked outside the apartment building when I arrive home after work on Friday morning.

Home. That's a dangerous word. When had I started thinking of Summer-Raine's apartment as my home? It's barely been a month since I moved in and it's not as if there's any trace of me in the furnishing or décor of the place. The photos in the frames aren't of me and they're not even my sheets on the bed.

No. It's not my home. That was a Freudian slip.

The sounds of giddy laughter and high-pitched screams reach me as I walk down the dimly-lit corridor and let myself into the apartment.

My lips stretch into an unstoppable grin as I'm greeted by Summer-Raine chasing two tiny humans in dinosaur pyjamas around the coffee table in the living room.

I'm stunned by the sight of her smile. It takes the breath

straight from my lungs. *My god,* I haven't seen her smile like that for so long. I thought I remembered how magnificent it is, but none of my memories, even the most vivid, do it justice at all.

I've missed it so much.

There was once a time that I could make her smile like that, but I can't anymore. I know because I've tried. It's embarrassing actually, how hard I've tried. It's just that there is just nothing in this world as spectacular as the sight of Summer-Raine's smile.

Especially the one she's wearing right now.

It's such a stark contrast from what I've grown used to seeing from her over the past few weeks. Since I've been staying here, I've only known her to be steeped in sadness. Her depression is so palpable it's almost tangible, like a thick black fog that follows her everywhere she goes. I'd listened to her cry herself to sleep after our argument the other night and, though I'd longed to go to her, I'd simply sat by her door and waited for the sobbing to stop. So, the sight of her smiling in this way now, so brilliantly and unrestrained, is possibly the very best thing I've seen in my entire life.

I catch Winter observing me from over the rim of a steaming cup of coffee, her eyes narrowed as she watches me watching Summer-Raine. Ignoring the accusatory expression on her face, I close the front door behind me and throw my keys on the console table.

"You're here early," I say to Winter, joining her in the kitchen and pouring myself a cup of coffee.

I'm staying at Cara's tonight, so Winter agreed to bring her sons round for a "family sleepover".

She shrugs. "The boys were excited and we weren't doing anything else." We both look over to where Cooper and Carter have tackled Summer-Raine to the floor and bundled themselves on top of her. "Besides, I figured you'd appreciate getting to spend some extra time with your girlfriend."

"Oh right." I nod absentmindedly. "Thanks."

But my attention is focused wholly on the golden-haired goddess rolling out from under her nephews and pulling them both into her arms at once, tickling them until they can't breathe.

This is a side of her that I have never seen. Even back in senior year when we were at our happiest. In fact, I didn't even know she liked children at all. Our plans for the future had never gotten as far as deciding whether or not we'd have kids. I guess I'd always just assumed we would someday, but we'd been more excited about spending the rest of our days wrapped up in one another to think any further than that.

Now, I can't help but think that had things worked out between us, she'd have been the most incredible mother to our children.

"What are you doing here, Auden?" Winter asks, distracting me enough that I turn to her and find that judgemental look back on her face.

"Staying here?" I say, confused. "To keep an eye on your sister."

She shakes her head. "No, I mean what are you doing with Summer-Raine? I see the way you look at her, Auden. You might pretend that you're not still in love with her, but I can see straight through you. You forget that it's me you've been relentlessly calling for the last five years to keep tabs on her."

My defences rise automatically, but I take a deep breath to calm myself. "I'm not doing anything, Winter. I'm just trying to help her get better and keep her from harming herself again. Just like you asked me to, remember?"

"So you deny that you're still in love with her?" she probes, eyebrows raised as if daring me to lie.

"That's not what this is about." I drain my coffee mug and rinse it out in the sink. "I'm just doing what I can to help Summer-Raine. There's nothing more to it than that."

"What does your girlfriend think about you living with your ex?"

"She's fine with it." *Because she thinks Summer-Raine is my cousin.*

Winter scoffs. "She doesn't know, does she?"

I scowl but don't respond, staring down at the basin of the kitchen sink.

"Jesus, Auden." She releases a bewildered laugh. "I thought you were better than that."

"Yeah?" I turn to her. "Well, what would you have done?"

"I don't know." She throws her hands in the air. "Told her the truth? Done the kind thing and broken things off with her the second I realised I was still in love with someone else?"

My lips purse as I shake my head, desperate to defend myself against her attack. But the truth is, she's not wrong. Everything she's saying is bang on the money. I haven't been fair to Cara at all. Not only have I lied to her, but she's barely crossed my mind since the day I moved into this apartment.

God, what kind of man have I become?

I'm not a liar, I don't lead women on and I'm certainly not a cheat. So why is it that I seem to lose all sense of my morals when Summer-Raine is involved? Because I may not have physically cheated on Cara, but betrayal can be psychological too. I've continued our relationship, called her every other night and listened to her tell me that she loves me, all while obsessing over another woman.

In fact, if I'm being really honest with myself, I've been deceitful since even the very beginning of our relationship. How would she feel if she knew that I'd imagined another woman's face every single time I made love to her? She deserves so much better than what I've given her.

Shame overwhelms me and I know what I have to do.

"You're right," I tell Winter, hanging my head. "I'll fix it."

"Good."

We fall into a surprisingly comfortable silence given the verbal lashing she's just given me. But Winter has never been one to filter herself or mince her words and I respect that about her.

"How's she doing?" she asks, nodding in the direction of her sister who's lying on her back on the floor with rosy cheeks and a peaceful smile on her face. The two little boys giggle as they both curl up against her to cuddle until they calm down.

"Better than I was expecting," I tell her truthfully. "She's only had one episode since I've been here and I managed to intercept her before she was able to leave the apartment."

It was about three am one night last week. One of the motion sensors I've hidden around the apartment had triggered the alarm on my phone and I'd stumbled half-asleep out of my room to find her clawing at the front door to get out. After she'd finally regained her lucidity and gone back to bed, the tortured vacancy I'd seen in her eyes had haunted my dreams for the rest of the night.

But aside from that one occasion, the stability of her condition has had me pleasantly surprised.

Winter nods thoughtfully. "Is she cutting?"

"No." I know, because I routinely check her for fresh scars.

"Good." She turns to face me, her fingers tapping nervously against the kitchen counter. "I should confess, I kind of had a suspicion that you being here would help her and not just because you're looking out for her. I guess I just knew that you being back in her life was what she needed to kickstart her recovery."

My eyes widen. "So you begging me to do this because I was the only person who could was just bullshit?"

She shakes her head. "No. Well, not completely. We probably could have worked something out, but it would have been a struggle. It's just that even if we did have other options, I still would have asked you."

"I feel weird about it." I tell her, rinsing my hands over the sink just to have something to do. "Like you've deceived me or something."

She rolls her eyes. "I didn't, not really. But are you saying that if I'd told you this before then you wouldn't have agreed to stay here?"

I stay silent because she knows the answer. No, of course I wouldn't have shut her down. Summer-Raine needed help and

I'd have given it to her no matter the reason for me being asked.

"I need to get ready for my date," I grumble.

A gentle snore pulls our attention to the bundle of sleeping bodies still lying on the floor in the dining area. "And I need to get the boys to bed. If I don't see you before you leave, have a good night."

"Thanks, I will," I say, despite knowing otherwise. "You too."

I leave her in the kitchen and disappear to the room that's become mine to shower and change. It takes more thought than usual to pick out my clothes for the evening. I worry needlessly over what shirt to wear, as if the colour I choose will influence how Cara will react to what I have to tell her tonight.

In the end, I opt for a linen shirt in aqua after remembering that blue is considered to be the most calming colour. I read an article once about how doctors tend to wear blue scrubs because the colour helps soothe their patients. I don't know if there's any scientific truth to that, but I've seen Cara when she'd pissed off so I'll take all the help I can get.

The sound of feminine voices reaches me as I step out of my room and walk towards the living space. When I recognise who they belong to, my stomach twists in panic.

"You'll have to tell me all about what Auden was like as a child," Cara is saying. "I've just been *dying* to hear all of his embarrassing stories."

"Oh, um, I didn't know Auden when he was little." Even from here I can hear the confusion in Summer-Raine's voice.

"Really? That's crazy."

I speed walk down the hallway until I'm in sight of the

front door. Summer-Raine blocks my view of Cara as she stands with her back to me, her stance confident and self-assured despite her being dressed in pyjamas with one hand cocked on her hip.

"Is it?"

"Yeah. I've known all my cousins since I was a kid."

"Cousins?"

Oh shit.

"Yeah. Auden told me you were cousins."

I launch myself towards them but I'm too late.

"Um, no?" Summer-Raine looks over her shoulder and meets my wide and panicked eyes. Hers narrow in confusion. "We're not cousins," she says, turning back to my girlfriend.

I finally reach them, setting a hand on Summer-Raine's waist without thinking to gently move her to the side and make room for me. Cara's already fuming eyes follow the movement. I instantly move my hand to rest on the top of the doorframe.

"How do you know each other then?"

Summer-Raine swings her gaze to me, her brows raised and I swear I detect a slight glint of amusement twinkling in her emerald eyes. "Er, I think I'll leave Auden to answer that one," she says, tapping me twice on my bicep as if to wish me luck, before ducking under my arm and disappearing to give us some privacy.

"What the actual fuck, Auden?" Cara stands on the other side of the threshold with her fingers on her hips and murder in her eyes. "If she's not your cousin then who the fuck is she?"

"Um," my voice croaks, "I think we should talk about this somewhere else."

Her red-painted lips fall open in shock. "I think we should fucking talk about this now."

I cast a glance over my shoulder to find Summer-Raine staring right at me. She looks away instantly, but it's too late. I already caught her watching us.

I'm a couple of seconds too slow to drag my gaze back to my girlfriend. "What are you doing here anyway?" I ask, taking in the sight of her in her white tuxedo style suit and sky-high red stilettos. She's wearing nothing underneath her blazer, not even a bra by the looks of things, and the fastened buttons are the only things protecting her from exposing her breasts. She looks incredible. Like an A-list celebrity or catwalk model.

So, why is it that I had a stronger physical reaction to Summer-Raine's fresh face and pink gingham pyjamas?

"I can't believe this," Cara says with an exasperated shake of her head. "I came by to surprise you and see your new place before our date tonight. I wasn't expecting to find out that my boyfriend is a goddamn fucking liar."

I flinch, but it's in response to her continuous swearing rather than from being caught out. "Come on," I talk gently, reaching out to take her elbow to guide her down the corridor away from the apartment. I curse inwardly when I realise that I've forgotten my keys.

Just great.

Even if Cara were to forgive me tonight, it wouldn't be fair to let her. I've treated her too badly to allow this relationship to continue regardless of whether or not she'd want to stay with me after learning who Summer-Raine really is to me. Because I've sworn to myself to answer any and all questions that Cara hurls at me tonight. I owe her that much at least.

And later, after I've dropped her back to her apartment for the last time and dried the tears on her cheeks gently with the back of my hand, I drive back home. I know that I should use the time to reflect on my failed relationship and the way I broke Cara's heart, but I don't. Because my thoughts are too full of someone else, the way they always have been.

But I guess I shouldn't be surprised. I've spent the last five years thinking about Summer-Raine, why would that change now?

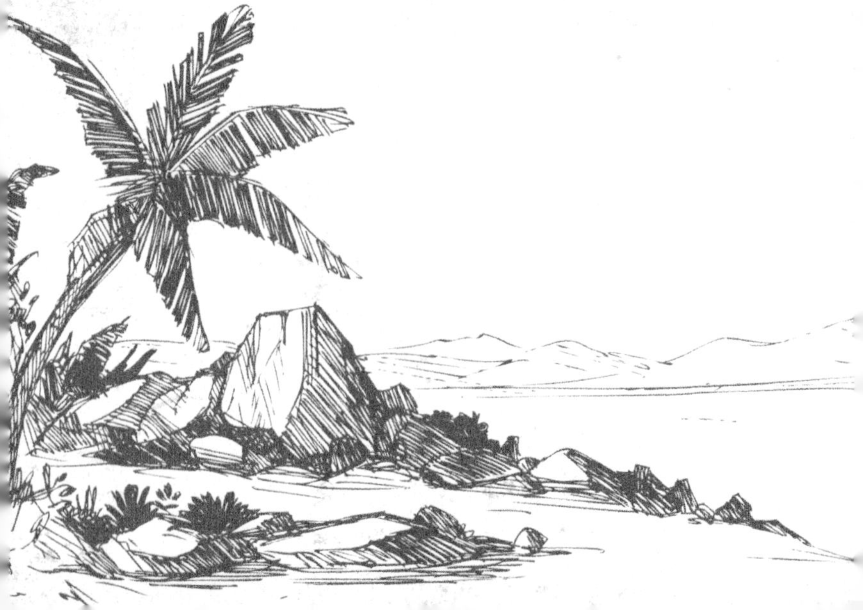

Chapter Twenty-Two

SUMMER-RAINE

I shoot up in my seat at the sound of keys in the door.

Auden stumbles into the apartment and curses as he stubs his toe forcefully against the doorframe. I can't help but smile at the sight of him hopping up and down. I breathe in the colour of his shirt that is the perfect shade of blue to bring out his eyes and the way his hair sticks up in all directions like he's been running his hands through it all night. It reminds me of the way he used to look in the mornings after making love to me all night.

I would worry that his dishevelled appearance is due to him fucking Cara in an alley somewhere if it weren't for his hunched shoulders and downturned lips. He's not wearing the expression of a man who's been freshly fucked, though he brightens when he catches sight of me sitting on the couch.

"Thanks for leaving my keys out for me," he says, the gentle smile on his face morphing into that cocky smirk I love so much as he breathes in the sight of me sitting cross-legged on the couch. "Did you wait up for me?"

I don't even try to deny it, just shrug my shoulder. He lifts a brow at my obvious lack of denial, but says nothing more about it. Instead, he walks the few yards to the kitchen and pulls two beers from the fridge, uncapping them both and passing one to me.

"Bad night?" I ask once he's taken a seat in the armchair across from me.

He freezes with his bottle halfway to his lips, his long eyelashes fluttering as he blinks at me. "Wasn't the best."

I'm dying for him to tell me more. What happened when he told Cara how he really knows me? Did he even tell her the whole truth or placate her with another lie? I worry my bottom lip painfully between my teeth at the possibility of them having broken up, or worse… at them having made up.

My heart had stopped when I opened the door to her earlier. There I stood in my pyjamas with unbrushed hair as this willowy gazelle of a woman with flawless skin and sleek, shiny hair looked me over with narrowed eyes. It was only when she'd obviously decided I was no threat to her that she'd allowed herself to smile.

I'd hated her instantly.

"Did you work things out?" I ask hesitantly, avoiding meeting his eye though his gaze never wavers from my face. I watch him watching me from the edge of my periphery.

"Not really your business, is it?"

"Oh." I gulp, hating the way his words instantly make me nauseous. "Sorry."

"Are you?" he asks and I finally allow myself to look at him.

Though the events of the evening are clearly weighing on him, he seems lighter somehow. His face is slightly haggard but his eyes are shining brighter and it's that extra little twinkle that encourages me to answer his question honestly. "No."

Despite being able to see the answer on my face, his brows shoot up in surprise at my candour. I've never been able to hide my emotions from him. He's always had the ability to read me like a book no matter how hard I've worked to keep my secrets hidden. He's always just been able to see me in a way that no one else ever has, not even Winter.

"I bet you're so happy, aren't you?" He says, surprising me, his voice taking on a darker tone as he stalks towards me.

"N-no," I stutter, instinctively leaning back into the soft cushions of the couch to put a slither more space between us.

"I bet you were beside yourself thinking I was breaking up with her, weren't you? I saw you watching us. I saw the little smile on those lips when you heard her yelling at me." His gaze falls to my lips and lingers there.

"No, Auden. Of course not." I shake my head wildly.

But he carries on. "And now here you are, huh? Sitting here waiting for me to come home all so you can hear about what happened tonight."

I say nothing because he's right. That's exactly what I'm doing.

He leans over me, bracing his hands on the back of the couch either side of my head.

"You want to know if she ended it? Or if we kissed and made up?" His face moves to my neck as he runs the tip of his nose along the long column of my throat. "Maybe we did more than that. Maybe we fucked, would you want to hear about that?"

I screw my eyes shut, white hot jealousy coursing through my veins and burning me from the inside out.

Did he really have sex with her?

I was so sure after the lie he told her that it'd be over between them. And yeah, maybe it makes me a bitch to have been happy about that, but after meeting her earlier tonight, it's clear she's not right for him anyway.

"Answer me," he growls.

"No," I whisper. "I don't want to hear about that."

He chuckles to himself, though it's not his usual laugh. It's a cruel sound. Taunting, deep and scornful.

"But you must have known when you *set me free*," he rolls his eyes at that, "that I'd end up fucking other women. You couldn't have thought I'd never touch another woman again. You want to know just how many women I've been with since you, Summer-Raine?"

My eyes burn.

God, I wish he'd stop talking like that.

I can't even look at him.

Who even is he right now?

This isn't the Auden I know with his warmth and kindness and sweet disposition. This man is harsh and cold, and I don't recognise him at all.

"Stop," I beg, a tear spilling down my cheek.

"Why should I?" he seethes. "It's because of you that my relationship could be over, after all."

My eyes fly open at that. I'm on my feet in a flash, barely giving him a chance to step back before I'm in his face and backing him against the wall of the living room.

"Don't you dare." I jab my finger into his chest. "Whatever's going on in your relationship right now is your fault, Auden. *You* were the one who lied, so don't you dare try and pass the blame over to me."

He moves like a jaguar. Dark and fast as switches our positions, pinning me against the wall before I even have a chance to blink.

My heart thunders in fear as a low, dull ache begins to pulse between my legs.

His eyes are black, his teeth bared as he looms over me. He's a predator and I'm his helpless prey.

But I don't cower away or hide myself from his fury. Standing on my tiptoes to give me as much height as possible, I meet his blazing glare and match his fire with my own.

"It is your fault," he roars. "It's your fault that I couldn't stop thinking about you enough to focus on my own girlfriend. It's your fault that with every woman I've taken to bed since you left, it's you that I've imagined beneath me. It's your fault that I'm too hung up on my damn high school girlfriend to love Cara the way she wants me to. The way she *deserves* me to. All of it, every single second of the pain, misery and suffering I've faced over the last five years is because of you."

"Take some goddamn responsibility, Auden. I didn't ask for you to still be thinking about me after all this time. You could have gotten over me, you just didn't. But I did, I got over you, it wasn't that fucking hard."

My rage and jealousy make the lie all too easy. It's just that in this moment, no matter how wrong it might be, I want my words to hurt him as much as his are hurting me.

He sucks his bottom lip into his mouth and shakes his head, laughing darkly. "I'm the only one who feels this, am I? Can you seriously look at me right now and tell me that it's not my face you picture every time another man makes love to you? That it's not my fingers you feel touch your soft skin, not my voice you hear whispering words into your ear, not my kiss you taste on your lips?"

He takes a deep breath, his chest heaving.

I shake my head, my lips pursed and nostrils flaring with the effort of not launching myself at him in furious lust.

He doesn't know how wrong he is.

"You can't, can you? Because you know it's true. You never did get over me. Who's the liar now, huh?"

"No." I stare straight into his pitch-black eyes. "No, it's not true."

"Stop lying," he growls through gritted teeth.

"I'm not." I blow out a long breath as I steel myself for my next words. "I'm not lying, because there were no other men, Auden. There has never been another man. My body has known no other touch, no other kiss but yours."

He blinks.

I can feel his chest rising and falling against mine. Heartbeat against heartbeat.

The only sound comes from our shallow breaths as we fight for air like we're drowning.

And then suddenly, I'm thrust into his arms. My legs close

automatically around his waist, muscle memory taking over as my ankles lock behind his back.

I smell the pinewood and old, worn books that have always made my head spin, the scent of him filling my lungs and threatening to choke me. It's a sweet kind of torture.

He buries his face in my neck, nipping and sucking every inch of exposed skin.

There's nothing gentle about the way he's handling me. There's no tenderness to his touch, no soft kisses or whispered words of affection.

It's his fury that's fuelling this fire and my own that ignites it like gasoline.

I claw at the lapels of his jacket as I work to get the material over his broad shoulders. I'm not careful. I don't care if I tear it. I just need it gone so I can rid us both of all the layers standing between us.

My breath hitches as I feel Auden's fingers creep into the opening of my pyjama shorts, a featherlight touch whispering up my thigh to toy with the lace trim of my panties.

"Fuck, these legs."

When he mercilessly thrusts two fingers into me, I scream.

"You better be quiet if you don't want to wake your sister," he growls into my ear, reminding me of Winter and her sons fast asleep in Auden's bedroom down the hall.

He hooks his fingers, hitting that magic spot deep within me that makes my toes curl and fingernails dig crescent moons into his neck. I don't care if it hurts him. In fact, I hope it does.

He plays me like a master musician. I have no choice but to surrender myself to the sensations he's forcing upon me, the waves upon waves of pleasure that threaten to overwhelm me.

Auden has always known how to touch me. But whereas before, he always handled me with a kind of unpractised, boyish charm, whatever he's doing to me now is the definite ministrations of a man.

But he doesn't let me come.

I snarl as he pulls his fingers out of me and sucks them straight into his mouth.

"Don't worry, baby," he smirks, pulling open his belt and tugging down his dress pants and boxer shorts so that his cock stands tall and proud against his lower abs, "it's not over yet."

He tears my satin shorts straight from my body and pulls my panties to one side, the thick head of his cock sliding against my opening. Rubbing, teasing, but not entering.

"Is this what you want, baby?" he snarls. "You want me to fuck you? You want to come all over my cock for me?"

My eyes widen. I don't know who this man is. Don't know if I love him or hate him, but I do know that I want everything he's saying.

I need him inside me.

And I need it now.

I nod and that's all he needs. In one perfect thrust, he's buried inside me to the hilt.

"*Fuck*," he groans, the harsh grip of his fingers on my thigh surely leaving bruises.

I'm hit with a searing pain as he fills the part of me that has been empty for so long. It burns, almost agonizing, but nothing could make me stop this right now.

He gives me no time to adjust to the stretch of him,

just pounds into me relentlessly, his breath rough and brows furrowed together in concentration.

It's not long before the pain melts away and turns into extraordinary pleasure. I bite my lip hard out of fear of making too much noise, drawing blood and tasting iron in my mouth. But it only heightens the experience.

My head falls back against the wall and bangs against it with every punishing thrust. The orgasm he denied me of before begins to crest again. Growing and swelling like a tidal wave, it drowns me. My entire body vibrates. Tremors wracking through me as excruciating pleasure pulses like a drum beat and momentarily blinds me.

I'm only faintly aware of Auden finding his own release, too far gone in the throws of my climax to realise that he hasn't kissed me.

Breathing hard, he slips free of my body, finding my ruined pyjama shorts on the floor beside us and using it as a rag to clean between my legs.

Exhausted, I collapse to the floor and slump against the wall. Auden does the same. Despite what we've just done, we sit more than a metre apart, more than just physical distance between us. The anger from before is gone, but an uncomfortable tension still lingers.

"I broke up with her," he says quietly after a long period of silence.

I let the confession linger like smoke for a little while as I work to calm my thundering heart and racing thoughts.

"Why?" I whisper.

"You know why," he says it simply like it invites no further questions. "Besides, I didn't treat her the way I should have done anyway."

That doesn't make sense to me. Because in the time that I was blessed to be his girlfriend, not once did he treat me like anything less than a queen. Even when I fucked up and hurt him, he'd still reassure me of his love like nothing I could do would ever change the way he felt about me. So, the idea of Auden not treating a woman the way she deserves doesn't compute in my mind at all. It goes against everything I know to be true about him.

"You told her we were cousins." It's a statement, but he can read the question behind it.

He nods. "I knew she'd never let me stay here with you if I'd told her the truth."

"Was babysitting me that important? Enough to risk your relationship?"

Please say yes.

The thought is a selfish one, I know that. But despite not regretting letting him go, I'll always have that part of me that hopes he still cares about me.

He tuts. "Don't call it babysitting, that's not what this is."

But it is. That's why he's here. It's the reason he's installed motion sensors around the apartment. It's why he checks my arms and legs for fresh cuts every night. He never finds anything, but that's only because he's looking in the wrong place. Over the years, I've learned how to better hide my scars. If he started asking to see the soles of my feet, he'd confiscate the razor in my bathroom.

I ignore him and ask again, "Was it so important to risk

your relationship, Auden?"

He tilts his head to one side and assesses me, thinking over whatever it is he wants to say. "Yeah, Summer-Raine, it was."

"But why?"

I don't get it. Why would he go against the morals that he's always taken so much pride in and lie to the woman who loves him? I saw her. She's every man's dream woman. Why in hell would he risk losing her?

He looks at me then. *Really* looks at me. I can feel the heat of his stare from here. The warmth of him wraps around me like a quilt and I wish that I could lie in it forever.

When he finally speaks, I almost wish he hadn't with the hurricane of emotions his words awaken within me. "It doesn't matter how much time passes between us, if you need me, I will always come for you."

"I didn't need you."

It's a lie and he knows it as well as I do.

Because the truth is, I've felt more at peace since he's been here than I have in half a decade. Sure, his presence hasn't magically stopped me cutting the bottoms of my feet or slipping pills into my mouth to help me sleep at night, but I can't deny that life looks a little brighter now that he's back in it. The darkness isn't so dark. My hollowness isn't so empty. It's as if he's poured caulk over the holes in my heart and slowly started to piece my shattered edges back together.

I may not have ever admitted it to myself before, but I did need him.

And he came.

"Why?" I whisper, looking down at my lap. "Why would

you still want to help me after what I did to you? Why would you agree to move in with me when we haven't been in touch for so long?"

I'm so confused. It's like I'm submerged in cold water. Every answer he gives me only serves to pull me further beneath the waves. Every question I ask only perplexes me further. Nothing he says is making sense to me.

Auden stands and walks to me, holding out his hand to help me up.

"You may not have been in touch with me, but—" he pauses, closing his eyes and inhaling a breath, "I've always been in touch with you."

I shake my head, blinking. "What does that even mean?"

"I've called your sister every month at least since the day you left." My mouth falls open at his confession, but he doesn't give me a chance to respond before carrying on. "At first, I told myself it was simply to make sure your injuries were healing okay, that you were recovering from the accident, but when a year had passed and I was still calling, I realised I couldn't keep using that as an excuse anymore. I guess the simple truth of it is that I was an addict. You were my drug and I couldn't go cold turkey just because you'd decided to take yourself away from me. So, I'd torture myself every few weeks by calling Winter, if only to hear your name said out loud by someone who wasn't me. She'd give me some abridged version of whatever you were doing and I'd be happy just to imagine you sitting in class at college or eating pistachio ice cream until I needed a fix of you again. I guess it just became habit after a while. Those phone calls with Winter became so entrenched in my routine that it would have been impossible to stop them. I'd make her tell me if you were going through dark patches and the urge to come to you and take away your pain would wither me, but I never did. Not until she asked me to. Not until now."

I suck in a lungful of air only to still feel breathless.

All this time he's been using my sister to keep tabs on me. I chew at the corner of my fingernail as I consider how I should react to that. Though, honestly, I don't even know what to think right now, much less what my response should be. The inside of my brain is a patchwork of undecipherable emotions.

I don't even have the mental capacity to be pissed at Winter for going behind my back for so long.

My thoughts are occupied by the fact that everything he's just said was in past tense. *You were my drug.* My brain's only focus is how I wish he'd used "are" instead of "were". Because he's not the only one who had an addiction. I guess the difference is that my need for him never lessened at all.

"You're wrong."

Now it's his turn to be confused. His eyes narrow, searching my face for meaning and coming up empty. But I take a few moments to breathe before I say what's on my mind, the coming confession one that I thought I'd never have to make. No one knows this. Not even Winter.

"You said I didn't keep in touch with you. You were wrong. I did."

"What?"

"Your football games. I once made you a promise that I'd never miss one." I stumble over the words as my throat constricts. "I didn't break it."

"I don't understand."

"I watched you, Auden, at every game. I came to every single one. From the first game of the season in senior year to the last one you ever played in college, I was there. I still don't understand football at all, or even enjoy watching it to be entirely honest, but I'd made you a promise and I wanted to keep it. God knows I owed you at least that."

He leans into me as I'm talking, focusing on my lips as I talk.

"I actually thought you saw me once," I continue, "when you played the Florida Knights and scored the winning touchdown at the eleventh minute of the last quarter"

He'd looked straight at me. I was in the stands, wearing his high school football jersey that he'd given me pretty early on in our relationship. It was the wrong colours for the Gators, but I didn't care. All that mattered was that I had his name on my back. I was there for him, not the team. Only him.

It was just after he'd scored that touchdown. I'd watched with a smile on my face as he'd celebrated with his teammates and then with a broken heart as he blew some redheaded cheerleader a kiss across the field. Then his gaze had swung over the stands and caught mine.

That moment was one that seemed to never end though likely didn't last more than a second or two. It was like the thousands of people around us disappeared, their figures blurring in my vision until I was unable to make out the shape of them at all. It was just Auden and I in that stadium, our eyes locked on one another for the first time since we'd broken up.

But then one of his teammates clapped him on the shoulder

and the moment was broken. He didn't look in my direction again.

"I did." His voice is so quiet I can hardly hear it at all. "I thought all this time that I'd imagined you, but I didn't. You were there. I saw you."

We fall into a soft silence, the air between us thick with the weight of our confessions. I self-consciously tuck a wayward lock of hair behind my ear, wishing that he'd done it for me like he'd always used to do, and distantly wondering if he even gets the urge to do it anymore.

"I thought you didn't come to that game in high school," he says after a little while, a small frown marring his perfect features.

It was the game he played on the day of the very first night he'd spent with me on my balcony. He'd asked me days before if I would come to watch him play and I'd told him that I'd cheer him on from home, but later changed my mind. I never admitted to him that I'd actually gone.

Back we fall into silence, but despite all that's happened tonight it's an easy one. The kind of silence that only occurs when two people are completely comfortable with one another, when they understand each other in a way that no one else does.

We just simply stare at each other for a while.

"I should get to bed," I say after a while. It must be the early hours of the morning by now. "Will you be okay out here?" Given the fact that he was supposed to be staying at Cara's tonight, Winter and the boys have set up camp in his bedroom, leaving Auden the couch to sleep on tonight.

"I'll be fine." His features pull tight as he deliberates something in his mind. I'm not the only one of us who thinks loudly. "Goodnight, pretty girl," he says gently and then he bends down to press a kiss to my forehead.

The kiss only lasts a second or so, but it sends every nerve in my body haywire. I haven't felt his lips on me for so long. It's like I've been naked all this time and only now his lips have touched my skin again do I realise just how bitterly cold I've been without them.

He might have just fucked me, but nothing has ever compared to the power of Auden's kiss.

"Night, quarterback."

I'm still dazed when I make it back to my bedroom and get undressed. I absentmindedly cut my nightly line in blood on the underside of my foot, but I barely even register the pain. My head isn't in it tonight. I'm just following the motions.

Even when I take out the Ambien I keep hidden in the seam of a coat I have hanging in the closet, I'm too caught up in the memory of Auden's mouth to register that my supply is almost empty. It doesn't occur to me to worry about what will happen when the pills run out.

Because it's not as if I'll be able to get more. I wasn't exactly prescribed them and I won't be able to contact my dealer without Auden finding out. But right now, I'm too blissed out on the high of the kiss on my cheek to give it any thought.

It's a problem I'll save for another day.

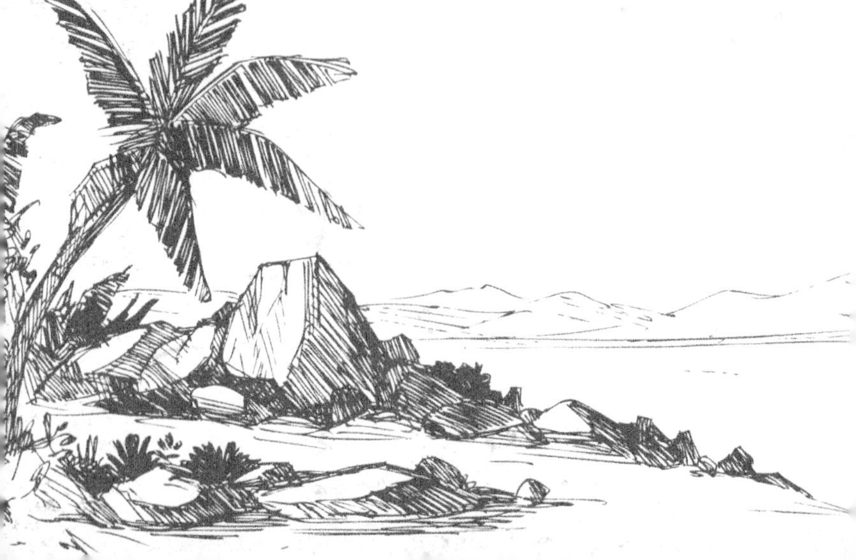

Chapter Twenty-three

AUDEN

The dying sun pours in through the wall of windows and drenches the apartment in violet light. I sip distractedly from a cup of hot tea, my thoughts fixed on the girl asleep down the hallway.

Summer-Raine has spent the last several days hauled up in bed. She's sick. Really sick, if her incessant vomiting and uncontrollable sweating is any indication. Though bizarrely, she doesn't have a temperature. I know, because I've been checking every couple of hours. And when she isn't sweating or vomiting, she's either sleeping fitfully or sobbing into her pillow.

I don't know what's wrong with her, so I don't know how to help. Of course, I've been doing all the usual stuff you do when someone is sick. I've spoon-fed her chicken soup, made sure she's having enough fluids and carried her to and from the bathroom every time she's needed to go. But we're five days in now and she isn't showing any sign of getting better.

Something isn't right. I can feel it in my gut.

I check the time on the oversized clock on the wall. It's been two hours since I last checked on Summer-Raine, so I grab a bottle of water and some crackers from the kitchen and carry them through to her bedroom.

She's laying on her stomach in the centre of the bed, her face buried in a pillow as she groans in pain. The sound goes through me and turns my stomach. I could be sick from how worried I am about her.

"Summer-Raine, I brought you a snack." I perch on the edge of the bed and slide the plate of crackers towards her. She doesn't even glance up. "Come on, you need to eat something."

She releases another groan and presses her face deeper into the pillow. She tries to say something that sounds like "go away", but she's trembling so much that the words are barely audible.

I hate this. If I could take it all away from her I would. I've never been able to handle seeing her in physical pain, perhaps because I know how much it takes for her to be affected by it, so I know that whatever's happening to her is bad.

"Please," I beg quietly. "It'll make me feel better if you do."

Finally, her sunken eyes rise to meet mine and she nods once. A tiny movement that I almost miss, but it happens and I waste no time holding a cracker to her lips for her to take a bite as she adjusts herself into a more upright position. I don't move my hand away until she's eaten it all and taken several sips of water. But not twenty seconds after she's finished is she retching over the side of the bed.

"Fuck," I curse, jumping up to grab a trash can for her to aim into, before swiping her hair away from her neck and rubbing her back until she's done. "What can I do to make this better?"

She swipes the back of her hand across her mouth. "Nothing," she rasps. "You can't make it better." At the crestfallen look on my face, she whispers, "I've done this to myself."

But I don't know what she means by that and her eyelids are growing heavy again, so I help her lay back down and tuck the blankets in around her. Then I lightly stroke the side of her face until she falls asleep. Longer, even, if I'm being truthful. It's just that my hands have been without her for so long that they don't feel right if they're not touching her, so I take the opportunities when I'm presented with them.

I don't even mind that her skin is clammy under my touch. She's been sweating so much that her hair is claggy with it and it sticks to her neck in tangled clumps. It occurs to me that even like this, with her complexion so pallid she almost looks grey, she is still the most beautiful thing I've ever seen.

Not even the sunsets we used to watch together can hold a candle to her.

I'd rather sit here in a room that smells of sweat and vomit if only to look at her than ever see a Floridian sunset again.

Since the night Cara and I broke up, I haven't stopped thinking about what happened with Summer-Raine. I was so cruel to her. The things I said, the way I acted, I was awful.

Yet, I find it hard to regret any of it.

Because being inside her after so long, being surrounded

by her body and her warmth and her smell, it's the first time in five years that I've felt like I can breathe.

"Auden," Summer-Raine murmurs, her eyes still closed. "Auden," she moans again, my name a pained plea on her dry, cracked lips.

I stroke my fingers through her hair to soothe her. "Shh, baby, I'm here."

"Don't go."

Never.

The thought is automatic and I have to fight myself not to say it aloud. Because as much as I wish I could make that promise, I know that I can't. We're not together anymore. We haven't been for a long time. And no matter how much I've come to accept the reasons for Summer-Raine breaking my heart so long ago, a part of me still can't forgive her for the pain she put me through. Maybe I never will.

But more than that, I have no idea what's going to happen when the doctor signs off that Summer-Raine doesn't need twenty-four-hour supervision anymore. I don't know if we'll stay in touch. Who knows if she'll even want to, let alone work on starting things up again and rebuilding our relationship? Truth is, I don't even know what I want.

All I know is that right now, she needs me. So, I lay down beside her in the bed and wrap my arm around her waist. She instantly curls into me, chasing the warmth of my body despite the sweat still beading on her forehead. I rub my hand up and down her back, happy just to listen to the sound of her breathing.

"Please don't leave me."

"I'm not going anywhere." Right now, at least, I know that to be true.

"*No, Auden, please.*" The anguish in her voice has my heart beating faster. I shift until I can see her face and find that her eyes are scrunched shut. "*No, no, no. Don't leave. Please don't leave me.*" Her body starts to thrash as she grows more distressed. It's only when I realise that she can't seem to hear my gentle assurances does it dawn on me that she's dreaming. It's not the first time in the last few nights that I've heard her call out in her sleep, but it's the first time I've heard her say my name.

Despite knowing she can't hear, I keep whispering quiet reassurances into her hair. "I'm here, baby, I'm right here."

She claws at me in her sleep, her nails digging into the skin on my chest but I don't flinch or pull away. Because whatever she's dreaming about, whatever's putting her through this much pain is hurting me as much as it is her.

Finally, her panic starts to ebb away. Her body relaxes and her face takes on that look of perfect peace it's always had when she sleeps. I pull her into me, relishing the feel of her skin on mine as she buries her face in my neck. She's so hot it's like I'm cuddling a furnace, but I haven't been so comfortable since the last time we shared a bed together. It makes it all too easy to close my eyes and fall asleep beside her.

But just before I fade into unconscious, Summer-Raine breathes out a sigh and whispers in her sleep, "I love you."

And maybe it's because I know she can't hear me and will have no recollection of this tomorrow that I say, "I love you too, pretty girl."

It's another week before Summer-Raine starts to get better and I've slept beside her every night, convincing myself it's simply to make sure that she's okay.

On Wednesday, having taken the week off work to care for her, I was so overcome with worry for her unchanging condition that I called the doctor. Summer-Raine had been furious when she found out, but she needn't have worried. He really didn't do all that much to help. He couldn't work out what was wrong with her, so he took some tests and promised to call with the results the next day.

Well, that was three days ago and I'm yet to hear from him.

I'd have called in blind fury if it weren't for Summer-Raine showing signs of improvement. Yesterday, I was even able to convince her to take a shower while I fumigated the room and this morning, she joined me in the kitchen for pancakes and bacon. She didn't even throw it up afterwards.

Now, she's curled up on the couch with a book in her lap. Like it is most of the time, her hair is heaped in a messy pile on top of her head with loose tendrils falling to frame her face. She holds a cup of hot tea in one hand, but she hasn't sipped it in all the time I've been watching her. It must be cold by now.

It's such a domestic picture that I forget momentarily this situation is only temporary.

But it's just so easy to imagine her like this, lounging on a couch in a house that we both own. A house where there are photos of us smiling together in frames and a shared closet where we both hang our clothes. It's even easy to picture a nursery down the hall where a baby girl who looks just like her will sleep and play.

They're dangerous thoughts. They're thoughts that could get my heart broken again and I don't think I could survive it a second time.

It's this that's going through my mind when the doctor calls to say that Summer-Raine's test results came back. I'm sitting in my armchair and looking her straight in the eye when he says he found traces of Ambien in her blood. A prescription drug that she doesn't have a prescription for.

Substance abuse, he says.

The illness she's been suffering with for over a week turns out not to be an illness at all, but symptoms of withdrawal. Her trembling, sweating, nausea, insomnia, it all points to the same thing. She's been buying and taking sleeping pills that should only ever be used under the supervision of a doctor and only on a short-term basis.

All the colour drains from my face. I've been here for over a month now and not once did I notice that she's been self-medicating. I had one job. To keep an eye on her and make sure she's not doing anything to hurt herself. And I failed.

The phone slips out my hand onto the cream shaggy rug. I'm not even sure I disconnected the call. The doctor could still be on the other end of the line for all I know. But I don't care.

Summer-Raine stares at me with terror on her face. She watches me in silence, tracing every minuscule movement and flinch my body makes. She's holding her breath and I realise that I am too.

"Is there anything else I need to know?" My voice is numb with shock.

She shakes her head vehemently. Her eyes bulge in fear of my reaction, like a child who's been caught out in a lie. She looks so small like this. She's visibly shrunk in on herself, her shoulders hunched as she tries to sink into the back of the sofa. It's the first time since I've been here that I realise how ill she really is.

I've been naïve up until now. I thought that I could still read her well enough to know what's going on in her head. That I still knew her enough to know what she's thinking without needing her to tell me.

Now, I see that I really don't know her at all.

It's a realisation that's as stark as it is devastating.

"Please don't look at me like that," she whispers.

"Like what?"

"Like you don't recognise me anymore."

I shake my head. "I don't."

She shoots up out her seat and rushes to me. There are already tears falling down her cheeks when she reaches me and climbs onto my lap in blind panic. She's frenzied, her eyes wild as she clutches my face in her hands and forces me to look at her.

"Yes, you do, Auden," she sobs. "You know me. You're the only one who has ever known me."

My eyes close. I've always felt the same about her. When we were younger, she saw me in a way no one ever had before and no one ever has since. Even Cara, for as much as I believe she loved me, she didn't know me in the way Summer-Raine did. But this feels so much like a betrayal.

"I feel like you've lied to me."

"No, no, no. I haven't. *I haven't.*"

Tears splash onto my skin as she presses her forehead to mine, pleading for me to look at her. But I can't. It hurts too much. This is all just too reminiscent of the way I felt after she left me. It's like I'm losing her all over again.

"You have, Summer-Raine." I sigh. "You let me believe you were doing better."

"I *am* doing better, Auden, don't you know that? This is the best I've been in five years."

"How can I believe that when you've been taking prescription drugs this whole time and hiding it from me?"

She sniffs and wipes her nose with the back of her hand. "I didn't mean to. I didn't buy any more because I didn't want to keep doing it, I wanted to get better for you."

"Can you look me in the eye right now and tell me that you haven't lied about anything else?" I ask, finally opening my eyes to look into hers, desperately hoping that she keeps the connection, that she doesn't look away.

But she does. And my heart shatters all over again.

"I'm sorry," she stutters, fresh tears falling freely down her crestfallen face. She climbs off my lap and stumbles backwards, her hands covering her mouth as she fights to calm herself down. "I'm so sorry."

I'm as devastated as she is, but it doesn't show on my face. I'm rigid, my expression stony. My voice, too, is cold and Summer-Raine shivers when I speak. "Tell me."

But she shows me instead.

I'm confused at first, as she sits back on the couch and takes off her socks. But when she lifts up her feet to show me the undersides, it becomes gut-wrenchingly clear. Every inch of the skin on the soles of her feet are covered in faded, bloody slashes. The marks aren't fresh, but they've definitely been made recently.

I've been checking her arms and legs religiously for cuts and stupidly celebrating that they've been clear at every inspection. Turns out, I was just looking in the wrong places.

"Fuck," I choke.

I can't help myself, I stand and go to her, taking her feet in my hands and tracing my fingers over every jagged line. God, she must have been in so much pain every time she took a step. How the fuck did I not notice?

"I'm so sorry, baby," I say, the sheer size of my failure crashing into me like a forty-tonne truck.

Summer-Raine blinks. "What?"

"I should have known. I should have realised." I slam the heel of my hand into my forehead as I scrunch my eyes shut. "I was supposed to be looking after you and I failed. None of this is your fault, the drugs, the cuts, nothing. It's all on me."

The touch of her soft hand to my face encourages me to look at her. She slides off the couch to meet me on the floor and slides her other hand round to the back of my neck.

"Don't be silly," she whispers, only a breath away from my lips. "If an addict wants to hide something from you, best believe they'll find a way to do it."

"But you're not an addict."

"I am." She smiles sadly. "I'm addicted to pain."

"God, Summer-Raine. I truly thought I could help you."

She releases a soft sigh. "Don't you see? All I do is hurt you and all you do is try to piece me back together. It's why I left. It's why you and I can never be together."

Fuck, she's right.

It's the first time I've truly accepted it.

How could we ever be together when our relationship is centred around me trying to fix her? And yeah, maybe some of that is because of my own emotional baggage. I could never give up on her because I'd never allow myself to turn my back on someone who needs me, like my dad did when he left my Mama.

As long as she's sick, I'll keep trying to fix her. And that's no basis for a healthy relationship. As long as things stay the same, we won't ever be good for each other. We could never make each other happy like this and maybe it's time I finally see that.

Maybe it's time I accept that it's time to say goodbye.

"I think maybe I need to move out," I say gently. Summer-Raine sobs quietly, but nods like she's decided the same thing too. "I'll still be here for you, baby, I always will be, but I think it's getting way too complicated with me living here. We're only hurting each other."

"I know," she cries. "I know."

I wrap my arms around her and pull her into me. She curls into my lap on the floor and tucks her head into my neck. The position is so natural to us, so right. It always has been.

It probably always will be.

Because even though I know it's time to let her go, I'll always love her. That will never change. I'll carry Summer-Raine and the memories of her in my heart for all of time.

"Auden?" she whispers tentatively, lifting her head to meet my eye.

"Mm?" I can hardly speak for fear of crying.

"If this is goodbye, can I ask you something?"

"Anything."

"Be with me one last time? Make love to me. If this really is the end, let me have this night and then I'll let you go."

Could I really do that? Could I touch her again, feel her skin and her lips and her body under my hands after everything and still leave in the morning?

But my body decides for me, because before I know what I'm doing, I've scooped Summer-Raine into my arms and I'm carrying her through to the bedroom.

This isn't how I thought we'd end. But if this really is goodbye, then I need to say it right.

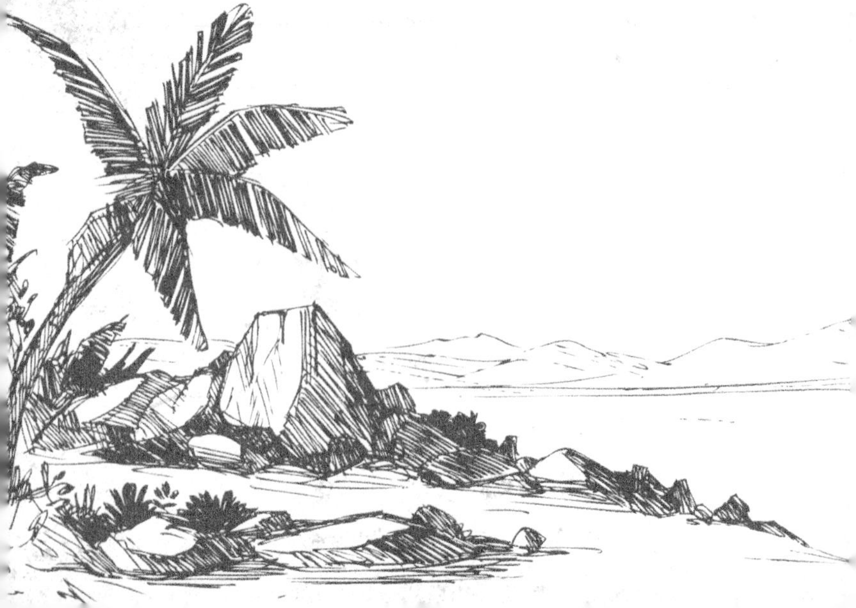

Chapter Twenty-four

SUMMER-RAINE

Auden lifts me like I'm weightless, like I'm treasured gold and lighter than air at the same time. He cradles me against him as he leads us to the bedroom where we've both been sleeping for the past week or so. Oh, how cold it will be when he leaves.

My eyes screw shut at the thought of saying goodbye to him for the last time. It's what's right, I know it is. That's why I made the choices I did back in high school. The monsters inside my head will never allow us to be together, I've known it for a long time. I'm just not sure I'll survive it this time.

"Stay present, baby," Auden murmurs against my hair. "Stay in the moment with me, okay?"

I hold his gaze as he lays me down gently onto the soft cotton bedsheets. His eyes are wild with desire and adoration, two orbs ablaze with the love he has never held himself back from showing me. I'm sure mine look the very same right now.

He sheds himself of his clothes as he stands before me, his

gaze never wavering. Even as he pulls his sweater over his head and slides his sweatpants down his legs, he looks at me like he's frightened I'll disappear if he dares to look away.

I know how he feels.

How long I've waited to feel his hands on me again, to feel the warmth of his body on mine. To feel the safety I've only ever felt in his strong arms. And now it's finally happening, it's hard to believe that any of this is real.

When he strips me of my clothes and presses his skin to mine, it's so burningly intense that I almost flinch in pain. It's even worse when his lips take mine in a kiss so searing and powerful, volcanoes erupt on the other side of the world.

Worse still when he enters me for the first time.

His head drops to my shoulder, both of shuddering as the sheer momentousness of the moment starts to sink in. The space between my legs burns with the sudden fullness. Maybe we should have taken some time to warm up first, but I needed him to complete me, to become one with me, more than my lungs need air to breathe.

I'm only whole when he's inside me.

It's not like when he took me against the wall. That was about hatred, this is about love. He doesn't fuck me. That's not what this is, not what our bodies are trying to say. Instead, we move together, our bodies grinding against each other like undulating waves.

It's almost too much. And yet, I can't help but wrap my arms around him and pull him closer to me.

It's overwhelming, what's happening between us. This reconnection of our souls. It's like my heart has spent the last five years beating out of time and only now with Auden's heart beating against it like a metronome is it finally able to remember its rhythm.

Our moans melt together as my ankles lock behind his back. He growls, carnal and fevered as his mouth takes mine and whispers silent words against my lips. My god, I'd forgotten what it was like to kiss him. It's extraordinary. The way he's so gentle yet commanding all at once. I've never known the kiss of another man, but I know that no man could ever kiss me like Auden.

It's unthinkable that I'll never get to feel this again.

My fingers tangle in his hair as I bury my nose in his neck, inhaling the smell of him while I still can. I'm terrified that one day I might forget it, though I know it isn't possible.

The smell of him will surround me when the wind blows through pine trees. I'll be reminded of him every time I open a book, walk through the woods or simply just take a breath.

I'll never forget it because it's locked in my heart forever. It's as familiar to me as my own perfume and it always will be.

Auden rolls us, trapping himself beneath me before guiding us both into an upright position. We're chest to chest and nose to nose. He's deeper this way. We're so tightly sealed together that we may well be one person.

My eyes close as I wrap my arms around his neck, seeking out his lips with my own.

"I love you," he whispers into my mouth.

It's the first time I've heard him say those words since I was eighteen and it feels just like it did back then. Maybe even better now. Like nothing bad can ever happen to me so long as

I have the love of Auden Wells.

His tongue finds mine and slides against it. I moan and he drinks it down, worshipping me with his kisses until I can't hold back the breathy sounds falling out my mouth.

"How will I ever be able to say goodbye to you?" he asks, pulling back to look me in the eye, and instantly, tears run in their thousands down my cheeks.

Don't.

Don't ever say goodbye to me.

And that's when I realise. I *can't* let him say goodbye. It's my sickness that won't allow us to be together, but what would happen if I got better? If I opened myself up to the possibility of recovery, *true* recovery, at an inpatient facility or somewhere that can offer the help I've always pretended I don't need, would a future together be possible for us?

I would stop hurting him and he would stop trying to fix me.

"Auden," I rasp, cupping his cheek.

Our bodies stop moving he stares at me, waiting for whatever I'm about to say, but he still remains inside me.

"What if I got better?"

"What?"

"What if I accepted help?" I stroke the hair at the back of his head as I talk. "What if I went to rehab and got better?"

"I don't understand," he whispers.

"What if this doesn't have to be the end for us?"

His eyes widen as he realises what I'm saying. I've always been so adamant that I would never go to a rehabilitation centre or actively seek help for my condition. I thought doing so would make me weak.

But maybe all this time I've been wrong.

Maybe the weak thing would be to let the love of my life go again because I'm too damn proud to admit that I need help. Maybe finally admitting that I'm not okay is actually the brave thing.

"But you said that you can't imagine anything worse than being locked in a place full of pyschos and crazies."

Yeah, I did say that. Word for word.

"I was wrong." I cup his face in my hand and he leans into my touch. "Nothing could be worse than losing you."

He blinks, tears of his own swelling in his eyes. They spill over and run delicate tracks down his rugged face.

"You'd really do that?"

I nod. "I'd do anything if it meant finally getting to love you the way you deserve."

I kiss him then, showing him with my lips how desperate I am for him to understand what I'm saying.

"Baby," he shakes his head with a small smile, "it's not like I'm innocent, is it? You deserve more than someone always trying to fix you."

"But if I get better, that won't happen anymore."

He tucks a loose strand of hair behind my ear and that one gesture says more than any of his words ever could.

"So, what are you suggesting?" he asks.

"That tomorrow we don't say goodbye, we say see you later."

His face lights up, a smile so beautiful breaking across his face that it takes my breath away. I feel him twitch inside me where we're still connected, his body responding to me just as powerfully as his heart.

"You think I'd ever say no to that? To the possibility of being with you again someday?"

He lowers his head to my shoulder and presses soft adoring kisses over my collar bone and up the length of my neck. My entire body trembles. I reflexively clench around his dick and his head falls back as a low groan slips rumbles in his throat.

My breathing picks up and I clench again. His hands shoot to my hips and his fingernails dig half-moons into my skin.

"Shit, baby, stop." He clenches his jaw. "I can't concentrate when you do that."

That makes me giggle. It's the first genuinely happy sound I've made since I saw my nephews last.

"Sorry."

"Don't be." He rubs his nose against mine in a gesture so innocent and childlike I almost giggle again. "So, you're really going to do this?"

I don't even hesitate. "Yeah, I think I am."

It's a weird sensation, this epiphany I'm having. It's anticlimactic, yet world-changing at the same time. It has shifted my entire perspective on life and yet it's so glaringly obvious that I can't believe it hasn't occurred to me sooner.

Why should I have to live without Auden if I can do something to keep him?

For so long I have read poetry that make bullshit claims like *you are the master of your own destiny*, but now is the first time I'm stopping to think that maybe it isn't bullshit at all. Maybe I really am the captain of my soul.

He grins, this glorious smile that could light up the entire city, before flipping us over to lay over me again.

He flexes his hips, driving himself into me. And just like that the conversation is over. The tears on our cheeks dry as our hearts come alive with light and love and hope. It's such a stark difference to the mournful, grief-stricken way we were making love before.

Before, we moved in gentle rolling waves.

Now, our bodies rut against each other in frenzied desperation. It's primal, this thing we're doing together. It's not sex, it's more than that. It's an apology for the past and a promise for the future. It's everything that we are. Messy. Stormy. Tempestuous.

When we find our ends together panting and moaning in harmony, I've never felt such euphoria. In his arms, I am finally alive. And I know in this moment that there is nothing I won't do to have this feeling for the rest of my life.

"So, what happens now?" I ask Auden later, my head on his bare chest as my fingers draw love hearts around the freckles on his skin.

He looks down at me with his arm bent by his head, cheek resting on his fist. "You tell me, baby."

"There's a rehab facility in Tampa that I'll check myself into tomorrow."

"I'll drive you," he says instantly.

"You don't have to do that," I whisper.

He presses a kiss to the top of my head. "Try and stop me."

"You know," I roll onto my front and rest my chin on my hands, looking over at him. "I don't know how long I'll be gone. It could be a while."

"Doesn't matter."

"You could meet someone else."

The thought alone is devastating, but it's true. I could be gone weeks, months or years. Who's to say he won't fall in love before I have a chance to come back for him?

But he laughs like the idea is ridiculous. "Pretty girl, listen to me. There is no one else in this world for me but you. It has always been you. And I will wait as long as you need me to until you show up on my doorstep and tell me its time. I'll wait forever, baby. *Forever.*"

I blink back tears at his words.

This is really happening.

I'm going to go to rehab, the one thing I swore I'd never do. I'll do whatever needs to be done to get better and only once I'm ready, only once I know for certain that I can love Auden the way he deserves, only then will I come back for him.

And, *my god*, will the wait be worth it.

"Promise?" I ask, tangling my fingers with his.

"I promise."

Part III

Two years later

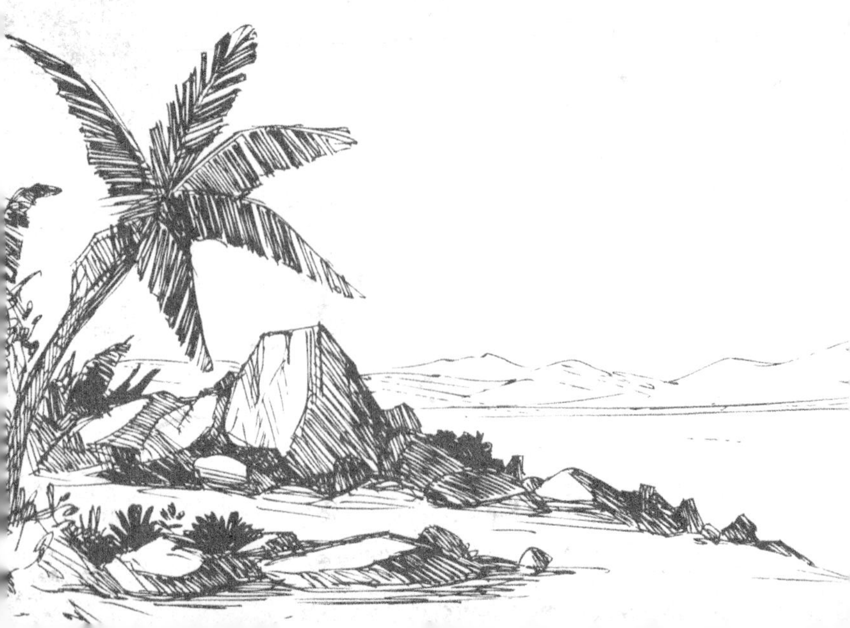

Chapter Twenty-five
SUMMER-RAINE

"Order for Summer," the barista yells, setting my venti caramel macchiato down on the bar before moving swiftly onto the next customer.

For the last few months, I've come in every day at seven-thirty to pick up my morning dose of caffeine. The Grind is this cute little hole in the wall tucked into a backstreet and I'd thought it was one of the city's hidden gems until I'd turned up this morning to find all of Tallahassee's female population waiting in line for a cup of artisan coffee.

"Is something going on?" I ask Max, who's wiping down a table to the right of me in his uniform of a black shirt buttoned to the collar and a forest green apron. He's actually the owner of the café, but he never takes a back seat when it comes to the running of his business. He likes to get his hands dirty and lead from the front.

"Our feature in Sunshine Living came out yesterday." He

grins, white teeth sparkling. "Guess that awful interview and photoshoot I was subjected to was worth it after all."

"What interview and photoshoot?" I take a sip of my coffee and moan as the caffeine enters my bloodstream.

Max eyes me closely, gaze dropping momentarily to my lips. "The one I told you about last month, remember? With the journo who kept trying to make me take my shirt off."

"Ah, yes." I laugh. "I remember now."

He'd actually met the reporter for Sunshine Living on a blind date. He'd taken her back to his place and shown her the time of her life, making her fall so deeply in love with him that she'd been desperate to get The Grind featured in the magazine. Or that's how he tells the story, at least.

"Tell me they didn't use a topless photo of you in the article?"

"Why else do you think all these women are here? It ain't my milkshake bringing all the girls to the yard." He winks and I groan. "Seriously, look at this shit."

He takes a rolled-up copy of the magazine out of his apron and lays it out on the table in front of me, flicking to the double-page spread and motioning for me to look.

He wasn't joking.

Almost an entire page is taken up with the image of Max sitting on a stool in faded jeans, branded coffee cup in hand and shirt nowhere to be seen. The photographer has caught him mid-laugh and the joy on his face leaps off the page and infiltrates my body. The photo makes me happy. I can see why they used it.

"I look good, huh?" he says, flashing me a cocky grin.

In the short time I've known Max, I don't think I've ever seen him without a smile. He's one of those people who just radiates sunshine and rainbows. It's why I've gravitated so much towards him. Being around him makes me feel good and I need more people like that in my life.

The first time I came here, he'd served me at the counter and made a joke that I can't remember now, but I do remember that it had made me laugh. He'd hit on me and handled it well when I rejected him and somehow, we became fast friends.

He still makes a pass at me every time we see each other though, but I've sort of come to love it. He's a serial flirt, but completely harmless.

"You know you do."

He does. My heart may belong to another man, but I can't deny that Max isn't incredibly handsome. With his curly dark hair and perpetual boyish grin, he's an absolute dead ringer for Harry Styles.

"Good enough to let me take you out?" he asks, batting his eyelashes dramatically and making me roll my eyes.

"We've been over this, Romeo. I'm spoken for, but good try."

He sighs wistfully. "Your man doesn't know how lucky he is."

No, he doesn't. But that's because he's technically not my man yet.

I've been out of rehab for a year now, but I haven't been to see Auden yet.

It's not that I've had second thoughts, quite the opposite actually. I've never been so sure of anything in my life than I am about living the rest of my days with him by my side. Being without him for so long has been like living with a dagger in my heart.

It's just that I don't want to start our life together until I know with absolute certainty that I'm ready.

It's been two long years of self-reflection and accountability, staring my demons straight in the face and learning how to live with them.

It hasn't been easy. It's been debilitating, actually. There have been more moments than I can count when I've contemplated giving up, but then I would remember the promise Auden made and the future I'm working towards and I'd get back up, dust myself off and get back to work.

Of course, I'm not magically cured of my condition. My depression is still as real as the air I breathe, but I've spent hours and hours with psychiatrists and in group therapy sessions learning how to manage it.

I'm also on a shit tonne of medication, which is something I never thought I'd say. But I've come to learn that there's no shame in it.

Mental illness isn't a choice. No one wakes up one morning and chooses to be depressed. I certainly never wrote 'depression' on my Christmas wish list, but I was gifted it nonetheless. So why should I be ashamed to take a few prescribed pills if they help to keep the demons at bay? Especially if they help me live the life that I'm desperate for, if they help me love Auden the way I have always wanted to, but couldn't.

"One of these days you're going to say yes to me, Summer," Max says with a wink.

But I won't.

Even if agreeing to dinner with him wouldn't technically be doing anything wrong. Auden promised to wait for me, but he never promised abstinence. It's a detail I hadn't thought to cover at the time, but I don't think it was needed.

In two years, I haven't felt even a twinge of attraction towards another man. My heart, my longing, my desire all belongs solely to him.

I laugh and swat Max playfully on the arm. "Keep dreaming."

Smiling, I say my goodbyes and start the walk back to the building where I both live and work.

The week after I was discharged from rehab, I used the entirety of my trust-fund to set up a non-profit organisation for people with mental health difficulties who can't access medical help or just don't want to. It's a place where people can come and be safe, unjudged and in the presence of those who understand.

I've set The Rainey Days Foundation in a restored building that had been a bank once upon a time. The entirety of the downstairs is dedicated to the organisation, with a large communal space, kitchen, dining area and a number of small side rooms leading off the main area for the different services we offer.

We host group activities and lunches and regular group therapy sessions. Every day, there is at least one psych on sight for drop-in appointments as well as volunteers who help me keep the centre running. But my favourite part of the whole building has to be the small rooms that I had set up with daybeds and book shelves and comfy chairs, for those who want to be on their own while also being surrounded by people.

And the best thing about the foundation? It's one-hundred-percent free for everyone who uses it. We rely solely on the money I feed into it, donations and fundraising.

I don't even take a salary.

During my stay in rehab, the councillors encouraged us to write about our experiences. I don't know what made me do it, but I started uploading my daily journal entries onto an online blog. I wasn't expecting anyone to read it, but after only a few months I had such a large following that I was able to monetise it, which is how I'm able to run the foundation without taking any money out for my living expenses.

It's a magical kind of irony. How the demons in my head are the reason that I'm helping other people learn how to live with theirs. For so long, I've hated my monsters. I've blamed them for the pain I've felt, the mistakes I've made, the times I've hurt the people I love. I've always thought that it was because of them that I couldn't be with Auden.

But that's not true.

It's not my condition that was the problem, but how I dealt with it. Having depression didn't make me any less deserving of Auden's love, but the way I treated him did.

I know that now.

It's why I've waited so long to go to him.

Because it wasn't my monsters that were hurting him before, it was me, and I need to be sure that I'll never put him through it again.

And if I'm being totally honest, maybe I'm a bit scared.

Auden and I have been seven years in the making. It's overwhelming, knowing that our past really can be left behind us now. Maybe there's a part of me that still clings to the darkness because it's safe and familiar. I'm a recovering addict after all. Pain will always call to me like a siren in the night, but I'm strong enough to resist it now.

I'm ready.

Finally, my heart is strong enough to withstand the weight of mine and Auden's love. Because together, we burn like wildfire. We love with the light of a million stars. We're fierce and chaotic and powerful and until now, I never had a hope in hell of surviving it. But I do now.

I don't know what our new reality will look like, but I know that the flames of our love will burn forever and light our way through the dark.

It's time, I realise.

No more waiting.

We've waited for each other long enough and I have no excuses left to hold out another day or two.

So tonight, I'll go to him.

I'll show up at his apartment and open the door to our new life. And in the morning, I'll wake up in the place I've been dreaming of for the last two years, his arms.

And finally, we'll be happy. Finally, we'll be together.

Finally, I'll be home.

This is it.

I let out a hot breath as my palms sweat and my heart thuds wildly in my chest.

God, I don't think I've ever been so nervous.

The apartment building my sister told me he lives in now looms over me, twenty floors of and reinforced concrete and glittering glass windows. It's one of the most sought-after buildings in the city to live in. I know, because I tried to rent an apartment of my own here when I first moved to the city years ago.

Auden must have done well for himself in the time that I've been away to land a place here and be able to afford it. My heart swells with pride for him.

I know nothing of his life over the last two years. We haven't had any contact since he dropped me off at the rehab facility in Tampa with whispered words of love and soft kisses to my lips and forehead.

We thought it would be better that way. Knowing that the next time we spoke would be the first day of the rest of our lives. Texting would have only cheapened our experience when what we were going through was so intense. And sure, we could have written letters, but I kind of loved knowing how much we would have to talk about when our day finally came.

And here it is.

I can hardly believe it.

I walk straight past the doorman to the elevator and tap the button for the fifteenth floor. With every rising number I see on the indicator, I get a little bit sicker with nervous energy. It feels like an age has passed when the elevator bell finally dings and the doors open.

With tentative steps, I walk down the brightly lit hallway to the door embossed with the number I was told belongs to Auden.

My stomach flips. This is it. I'm so nervous, so overwhelmingly excited, that adrenaline courses like neon liquid through my veins and sets my body aglow. I'm vibrating with the anticipation and I can't wait a second more.

I raise my fist to the door and knock.

There's a shuffling inside followed by the clip-clop of footsteps, like high heels on hardwood floors.

"Just a sec."

The voice is acutely feminine, but my brain hardly has a chance to register the significance of that fact before the door is swinging open and I find myself staring into a pair of familiar eyes.

But they're not the eyes I've been dreaming of for so long.

Instead of a brilliant blue, they're deep brown. They're not wide with happiness at the sight of me, but narrowed in hostility.

Because it isn't Auden standing there with open arms ready to welcome me home, it's Cara with hatred on her face and a sparkling diamond on her finger.

Her *ring* finger.

I turn on my heel and run, white hot pain searing through me like lava, burning me alive from the inside out. All the ways I imagined this moment could go, his ex-girlfriend opening the door was not one of them.

Only, it doesn't look like she's his ex-girlfriend anymore.

It looks unmistakably and irrevocably like she's his wife.

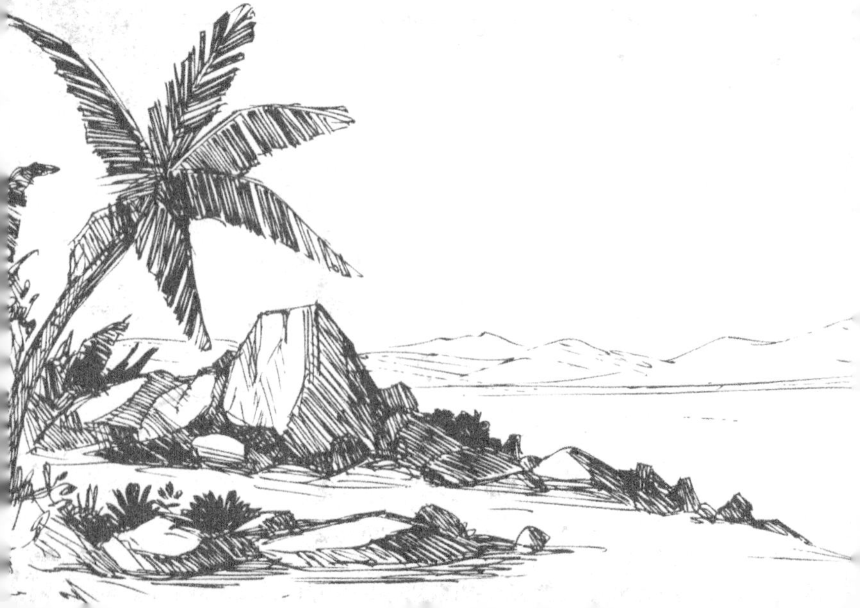

Chapter Twenty-six
AUDEN

Peaches and bergamot.

The smell assaults me while I'm folding laundry in my bedroom. At first, I think I'm imagining it, but as the scent grows stronger, I realise with blinding clarity that it's real.

She's here.

I follow the sweetness down the hallway, my heart flipping over and over the closer I get to the front door.

But it's Cara who gets there first.

I watch in wide-eyed horror as she opens the door in only her nightwear, her body seizing with hostility as recognition dawns. I can't see the person on the other side of the door, but I know who it is. A smug smile spreads across Cara's face as she positions her hand on the doorframe so that her wedding band and engagement ring are on full display.

It's a petty move, cruel even, but it has the desired effect.

Because the girl on the other side of the door releases a gasp as if in excruciating pain. The sound cripples me.

This shouldn't have been how she found out.

I should have been the one to tell her.

But I've had over a year to reach out and I haven't. I'm a coward, I know that. I fucked up by not telling her. God, I fucked up by doing a lot of things. But allowing her to be blindsided by this is possibly the worst fuckup of them all.

She doesn't deserve any of this.

My poor sweet Summer-Raine.

I'm blinded by a flash of gold as she turns and runs. I can hear her sobs from here as she hurtles down the corridor and presses the button to call for the elevator.

I'm right behind her.

I ignore Cara's scowl as I charge past her, my heart in my throat and panic in my gut. I don't bother waiting for the elevator, it's already gone, carrying Summer-Raine further and further away from me. I bolt into the stairwell, flying down flight after flight until I crash through the door to the foyer and out of the building.

But the second I feel the fresh air on my skin, I slow to a stop.

Summer-Raine stands just metres away, hunched over a three-foot wall as she wretches over it. Her hair catches in the wind and blows across her face, strands getting caught in the path of her vomit.

It doesn't make her any less beautiful.

Even like this, with her eyes red and puffy, makeup streaming down her cheeks in murky black waterfalls and vomit in her hair, she's still the most beautiful thing I've ever seen.

She may not be mine anymore, she may never be again, but it doesn't make that fact any less true.

I'll still always rather watch her than the sunset.

"Summer-Raine," I whisper.

"Don't."

She won't look at me. She just stays there, hand resting on the wall, her eyes clenched shut as she sucks in short breaths. Every so often, I hear her whimper. It's a sound as gut-wrenching as the noise a dog makes when it's kicked or the cry of a frightened child. Now I know what it sounds like when a heart breaks and I never want to hear it again.

I ache to go to her, but I don't. I *can't*. I have no choice but to watch on helplessly. Because I did this to her. I could have spared her some of this pain, if only I'd been brave enough to tell her about Cara sooner.

I don't know how long it is but finally, she steels herself and stands to her full height. Her breaths have evened out now, though I can tell she's fighting to keep them steady and her hands are clenched into fists at her side as if preparing herself for a fight.

"When?" That's all she asks.

But she still won't look at me. She won't even open her eyes.

"About fourteen months ago."

She flinches. It's only a small movement. So slight, it's almost imperceptible. But I notice it. I notice everything about her.

I watch her face as she does the math, working out how long after she left for the rehab centre that Cara and I got married.

Her eyes fly open. "Ten months?" she fumes, nostrils flaring in blazing fury. "Ten fucking months?"

She advances on me, her eyes wild. She comes to a stop in front of me and beats her tiny fists against my chest. I stand stock still and let her do it. If she needs to hurt me for the pain I've caused her, then she can. I deserve it.

Hell, I deserve more.

But even in the midst of her madness, she holds herself back from using too much force. She's strong, I know that. She always has been. If she wanted to, she could hit me hard enough to actually hurt me, but she doesn't.

Even with all the pain I'm putting her through, she's resistant to return it.

It makes my betrayal feel even worse.

"How?" she screams, drawing the curious eyes of city goers as they pass us on the sidewalk, but I don't care. "How could you do this to me?"

God, I hate this. But I hate myself more.

Truth is, it was easier to live with what I'd done when I didn't have to face the consequences. Maybe that's why I never told her. Because it would have made it all real. And now, there's no escaping it. I have to live with my decisions and the guilt they bring me, the pain they cause the last person I'd ever want to hurt like this.

"You told me you'd wait for me," she sobs. "Did you even wait at all?"

Taking a deep breath, I look to the skies and pray to a higher power that I've never believed in for a way to make this better.

"I tried," I say quietly, my voice trembling.

"You tried?" she blinks. "*You tried?* Tell me how marrying your ex-girlfriend ten months after I left is trying?"

Fuck, I can't do this. I shake my head. "You don't understand."

She scoffs. "Of course, I don't fucking understand."

"Summer-Raine, please," I beg, though I don't have the right and I don't even know what I'm begging for. For her to stop crying? For her forgiveness? Or just for all of this to end? "I'm sorry. I'm so fucking sorry."

"Why?" she whispers, finally looking me in the eye. The hurt and betrayal I see in them sucks all the air from my lungs. "Why did you do it?"

"Because I had to."

The truth is as simple as that.

"Was I too hard to love?" Her bottom lip shakes as she speaks and her gaze dips away from me again, her anger gone now and replaced by choked desolation.

I can't help myself. I tilt her chin back up with two fingers, letting them linger there as I say my next words. "Loving you was never the hard part, Summer-Raine. That's always been as easy to me as breathing. It was never a choice or a decision I made. I fell in love with you because my heart didn't know how to do anything else. Loving you was the only thing that ever made any sense to me. Please don't think you were hard to love, baby, because that couldn't be further from the truth."

She blinks away tears. "Don't call me that."

Confused, I think back over what I just said with a furrowed brow, understanding dawning as I realise the slip-up I made. Even now, after all I've done, calling her baby is as natural to me as the soil in the earth and the clouds in the sky.

I let my fingers fall away, remembering that I have no right to touch her anymore.

God, how differently I pictured this day going two years ago. Driving back from the rehab facility after dropping her off, I imagined us reuniting with incredible smiles and tearful eyes. She'd have run to me and I'd have scooped her up, wrapping her legs around my waist as I kissed her like I'd never kissed her before.

I was going to propose.

And then everything changed.

"Sorry," I rasp.

She rolls her eyes. "You can stop saying that too. Sorry doesn't change anything."

I nod silently. She's right. There are no words I can say to make this better.

Her eyes widen as she spots something over my shoulder. I follow the trajectory of her gaze to find Cara watching us with pursed lips and a hand on her hip. She clears her throat and stares at me accusingly.

"I think you're needed," Summer-Raine says, her voice flat.

In the few seconds I was looking away, she's managed to school her features into a blank expression that gives nothing away. She's shut herself down. There's no anger on her face anymore, no pain or sadness, no emotion at all.

It was better when she was screaming at me.

"Ignore her."

"She's your wife."

"I don't need reminding."

She laughs quietly, but there's no amusement in it. It's a cold laugh. Hollow. Almost sinister. My heart drops as she takes a step backward, turning around to walk away.

I resist the urge to clasp her wrist to stop her.

"Where are you going?" She doesn't answer. I watch her take a few more steps before I call out, "Summer-Raine."

"Go back to your wife, Auden." She doesn't even turn around, just throws the words over her shoulder as she gets further and further away from me.

Though I can feel Cara's glare burning into my back, I don't go to her. Instead, I watch the woman I once thought would be my forever walk away from me. Every step she takes is another step away from everything we could have been.

But maybe there was never any hope for us anyway.

We've both fucked up over the years. We've both hurt each other when we shouldn't have and caused more pain than either of us deserved. And that's our problem, isn't it? It's like we can't help ourselves. We fuck up time and time again. It's been seven years since we were first together and we still haven't learned.

We're a tempest. A storm raging over wild waves. Loving Summer-Raine has always been like that. Like a natural disaster. As fatal, devastating and inevitable as a star burning out.

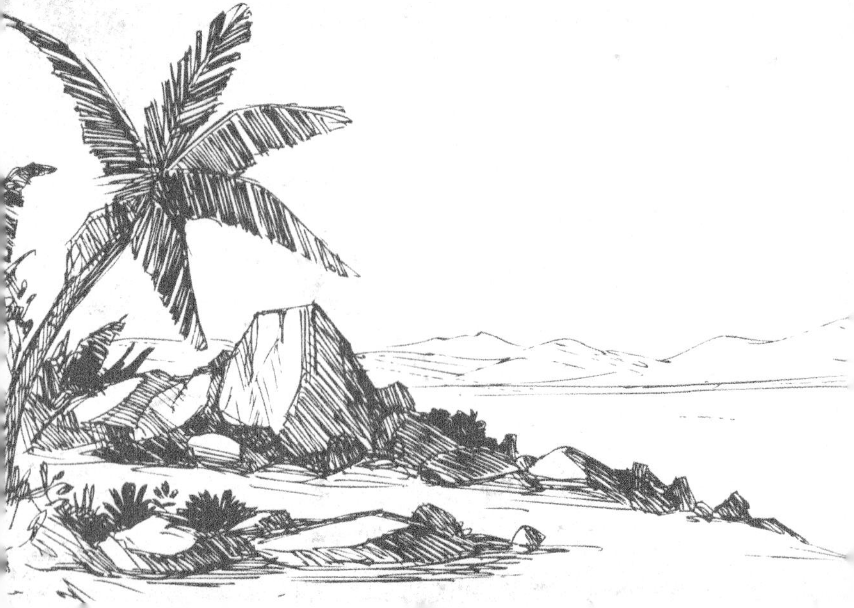

Chapter Twenty-seven
SUMMER-RAINE

"Come on girl, it's been two weeks. You've gotta get out of bed," Marlowe says, throwing open the drapes and drenching the room in blinding light.

I whimper, the sunlight bringing me physical pain. It's been fourteen days since I last saw it.

Not long after I got back from rehab, I bumped into Marlowe in the grocery store. I'd somehow convinced her to have a coffee with me so that I could explain why I fell off the grid after high school. It had taken some grovelling on my part, but she'd eventually accepted my apology. Fast forward a year and she's insisted on moving in for a while to help me cope with Auden's betrayal.

"It hurts so much, Mar."

She takes a seat beside me on the bed and strokes her hand through my matted hair. "I know, Summer. I know."

My eyes burn, but nothing leaks out. I guess I've got no tears left to cry. All I've done for the last two weeks is weep. It's been relentless. I'm dehydrated, I have a permanent migraine and I feel so weak that I don't know if I'd be able to stand if I even wanted to get up.

"It's two-thirty in the afternoon. Let's grab a coffee at The Grind and take a walk? Just for a little while."

I bat her away. "I don't want to go out."

"Come on." She throws the covers off of me and tugs at my arm.

"I swear to God, Marlowe. If you don't fuck off right now, I might end up hitting you."

"Good." She chuckles. "Then at least you'd be out of bed."

I wish she'd go away.

I don't know who came up with the phrase "misery loves company", but they obviously never knew the pain of heartbreak. The way the shattered fragments of your heart seem to float around inside of you, puncturing your organs and lodging in your veins. It kills you slowly. Like arsenic poisoning or a severed artery that's left to bleed out.

There's nothing worse than company when you feel like that.

I don't want Marlowe in here trying to make me go out.

I just want to be in the dark.

"Think of how far you've come, Sum. All the work you've put into being healthy and getting better. It would kill me to see it all go to waste."

"It *has* all gone to waste. He married someone else, Marlowe. Everything I've done has been for fucking nothing."

"Don't you dare say that, Summer." She looks at me furiously, shaking her head. "Don't you dare let a guy be the reason you lose all the progress you've made. He may have been the motivation but you didn't go for rehab just for him, did you? You went for *you*. Please don't let this ruin you. You're stronger than that, I know you are."

I look up at her, exhausted and defeated. "I don't know how to stop feeling like this," I say quietly, my voice catching in my throat. "I don't know how I can ever be happy without him."

Her eyes shine with sad understanding. "I know it feels like that now. I know it feels like all you want to do is go to sleep and wake up when the pain has stopped, but I promise that eventually it will get better."

"How?"

I don't understand how it could ever get better.

For two years, I imagined what my future would look like with Auden. I dreamt of the house that we'd call our home, a place by the ocean with a balcony where we would watch the sunsets together and fall asleep in each other's arms every night. I'd try to picture the faces of the children we'd have. A son who looked just like him and a daughter who looked just like me. The vacations we would take together, the holidays we'd celebrate, the way our family home would forever be my sanctuary. The place where I'd feel safest.

But I'll never know what it's like to have any of that. Because that future doesn't belong to me anymore. It belongs to Cara.

He chose her over me in a competition I didn't even know I was a part of.

She'll get the house on the beach with the sunsets and the children and the holidays. She'll know the safety of Auden's arms for the rest of her days and the comfort of breathing his air.

And all I'll have is my shattered heart to try and put back together.

"You can start by getting coffee with me," Marlowe says, taking my hand and laughing when I roll my eyes. "Come on. We'll get coffee and come straight home. I promise. I just think you'll feel different when you're in the fresh air."

"Fine."

"Great." She smiles triumphantly. "And have a shower, you fucking stink."

It takes severe effort but I do as she tells me, heaving myself out of bed and into the bathroom, where I wash the last two weeks of misery off my skin. Then I change into trackpants and a baggy tee, and meet Marlowe to leave.

She looks me up and down with a raised brow. "You could have made a bit of an effort."

"For what? We're getting coffee."

She rolls her eyes, standing there in a summer dress with her raven-coloured hair styled perfectly into waves. She's no longer the meek teenage girl she was in high school, she's a woman through and through. While she's undoubtedly gorgeous, it's her confidence that has had the best transformation. "You haven't even dried your hair."

"Whatever." I push past her. "Wanna do this or not?"

We walk the short distance to The Grind in comfortable silence. The late summer sun beats down on me and it's so unbearably hot that by the time we make it to the coffee house, my forehead is dripping in sweat.

Max spots us the second we step inside, flashing us his signature smile that he uses to charm the panties off women. I lift a hand in a small wave before turning my back on him to order my drink at the counter, an Americano despite the humidity.

"That poor boy has got it bad for you," Marlowe whispers into my ear as we order our drinks.

"No, he doesn't." I tut.

"Then why is he staring at you?" She casts a glance over her shoulder to where Max is making light conversation with an elderly customer. His body faces the woman, but his twinkling eyes are on me.

I scoff. "Probably because I look like a hot mess. Stop reading into things cause you're reading it all wrong."

"Am I?" She looks at me in amusement. "I guess you've got a chance to prove me wrong because he's coming over here."

Max saunters across the room towards us, his hands shoved into his pockets and a cheeky smile on his lips. He's clean-shaven, accentuating the deep dimples in his cheeks that remind me of another man. A man I may well never see again.

The thought threatens to send me spiralling back into darkness.

"Hey, gorgeous." He bends down and drops a flirty kiss on my cheek, unknowingly bringing me back to the light.

"Oh, shut up." I bat him away with a scowl. "I look like shit and you know it."

He throws his head back and laughs like my words are

hilarious. "Sweetheart, you could have grease in your hair and grit in your teeth and I'd still think you were hot as hell."

Marlowe raises her eyebrows, looking at me pointedly and I stick my middle finger up at her when Max glances away.

"Whatever," I grumble, perching my ass on the corner of a table beside me as they both make small talk and toss flirty little comments between them as if they're playing ping pong. It pisses me off. "Maybe you two should go out."

Max swings a confused stare round to me as Marlowe chokes on her coffee in surprise.

"I don't think I'm the one he's interested in, Sum," Marlowe says, chuckling wryly to herself and earning a glare from me.

Why is she enjoying this so much?

"Jesus, Mar. He doesn't even like me like that."

"Then why does he ask you out all the time?" Her hand drops to her waist and she juts her hip out, making me regret ever telling her about Max and his affinity to asking me on dates.

"Because he asks out everyone." I toss my hands into the air with an exasperated sigh.

Max, who until this point has been watching the entire exchange with raised brows and a smirk on his face, gapes at me like I'm stupid. "No, actually," he says slowly. "I don't."

I blink at him.

"I asked you out originally because I actually really wanted you to say yes, but you said you weren't available. The only reason I carry on asking is because it makes you smile." He pauses and then says quietly, "And I like it when you smile."

Marlowe swoons beside us and I roll my eyes at her. "She's

not unavailable anymore," she says, her eyes twinkling. "Maybe you should ask her out again."

My eyes widen in astonishment. I don't even know how to react.

What in hell is she playing at?

"What happened to your man?" Max asks, his head tilted to one side.

Marlowe chews on her bottom lip as she looks at me worriedly, wondering whether she's gone too far.

"He married someone else," I whisper, averting my gaze from his concerned one.

"What?" He laughs in shock. "Are you serious?"

I nod, but don't reply.

"He's an idiot." I roll my eyes. "No, seriously, he is. If I had your heart, the only woman wearing my ring would be you."

I smile up at him, a slight blush pinking my cheeks. "Thanks."

"Maybe I should ask you out again."

"Yes." Marlowe claps her hands together triumphantly. "You totally should."

"What are you doing?" I growl at her, but she ignores me.

"In fact," she says, despite the daggers I'm firing through my eyes in her direction. "She's free Saturday. Her favourite food is Italian. I'll leave you the address and you can pick her up at eight."

My mouth falls open in horror, words of refusal desperate to escape but dying silently on my lips. I'm going to kill her. In what world would be a good idea for me to go on a date two weeks after getting my heart broken?

But I'm too late to put a stop to her madness, because she's already scribbling my address down on a napkin. I make a grab for it, but she swipes it up quickly, folds it into four and tucks it into the pocket of Max's apron.

"Guess we're going on a date then, sweetheart," he says with a smirk, sauntering away before I'm able to set him straight.

Marlowe is particularly skilled in two things; driving me insane and convincing me to do things I don't really want to do.

It's because of the latter that I find myself sitting opposite Max in a trendy Italian bistro on Saturday night, the lights low and twinkling guitar chords carrying atmospherically around the room.

I study him in the glow of the flickering candlelight. His hair, as always, is curly in a deliberately wild kind of way and his rich hazel eyes sparkle like diamonds whenever the flames dance across them. He's an undeniably beautiful man and yet it isn't him who I see sitting across from me.

It's the seventeen-year-old boy who took me on my first date all those years ago. The boy who introduced me to Captain Arthur Harris—who must be long dead by now—and walked barefoot with me on the sand. The boy who tasted like first loves and lemonade when he kissed me at the end of the night.

I could be sitting in that very same restaurant right now with how vivid the memories are.

"You're distracted," Max says with a gentle smile, pulling

me back to the present. His voice, like his expression, is kind rather than chastising and it makes my stomach twinge with guilt that I've been sat here wishing he was a different man.

"I'm sorry." I look down at my barely-touched plate of pasta.

"Don't be. I've been where you are, I get it."

But before he can elaborate, we're interrupted by a woman I hoped I'd never have to see again as she struts towards us in heels higher than I could ever walk in. I resist the urge to look down self-consciously at the chucks on my own feet.

Cara reaches the table, towering over us in her designer shoes, and it takes everything in me to stop my eyes tearing at the sight of her.

She's stunning in a severe kind of way. Her face is a picture of sharp lines and rigid angles, straddling the line between modelesque and gaunt. If she's wearing makeup, it's been applied by an expert hand to make her appear fresh-faced, with the exception of her lips that have been painted the boldest shade of red to match the colour of her skin-tight dress.

"Summer." Her lyrical voice goes through me like microphone feedback.

"Cara."

My heart jumps.

Is he here too?

I fight to remain expressionless, refusing to give her the satisfaction of seeing the depth of my heartache. She's looking for it though, my pain. I see her studying my face with arrogant, triumphant eyes.

She got the guy.

She won the game I didn't even know I was playing.

She stole the only chance of happiness that I will ever have.

"And who's this?" Her smug gaze rakes over my dinner date.

"Max." He stands and holds out his hand for her to shake.

She fakes a laugh and leans into him. "I'm a woman, Max," she says, as if he hadn't already noticed. Every man in this damn place is well aware of her womanhood if the gaping mouths and floppy tongues are any indication. "I do hugs not handshakes."

My hands clench into fists underneath the table.

Max though, to his credit, frees himself from her grasp and sits down awkwardly, reaching across the table with his hand palm side up. I stare at it for a minute before realising his intention. My hand slips into his.

Cara eyes the movement with a creased forehead. "Are you together?" she asks, looking only at him.

"We're together right now." I blink at her like she's stupid.

"Just seeing how things go," Max answers vaguely, winking at me across the table.

I blush despite my discomfort.

"Oh, wow, isn't that just lovely?" Cara exclaims, though her expression says she thinks it's anything but. Too obvious to be unintentional, she clasps her hands in front of her and twists her wedding band round her finger.

My stomach plummets, the tiny amount of food I've eaten tonight threatening to make an appearance all over her scarlet dress.

I should never have come tonight.

Cara slaps her hands together just as I'm taking a long glug of wine, startling me. "I've just had a thought," she says. "My husband and I", her eyes swing to mine and she smirks, "are hosting a dinner party next weekend. You two should come."

It's such a ludicrous suggestion that I almost spray my mouthful of merlot across the table.

"We'd love to." Max grins, a mischievous glint in his mahogany eyes. "Wouldn't we, baby?"

"Um, no actu–"

"Yes," he cuts me off. "We'll be there. But would you mind leaving us to finish up? I need Summer to eat if she's to have enough energy for what I've got planned tonight."

I choke on my wine.

What the hell?

Cara's eyes widen in shock as her cheeks flame in embarrassment. Though I get the feeling her discomfort has less to do with Max's crudeness than the surprise of being dismissed by him. She probably doesn't get the cold shoulder from men very often, looking the way she does.

She was beautiful enough to make Auden fall in love with her after promising himself to me, after all.

"Very well," she laughs lightly, composing herself. "I'll have an invitation sent out to you." She nods and with not another word, turns on her red-soled shoes and takes a seat at a table with three other women, all dressed as glamorously as her.

She's not here with Auden.

I feel my body relax in relief. At least I won't have to face seeing them together. I won't have to watch as he looks at her the way he used to look at me, or tucks a loose strand of hair behind her ear.

I wouldn't have been able to survive it.

"What the fuck was that?" I demand, snatching my hand

out of his. "We're not going to that dinner."

"Yes, we are," he states simply, not even looking at me as he tucks back into his dinner.

"Max" I sigh. "I don't know what impression I've given you, if you think I'm more into this than I am, I don't know. And if I've led you on, then I really am so sorry because that was never my intention, but—"

"That was her, wasn't it?" he interrupts me for the second time this evening.

"What?"

"The woman he married."

I blink at him in shock. *How could he have possibly known that?*

"It was obvious," he says, reading the thoughts displayed on my face. "You were so uncomfortable with her presence that your skin was basically grey and the hatred on her face when she looked at you was unlike anything I've ever seen."

I scoff. "She has no reason to hate me."

"Sure, she does." He pulls a card out of his wallet to pay for dinner, batting me away when I reach for my own. "Look, I don't know exactly what happened between you and that guy but for whatever reason, she sees you as a threat."

I shoot him a sceptical raise of my eyebrows.

"And no, Summer, going back to what you said before, you haven't led me on." He rolls his eyes. "I'm under no illusion that this is anything more than a dinner between friends, despite how much I enjoy flirting with you. But regardless, I care about you and I hate to see you so destroyed by this. So, you're going to go to that dinner party with me by your side and your head held high, and we will eat their food and drink their wine and make fun of them at every opportunity. And if you need to, you can spend another two weeks in the dark afterwards. But if you want any chance of moving on, then you need to face them. Trust me, okay?"

I nod mutely.

I get what he's saying. I understand where he's coming from. But I'm not sure I'll get the closure he thinks I will by sitting in Auden's home as I watch him with his wife and their friends.

It's easier to pretend it's not real when I don't have to see them together. I can just go about my life, pretending that he's still waiting for me to show up at his door someday.

But maybe Max is right.

I won't be able to move on until I've faced my new reality. That's how grief works, right? You work through the stages until one day, you finally reach acceptance.

I'm not sure I'll ever get there, that I'll ever accept that Auden's heart doesn't belong to me anymore and never will again, but I have no chance if I keep allowing myself to live in a fantasy world and pretending that none of this ever happened.

I need to see for myself that he's happy without me, that his betrayal wasn't in vain. God, it's going to kill me, to see Cara live the life I thought would be mine. To watch her touch Auden and kiss him and love him the way I ache to do.

But I need to.

If I want any hope of rebuilding a future for myself, then it's what I have to do.

And maybe then, after all these years, I'll finally let him go.

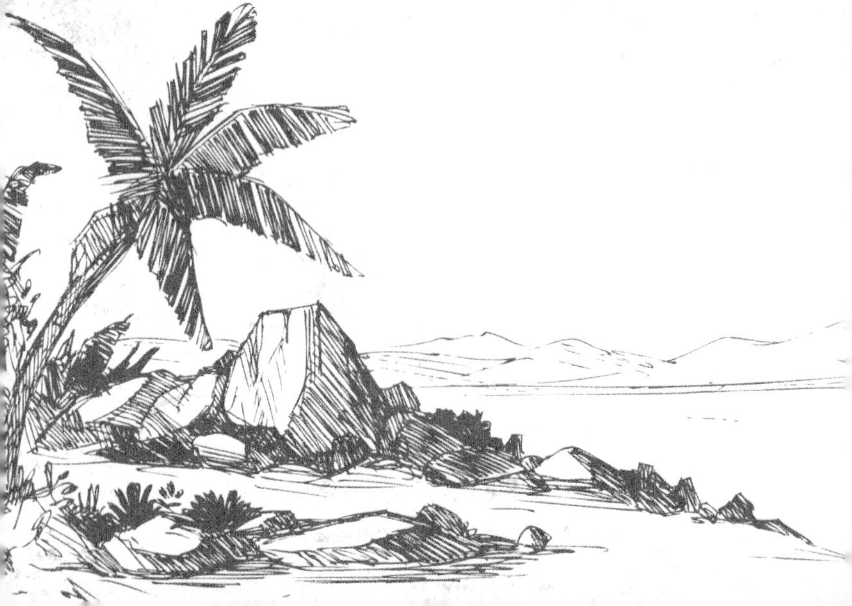

Chapter Twenty-eight
AUDEN

I've never hated a person more than the man currently sitting opposite me with his arm wrapped around the back of Summer-Raine's chair.

My eyes zero in on the movement of his fingers as they toy with the golden strands of her hair and it makes me murderous.

Mine.

That's the word screaming in my head repeatedly like a siren.

Mine. Mine. Mine.

My hands are clenched into tight fists underneath the table. There is so much rage coursing through me that I don't dare reach for my wine, for fear that I'll shatter the glass with the strength of my grip. And all because he's touching what doesn't belong to him.

But… she doesn't belong to me either.

That fact only serves to make me more furious, more violently jealous.

He knows it too, the man who's touching her. He knows what it's doing to me. I see him watching me through the furthest corner of his eye as he laughs at a story Fred, my best friend since high school, is telling. I see the way his lips twitch smugly every time I flinch or flare my nostrils.

Fuck, I hate him.

I can't help thinking that his stupid face would look better if I stuffed it into the silver-plated gravy boat Cara and I were given as a wedding gift.

I've never really had violent tendencies. As a teenager, I'd channel any anger I felt into playing football. But even when I gave up playing after college and lost that outlet, I didn't experience any bursts of aggression like I am right now.

It's just that the sight of him touching her, even though it's just her hair, is too much for me to deal with. It makes me wonder if he's touched her anywhere else. If he's touched her in the places that were supposed to only ever be touched by me.

Two weeks ago, she showed up at my door. Has she really gotten over me in that time? Has she really moved on with this smirking, arrogant asshole who looks like a member of a One Direction tribute band?

If she has, I think I'll kill him. And I don't mean figuratively.

The thought of wrapping my hands around his neck and choking the life out of him is almost as exhilarating as the thought of divorcing Cara.

Speak of the devil, my wife lays her hand on my wrist and digs her impossibly sharp nails into my skin. I curse. Witch made me bleed.

I glare at her and she gives me a smile in return that is nothing but wicked and fake.

"Honey," her sweet, caramel voice is sharp in my ears. "I was just telling Max and Summer-Raine that they should consider Antigua for their first vacation. You remember how beautiful it was, don't you?" She doesn't give me a chance to respond before she turns back to our guests. "We took a catamaran out one evening to watch the sunset. Auden said he'd never seen one like it and it was so romantic that we just couldn't help but make love underneath it. Sunsets are our thing, you see."

Summer-Raine whimpers.

It's so quiet, this musical little squeak that's hardly audible, but every single person in the room hears it.

"Excuse me."

Chair legs screech on the oakwood floors as she all but runs from the room.

"Oh, dear," Cara giggles. "Did I say too much?"

No one answers her.

I'm furious, almost shaking with it. I knew this was why she invited Summer-Raine and her asshole of a date Max. To rub our marriage in her face. To laud the victory over her and make her feel the pain of it.

Cara's vindictive like that and she's always hated Summer-Raine.

I take a large swig of my wine before excusing myself too, ignoring the burn of Cara's glare as I go in the direction of Summer-Raine.

I don't know what I'll say when I find her, I haven't spoken to her all night or even made eye contact, but I know that right now she's in pain and I've never been able to ignore it when she's hurting.

When she hurts, I hurt.

It doesn't matter that I'm married to someone else, that's just the way it is. The way it's always been and the way it always will be. My signature on the marriage certificate doesn't stop it being true.

I follow the sound of her footsteps down the hallway, but I still can't see her. She must have found the bathroom. I resign myself to returning to the dinner party when I notice light shining into the hallway through a door that shouldn't be open.

That door hasn't been open in almost a year.

Though my heart aches, I allow my feet to carry me to the threshold of that room. My breathing grows laboured, but I refuse to turn around. I guess now is as good a time as any to finally face the memories that lay inside the room.

"You're a father."

For the first time tonight, I look into Summer-Raine's eyes. Those spheres that are usually so vibrant and colourful are almost completely dull. It's as if she's past the point of devastation. Too overwhelmed by the significance of what she's just discovered to allow herself to really feel the emotions that the discovery brings.

Her hand skates across the side of the bassinette, reaching to softly touch the mobile suspended above it. She accidentally knocks the on switch and a quiet lullaby begins to sing around the room.

The twinkling notes bring tears to my eyes.

I watch as she picks up a soft toy, a bunny just like in The Velveteen Rabbit, and brings it to her face, burying her nose in the fur.

"Was."

"What?" Her vacant eyes meet mine again.

"I *was* a father. My son," I stop to swallow a sob, "he passed away."

And just like that, life rushes back into the emerald depths of her irises. Her eyes are no longer glassy and blank, they're as deep as the ocean with unspoken questions.

"I don't understand," she whispers.

She does. She just doesn't want to. And I get it. I was like that for a long time. Still am, really.

Finally, I step across the threshold into the room, moving to the chest of drawers where picture frames are displayed on top of it. I pick up a photo that was taken not long after my son was born. I'm lying on the sofa with him on my chest. The downiness of his hair brushes against my chin as I smile widely down the camera lens. I can still feel the softness of it and smell the milkiness of his skin even now.

It's a perfect moment in time frozen in black and white.

I set it back down again.

"When he was twelve weeks old, he got sick," I tell her, closing my eyes as I'm assaulted by the memory. "He was fine when we put him to bed. There was nothing to suggest there was anything wrong, he'd been smiling that day and everything. But a few hours later, we were in the emergency room and by the morning, he was gone."

I don't even know I'm crying until I feel Summer-Raine's

fingers catching the tears on my cheeks. The touch of her skin on mine is more comforting than anything I've felt since the day it happened.

When I blink my eyes open, I find that she's crying as well.

"Don't cry for me, Summer-Raine."

She blinks up at me. "How can I not?"

Though I have no right to touch her, especially here, in my marital home, in he nursery of the son I had with my wife, I take her face in my hands. "You should hate me."

"I do." She says it so earnestly that I almost take a step back. "I hate you for having a child with a woman who wasn't me, but you don't deserve this. In no world would I ever wish upon you the pain of losing your child."

My gaze dips as more tears fall.

She lets me cry in silence for a little while, my hands still clutching her face. The feel of her is enough to ground me in the moment and stop me spiralling into the endless pit of grief that I fall into most hours of most days.

"What was his name?" she asks on a whisper.

"Oscar." I look at his little face in the photos on the chest of drawers beside us. At his button nose and cupid's bow lips. The way his lashes rest on his little cheeks as he sleeps. "After Oscar Wilde."

"He's so beautiful, Auden." She sniffs, bringing her hands up to cover mine where they still cup her face. "He looks just like you."

"Yeah? You think so?"

"I really do."

Her eyes stare into mine, deep and understanding. The

moment is so thick as we share in my grief that it would take an Obsidian knife blade to slice through it.

Several minutes pass before Summer-Raine coughs and steps out of my hold. The reality of our situation seems to return to her. I watch as the memory of my betrayal takes root, her eyes clouding over once more, the emptiness in them returning.

For a few long moments, I got to see her without the shields she erected two weeks ago. It was a privilege I didn't deserve, no matter what I've been through in the time she's been away.

But now, she's closing herself off from me and I feel it like a chill on my skin.

"Thank you for having us, but I think Max and I should go now."

My jaw ticks at the mention of that asshole.

"Is he your boyfriend?" I can't help myself. The question is out before I'm able to censor it and the severity of my voice goes undisguised as well.

She looks at me with narrowed eyes. "I can't see how that's any of your business."

I scoff, anger rising like a sea storm and I have no hope of stopping it. "It was only two weeks ago that you were showing up here to be with me."

She blinks, stunned.

I can see the confusion on her face. She doesn't understand how my mood has changed so quickly. She can't pinpoint the trigger that made me switch.

But she doesn't know just how much I've changed in the years since she's been gone. I'm not the jovial, easy-going

Auden I was back then. I'm cold and angry and cruel.

It's because of that, that I say, "You move on quickly, that's all. Or is that why it took you so long to come for me? Because you were fucking him already?"

The slap comes so fast I don't see it.

"Don't you dare talk to me that way," she spits. "You have no right to make those accusations. Not when you got married to another fucking woman while you were supposed to be waiting for me."

"She was pregnant," I roar.

"You should never have fucked her in the first place."

I shake my head, my hands ripping at the wild strands of my hair. I'm sure everyone can hear us, but I'm still lost in the red mist of my rage to give them any thought.

"You're unbelievable."

"I'm unbelievable?" She laughs in disbelief. "It was you fucking another woman while I was in rehab, wasn't it? What, did the two of you laugh together as you imagined me in that centre, going to therapy and taking my meds? Did you think it was funny that all I cared about was getting better for you? Were you excited for me to show up just so you could break my fucking heart? I bet you even planned for Cara to answer the door, huh? For maximum damage and all that."

I have her pinned up against the wall before she even has a chance to take a breath. "Listen to me right now, Summer-Raine, because I won't repeat myself."

Her chest heaves, her chin tilting in defiance but she doesn't respond. She just waits for me to continue.

"Cara was already pregnant when you left. I haven't slept

with her since before we ended things two years ago. Not on our wedding night, not on our honeymoon. I haven't been inside another woman since *you*, do you understand?"

"That's not what she said at the table."

"She fucking lied."

She shakes her head, looking away from me. She's still angry, it emanates from her like steam from a kettle as she fights to slow her breathing.

We're so close, our noses almost touching. I can taste the sweetness of her even from here, can smell the peaches on her skin and the citrus in her hair. The natural scent of her is better than any perfume Cara has ever owned.

Neither of us says anything as my words settle over her. She's fighting it, but I know that she believes me. I wouldn't lie to her and I think she knows that. Not about something as big as this.

But still, she doesn't give up the fight. Her body is still posed for combat, her glare is still deadly enough to stop my heart if she looked at me for long enough.

Finally, after a lifetime of staring at one another with so many words unspoken, she pushes away from the wall and tears herself away from me.

"I can't do this right now."

She runs from the room and I let her go. It isn't until my heart rate has returned to normal and the storm within me stops raging that I go after her.

I don't know when I'll next be able to see her and I can't leave things like this. My soul won't settle until things are somewhat okay between us.

I don't even acknowledge my wife as I rush through the main living area to the front door, running down the corridor to the elevator. I know that Summer-Raine has already left since she wasn't with the rest of the guests at the table, but I shouldn't be too long behind her. Hopefully, I'll catch up to her in the lobby.

And I do.

But I'd forgotten that she hadn't come here tonight alone. I don't know how, but Max's existence slipped my mind the moment Summer-Raine and I had started screaming at each other.

They're standing just inside the doors as they wait for a cab. Summer-Raine's back is to me, but Max is staring straight into my eyes. He holds my gaze for a moment and smirks. And then, as if in slow-motion, I watch as he tilts her chin up so that he can lower his lips to hers, wrapping her up in a kiss so intense that it can't possibly be the first time it's happened.

And, like a dagger to the heart, I watch as the woman who should be mine wraps her hands around his neck and kisses him back just as deeply.

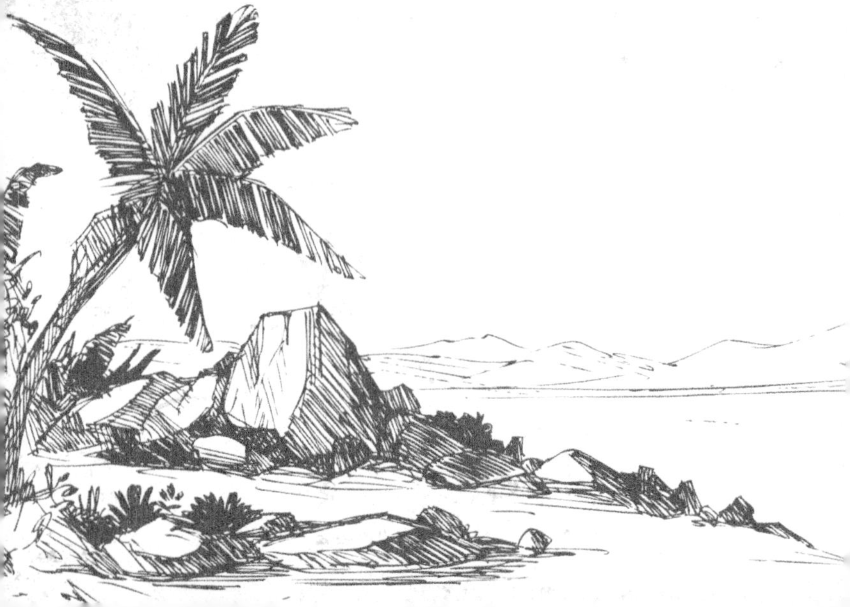

Chapter Twenty-Nine

SUMMER-RAINE

"What the hell are you doing?" I yell, coming to my senses and shoving Max away from me.

I stumble backwards, breathing hard as I fight to calm myself down. *I kissed him back.* Until now, I have only ever felt the kiss of one man. Only known the taste of Auden's lips and the touch of them against mine. And though he's married to another woman, I can't help but feel like I've betrayed him somehow.

It's stupid, I know. How can I betray a man who belongs to someone else? And yet, guilt festers in my gut like a stomach virus.

I haven't been inside another woman since you. He'd said that, hadn't he? Or did I imagine it? And if I didn't and he was telling the truth, that he really hasn't slept with Cara since before I left, does that mean he hasn't kissed her either?

Maybe the answer doesn't matter anyway.

He married her, that's the important thing. He put a ring on someone else's finger when he was supposed to be waiting for me. And that's betrayal enough.

But she was pregnant.

I wish I could silence the voice in my head that reminds me of that fact. Because it's so much easier to be angry with him for betraying me than it is to accept that he had a good reason for breaking my heart.

She was pregnant with his child, so he married her. It was the right thing to do. Or, at least, he thought it was. I've never been of the opinion that parents should be married for the misguided notion that their children will be better off even if the union is a miserable one, but I understand why Auden would be. After growing up with an absent father, of course he'd want to give his child as much security as he can offer.

But that doesn't stop it hurting.

I might understand his decision, but it still tears me apart. I still hate him for it. And truthfully, I don't think I'll ever forgive him, but that doesn't stop the guilt coursing through me that I let myself get lost in the kiss of another man.

For just a moment, I'd let myself believe it was Auden's lips on mine. But reality had come crashing down the second Max slipped his tongue into my mouth. It didn't feel right. Didn't taste the way it should have.

I turn away from Max just in time to meet a pair of devastated blue eyes. Auden stands inside the elevator, staring right at me. Had he seen Max kiss me? Had he seen me push him away?

I'm frozen. My brain tells me to run to him but my feet stay rooted to the ground. All I can do is stare back at him with panic in my eyes as the elevator doors close and he rides it back up to his floor.

"He was watching." Max shrugs with a sheepish grin. "I saw an opportunity and I took it."

"Opportunity for what?" I swing my gaze back round to him.

"To fuck with your man a bit."

My forehead creases in confusion as I blow out a frustrated sigh. "Why would you do that?"

"Didn't you see how he was looking at me at dinner?" I didn't. Mainly because I was doing everything I could to avoid looking Auden's way at all. "It was like he wanted to kill me. You don't have that kind of hatred for a man you don't know unless you see him as a threat. Guess I wanted to exploit that. Provoke him a little, you know?"

"Jesus, Max. It's not your place to do that. And besides, he's married to Cara. He isn't thinking about me at all."

Though after the argument I had with Auden tonight, I'm not entirely confident in the truth of that statement.

Max chuckles. "Trust me, Summer, that woman might be wearing his ring but it's not her he looks at like she's the centre of his entire universe."

My heart jumps at his words. Is that true? Does he really still look at me that way?

I shake myself clear of the thoughts. I can't allow myself to wonder about stuff like that. It'll only cause me more pain in the end. Because, no matter his reasons, he's still married to another woman. And I can't see how that's going to change.

"Look, I appreciate you coming here with me tonight, I really do, but you had no right to do what you did. This was supposed to help me find closure, but it's only made me feel worse. Because now I'm the one left feeling like I've done something wrong."

He reaches for me but I flinch and his hands fall back to his sides. I don't want him to touch me.

The taste of him is still on my lips and I itch with the need to scrub it off. If I was any other woman, I'd probably be elated to have had a man like Max kiss me the way he just did. But not me. His touch was too foreign, too unfamiliar. *Wrong.* The only way that kiss could have felt right was if Auden was the one who had given it to me.

And maybe that makes me pathetic, I don't know. Frankly, I don't care at this point. Because even though he legally belongs to another woman, my soul still knows that his heart belongs to me.

"Sum, I'm sorry." Max hangs his head. "That wasn't my intention at all."

"You know what, it's fine. Let's just—"

I'm interrupted by my phone ringing. I pull it out, brow crinkling in concern when I see my sister's name flashing on the screen. It's almost eleven pm. She never rings this late.

"Summer?" Winter's voice is shaky and solemn. "It's Mom and Dad."

Burying your parents is a strange thing to do when your feelings towards them are mostly fuelled by resentment. It feels wrong somehow, like I shouldn't be the one to do it. Maybe one of their business colleagues or highbrow socialite friends would have been the better choice.

And yet, I find myself holding a fist of dirt over their shared grave anyway.

Is this the point that I'm supposed to make a speech? Or, at the very least, say some long emotional goodbye to them in my head, tell them all the things that I'll miss about them and thank them for everything they've given me in life?

Truth is, I can't think of anything of note that they've given me. Sure, I have a trust fund and now half of a pretty hefty inheritance, but it was never money I wanted from them.

It was love.

But I haven't seen them since I was eighteen and I have minimal memories from before then that evoke any kind of positive reaction within me. All I have are the scathing criticisms they'd throw at me across the dinner table and the emptiness that has always lingered inside me from being a child unworthy of her parents' affection.

And though I am now twenty-five with friends, a career and a purpose, I am still very much that child who is desperate to be loved.

I cast a glance to Winter, who stands on the opposite side of the grave. Her eyes are closed, her brow furrowed. Looks like she's having the same difficulty I am.

A hand slides into mine.

It's soft, it's warm, it's familiar. As familiar to me as my own hand.

I blink into the sparkling blue depths of Auden's eyes as he smiles down at me reassuringly. He's here. In Islamorada. At my parents' funeral. But why?

It doesn't matter how much time passes between us, if you need me, I will always come for you.

They're the words he'd spoken to me two years ago. I remember like it was yesterday. I didn't really believe the truth in them back then, but I guess there's no denying it now.

I didn't even think he knew that my parents had died at all. It certainly wasn't me who told him about their car accident.

I didn't ask him to come, but he's here anyway. Holding my hand and smiling as if to tell me that I'm strong enough to do this.

I hold his gaze as my fist opens and the dirt that I'd been clinging to falls six feet down to scatter across their coffin.

Even now, after everything that's happened, it's like he can sense what I need before I know myself. He tugs gently on my hand as he leads me away, through the graveyard to a wooden bench sitting quietly beneath the weeping branches of a willow tree.

"You're here," I whisper, sitting down and looking through the small gaps in the leaves to watch the end of my parents' service, though I'm too far away to hear anything.

Auden shifts from foot to foot with his hands shoved into his pockets. "Winter called me."

I roll my eyes. "Of course, she did."

"Are you mad?"

"She needs to stop interfering, but no. I'm not mad."

His shoulders visibly relax and he finally takes the seat beside me, but he doesn't touch me again. He clasps his hands together between his legs as he leans forward and rests his elbows on his knees. The golden sunlight catches on his wedding band.

I look away.

"How are you coping with everything?" he asks, staring straight ahead.

I peek at him through the corner of my eyes, studying all the ways the years have changed him. He still has that boyish charm that makes him seem ageless, but there are creases in his skin and a lasting sadness to his features that weren't there when he was eighteen. His eyes don't sparkle like they used to either.

The changes are so subtle, I doubt anyone would notice them. But I do. I notice everything about him.

"I'm okay."

He turns to me, brows raised sceptically. "It's okay if you're not, Summer-Raine."

"No, I really am." But even as I say it, my eyes sting and a single tear spills inexplicably down my cheek. I brush it away, sniffing. "I don't know why I'm crying. It's not like they were a huge part of my life. I didn't even like them."

More tears leak from my eyes and I bury my face in my hands as they fall. Auden sits silently beside me not speaking or touching, but comforting me just by being there.

"I don't understand," I sob. "Why am I sad?"

He reaches for me then, taking my hand and settling it in his lap where he rubs his thumb over my knuckles in small soothing circles.

"Because they were your parents," he says simply. "And even though you didn't like them, you still loved them."

"They didn't deserve for me to love them."

"Probably not, but you did anyway."

For just a moment, I let myself forget that he's married to someone else. Sucking in a long breath, I rest my head on his shoulder and use the woodsy smell of him to calm myself down.

Our hands are still clasped together, resting on his legs. It takes everything in me not to splay my fingers out across his thigh like I own it, like he's mine and I can touch him whenever and however I want. He must feel me twitch because he turns over my hand and traces the lines on my palm with his fingertips.

"Where are you staying tonight?" I ask so quietly it's almost impossible to hear over the gentle rustling of leaves as the breeze blows through them.

"I'm not. I'm driving back home tonight."

"What?" I sit up and gape at him. The drive between Islamorada and Tallahassee takes eight hours. If he left tonight, he wouldn't make it home by tomorrow morning and that's not even factoring in breaks. "You can't do that."

"It's fine." He shrugs. "I've got nowhere to stay anyway."

"Stay at the house." The words are out before I've really considered them.

"Yeah?" The smile he gives me is small and shy.

"Yeah. You drove all the way out here just to make sure I'm okay, giving you a place to lay your head tonight is the least I can do."

He worries his bottom lip between his teeth as he thinks it over.

"Winter and the boys will be there too," I say, sensing that the reason he hasn't immediately agreed is because he's concerned about it being just the two of us. "So, there'll be a buffer between us." I try a laugh, but it falls flat.

He finally nods, though his eyes are sad. "Yeah, okay. That'll be great, thanks."

Later, when he's gone to bed in one of the guest rooms that I had made up for him, I try my hardest not to knock on his door and beg for him to sleep with me instead. To let me bury my face in his neck and fall asleep to the sound of his breathing like I did the last time he spent the night in this house.

Instead, I take a seat in the wicker chair on my balcony where we used to sit curled up to watch the sunset together. And with tears in my eyes, I watch the sky bleed on my own.

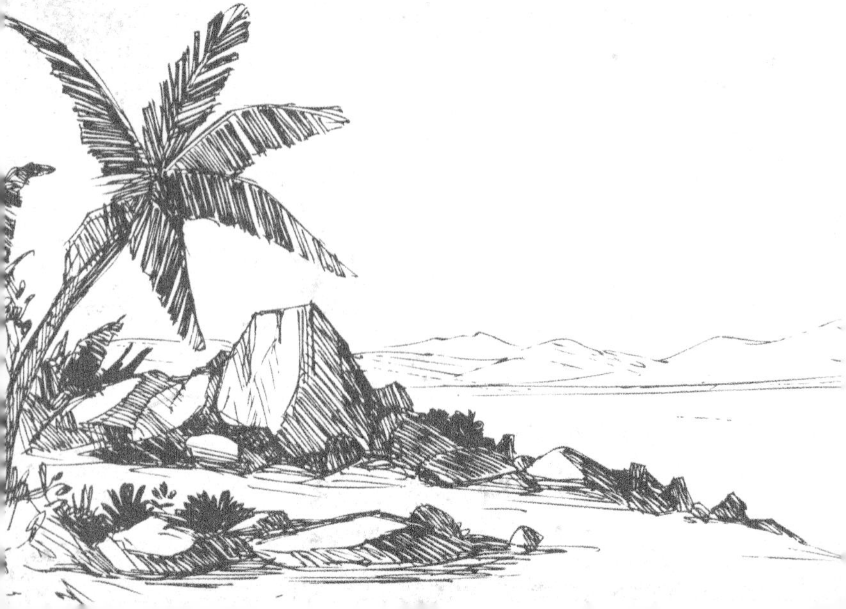

Chapter Thirty
AUDEN

*D*on't go to her.

I say it to myself over and over again as I lay on the bed in Summer-Raine's guest room and stare at the ceiling. But no matter how many times I repeat the words, the urge to make the walk down the hall to her bedroom is too much to bear.

Though we're on opposite sides of the house, I'm sure I can smell her peachy sweetness from here. It entices me, taunts me. The scent is so damn irresistible to me, I'm like a dog with a bone.

Don't go to her.

I say it again, out loud this time, as if hearing it will make it easier to resist her pull. But it doesn't. It does nothing.

I just want to make sure she's okay, I tell myself as I swing my legs out of bed and pad down the hallway to her door. She buried her parents today. It would be wrong of me not to check on her.

But there's no answer when I knock. So, I knock again, but

still nothing.

Maybe this is where I should turn around and go back to my room, take the silence as a sign that she's sleeping and try and ignore the irrepressible citrus scent of her as it drifts to me as if caught in the breeze.

But I don't. I crack open the door and step inside.

Summer-Raine's bedroom is just as I remember. Literary postcards still cover every square inch of the walls and the sheets on her bed are still the same pastel shade of blue that they were seven years ago.

They're empty though, the sheets. Summer-Raine isn't wrapped up in them and I take that to mean she's somewhere else in the house when a draft alerts me to the balcony doors being open.

The wooden floorboards creak as I step through the doorway to the place that holds a handful of my happiest memories. As soon as I feel the warm ocean air on my skin, it's like I'm transported back in time.

Suddenly, I'm eighteen again. I can feel no wedding band on my finger, Mama is still alive and I still have the heart and love of Summer-Raine. She's still mine. No complications, no complexities. She's mine and that's all there is to it.

"Auden?" her surprised voice cuts through the gentle breeze and reality sets back in.

Words escape me now that I'm here, now that she's looking at me with those wide eyes and sad smile that makes my heart ache every fucking time I see it. I can't remember the last time she showed me her real smile. God, the things I'd do to be able to see it again.

"Mind if I sit?" I motion to the chair beside her and fold myself into it when she nods.

The sky is still a painting of vibrant reds and purples, though the dark stretch of night isn't far away from spilling black all over it.

We watch it for a while, the way we used to do, though she's not curled up in my lap like she would have been back when she was mine.

We don't say anything. We don't need to. We just live in this moment together, breathing in the memories of a time when things were simpler.

"Do you ever wish we could go back?" Summer-Raine asks.

"Everyday."

She sighs and it's this sorry wistful sound that makes me want to cry. "Me too."

I look down at my hands and the gold ring on my finger. That awful piece of metal that connects me to a woman I don't want to be with. God, I ache to wrench it off my finger and hurl it into the depths of the ocean.

"Do you love her?" She asks it so quietly I'm not even sure I hear her right.

"What?"

"Cara." She refuses to look at me, her hands rubbing nervously together in her lap, like she's scared to hear my answer. "Do you love her?"

I don't answer straight away. Truth is, it's not a question with a clear-cut answer.

I can't stand Cara as a person and I've never been *in* love with her, but when you have a child with a woman and then go through the shared trauma of losing that child, it's difficult not to carry some feelings of affection towards her.

"Not in the way I love you," I say finally.

I hear her gasp despite her attempt to disguise it with a cough. The way she's looking at me, like I'm breaking her heart and holding it in place all at once, steals the very breath from my lungs.

I feel it too. That ache in my chest that only ever exists around her. Like I'm shattering into a million tiny pieces despite only ever feeling whole when I'm in her presence. It's dizzying.

"Then why are you still married to her?"

I turn away and look out over the sea. The sun has completely set now, the only natural light coming from the celestial glow of the moon. It dances across the waves and distracts me from the conversation just enough to get my heartbeat under control.

I hate talking about my wife with Summer-Raine.

"What kind of man would I be to divorce a woman who's still mourning the death of her baby?"

Beside me, Summer-Raine releases a shaky breath. "But what about you, Auden?"

"What about me?" I look at her again and find her jade eyes sparkling with unshed tears.

She shakes her head mournfully. "What about what's best for you? What about what you want?"

"It doesn't matter what I want."

She leaps out of her seat and comes to stand in between my legs, crouching down to bring herself eyelevel with me. "Of course, it does."

Her hand raises to cup my cheek. I don't even think she realises how easy she finds it to touch me, but every time we see each other, we somehow always find a way to physically connect. It feels unnatural to be together and not touch.

"You're grieving too," she goes on, her voice rich with sorrowful compassion. "Your needs matter too. You can't always live your life for others, Auden."

"I don't."

"Yes, you do." Her thumb strokes softly over my cheekbone. "You stayed with me even when I made you miserable. After my suicide attempt, you dropped everything to come and look after me. You were going to choose your college major based on what would help your mother the most, you married a woman you didn't love because you got her pregnant and now, you're staying with her because you're scared of adding to her pain even though being with her clearly makes you miserable. When will you start making decisions based on what *you* want?"

At some point during her speech, she'd began to cry. She stops, heaving in a breath and then asks the question I know she really wants the answer to, "Why won't you leave her and be with me?"

"Please don't ask me that."

"Why?" Her hand falls away from my face. "Why not?"

"Because I can't!"

"Yes, you can." Tears fall freely down her face, violent and relentless. "You just don't want to."

"That's not fair." I stand and clutch her by the shoulders, looking straight into her devastated eyes as I speak. "I can't do that to her, Summer-Raine. I can't hurt her like that."

"But you're hurting *me*," she yells, her voice echoing around us as powerful as the tide washing waves up on the shore below us.

"I can't win, can I? If I file for divorce, I'll hurt Cara and if I don't, I'll hurt you. There's no situation that I can win here, so what exactly do you want me to do?"

"I want you to choose me."

God, I can't bear this. The pain in her voice, the questions she's asking, the answers she's demanding from me. It's too much.

"I can't." I close my eyes, wishing there was something I could do to make this end somehow. "Christ, you think I don't want to? But I made her a promise when I married her."

"You made me a promise too, Auden. Or did you forget?"

I collapse back into the chair with my head in my hands.

"I don't know what to do, Summer-Raine. This is so hard. Why does everything have to be so fucking hard?" I slam the heel of my hand into my forehead.

I hear the scraping of chair legs across the wooden floorboards as she drags her seat closer to mine and flops down into it.

She's calmed down a little, it seems. The tears have dried on her cheeks, which are still flushed from her frustration but slowly starting to regain their usual colour. She sits beside me in silence and stares out at the sea beyond us.

My God, does she have to be so beautiful?

Sadness pours from her, so visceral I can almost see it. And when the wind rolls over the ocean, it catches in her hair and blows the strands around her face like a glowing halo of gold.

She's a weeping angel. Breathtaking, despondent and divine.

"I think of you every day," I find myself saying, though the words flow freely and without thought. "The moment I wake up until the moment I fall asleep, it's you who plagues my every thought. I wonder what you're doing, if you're okay, if you're with *him*." I growl that last word, jealousy overwhelming me as I remember watching Max kiss her.

I'd been so furious in that moment, so broken by what I'd witnessed, that I'd immediately turned away. And then I'd gone back up to the apartment and gotten myself so blindingly drunk that I'd done something unforgiveable.

I don't remember it. I don't know how it started or how I even let it happen at all.

All I know is that I woke up the next morning with Cara naked and victorious beside me.

"I get lost in memories of your touch on my skin and the way you felt beneath my hands. I remember the sunsets and the poetry, the brightness of your smile and the way you used to look at me like I was the only good thing left in the world. You don't look at me like that anymore. I even still carry that piece of lavender I had frozen into glass around in my wallet. I still take it out and touch it every time I watch the sun setting."

I can feel her looking at me, but I don't turn to meet her eyes. I keep talking though, just staring straight ahead into the darkness.

"It hurts me, you know? To have you so near and not be able to touch you the way I ache to. You probably don't think it does, but it destroys me knowing how close we came to finally being together. My heart broke that day too, it really did. And yet, I can't allow myself to wish that things were different. Because if that accident hadn't happened two years ago, my son would never have been born. And I can't wish for that, no matter how much pain it caused me to lose him. But that doesn't stop me loving you, Summer-Raine. It doesn't stop me hoping that one day, we'll have our chance again."

"I don't understand," she whispers. "Why not now?"

"My son hasn't even been dead a year. How could I leave his mother all alone while she's still drowning in the depths of her grief? I can't do what my dad did to Mama. I can't be my father, I just can't."

She doesn't say anything, not for a long time. So long, in fact, that I'm sure she's fallen asleep, until I chance a glance at her and see that she's got her knees tucked into her chest as she rests her chin on top of them and stares out into the distance.

She's given up the fight. It's evident in the hunch of her shoulders and the paleness of her skin, as if the life is draining right out of her.

I get it. I feel that way too.

"There's a word for people like you, you know?" she says, her monotonous voice is flat and completely devoid of emotion.

"What?" I raise an eyebrow in question.

"Martyr."

And with that, she turns and heads back inside. I hear the shower turn on in her bathroom, but I don't go back to the guest room right away. Instead, I let myself breathe in the salty air on Summer-Raine's balcony for the last time.

Once the house has been sold, there will be no reason for her to come back here. No reason for me either, since Mama's house was sold to an architect looking to flip it shortly after her death. There's nothing left for either of us here in Islamorada.

Selfishly, I wish that we could have forgotten our situation for just one evening and sat curled up together in the same chair the way we used to. To say have said goodbye to our special place in each other's arms, surrounded by the sounds of the sea and the memories we made here.

To have had just one more magic moment out here before I return to life without her. To the life that makes me miserable because every day I wake up without the woman I love by my side. Because, even though I meant everything I said about needing to be there for Cara, there's a part of me that believes I don't deserve a happily ever after of my own.

So, was Summer-Raine right when she called me a martyr?

Yeah, I think she probably was.

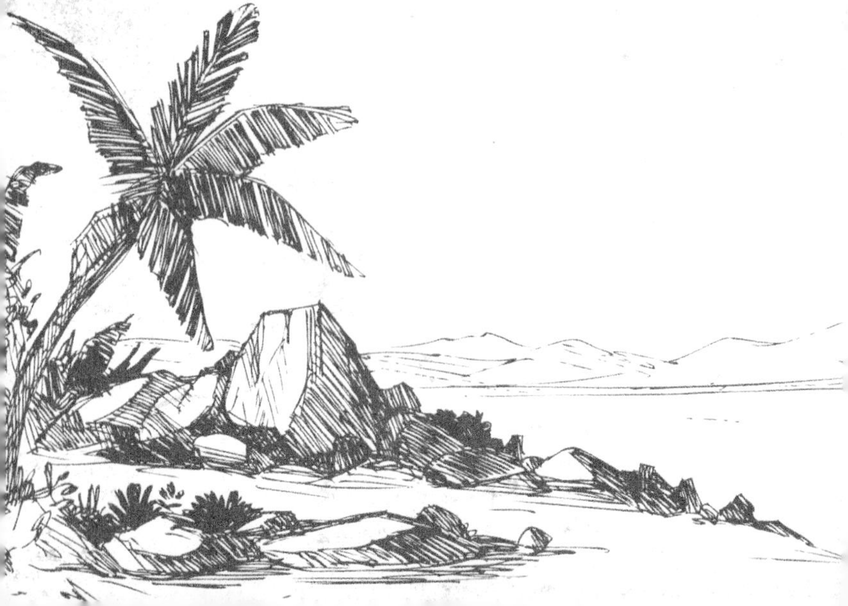

Chapter Thirty-one

SUMMER-RAINE

It's been a month since I buried my parents.

And a month since I saw Auden last.

He left my room that night after I'd hidden myself away in the bathroom, and began his drive back up to Tallahassee the next morning while I was still asleep. We haven't spoken since.

Being with him out there on the balcony was almost as painful as the moment I learnt he was married. Because it had always been the place where we were at peace. Nothing bad could ever touch us out there. When we were together on that small strip of wood, wrapped up in each other's arms as waves crashed and gulls beat their wings in the sky above us, we were untouchable. It was our safe space.

It was ours.

But now the sanctity of that sacred place has been lost. And yeah, okay, maybe that's on me for begging him to do things that I knew went against every one of his instincts. His need to save and protect is what makes him the person he is. It's both the best and worst thing about him, his selfish selflessness.

It's hard to hate him for it.

I do though.

I hate him because despite everything, I still love him with every shattered shard of my soul.

A knock at my office door has my head snapping up to find Marlowe leaning against the doorframe with a glint in her eye. I'm supposed to be balancing the accounts for the foundation and drafting ideas for a big fundraiser we're planning to host next month, but in two hours I have achieved next to nothing.

"Distracted?" Mar asks, coming round to perch on the edge of my desk.

She knows full well that I'm distracted. I've been distracted since the day I showed up on Auden's doorstep only to be greeted by Cara and her diamond ring instead.

"Do you ever wish you'd never met somebody?"

She looks down at me with sad eyes. "Yeah."

Of course, she does. Her ex-husband, Tyler, was an abusive asshole of epic proportions. For a long time after learning about how he treated Mar, I'd struggled with my guilt for encouraging their relationship back in high school.

But no one really knows what happens when the doors are closed, I guess.

Doesn't make me feel any better about it though.

"But, Sum, you might think you do, but you don't feel that way about Auden. Not really."

"Yeah, I do. At least if we'd never met, I wouldn't have

this permanent emptiness in my heart now, like there's a hole that can never be filled. No, fuck that, it's no hole. It's a damn chasm."

"You'd really give up everything you had when you were kids? Sum, you forget that I knew you back then. I saw with my own eyes how happy you and Auden were. And yeah, maybe everything did go to shit. But isn't it better that you got to have that experience, that all-consuming, death-defying love, than to have never had it at all?"

I shake my head. "Mar, if I could go back to that day on the beach when he spoke to me for the first time, instead of sitting there reciting fucking poetry, I'd tell him to leave me the hell alone."

She holds my gaze for a long moment, conveying with her eyes what she doesn't say out loud.

That I'm a liar.

"You wish you'd never met me?"

I gasp as the hurt voice cuts through the room. Turning, I find Auden staring at me with pain in his eyes from the threshold of my office. I stare back at him in shock.

Four weeks since we last spoke and this is the moment he shows up?

"I told you to wait outside," Mar scowls, marching over to him and poking him hard in the chest.

Auden ignores her. "You seriously wish that you'd never met me?"

"How long have you been listening?" I ask, crossing my arms defensively in front of me.

"Doesn't matter." He strides towards me. Long, purposeful

steps that make me lean further back in my chair. "Answer the question, Summer-Raine."

I ignore him.

He doesn't get to choose another woman over me, no matter how gallant his reasoning, and demand answers from me.

"Answer me," he growls through gritted teeth.

I meet his glare with a defiant one of my own.

"Yes."

I don't mean it though. I realise it as soon as the word leaves me mouth.

Auden visibly crumples in front of me. Like a scrunched-up piece of paper, he folds in on himself as if I've punched him in the gut.

Marlowe was right.

No matter the pain I'm in right now, I'd rather drown in it for a thousand life times than have never known the sheer magic of Auden's love at all. Those handful of months that we were together, *truly* together, were a miracle most people never get to experience.

Some spend their lives chasing it, only for it to always remain out of reach.

Others are so mystified by the concept that they waste away trying to define it or explain it in words as if it can be done.

It reminds me of the poem that started it all. The one Auden and I recited on the sand in Islamorada, holding tubs of melted pistachio ice cream and looking at one another like our souls were finally home.

When it comes, will it come without warning,
Just as I'm picking my nose?
Will it knock on my door in the morning,
Or tread in the bus on my toes?
Will it come like a change in the weather?
Will its greeting be courteous or rough?
Will it alter my life altogether?
O tell me the truth about love.

At the beginning, Auden's love swept me away like a whirlwind. It spun me until all I could see was him and his eyes and the dimples in his cheeks. We were the only two people who existed in the world. It was just him and me, lost in the vortex of our infatuation.

And then one day, the turbulence came.

I remember it like it was yesterday, that numbness that settled in my soul and ruined everything. It shook me loose from the safety of his storm and I fell from the sky alone, only to be replaced by another woman several years later.

But I wouldn't give up my time in that tornado for anything. I know that now.

Auden takes a long, heavy breath before he rights himself and turns blazing eyes on to me. I don't know how, but the inferno flaming in his irises forces me out of my seat and brings me to stand before him.

"You don't mean that."

I dip my eyes in shame and whisper, "No, I don't."

"Good." He heaves a sigh of relief. "Because I came to tell you something." His eyes swing over to Marlowe who has apparently been watching our exchange the entire time from the corner of the room. "Is there somewhere else we can talk?"

"Yeah." I nod, trying not to throw up as I wonder what on earth he has to talk to me about.

Without saying anything else, mainly because I'm too nervous to speak, I guide him through the building to the private staircase that leads up to my apartment, without once looking back to check that he's following.

He is though, as becomes evident when I feel the brush of his breath on my neck as I unlock the front door. He's not even standing that close to me and yet my body is hyper-aware of him. Every miniscule movement he makes I can feel on my skin like he's touching me directly.

All the drapes in the apartment are still closed despite it being early afternoon, so it's hard to make out much as I step from the well-lit hallway into the darkness of the room.

"Why aren't the curtains open?" Auden asks gently, walking over to one of the large wood-framed windows and throwing open the drapes.

"I don't like the light anymore," I answer simply, my eyes watering from the sudden assault of the daylight.

"Oh, baby."

"Don't call me that," I snap immediately.

He ignores me, turning away to take in the place I now call home. My old apartment was all glossy finishes and luxury furniture, as insisted upon by my late mother, but my new home couldn't be more different.

It's a vast, open space, with everything but the bathroom existing in just one room. The walls are exposed brick that have faded in colour throughout the years, bare lightbulbs dangle from wires above us and the old floorboards are covered by a large vintage rug that I picked up second-hand. My queen bed has a headboard upcycled from someone's tossed out rattan furniture, and is dressed in white waffle knit sheets and throw pillows in every colour the human eye can see.

It's eclectic and rustic and *me*.

Auden skims his fingers across the countertops in the kitchen with a look on his face that I can't interpret. He picks up a mug from the side and turns it over in his hands.

"This is cool," he says, studying the hand painted figures dancing together across the ceramic.

"Thanks. One of my regulars made it for me."

I smile, remembering the day I was given the gift. It had been a shitty morning about three weeks ago and the weight of living without Auden had been sitting heavy on my heart.

Connor, a military vet struggling to adjust to civilian life, came to my office and slipped the mug into my hands without saying a word. He didn't need to. The fact that he'd wanted to make something for me like that, something *at all*, made me smile during a time that I didn't think I'd ever smile again. I'll be forever grateful to him for that.

And now I won't drink my coffee out of any other cup.

"You're doing amazing things, Summer-Raine."

His eyes sparkle with warmth and I turn away, unable to bare it.

"You can't look at me like that."

"Like what?"

"Like you're proud of me."

He laughs quietly and the sound brings goosebumps to my skin.

"I am proud of you, baby, so fucking proud."

A growl rumbles in my throat, but he ignores it and keeps talking, walking slowly across the room towards me. I'm still not looking at him, but I trace his movements by listening to the sound of his footsteps. My heart beats harder the closer they get.

"I followed your blog, you know? I read every entry, still do. I've set it so that I'm notified as soon as you upload a new one. For two years, I've poured over every word you've written, cried with you, laughed with you, longed for you so fucking much that at times it made life unbearable."

He's close to me now. I can see the toes of his leather shoes, can taste his familiar scent on my tongue.

"The day you came home from rehab, all I wanted to do was come and find you. See your face. Touch your skin. But I knew that the second I did, I'd have to tell you what I'd done. That I'd married Cara, that she'd been pregnant with the child I always thought I'd have with you. And I couldn't do it. Because I knew that once you found out, your heart wouldn't belong to me anymore. It was selfish, I know, but the thought of you not loving me anymore was intolerable. For that, baby, for *everything*, I'm so fucking sorry."

His footsteps stop in front of me. And yet, I still can't look at him.

I don't want him to see the pain in my eyes, the way they're burning with unshed tears. If all I have left is my pride, then I'm going to cling to it with all the strength I have.

"Look at me, Summer-Raine."

"No." But instead of the word sounding strong like I'd intended, it comes out soft and weak.

"Baby, look at me."

He doesn't give me a choice. With the tips of his finger and thumb, he tilts my chin up and angles my head so that I have no option but to stare right into the glorious blue of his eyes.

"I'm leaving her."

My heart stops. "What?"

"I'm leaving Cara."

I stumble backwards, my knees giving out. Auden swoops me into his arms and crushes me against his chest before I have a chance to fall.

The thunderous beat of his heart thuds against me and it's just as wild and out of rhythm as my own.

I can't believe what I'm hearing.

"As soon as I leave here, I'm going to tell her," he says, stroking his hand through my hair. The way he's holding me, clinging to me so strongly yet softly at the same time, it's as if he's scared to let go out of fear that I'll disappear.

"She doesn't know?"

I feel the shake of his head above me. "I've been staying at Fred's for the past week while I've been thinking about everything. We haven't had the conversation yet."

I nod, but say nothing.

This is all too much. I'm so overwhelmed by what he's telling me that I'm not even sure this is happening at all. I'd be more inclined to believe that I'm having another delusion, the kind my medication helps prevent. That this is all just a figment of my imagination and I'm making it up in my head.

He's really leaving Cara?

It feels too good to be true.

But when I look back into his eyes, it's only sincerity I see.

"Summer-Raine, you were right about everything, I was just too stubborn to see it. I thought leaving Cara after losing our son would be the worst thing I could ever do, that I'd be just as bad as my dad if I did. But in the weeks following your parents' funeral, I couldn't stop thinking about what you said."

He pauses and takes a long breath.

"There was this one night, I can't even remember exactly what it was really that sparked it, but Cara and I were eating dinner in total silence like we always do and something in my head just clicked. I finally fucking realised that forcing myself to stay in a marriage where neither one of us is happy isn't helping anyone at all."

His thumb shoots out to catch a tear as it rolls down my cheek. I didn't even realise I'd started crying.

"You chose her over me," I choke, remembering how shattering it was when he refused to even entertain the idea of being with me a month ago.

"No, baby." He holds my face in his warm hands and softly brushes his thumbs across my cheeks, soothing me. "Even if I decided to stay in the marriage, it would be impossible for me to choose her over you. Because, Summer-Raine, there is no option for me but you. It's *you* who has my heart, it's *you* who owns my soul. I belong to *you*. I will only ever belong to *you*. My marriage was born out of obligation and it has never been anything more than that."

I sniff, gazing up at him.

His lips are so close to mine that if I angled myself just an inch closer towards him, I'd be able to touch them. I wonder if they're still as soft as they were the last time I felt them. I wonder if he still tastes as sweet, or if he's been soured by all the trauma he's endured over the years.

He's looking at my lips too.

And his eyes take on that kind of dark, hooded look they used to get whenever he was about to kiss me. His tongue darts out to wet his lips and then he's closing the distance between us.

But I can't let it happen.

With all the self-control I'm capable of, I set my hands on his chest and gently push him away.

"I can't kiss you while another woman still wears your ring, Auden," I whisper.

He was moments away from kissing me. After all this time, after everything that's happened, the man who I've loved since I was seventeen was about to kiss me. And I stopped him.

He nods once, then clears his throat into a clenched fist. "Yeah, I get it."

Even though I pushed him away, I can't stop myself reaching for him again and taking his hands in my own. Now that I've felt his touch again, I'll die if I have to endure another moment without it.

"Tonight," he says, walking towards my front door. "I'll be back tonight, if you'll have me?"

I laugh, because I've never heard a more ridiculous question. "Always."

"And then you'll be mine again?"

"I already am, quarterback." I smile through happy tears. "I already am."

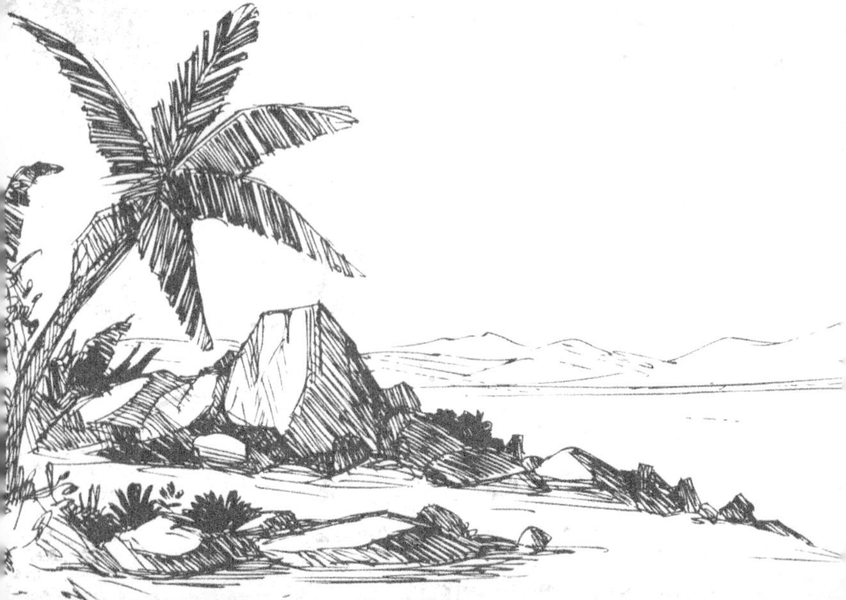

Chapter Thirty-Two
SUMMER-RAINE

I should have known something was wrong.

Rain has been pelting at the windows for hours now, but it hasn't brought me peace the way it usually does. Normally, I find it grounding. Today, it's only added to the strange, sinking sensation I feel in my stomach.

They say you should always trust your gut and yet, like an idiot, I ignore it.

Instead, I busy myself in the kitchen making dinner for me and Auden. I've never been particularly skilled at cooking, but I'm trying my best. There are meatballs heating on the stove and I know it's not the most romantic meal, but I figure we can re-enact the spaghetti scene from Lady and the Tramp. It's the kind of thing we used to do when we were younger.

I've laid out a blanket on the floor surrounded by tealights and pillar candles in varying sizes. I bought his favourite red wine and a cheesecake for dessert that we can feed to each other before he makes love to me in the bed where I've slept alone for so many years.

But eight o'clock passes with no sign of him. Then nine, then ten.

The food is cold on the counter and the candles have long burned out.

By eleven, I've opened the bottle of merlot and am sipping from my second glass.

When midnight strikes, I change out of the black dress I'd put on just for him and into baggy sweats and an old t-shirt.

He's not coming.

I should have taken notice of that stirring in my gut, that twinge in my spine that said something wasn't quite right. I shouldn't have let myself get swept up in the fantasy of a happily ever after, because that's all it is. A fantasy.

It's a lesson I thought I'd learnt when I found out about his marriage. But apparently, I didn't. Because I've spent the last several hours barely able to function with all the excited energy coursing through my body like caffeine at the thought of being with Auden forever.

It's the middle of the night when there's finally a knock at the door.

I don't hear it at first. At some point I must have fallen asleep, because I wake up on the blanket I'd laid out on the floor with backache from the hard surface. I guess it was the rhythmic thudding that rose me.

Disorientated, I drag myself to the front door and open it.

Auden stands before me, his hair wet from the rain and sticking to the sides of his face. The darkness in his expression, the downturn of his plush lips and dullness to his eyes confirms that my instincts were right all along.

Whatever I thought would happen tonight, the spaghetti kisses and lovemaking, isn't going to.

"Good of you to show up."

I rest my hip on the side of the doorframe and look up at him with seething eyes. He scrubs a trembling hand down his face, before pushing past me and into my apartment.

I watch as he takes in the setup, the candles and the cushions and the wine. And then, with no warning, he picks up one of the glasses and hurls it at the wall. The resulting smash is ear-splitting.

But I don't flinch.

I'm used to it anyway. The sound of a breaking heart is remarkably similar and I've heard it enough that I'm desensitized.

I'm frozen in place by the door as Auden claws at his hair and roars as he falls to his knees.

"She's pregnant."

And just like that, the world around me collapses. If I thought I knew pain before, it was nothing compared to this. This blinding agony, it flows like venom in my veins. I can feel it poisoning me, shutting down my organs and stealing the very essence of my soul.

By the time the words have settled, all that's left of me is a broken shell.

Because not only has he built my hopes up just to shatter them again, he's lied.

"You said you hadn't slept with her." My voice is barely a

whisper, but he hears it all the same.

"I hadn't."

"Then how is she pregnant?"

When he looks at me, his eyes tired and devoid of colour, I see it. The guilt. The shame.

"The night of the dinner party, I saw you kiss Max," he says, gritting his teeth as if he can't bear to say that name. "I was so jealous, so fucking possessive of you in that moment that I swear I could've killed him. But I didn't. I got drunk instead. And when I woke up in the morning, Cara was naked beside me."

I can't stop the horrified gasp that leaves me.

I stagger backwards, my legs collapsing underneath me. With my head in my hands, I slide down the wall and hug my knees to my chest.

He didn't see me push Max away.

Auden stays rooted in the centre of the apartment, keeping me locked within his unrelenting stare.

"I don't have any memory of it at all. Everything after you left that night is a black void. I have no recollection. Nothing."

His chest heaves. I can hear his heavy breaths resonating around the room, the intensity, the force of them. They're so very different to mine.

I don't feel like I can breathe at all.

I don't think I'll ever breathe again.

And then something bizarre happens. I start laughing. This high-pitched hysterical laugh that sounds almost like a scream goes on and on until tears are streaming down my cheeks.

"I should have known."

Auden watches me with wide eyes, hesitant, almost wary. As if I'm a wild animal whose actions he can't predict. He's right to look at me that way. I don't know what I'll do either.

"What?" He blinks.

"Me and you," I say through the hysteria. "We were always a pipedream, weren't we? Guys like you don't end up with girls like me, the fucked-up ones with more baggage than you can carry. No, it's women like Cara you all go for in the end. Joke's on me for ever thinking it could be any different."

"Don't do that," he growls, storming over to me and crouching down to my level. "Don't say shit like that. It's not true, you know it's not true."

"Isn't it?" I shake my head. "So, you're not here to tell me that you're staying with her?"

He immediately looks away.

I scoff. "That's what I thought."

He says nothing and the silence gives me a chance to calm down. I take in long breaths until my heartbeat slows and my blood stops thrumming in my ears.

And then, once my body is finally quiet, I resign myself to what needs to happen now.

"We can't see each other anymore," I whisper into the dead air between us.

"What?" His voice is cold and rough. It's nothing like the caramel-smooth lilt that I'm used to hearing from him.

"When you walk out that door, it's for the last time," I say, staring straight into his eyes so he can see just how serious I am. "I mean it, Auden. This is it now. There'll be no contact, no calls to my sister to check up on me, no showing up to be my hero when I'm in a bad way. When you walk out that door," I take a breath, preparing myself, "it's the last time I'll say goodbye to you."

He stands up abruptly, rearing back. The look in his eyes is a deadly combination of menacing and wild.

"That's what you want?" he asks in disbelief.

"*What I want?*" I yell, standing to glare up at him. "*You think this is what I want?* It's not even close to what I want. What I want is to be with the man I love. For the guy who told me two years ago that he'd wait for me to have been telling the goddamn truth. To not have come home, ready to finally give you the love I always thought you deserved, to find you married to another fucking woman."

He shakes his head, refusing to hear the truth in my words. "And what, we can't be in each other's lives at all? We can't even be friends?"

"No, Auden." My voice is quiet now, almost calm. I can feel myself disassociating, drifting outside of my body to watch the scene like a ghost in the corner of the room. "I can't watch from the side lines as another woman lives the life I want with the man who was supposed to be mine. It would destroy me more than you already have. And I've made too much progress to put myself through that."

"Baby, please," he cries, reaching out and gripping my face between his strong hands. I allow myself a moment of weakness to close my eyes and feel the warmth of them. This is the last time he'll ever be able to touch me. "I can't be without you in my life. Not again."

Inhaling strongly, I close my fingers around his wrists and

tug his hands away from my face.

"That's the decision you made, Auden. No one's holding a gun to your head. We don't live in a world where parents have to be married anymore. It's not me forcing you to stay married to a woman you don't love. You made the choice."

"I don't have a choice!" he roars.

"We all have a choice."

"So, what? You're giving me an ultimatum?"

"No," I say as gently as I can manage. "You've already made your decision, you know that as well as I do. Now, I'm just making mine. I'm doing what I have to do to protect myself."

"And that means never seeing me again?"

I nod through uncontrollable sobs. I'm sure the makeup I put on when I dressed up for him earlier is now a mess of smudges and murky, black tears.

But I don't care.

Let him see what this is doing to me.

"I have no other option, Auden."

He's crying too. Not quite as violently as I am, but his devastation is clear all the same. I want to pull him into my arms and lay with him on the bed until the end of time.

But I can't.

"I love you so much, Summer-Raine. I always will." He sniffs, his hands fisted at his sides as if holding himself back from reaching for me. "I'll see you everywhere. In the bleeding skies and the sunlight as golden as your hair. I'll hear your laugh in poetry, I'll see your smile in the daffodils that grow outside my building. I'll taste your lips in every peach and smell you in every ocean breeze. The beach is ruined for me now, as is every balcony, every wildflower, every splash of summer rain. And just know, my pretty girl, that whenever you think of me, I'll be thinking of you too."

With that, he steps towards me and presses his soft lips to my forehead for the last time. Then he walks away from me forever.

And when I wake the next morning after crying myself to sleep, I find the lavender he's carried around in his wallet since the day I gave it to him on the floor just outside my front door. Beside it, a few scribbled lines on parchment paper. W H Auden poetry. Of course, it is.

> *The stars are not wanted now: put out every one;*
> *Pack up the moon and dismantle the sun;*
> *Pour away the ocean and sweep up the wood;*
> *For nothing now can ever come to any good.*

Finally, after all this time, Auden Wells is saying goodbye.

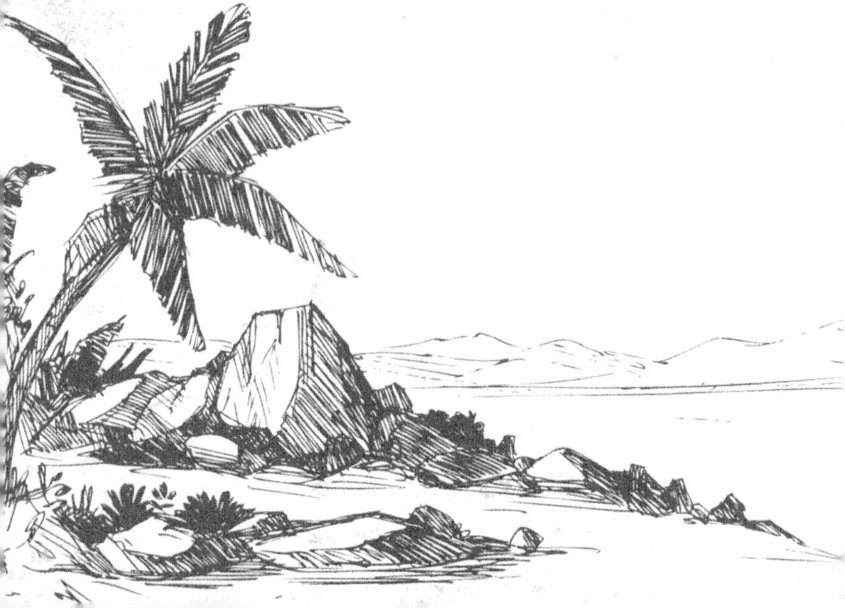

Chapter Thirty-Three

AUDEN

A son.

I'm having another son.

But for some reason, whether it's guilt about having another child after losing Oscar, I don't know, but I don't feel connected to this baby at all. And I have this terrible fear that I won't love him the way that I should.

I know it's normal to struggle bonding with a baby born after loss, according to Google anyway, but I'm not sure. This feels more than that, but I can't put my finger on why.

Cara reaches for me from the bed where the sonographer is performing an ultrasound, but I shrug her hand away. Three months it's been since she told me that she's pregnant and not once have I allowed her to touch me.

She scowls at me.

"Doesn't he look handsome already, honey?"

I fake a smile and check the time on my watch.

"I think he looks just like you," she carries on in that sweet-as-pie voice she uses only when we're in public.

"He's the size of a banana." I scoff. "You can't possibly tell already."

"Don't be boring." She pouts. "You're ruining it."

I sigh and stand up, drying my clammy hands on the front of my pants. "I'm just going to wait outside."

The sonographer shoots me a judgemental look, but I take no notice. Fuck him. He has no idea of the shit Cara puts me through, of everything I've given up for her and the child in her womb.

She's seething by the time she finds me leaning against the wall of the hospital with a cigarette suspended between my lips.

I started smoking the day I lost Summer-Raine.

Walking out of her apartment was the moment I stopped caring about myself. I don't care about developing lung disease and dying. I couldn't give a shit what happens to me now.

There is no life without her anyway.

I may as well be dead already.

"Smoking is bad for the baby, you know." Cara grips her hips with her hands.

"Then stand further away."

"You could at least pretend to care about him," she whines. "He is your son, you know?"

I take a short puff of the cigarette before stubbing it out with my shoe. I don't bother throwing the butt in the trash.

"I wouldn't be here if I didn't fucking care about him,

Cara."

"Could've fooled me."

I start the walk back to the car without checking that she's following.

A good man would offer his arm to support his pregnant wife. But I'm not a good man, not anymore. I'm barely a man at all.

I'm several strides ahead of her when I make it back to the black sportscar Cara bought on my credit card shortly after we got married. It's ridiculous and completely unsuitable for driving a kid around in, but she throws a hissy fit every time I mention getting something else.

At this point, I might just sell it behind her back to piss her off.

That's the type of guy I am now. Petty and cruel.

"You're such an asshole, you know?" she moans, climbing into the passenger side and frowning at me across the centre console. "You never used to be like this."

"People change."

"It's about her, isn't it? That bitch is always getting in your head and ruining everything."

My hands white-knuckle the steering wheel and my foot slams down on the break more violently than necessary as we hit a red light. "Don't you ever talk about Summer-Raine like that."

Cara rolls her eyes. "And what's with her name anyway? Fucking stupidest name I've ever heard in my life."

"I'm warning you, Cara," I growl. "Cut it out."

"God, you're still hung up on her, aren't you? Her pussy

must be made of gold to have you simping after her like you do. I really don't get it. She isn't even that pretty." She laughs to herself like a witch mixing spells in a cauldron. "She lost though, didn't she? You might pine after her like a pathetic little puppy, but it's me who gets to call you her husband. It's me who won in the end."

"Goddamn it, Cara. If that's how you want to look at it, then sure, you fucking won. But remember that I'm only here because I knocked you up the one and only time I've fucked you since we got married. And I don't even remember it."

I slam on the breaks outside our apartment building, causing the cars in the traffic behind to beep their horns and yell profanities at me through their open windows. I ignore them all.

"Don't be so caught up in your narcissism to believe that I'm here out of anything other than obligation. I'm trapped in a marriage with a woman I despise because I was stupid enough to get her pregnant," I continue, my words heartless and cold. "But you don't love me either, do you? You simply love the money I earned from the book I wrote about the woman you hate. Don't you see the irony in that? But one day, when the money dries up and there's nothing left, you'll be just as damn miserable as I am. So, yeah, if you think that makes you a winner, then I suppose I should congratulate you."

She blinks at me, her lips pursed and nostrils flaring.

"Get out the car," I say, my voice flat. "I won't be back tonight."

"Where are you going?"

"Out."

I wait until she's inside the building before I pull away. I might be a cold bastard now, but I'm not totally devoid of morals. She's still pregnant with my child. And for that, at least, I care about what happens to her.

Revving the engine, I do what I do on the days where missing Summer-Raine is especially painful. I drive through town and park across the street from the Rainey Days Foundation where, like a stalker, I watch her work through the windows.

Most of the time, the light shines too brightly on the glass to allow me to see through it, but it doesn't matter.

Just knowing she's close is enough to thaw the ice that freezes in my heart whenever I'm at home. Just feeling her proximity, even if through concrete walls, brings me a little slice of peace.

I've done this at least twice a week since the day I told her about the pregnancy.

I'm not breaking her rules, not trying to talk to her or make contact in anyway. She has no idea that I come here to feel close to her every couple of days.

And that's the way it will stay.

Because even though it kills me not to go to her, even though I wish she hadn't set the boundaries she did, I understand why she needs me to keep my space.

If the roles were reversed, I'd be the same.

The one time I saw another man lay their hands on her, I could have committed murder. I'd be sentenced to death row for all the crimes I'd commit if I had to watch her have a baby with someone else.

The doors to the foundation open and my breath catches.

There she is.

Her hair is loose around her shoulders, shiny golden waves that tickle her face with every bluster of wind. She's dressed in denim overalls with a cropped white t-shirt underneath, leaving a strip of skin around her ribs exposed to the breeze. I want to trace my lips over it.

Behind her, she drags two bulging trash bags.

It takes everything in me not to throw open my door and demand to help her with them. But doing so would go against the one thing she told me to do. Leave her alone.

So, I don't go to her.

But I still trace every ripple of her body as she picks up each bag and hauls them into the dumpster outside the building. They must be heavy—at least, they look to be—but Summer-Raine doesn't struggle at all.

In the years it's been since she admitted herself to the rehab facility, she's softened out and built up her strength.

I remember the shock I'd felt at seeing how tiny she was when I first saw her after the five years of no contact. Her ribs and hipbones were protruding, and the skin around her chest and collarbones was taught and grey.

She looked gaunt.

Sick.

And that had all changed when she returned from rehab. Her body had new curves, her hair was shinier and her skin clear. She looked alive again.

But in the months that have passed since our last goodbye, I've watched from across the street as the life in her eyes has dulled and the softness in her body has returned to sharp edges.

It kills me.

When she doesn't go straight back inside after throwing the trash out, I freeze.

Does she know I'm here?

Did she see me sitting here and I somehow missed her looking in my direction?

But she doesn't turn to me or show any sign of knowing that I'm watching her. Instead, she wraps her arms around herself and tilts her head to the sky.

It takes me back to that night in senior year when I saw her for the first time. I'd thought she was the most beautiful thing I'd seen in my life.

I still do.

But looking at her now, even as exquisite as she is, the harrowing pain that emanates from her almost makes me want to look away.

I've done this to her.

For the second time, I've chosen to stay with a woman I have no feelings for over the love of my life. I've made Summer-Raine feel second-best, inferior, maybe even worthless.

And simply because I have daddy issues that I've never dealt with.

I'm so terrified of turning into my piece of shit father that I've hurt the one person in this world that I would die for.

Because Summer-Raine is right, of course. This is just the first time I've realised it. We no longer live in a world where two people have to be married in order to raise their children. There is no reason that Cara and I can't parent our son while living in different houses. Dating other people.

Would parenting separately make us bad parents? Absolutely not.

Our son will still be safe, he'll still be looked after, I'm sure he'll still be loved.

So why have I spent so long convincing myself that divorcing Cara would make me the same as my dad?

Summer-Raine's mouth opens in a silent scream.

Her pain is so profound, I can feel it on top of that which I already bear.

It's excruciating.

I ache to run to her, hold her, kiss her. Touch her skin and feel her lips, breathe her air until we're the only two people left in the world.

And I will.

Not now, but soon.

Just like that, alone in a truck across the street from the love of my life, my fingers twitching with the need to touch her, my lips tingling with the need to kiss her, my heart pounding with the need to love her, the decision is made.

I'm filing for divorce.

It's an epiphany of extraordinary proportions. One that causes excitement and adrenaline to course through me as I throw my truck into gear and head back to the apartment.

I walk through the lobby that feels unfamiliar to me now and take the elevator up to the apartment that has never felt like home.

I'm so giddy that I almost don't notice the pair of men's shoes by the front door that don't belong to me. I almost don't notice the smell of foreign cologne, almost don't hear the sounds of blissful moaning.

Almost, but I do.

Elation turns to red hot anger as I follow the grunts and groans to the master bedroom, where I find my wife riding the ever-loving fuck out of some asshole who hasn't even taken off his sweater.

I slam the door to alert them of my presence. Panicked eyes snap to mine as I lean casually against the wall, my arms crossed in front of me.

"Please don't stop on my account."

Cara scrambles off the man, but doesn't bother to cover herself. In fact, she sits cross-legged on the bed with her shoulders back, pussy exposed and breasts thrust out in front of as if challenging me to look.

I don't.

It wouldn't have the affect on me that she thinks it would anyway.

Not that there's anything wrong with her body. The woman looks like a supermodel, but I've only ever had sex with her while thinking of somebody else.

She scowls when my eyes don't wander and finally grabs the bed sheet to wrap around her shoulders. The man beside her is slower to cover himself, laying there on the bed with his pathetic deflating cock as he glares at me like I'm the asshole.

There's a standoff of stares for a while before Cara huffs like a child. "You have no right to be mad," she says. "You're in love with someone else."

"I have no right to be mad?" I laugh sinisterly. "Big words

for the woman who's staring down the barrel of an ugly divorce."

"Look man," doucheface starts and I hold a hand out to silence him without looking his way, but he doesn't take the message. "What the fuck? You can't do that. Babe, did you see that? Tell him he can't do that."

"Get out, Graham," Cara snaps.

Ah, so that's his name.

I see his mouth drop open in shock through the corner of my eye.

"What?"

"Now."

I meet his eye as he looks at me, pleading for me to help him, as if I'm not the husband of the woman he just got caught fucking.

"You heard her."

Graham finally puts his dick away, doing up his cargo pants and throwing on an oil-stained shirt. Cara and I don't take any notice as he picks up his work boots, not bothering to put them on, and shuffles out of the room.

All the while, Cara looks at me with an arrogance that doesn't make sense.

She stands and saunters over to me, white sheet falling off her shoulders and exposing her nakedness to me once again. When she raises a hand to touch my chest, I catch her wrist and hold it in front of us.

"Don't fucking touch me," I snarl. "And put some damn clothes on, for Christ's sake."

She pouts, but does as I say, taking a satin robe out the closet and tying it in place. Then she flops into the chair where she usually sits to do her makeup and cocks an eyebrow.

"So, who's your friend?" I ask.

"Some guy I picked up at the construction site across the street after you abandoned me earlier."

"He know you're pregnant?"

She shrugs. "Told him I was bloated."

Jesus, this woman is shameless.

"Classy."

She rolls her eyes. "Well, what did you expect? I'm a woman, Auden. I have needs. And God forbid you'd ever be down for a fuck, we haven't even consummated the marriage yet."

Her hands snap to cover her mouth as if she's just said something she shouldn't.

"Of course, we have," I snap. "You're pregnant."

And then I see it.

The blush of panic on her cheeks, the glint of deceit in her eyes, both are a blinding indication of the truth.

She scurries backwards up the bed until she hits the headboard like a mouse running from its predator. "I meant apart from that one time," she says weakly.

"That one time that I have no memory of other than what you've told me?"

Fuck, the lie was there all along, wasn't it? I've never gotten so drunk that I've forgotten the night before, but I believed Cara when she told me we'd slept together without a second thought.

What the fuck have I done?

I watched Summer-Raine's heart shatter in front of me

the night I told her about Cara's pregnancy. For months, I've watched her from a distance. I've seen her weight-loss, the fake smiles she gives her clients and the moments she lingers too long at the dumpsters to cry where she thinks no one can see her.

I've ripped her apart.

And for what?

To be the hero for a woman who has been lying to me all along?

"I was scared," Cara cries, seemingly having realised the game is up. "It was a one-night stand and I didn't know what to do. I knew you were going to ask for a divorce that night and I panicked. You were always such a good daddy to Oscar, you loved him so much and in the months that he was alive, you didn't even seem to resent me that much. We were almost like a real family, you know? And I knew that you'd love this baby too, that you'd do the right thing and stand by us. So, I made you think that we'd slept together."

She screams as my fist sails into the wall, plaster exploding around the room.

I can't breathe.

In all my life, I've never felt fury like this. It's the kind of anger that leads to murder or world wars. The kind that makes you feel as if your head will explode from the impossible pressure in your skull.

She was going to trick me into raising a child that wasn't mine.

I'd have given up the kind of love that only comes once in a dozen lifetimes for a liar and a son that doesn't belong to me.

I shake my head, my tight fists hot and vibrating at my sides, blood trickling down my knuckles from punching the wall. I need to get out of here.

"You can't leave me!" she shrieks as I turn and start to head out the room. "You'd really leave me alone with a baby? That's not you, Auden. You'd never do that."

"I'll have my lawyer draw up the divorce papers," I say, my voice cold, not bothering to turn around to face her.

I don't ever want to look at her again.

"I'll contest it." She runs in front of me and tries to block the doorway with her body.

"Like fuck you will," I growl and stare her down with a glare so intimidating, she visibly shrinks in size.

She takes a tiny step to the side, but it's enough for me to get past her. Her sobs are growing uncontrollable, her wailing shrill and ear-piercing.

"Please don't do this to me," she begs.

"You've done this to yourself."

I can still her hear crying as I wait for the elevator to take me down to the lobby, but I feel nothing. Even when the smashing sounds begin and she undoubtedly starts destroying my things, I don't even blink.

There's nothing in that apartment that I can't replace anyway.

I've only ever had one thing that I considered irreplaceable and I returned it to the person who gave it to me months ago.

I can only hope that Summer-Raine will forgive me enough to let me have it back.

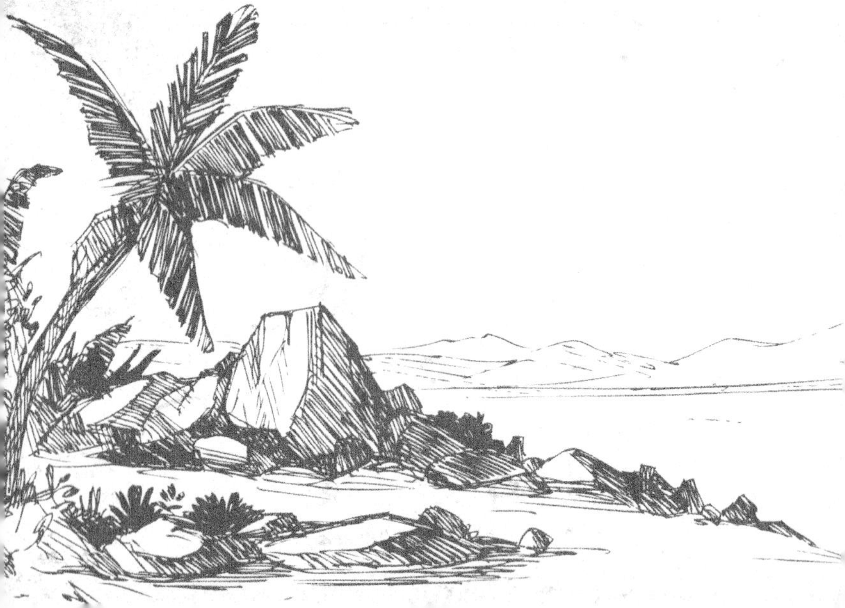

Chapter Thirty-four

SUMMER-RAINE

He wrote a book about us.

It was released well over a year ago, while I was still in rehab, I think. And I don't know how I've gone so long without knowing it existed because apparently, it's quite the global success. I guess that's how he made his money. I've even heard that it's being made into a movie.

The Sun After Summer Rain, that's what he called it.

He wrote our love story and shared it with the world. He changed our names, of course, but every magic moment on my balcony, every time he brushed my hair behind my ear or recited poetry with me, he wrote it all in that book.

It's unmistakably the story of us.

But he gave us a happy ending in those pages that we didn't get in real life.

I've read it three times now and I still sob like a damn baby every time, wishing that it was us who got the happily ever after instead of Sienna and Andrew from the book.

It's been months since he left and it hasn't gotten any easier. Whoever said *time heals everything* had obviously never had their heart broken by Auden Wells.

I've tried to move on, I really have. I've even been on dates. Not with Max, obviously. Things are messy enough between us after he kissed me in front of Auden. But I haven't been able to get through one nice dinner or couple of hours at the movie theatre without thinking I'd rather be there with somebody else.

It's worse, perhaps, because I know that the reason we aren't together isn't because he doesn't want us to be. My heart can still feel the beat of his, my soul can still hear his calling out for me. We belong to each other, hopelessly and infinitely, but duty binds him to another woman.

I wonder if their baby has been born yet.

And if it has, then I pray to the stars that that it's healthy. That it's okay. That it will *always* be okay. Because even though I hate the circumstances, I'd do anything to protect Auden from losing another child.

I lay back on my bed and stare at the ceiling.

Silence is my best friend on days like this. Days where missing Auden is particularly painful, when I can think of nothing but what could have happened that night if Cara hadn't been pregnant.

I drive myself crazy imagining what life would look like if things were different.

I scream and cry. I lay for hours in my eternal darkness. I hold ice in my palm to distract from the thoughts in my head.

That's something positive, I guess. Despite all that's happened, I haven't once diverted back to unhealthy coping mechanisms. I haven't taken a blade to my skin for years now and I celebrate every damn day that passes of staying clean.

Because even though I'm stronger now and have learnt healthier ways of coping, the urge to self-harm is still there. It still tempts me sometimes.

Ice satisfies that craving for me.

It helps me swallow down the desire for something sharper, for a harsher kind of physical pain. It's a life saver, especially on days like today.

A knock at the door startles me.

I ignore it at first, but when it sounds again, I huff and drag myself across the apartment. It's probably Marlowe coming up to ask me why I'm not downstairs at the foundation.

But when I swing the door open, I freeze in shock.

Because it's not Marlowe.

It's the one person I never thought I'd see standing on my doorstep again. Not after I told him I didn't want to see him anymore. Not after he left the lavender.

"Auden," I breathe, but the word is barely out of my mouth before his hands are on my face and his lips are on mine.

He kisses me ferociously. Like a wild animal unleashed from a cage. His hands are everywhere, on my back, in my hair, cupping my cheeks, grabbing my ass. Mine are fisting the fabric of his shirt.

For a while, I'm too stunned to kiss him back. I'm not even sure if this is happening at all, or if it's just a really vivid lucid dream.

But finally, I melt into him.

My lips part and his tongue slips between them, finding mine and entwining with it.

He tastes the same. Like home. Sweet and familiar, my favourite flavour.

But when he moans into my mouth, the sound shocks me out of my daze and I shove out of his hold.

"What the fuck are you doing?" I yell, breathing hard.

His eyes are wide as he drinks in my appearance. My hair, a ragged mess, is thrown back into a messy ponytail and my skeletal frame is drowned by his old high-school football jersey that still falls to my mid-thigh.

His gaze lingers on the parts of my legs that are visible between the hem of the sweater and the tops of my knee-high socks.

"Eyes up buddy," I snap, despite my lips still tingling from the thrill of his kiss.

Auden smirks. It makes him look like that teenage boy I fell in love with so many years ago. His eyes are the same sparkling blue they were back then as well. The way they were before he lost his son, before his mama killed herself, before I broke his heart in a hospital waiting room when he was eighteen.

Everything about him is different than it was when I saw him several months ago.

Lighter. Sunnier. Like a fog has lifted around him.

"I got divorced," he says, eating up the distance between us.

I blink at him.

"It was finalised today."

He reaches out to tuck my hair behind my ear, a peaceful smile on his face. And though the gesture makes my heart beat double-time, I flinch at the touch.

Auden's fingers instantly fall away.

In all the times I've allowed myself to fantasise about a moment like this, I always imagined that I'd leap into his arms, wrap my legs around his waist and cling to him so tightly that he'd never be able to leave me again.

But all I feel right now is anger.

"And what? You thought that you could just show up and I'd take you back like that?" I snap my fingers. "As if you haven't picked another woman over me, not once, but *twice?*"

Auden stares at me in confusion. I guess he was expecting a different reaction from me too.

"You thought that I'd just welcome you with open arms and no questions asked?" I carry on. "As if you aren't the reason for my broken, unmendable heart? Did you even stop to consider that I might have moved on? That I might *finally* be happy? That maybe I'd even met someone else?"

He rears back like I've shot him. "Have you?"

I let the question hang in the air between us. Maybe it's cruel, but I want him to hurt a little. I want him to think that maybe there really is another man warming my bed at night. That I'm not pathetic enough to have spent all this time crying over him in the dark.

"No," I say finally. "But the point is I could have done."

His shoulders relax.

"You can't keep picking me up and letting me down, Auden. It isn't fair. You can't play with my heart again, I won't let you."

He hangs his head, regret swimming in those gorgeous depths of turquoise. "Pretty girl, I'm so sorry. Please believe that the last thing I ever wanted was to cause you pain."

"But you did." I sigh. "You hurt me so bad I didn't think that I'd survive it."

"I was trying to do the right thing, baby. That's all I've ever tried to do."

"I know, but—"

"Please," he pleads, silencing me. "Let me say what I came to say. Just hear me out. And if, by the end, you want me to leave and never come back, then I will."

I purse my lips in thought, then nod.

I head to the couch, flopping down onto it with my arms spread either side of me. I stare him down with steely eyes and a blank face. It's taking a hell of a lot of control to keep my facial features so rigid, since it really is adorable when he's looking all bashful with an anxious smile and rosy cheeks.

"My dad ran out on Mama when I was five," he starts, breathing heavily, his hands rubbing together nervously in front of him. "I was too young to really understand what was happening, but one day he was there and the next, he was gone. Afterwards, Mama crumbled. She'd always struggled mentally, but it was like a damn broke when Dad left. She was imploding and I was just this little five-year-old boy watching his Mama get sicker and sicker, desperate to help but not knowing how."

Tears fill my eyes and they fall silently as he talks.

"I was seven the first time she attacked me, eight when she made the first attempt on her life. She became so sick that for a long time, I'd have to make all her meals, bathe her, even help her when she needed the bathroom. I was just a kid. And I blamed my dad for everything. What kind of man abandons his sick wife and leaves his young son to pick up the pieces?"

He sucks in a deep breath and pauses, the weight of the conversation hanging heavy in the air.

"I've spent my whole life doing everything I can to make sure I never become my father. Repelling anything that could even suggest I'm following in his footsteps is what I've been doing since the very day he left us."

He looks at me, the warm artificial light reflecting off his pupils. He shoves his hands into his pockets and shuffles from foot to foot, all the while staring straight into my soul.

He can see the tears on my face, I know it. But he doesn't comment or acknowledge them, he just carries on.

"Baby, I wasn't lying when I said I'd wait forever for you. I'd wait a thousand lifetimes if only to hold you in my arms one more time. I wouldn't touch another woman for the rest of my days if it meant touching your skin again just once. But I didn't know Cara was pregnant when I made you that promise."

He paces back and forth across the room, his brow furrowed, his hands trembling.

"I married her because I thought that I'd be as bad as my father if I didn't. I didn't leave after Oscar passed away because her grief reminded me too much of Mama and her sickness. And then that day when I told you I'd be back for you and Cara told me she was pregnant again, I swear I've never felt such resentment towards a person. I was weak. I thought the right thing to do was to stay miserably together rather than raise the baby happily apart."

"I don't understand. What changed?" I ask. "Why are you here now?"

"It wasn't my baby. She lied. I never touched her, Summer-Raine. Not since long before you went to rehab, not since the night Oscar was conceived. She just let me believe I did so that I'd think the baby was mine."

Relief like I've never felt settles over me, it floods my heart and fills my veins.

"So, you're only here because you found out it's not your kid?"

"No." He shakes his head forcefully, walking over to the couch and crouching down in front of me. "I used to drive here and sit in my truck across the street just to feel close to you, always hoping I'd catch even the slightest glimpse of you as you worked downstairs with your clients. There was this one day, when you took out the trash, looked to the sky and cried. I saw your pain so viscerally, I felt it in my heart so powerfully, that I realised in all my efforts to do the right thing, I'd only hurt you."

I sob at his words. Even after I told him to leave me alone forever, he still couldn't bring himself to do it. He still had to be near me, even if I didn't know he was there.

"And I realised that the fear of turning into my father isn't even close to justifying causing you that amount of pain, or any pain at all. It was then, in that moment that it dawned on me just how wrong I've been all along. So, it didn't matter whether or not Cara was having my baby, I'd be stood here right now begging you to have me back either way. I'm not mad at her for having an affair, I'm furious with myself for wasting so much time worrying about duty and honour when I could have spent it with you in my arms."

I reach for him, my hands finding the back of his neck and my fingers getting lost in the overgrown strands of his hair.

"For the first time in my life, I'm not worried about doing the right thing," he whispers, leaning into me. His lips are just a breath away from my own. I could taste them if only I poked my tongue out the smallest amount. "In fact, it's probably better for you if you tell me to go to hell, but I'm praying on every star in the sky that you don't. That you tell me to stay instead. So, will you have me back, Summer-Raine? Will you be my pretty girl again? Now, forever and always?"

And though all I want is to close the distance between us and answer his question with a kiss, I don't. Because I'm still so hurt. I still feel broken.

His words are pretty, but I'm still dealing with the emotional fallout of his actions. He's told me pretty words before and then chosen another woman.

What if I take him back so easily only for another damsel in distress to come along that he can't help saving?

I nudge past him and stand, my hands gripping the roots of my hair. "I need a minute."

He twists his neck to look at me, his body still angled towards where I'd been sitting on the couch. The look of sheer terror on his face crushes me, but I'm too overwhelmed to reassure him.

To tell him that I'm not saying no, I'm just not saying yes right now.

His head hangs.

"Yeah," he rasps. "Yeah, I get it."

I don't stop him as he stands and walks to the door. I don't say anything when he turns back to look at me as if pleading for me to call out and ask him to stay. I don't even breathe as he turns downcast eyes to the floor, nods sadly and leaves.

I suck in a breath as if I'm drowning, but my lungs still feel empty. Auden took the air with him when he left.

Because that's what he is to me, the air I breathe. It's what he's always been. In all the time we've been apart, I've been on the brink of passing out from lack of oxygen. I can't function, can't *live*, without him.

So why the hell did I just let him walk out the door?

Guess I'm still a masochist who's addicted to pain.

There's no other feasible explanation for not running after him when I can feel my heart splintering a little more with every step that he takes away from me.

It's like I've been frozen in place, the shock of him showing up at my door after believing that I'll never feel the warmth of his arms again paralysing me. I don't know how to deal with it.

I don't know what to do.

I ache to run to him and believe all his promises, but I'm terrified that they're empty. There's no way I'd make it through him letting me down again. It doesn't matter how much work I've done or how much progress I've made with my mental health, there aren't enough pieces of my heart left to survive another break.

And yet, how could I live with the decision if I let him go?

I couldn't.

It's not possible.

There is only Auden, there has only ever been Auden, and without him, I am nothing.

I don't think as I sprint out the front door and down the stairwell. I'm in such a state, panting and sobbing and aching for Auden, that I almost trip over him sitting on the bottom step.

He's hunched over, his head in his hands. His pain is palpable. I can feel it everywhere. It's so powerful, I can almost see it. Like swirling wisps of black smoke.

I lay my hand on his shoulder and with just that simple touch, air fills my lungs once more.

His eyes snap to mine, devastated.

"Yes," I whisper.

He stands, shooting up so fast that I instinctively move backwards, going up a step. It puts us at eyelevel.

I reach for his cheeks, holding them between my trembling hands.

"Yes, I'll be yours. I'll always be yours."

The words have hardly left my mouth before he's seizing my lips in a bruising kiss. It's frenzied. Almost feral.

Our animal instincts take over as he tears at my shorts, ripping them clean off my body. His cock is out before I can blink. It's big, so big, and pointed straight at me. *How did I forget how beautiful he is?*

He asks with pleading eyes if I'm okay with what's about to happen. It's so unnecessary that I almost laugh. I wouldn't be able to deny him if my life was about to end.

At my nod, he hooks my leg around his waist and buries

himself inside me.

And just like that, I can breathe again.

We gasp into each other's mouths as we finally become one again. I can't believe I went two years without this, without the touch of his hands and the love of his lips.

"Mine," he growls, his thrusts hard and rough. It doesn't hurt though. It could never hurt. "You're fucking mine."

Yes. Yes. Yes.

I don't know if I say it out loud. I'm too lost in the feel of him and the sounds of our moans as they echo through the barren walls of the stairwell.

I bury my face in his neck and wrap my arms around him, clinging to him as tightly as I can manage. Tears slip down my cheeks and meet with the sweat forming on his skin.

"Please don't leave me," I beg. "Please don't ever leave me again."

He stops. The hold he has on my thigh grows impossibly tighter as he lifts me, allowing me to wrap my other leg around his waist. I gasp at the deepness of the new position.

He pins me to the wall to support us.

"Look at me," he says, my face still hiding in the space between his chin and shoulder blade.

Slowly, I raise my head and meet his sparkling eyes. The look in his eyes is hot enough to burn me, yet soft enough to ease the lingering ache in my heart.

He strokes his thumb across my cheek, brushing away a tear.

"There is nothing that could take me away from you again. *Nothing*. It's me and you now."

I shudder at his words.

"Promise me?" I beg.

"I fucking swear it."

"Okay," I whisper, panting as he slowly begins to thrust into me again.

I don't know how long it will take for me to lose that persistent insecurity that he'll find some other reason that he can't be with me. I don't know how long it will be to fully trust him again.

But I believe that he means what he says.

And that's enough for now.

When his speed picks up and the ecstasy builds, my fingers dig half-moons into his back and my head falls against the wall behind me.

"I love you," he pants. "God, I love you so fucking much."

It's his words that push me over the edge. I come, pulsing around him and sobbing in pleasure.

"I love you. I love you. I love you." The words are unstoppable and barely coherent, but still I chant them over and over like a prayer. Because what Auden and I have may be flawed, it may even be toxic at times, but it's also sacred.

Later, he makes love to me again. In bed this time.

We fall onto the covers in a mess of tangled limbs and wet kisses.

Our clothes come off, our breathing labours. He slides inside me with no preamble or preparation. It isn't needed anyway.

And like that, connected as one person, we rock together. We let our bodies do the talking. We make promises with our lips and gentle caresses.

This is it now.

Me and Auden.

Finally, after all this time, we'll get our happily ever after.

Our story hasn't an easy one, but every obstacle, every bump in the road along the way has led us here to each other's arms.

We were always going to end up here. Whether it was almost a decade ago in high school or two years ago or several months ago. And maybe I didn't believe it until now, but there was never a possibility of us being apart.

Because our souls are connected like puzzle pieces, like metals of the strongest magnetism. We have no choice but to be together.

Belonging to Auden is so deeply entrenched in my being that I wouldn't know who I was if I didn't.

He fills the empty parts of me, he completes me in a way no one else ever could. With every touch and kiss and whispered word, he makes me whole.

And I think I do the same for him.

I don't know the truth about love for everybody. I guess it's different for everyone. But mine and Auden's is intense. It's wild and explosive and chaotic.

It's perfect.

And it's ours.

The end

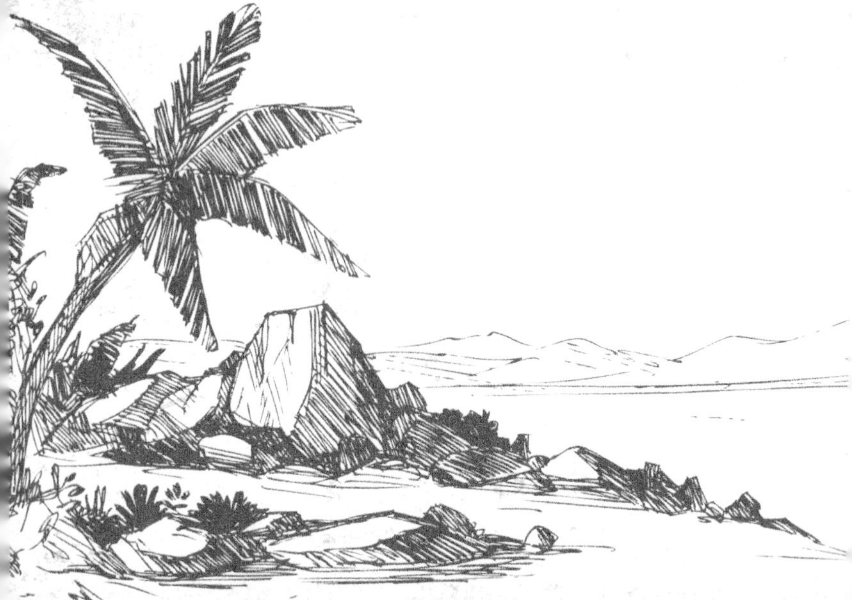

Epilogue

AUDEN

The first time I see her, she's being held up to me through a clear plastic screen. Her head is tilted backwards as she screams into the hospital room, announcing her presence to the world. Her tiny fingers are splayed, her little lips pursed, as she's wrapped in a fluffy white towel and placed into my arms, purple and slimy and a little bit gross. She's beautiful.

Perhaps the most beautiful thing I've ever seen.

With the exception of her mother of course.

I drop a kiss to Summer-Raine's forehead as she waits to have her stomach sewn back together. We weren't expecting a caesarean, but when does birth ever really go to plan? All I know is that I've never been more in love with my wife than I am at this very moment.

"Does baby have a name?" a nurse asks, snapping photos of us on my phone.

"Mabel." Summer-Raine smiles down at our daughter and shakily strokes her cheek with one finger.

"It means love," I add, but the nurse doesn't hear.

Mabel sleeps soundly in the bassinet beside the bed at our home in Islamorada.

Our house is three stories of blue weather-beaten cladding and white balustrades. On the second floor, a wooden balcony juts out over a private beach, with two wicker chairs sat side by side where my wife and I watch the sunset every night.

Not that she ever uses hers.

Like now, she's curled up on my lap with her nose nuzzling my neck as the sun burns red and the sky catches fire. Not that I'd ever complain. This is where I'm most at peace, with Summer-Raine in my arms on the balcony where she told me that she loves me for the very first time on her eighteenth birthday all those years ago.

It's why I proposed here. No other place would have been right.

I didn't even get down on one knee, just slipped the ring onto her finger as she lay cradled in my lap. She'd whispered *yes* into my mouth as she kissed me, and then I'd made her scream that same word over and over as I made love to her body and soul.

We married only a month later on the little strip of private beach below us.

This town, this house, was always meant to be our home. Yeah, we'd be happy anywhere so long as we're together, but on this balcony in Islamorada surrounded by all the memories of our teenage love is where we belong.

Neither of us wanted to stay in Tallahassee. There was nothing there for either of us but trauma and painful memories and we got out as soon as we could.

The Rainey Days Foundation still remains though, which Marlowe now manages for Summer-Raine, and we're actually in the process of converting the ground floor of our house into a second branch.

As for me, I found it in myself to write a second book. It seems that I have no issue finding inspiration when Summer-Raine is by my side and though it did well, it didn't have quite the same level of success as *The Sun After Summer Rain*.

I guess the world fell in love with our story, with the girl who had monsters in her head and the boy with a hero complex. The soulmates who were fated but could never quite get things right.

The movie comes out soon. It's set to premiere at Sundance Film Festival in August.

It's not a huge blockbuster, it didn't have a massive budget or world-renowned actors, but I like what the director did with it. It was beautifully done and a little sad in its aesthetic.

But that's what our love story is, I suppose. Sad, but undeniably beautiful.

I turn away from the sunset to stare at my wife. Her eyes like emeralds, her hair like woven strands of gold, her lips like blooming peonies.

There's never been a more spectacular sight.

Feeling the heat of my stare on her skin, Summer-Raine tilts her face to look at me.

"You're missing the sunset," she says.

"I don't care."

"You should. It's beautiful tonight."

"Not as beautiful as you."

"What a line." She laughs with a roll of her eyes.

My fingers brush a strand of hair away from her face and tuck it behind her ear. Then I cover her lips with my own and whisper, "Not a line."

Author's Note

Wow.

I can't believe we're here. It's been a journey and a half, if I'm honest.

Summer-Raine and Auden came to me in the shower one night while I was supposed to be writing the follow up to *Lovers in Lockdown*. And for a long time, I tried to ignore the way they were calling to me.

But I guess they just screamed too loud.

This story belongs completely to them. To me, these characters are real people. This story is theirs and I am simply the vessel through which they tell it.

It just means so very much to me. This is my second release, yet truthfully, I consider it my debut. *Lovers in Lockdown* was fun and it holds a special place in my heart because it was the first book I ever wrote. But this book just hits different.

It was while writing Auden and Summer-Raine's love story that I realised the kind of author I want to be. I want to write passion and fire and angst. I want to break your heart, then put it back together again.

So, if you'll have me, I'd love nothing more than to keep bringing you stories like this one.

See you soon,

Marlee Myers x

Acknowledgements

Crikey, where do I even begin?

You. Let's start with you. Thank you so much for taking a chance on a newbie like me. I can't tell you what it means to me to have you read my work and let me take you on this incredible journey with me. My dream is to do this fulltime and your support has done so much to bring me closer to making it come true. You're awesome and I love you.

Joe, my fiancé, father of my children and best friend, I think you're pretty cool. Thank you for loving me and giving me a romance hero of my own.

Nik, I don't even know what to say. Thanks for letting me send you random paragraphs with no context, getting semis over the sex scenes and believing in me. You're a real one.

My daughters, I will not be thanking you. You were both entirely unhelpful. But you're cute and I love you more than anything.

Gi and Kellie, my beta readers. Thank you for everything you did to help make this book what it is. The support you continue to show me is staggering. I don't know what I did to deserve either of you. I love you. I appreciate you. You're both angels.

My incredible cover designer, Sarah at okay creations. This cover is everything. It's perfect. I still can't believe it's mine.

Mary, Val and Julie at Books and Moods, thank you for making the inside as stunning as the outside.

And finally, Jess. God, I don't think there are enough words in the dictionary to completely express how thankful I am to have you. You have been my alpha reader, beta reader, editor, consultant, PA, marketing assistant, ideas generator and sounding board. But, most importantly, the most incredibly supportive friend I could have asked for. This book wouldn't exist without you. From the very bottom of my heart, thank you.

Stay Connected

Keep up-to-date with Maisie's latest releases on social media

Instagram – @maisiemyersauthor
Facebook Group – Maisie's Daisies
TikTok - @maisiemyersauthor
Goodreads – Maisie Myers

Hey, you.
Did you like the book?
If so, I'd be so grateful if you left a review.

Printed in Great Britain
by Amazon